MIDNIGHT IN DECEMBER

P.R. KEYS

E. Jackson Publishing

Publisher's Note:

This is a work of fiction. Names, characters, places and incidents are a product of the author's imagination. Locales and public names are something used for atmospheric purposes. Any resemblance to actual people, living or dead, or businesses, companies, events, institutions or locales is completely coincidental.

Ordering Information:

Quantity sales. Special discounts are available on quantity purchases by corporations, associations and others. For details, contact the "Special Sales Department" at the email address above.

E. Jackson Publishing/ PR Keys—1st Ed.

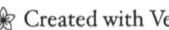 Created with Vellum

To my Daddy.

"The way to right wrongs is to turn the light of truth upon them."

— IDA B. WELLS

ACKNOWLEDGMENTS

I have so many to thank and acknowledge for this book. My fans, my mama, my husband, Kima and Alarra; you have all helped me through so many storms. But the true thanks for this book goes to my sons. Although you boys did more to distract me than anyone on this planet, your very existence served as priceless inspiration for this book. Thank you for teaching me so many precious lessons in this life. Thank you for slowing Mommy down and helping me smell the roses. I love you more than words can say.

PROLOGUE

Kingfisher County, Oklahoma
December 10, 1909

The rope's coarse strands grabbed the tender traces of the boy's neck and lifted until it pressed against his larynx. His jaw slacked in response to prevent the closure of his esophagus. He thought he should tiptoe or stand upright, but he was already on the balls of his feet and the wooden crate on which he teetered was close to crumbling under his bare, frozen feet.

The rags he wore did nothing to stop his body from shivering from the cold. He used every muscle in his posture to remain completely still despite its chilled state. One small and wrong gesture from him and his fragile, wooden lifesaver would abandon him. He would be dead in no time. The strong but silent oak tree that held his fate was the only thing that would live that day.

As time passed, he counted every beat of the pulse in his neck against the piercing rope. There was no other way to determine how long he had been out there in the middle of the forest. How could he know how many seconds he had left in his life? All he relied on was the sun shining over him. As long as there was sunlight, someone could find him.

But when the sun slowly distanced herself from him, he lost it. Two rogue tears dropped from his eyes and disappeared into his tether. His mind had begun to confront his death, as the wooden crate beneath him shook from the tremors in his body.

Darkness swallowed the light around him, causing his eyes to strain in every direction to search for hope. And just as he was about to close his eyes for good, his savior came toward him through the trees. He closed his eyes, convinced she wasn't real. He opened them again, and she stood before him. Then he heard her voice.

"I'm gonna getcha down. But you gotta listen to Mama."

While his mother shuffled through her leather satchel, he tried his best to remain still. But time had gotten the best of him and his big toe had given him all it would give. The wooden crate tipped to the right. He tried to pry it back to the left, but the rope lifted the base of his skull and threatened to separate from the rest of his body. His mother couldn't see this struggle. She was so intent on finding her knife in her satchel she didn't see him tip the crate back to the center. But she heard the crate collapse.

There was a sudden shock of his throat sharply closing at first and then a guttural twisting of his body, fighting against itself to stay alive. He jerked and swung until suddenly, his feet swung upward. He couldn't see her, but he could feel his mother push his legs up so that his body no longer pulled against the rope. He felt her cut his hands loose from the rope that tightly wound around his wrists. She shoved the knife into his hands next.

"You gotta cut it, baby," she croaked.

With the help of his mother, he rubbed the knife's blade against the rope's twists. It was then that he fell to the hard forest floor.

"Get up, boy. We ain't got no time to spare," his mother warned in a loud whisper.

They ran for their lives through the dark woods, praying that the monster who had strung him to that oak tree wouldn't catch them. After another hour of running, the woods opened up, revealing a familiar house ahead.

It was then that his mother spoke. "Look here, boy. This will be the last time we talk freely. You won't see me again after this. Ever."

"No, Mama. We can go together," the boy cried.

"Hush up. No time for that. Now, look. I'll make sure you have everything you need. You won't want for nothing and—"

The boy interrupted her when he said, "But the man who took me told me he wasn't trying to kill me. He said he was sending a message."

His mother stared ahead of him, miles away. She asked, "What message was that?"

"He said, ain't no deals between slaves and men."

His mother's eyes darted back to his, and she smiled. "Too bad you ain't no slave. You're a Freeman. And you might look like a boy, but you a man now. And there is one thing in this world that will kill a man, and that's greed. Don't let greed choke you. Now, I'm going to take you up to that house, and I will get you situated, but this is the end. I don't want you crying and carrying on when I leave. You hear me?" Before she finished talking, he hugged her body to his. "I love you more than life itself," she said as she gripped him.

And as she promised, she took him to that house. She told him goodbye as he hugged her again. He had tried to stretch the seconds into minutes, but eventually, time ran out. He never saw his mother again.

CHAPTER 1
THE BEGINNING

BALTIMORE, DECEMBER 10, 1928

"Spinster?" Bianca repeated softly, trying her hardest not to let outrage seep from her chest.

"I'm sure you prefer a nicer definition," Ms. Edison replied with a wave of her hand. Four loud and assorted sparkling gems covered her fingers to emphasize her conversational points. She waved her hand backward and forward, heralding her vast wealth from the moment Bianca sat down across from her desk.

It was not that Bianca was unaware of how rich Margaret "Mags" Edison was. The woman's holdings were the reasons Bianca endured her overbearing nature. But she needn't flaunt it. Everyone knew. She displayed her philanthropy as if it were her God-given purpose to bless the poor or as she called them, "undeserving." She was generous for sure, but she never gave a penny to anyone without the world knowing. And that was why Bianca was there. She needed the money—badly. The small news gazette she had built from the ground was one day away from bankruptcy. Her employees made ends meet by standing in breadlines and working part-time shifts in factories. So if Bianca had to endure Mags' polite belittling to keep her employees out of the poorhouse, she would endure it. But of all the words Bianca had expected to hear out of Mags' mouth, she had not expected to hear spinster. *Spinster?*

As if hearing her astonishment, Mags continued, "Perhaps a name like... modern might suit your fancy better? I'm not sure what you flappers call yourselves these days, but the legal term for a woman like yourself is spinster, a long in the tooth, unmarried woman."

"Long in the tooth? I'm twenty-five," Bianca corrected as calmly as she could. She'd had about enough of this strange woman. She was on the verge of showing her what a real spinster was.

Mags gasped loudly. "Twenty-five? Oh, dear girl, I thought you were at least twenty-three. But you are even older than I imagined. Why at your age I was already wed with a child. I enjoyed being married so much that I did it three times after the first."

Bianca blinked and swallowed her initial reaction. Instead, she continued with, "With all due respect, Mrs. Edison—"

"Ms.," Mags corrected. "I am recently widowed if you didn't know."

"My condolences. But I do not see why my marital status is important. I'm here to solicit your investment in a business venture. I have an up-and-coming newspaper with an all-female staff. As you can see, I have letters from several community leaders eager to get behind this."

"All that seems grand, but not enough to forgo common sense. You come into my office with your hair and your... pants and no collateral to speak of and no job—"

"The *Baltimore Beat* is my job."

"I'm sure it is."

"And about collateral. The landlord to the *Baltimore Beat* is willing to sell the building to me for a fraction of its value. I think it would be a lucrative investment—"

"That building isn't worth two cents," Mags replied dismissively. "And why are you doing this, anyway? Is it because you were fired from your job at a real newspaper, the *Baltimore Journal?* You were the only Negro writer, were you not?"

Mags had done her homework on Bianca and her life. She wouldn't have to guess that Bianca's departure from the *Baltimore Journal* was a sore spot. Imagine working hard day and night and still not being good enough. The day her editor scratched her name off an article and typed in her white friend's name over hers, was the day Bianca walked out the door and never looked back. She ran out the Journal's doors in a rage, unsure of where to take her life. It was her best friend, Daisy, who encouraged her to hang her own shingles and start her own newspaper.

"Are you crazy, Daisy?" Bianca remembered asking her after she suggested it.

"Maybe. But no crazier than you," Daisy returned with a shrug. "You have done it everyone else's way. Why not try your own? You don't need them."

And just like that, Daisy's words lit a fire inside of Bianca that wouldn't go out. Despite all the obstacles and pit holes she endured, she was still hell-bent on proving all her naysayers wrong.

Bianca shook thoughts of the past off and faced Mags. "I was wrongly terminated from the *Journal*," Bianca finally replied to Mags' accusation.

"It doesn't matter; the fact remains that you have no revenue."

"We make do. We distribute over two thousand editions weekly. It's nothing to scoff at."

"*Pish*! I don't know why we are discussing that gossip rag. Pennies," Mag scoffed. "You have nothing to show for your effort or any real collateral to speak of. It is all too much. Or, in your case, too little."

Mags settled her eyes on Bianca's composure and added,

"Cheer up, dear. I know all of this sounds harsh. But we women must help each other get on the correct path. I married at a young age. It makes no sense for you to do all of this on your own. A good husband with a sizable purse is not a bad thing. You are still pretty. A bit brown for my liking, but pretty. You have good breeding. Your father's reputation is notable. Oh dear, but then there is the awful scandal surrounding your sister. Tongues are still wagging about how she was on trial for murder just three years ago."

"She was acquitted."

"*Pish*! Maybe, but in the court of public opinion, she's guilty. At least she's married to a doctor. No doubt, the match has made it possible for her to show her face in public. See, that's what you need. A nice suitor to sort out the fray of things. Perhaps he can rescue you from bankruptcy and help you buy that building. He would certainly make your portfolio more appealing. Perhaps if you were connected to someone. Someone? But who?"

"Are you saying that if I were married, you would overlook my income and lack of collateral?"

"Well, I wouldn't put it as plainly. But there is an appeal to a woman who is backed by a strong man of means."

Bianca's mind skidded onto a desperate road. Desperation would be the only reason she considered saying what she said next. "Um, I never got around to telling you that I'm engaged." It was a bald-faced lie. But she said it because there were only twenty-six cents to her name and she barely had enough gas left in her tank to get her home. It was a stupid lie and one that she had no means of backing up.

"You are affianced?" Mags asked, her voice raised several octaves. "Why didn't I know that? I know everything and everyone. Who is he?"

Thank goodness someone knocked on Mags' door just before Bianca could think of a false person. Mags answered and continued to have a conversation with her assistant while Bianca's mind reeled. Who? Whose name could she use? Mags knew everyone in town. Could she make up a person? Would Mags want to meet him? Lying was such a terrible idea. Oh, goodness, why had she lied? No good would come of it. She would be easily found out and framed a liar forever.

"I'm afraid I will have to cut this meeting short," Mags announced, breaking Bianca's wild thoughts. "My apologies to you, my dear. I have another meeting to attend. However, I am having a Christmas soiree next Saturday. You can introduce this fiancé there."

Bianca blinked again and smiled. Somehow saved from immediate execution, she now had more time to figure out the specifics of her stupid lie. "Certainly, Ms. Edison. Thank you so much for your time."

Mags politely bid her farewell as Bianca walked out of her townhouse and to her car. Her rusted clunker sat offensively against the posh backdrop of Lafayette Square. Bianca untwisted the wire holding the driver's door closed. The loud sound of rusted hinges grinding against themselves could be heard for miles. They screamed when she slammed the door shut. However, she could not be so concerned about her antique car. Her thoughts were on the sad state of her affairs.

Damn. All that stood between her and her dream was a lie. A little white lie. No, a big fat lie. How in the world could she do such a stupid thing and make such an audacious claim? And better yet, how was she supposed to back it up? There was no backing up a lie about a man who didn't exist.

Well, it is not as if he couldn't exist, Bianca mused to herself. Nothing was impossible, and a made-up man with a made-up background was doable. She was a writer and the most infamous gossiper in the city. She had cooked up taller tales than this one would be.

Just as Bianca's mind baked on some ideas, a sudden movement caught her eye. Still parked on the street in front of Mags' house, she saw a man standing outside of a window on the second floor of another house. Bianca blinked for good measure as she watched the man lean into the roof's shingles to avoid the eyes of another man peering out the window.

"What in the world?" Her words hung in the air while she watched the man jump down from the roof, roll onto the ground, and leap to his feet. Just as she was about to turn away from this oddity, she noticed the strangest thing—he was rushing to her car.

"What's he doing?" she yelled to herself.

Her alarm bells rang as she watched the man yank open her passenger door and climb inside her vehicle. Now that he was much closer—a darn arm's length away—she recognized him. He was Victor Carlson, the most beautiful man in all of Baltimore.

Her mouth slacked in wonderment as he smiled at her and declared, "Hello, pretty. I'm going to kiss you now, so don't fret."

And to her utter shock, he did.

ONE HOUR EARLIER...

Victor laid his sleepy head against a soft, silk-covered pillow. The feather cloud expelled a soothing, light puff of flowery aroma. His belly was full of an exquisite meal prepared by the hands of his paramour. And after drinking the last drop of a delicious port from a crystal decanter, he was ready to go to sleep. This was surely how one could be foolish enough to make his bed in hell. To do something this foolish, one must lull himself into believing one is in heaven's bosom instead of in the belly of Hades. Why else would a person do such a thing as to sleep?

There were rules to his lifestyle. And he was breaking them all. He had allowed himself to do the one thing he had vowed never to do with his ladies—relax. No, he mustn't allow himself to be drawn into the cool silk fabric and warmed by the soft, lush body next to him.

As if feeling his hesitance, the bait spoke. "Aren't you tired, darling?"

"Yes," he replied through expelled breath. "But I should be going."

"Humph! You never stay for a spell. Where are you going now?"

Victor chuckled as he rose to sit on the edge of the bed. "Jealous little thing, aren't you?" He turned to tap her nose playfully.

"I hate when you leave just after we make love," she said with a full-on pout.

Victor smiled at her as he began to dress. She was beautiful. Even more so after they made love. Her wild and curly blond tendrils framed her heart-shaped face. Their amorous kissing left her usually pink lips swollen in a mauve color. She always donned her silk robe that barely covered anything. He delighted in catching her soft curves peek out from every move she made.

"Angel, your husband will be home any minute, and you know it," Victor remarked. His attention now focused on finding his clothing in the littered piles on the plush carpet.

"Not for hours, and you know it. Edmund has meetings all day. And that does not explain why you are leaving so soon. I know it's because you are seeing that Negro girl who works at the library. Or you could be going over to your favorite, that loose one at the club."

Victor stood in the full-length mirror, adjusting his tie. He eyed Angel's reflection in the glass and tried his best to stifle his smile. "Ms. Anderson is hardly a girl, and I have no idea who else you are talking about. Where do you get this stuff from, anyway? Please don't tell me you still read that rag. What's it called again? The *Baltimore Street?*"

"*Baltimore Beat*," she corrected. "Of course, I do. Lady Noire is the biggest gossip in Baltimore. Everybody knows that. All the speakeasies distribute her columns. I don't leave without one." She reached down into a drawer and pulled out a newspaper and read. "Rich he might be, but sensible he is not. The well-known banking bachelor changes women as often as he changes clothes. With all this foot traffic, how in the world does he have the time to do any work? I wouldn't trust him with my money.'"

"Ouch!" Victor winced as he fumbled with his cuff links. "I'm glad she isn't talking about me."

"What? This can only be you. Banking? Everyone knows you and your brother are the Carlson Brothers of Carlson Brothers Bank. And everyone and I mean everyone knows you have a lot of women."

"Angel, this is silly. Are you giving a gossip-monger credence? Some nosy broad? Let's talk about something else, like... when I see you again, I want you to wear that purple number."

"Well, I won't be wearing anything anywhere if you don't tell me where you are going."

"Angel... where is all this coming from? You've never questioned me before."

Angel stood behind him and wrapped her arms around his middle. "That was before you made me like you. I ask you all the time about us, and you never answer. Is it because of Edmund? I told you I would leave him if you asked me to."

Victor stifled his laugh. A divorced white woman and a womanizing Negro. His brother would kill him before the world even got the chance to. Angel was sweet, but she wasn't worth his life. Besides her ethnicity, he had no intention of marrying anyone, anyway.

After politely pressing his way out of her grip, he turned to her and blessed her with a kiss of assurance. That was really what she wanted, he surmised. She wanted to know if he would come back to her. She feared what most women feared, that someone more beautiful than she would draw him away. There was no way to tell if he would or wouldn't. Until such time, he would leave her with a pacifying kiss to ease her mind. With any luck, she would give him peace and let the whole thing go.

A firm knock at the door broke his spell. They both heard

the words they dreaded. "Your husband's car just pulled up downstairs, Mrs. Talley."

Angel ran around him in five different circles as he calmly pulled on his shoes and made his way to her bedroom door.

"Are you *crazy*? He'll kill you!" she hoarsely shouted.

"I don't plan on dying today, but where the hell am I supposed to go? I ain't getting under that bed again. I learned my lesson last time."

They both stared at each other while listening to Angel's husband argue with her maid, who was stalling to keep him from entering Angel's boudoir. Angel swallowed before nodding to her window.

Oh, the things that cross a man's mind as he stands outside of a woman's window, hoping to avoid that woman's husband. None of those thoughts were fear. Edmund was not the first angry husband Victor had dealt with. What crossed his mind as the cold wind whipped by his nose was boredom. At the age of thirty-two, getting away by the skin of his teeth had lost its appeal. Constantly dodging fists and squirming out of scuffles had gotten dull. Standing outside of a window in wing-tipped shoes, sliding down sloped shingles was boring and overdone. And though he should have fought to keep his body from rolling down the side of the roof, he could not really stop it from happening. It was just as well. He almost yawned as he stood up from the cold ground and wiped the dirt off his overcoat.

As he was about to make his trek around the corner to his hidden car, he heard a booming voice behind him and knew without a shadow of a doubt it was Angel's husband, Councilman Edmund Talley, who had undoubtedly caught on to their hoax.

"You there! Stop!"

Without bothering to turn around, Victor quickly scanned the area for a way of escape and found one in the form of a rusted jalopy parked across the street. Upon closer inspection, he determined that the driver was a woman—even better. With a sense of urgency, he ran to her car door and opened it, and with quick thinking, he kissed that woman. Luckily, her lips were warm and soft. And she smelled good.

"Now look here, we can get acquainted later, I promise you. But right now, I have a little problem that I need your help with."

Her eyes darted to the window behind him and grew large. And for a good reason, Angel's husband was now standing beside the car with a pistol pointed at his back.

Victor smiled at her before pulling her body into his embrace. "Hello, sir. May we help you? The wife and I were just on our way."

"Don't play with me, you son of a bitch," Edmund grumbled. His long mustache hid his mouth, but his words were well received. "I saw you running from my house just now."

"Me? Oh, that? I was just here to see about a job for the old ball and chain here. She's looking to be a maid."

"That ain't your wife, and you know it, boy!" Edmond yelled as he loudly cocked his pistol. The sound caused the poor woman next to him to shiver and tuck herself under him.

"I'm afraid so. Got myself a homegrown ole-fashioned wife. Not too much on the makeup and charms, but that's how I like 'em. She might be dull, but she's shy and sweet. Just for me. If you don't mind, sir, we'll be on our way."

Edmund narrowed his eyes and continued to point his gun in his direction for what seemed like hours. It was not until Angel appeared that the man finally blinked awake.

"Edmond!" she called. "What are you doing? You are embarrassing us out here with this carrying on. Leave these good people alone and let's go home. Really, Edmund! What's gotten into you?"

Edmund's eyes never left Victor's. "All right, then. Be on your way," he said before stowing his pistol and walking away.

Angel ran behind him after giving Victor a slight nod.

With his peace returned, Victor turned back to his little

savior next to him. He felt her exhale once Edmund was out of sight. Poor girl. He should make it up to her. So he pressed a fifty-dollar bill into her hand. "Sorry about all the fuss, miss. These things happen, you know."

He heard the crack across his face before he felt the hard, stinging bite of her palm. He had not expected that at all.

"Get your ass out of my car, Victor," she said before balling up his money and throwing it in his face for emphasis.

Victor shook his head in surprise. "You know me? Don't tell me we've been intimate and I don't recall. That would be a shame." Another crack across his face happened. "Okay! We must have met. I take it I didn't make a good impression when we did."

"I know who you are, and I want you to get your black ass out of my car before I scream and your woman's husband comes out here to put some real bullets into your back."

"All right!" he said with his hands up in the air. "Can you just take me around the corner to my car? I will be out of your way. No more kisses."

He saw her brown eyes light with fire as she roughly pressed her foot against the clutch. When the engine remained silent, she jerkily pressed her foot down and almost stood up in the car.

"Maybe you should shift it to neutral..." He stopped his words when the fire brown in her eyes bore into him to shut him up. And with a jerk to neutral and another smash at the clutch, the car sputtered along. He eyed her proud profile with a quiet smile. She knew him. For some odd reason, he found that he did not like the idea that she knew him. A jilted paramour, maybe? He couldn't tell. He would certainly remember this little fire starter with her pouty lips and her cocoa skin. Shame on him for not. Before he could muster the will to ask her name, she stopped her car and pointed to his door.

"Get out," was all she said, her finality clear.

Victor pushed open the door and climbed out. He stared at

her profile, willing her to turn to him so he could get a good look at her again. He had to remember.

"May I at least have your—" Before he could finish, she drove off, with her middle finger up in the air, leaving him with his own words in a dusty smoke cloud.

"Name?" he finished with a smile.

CHAPTER 2

THE PROPOSAL

She was no raving beauty; he decided as he drove up the narrow path leading to his brother's palatial home. She might be pretty, but not beautiful. The road's brown dust swirled around his Packard Roadster, making him recall that the woman's skin. That must have been the reason he was still thinking of her during his ride from Angel's house. He had a certain affinity for ladies with bronze complexations. Otherwise, there was no reason for her to be on his mind.

Maybe it was the fact that she knew him. Did he know her? She acted like he should have known her. Had he known her in the biblical sense and just forgotten? He hoped not. His mind pondered over the possibility of his having a dalliance with her, one that was probably wonderful for her and not even the least memorable for him. And if that were the case, she had a genuine reason to hate him. For some strange reason, he didn't like her disregard for him.

After a quick entrance into his brother's iron-rod gate and a ride up to his driveway, Victor shook his head to erase thoughts of the strange woman from his mind. She was neither here nor there or anywhere relevant. After shaking the dust from his jacket and removing his driving gloves and goggles, Victor pulled his brother's bell, knowing fully well he was tardy for this meeting. It surprised him to see the figure behind the frosted glass was not his brother's butler. He smiled inwardly as his greeter opened the door with a bright and beaming dimpled smile.

"You ole' devil," his sister-in-law's voice rang. "You just had to ruffle your brother's feathers today. You just couldn't do right and be here on time, could you? Well, don't just stand there like a log. Get in here, you demon."

An amused smile appeared on his face as she pulled him into the foyer. Anna was the only woman who talked to him in such a way, and he loved every minute of her treatment. She dramatically smacked him with a rolled-up newspaper she gained from the foyer's middle table, causing him to remember that his brother was a lucky man. To this day, he had no clue why Anna had picked his brother, Wesley, over him. Wesley was shorter than Victor and, even worse, shorter than Anna. Wesley wore spectacles and was the biggest square Victor had ever known. Regardless of his outward flaws, Wesley had won Anna's heart as he had with most things.

"Anna, my girl," Victor purred over her dramatized hysterics. "Sweet, Anna. The way you're behaving could give a man ideas."

She smacked him this time with much more vigor before stopping to put her hands on her small but round hips. Victor chuckled as he gave his coat, goggles, and gloves to their butler's waiting hands.

Anna didn't wait for Victor to settle in before exclaiming, "Ahem! Why are you late? Your brother is going to kill you. Your guest has been waiting for some time now. I'm sure he has made all the excuses that he could think of."

Victor's eyebrow lifted with interest. "Guest? She's a guest now? Well, aren't we being cheeky, Mrs. Carlson?"

"I am not sure what else to call her," Anna replied. "And she is not even a considerable one. I hate it when she comes around. She puts the whole house on edge. But not you. Why is that?"

Victor found the nearby glass bar and gave himself a considerable pour of aged scotch. After a huge gulp, Victor offered Anna a sly smile. "I keep my wits about myself when women are around. I don't get on edge." He eyed her for a moment before he continued, "Speaking of my brother, why'd you pick him over me again? It's been years and I still can't figure out what you saw in him. You know it's not too late for you, Anna. I could save you from all this and steal you away."

Anna returned a small, knowing smile. "Your brother may not be the tallest or even the prettiest, but he has his way of stirring my blood. And besides, you were too much in love with everybody else."

Victor quietly paused, realizing the countless times women had poured their love into his cup, but the damned thing was still empty. *He* was still empty. He moved to shake off the forming fog and sojourned on with, "Where are they anyway? I planned to make my appearance and then leave. The lovely Ms. Anderson is waiting, I'm sure."

Anna chuckled, "Isn't it Tuesday? I thought that was Angel's day."

"No, Monday is Angel's day. Except we got things switched, because Ms. Anderson had her lady's monthly, so I had—"

"All right, all right! Never mind. I get the picture. I can never really go there with you. You get an inch and go all the way." When his mind ran to a very naughty place, she quickly caught on and punched his shoulder. "All right! That's enough. Get in there right now." This time she shoved him toward his brother's study and walked away, shaking her head.

Victor gave the double doors a vigorous shove and smiled at the surprised looks that met him at his entrance. His brother's angry face met him first. Victor nodded hello and then looked to the lady of the hour.

"Mags," he boldly drawled as he neared the aging woman to

take her diamond-laden hand; unsurprisingly, she refused to offer it to him. *Old bird,* he thought to himself.

"Playing hard to get?" he asked with a smirk. "Not your style."

"Victor," she began with an operatic tone of voice that reached the rafters. "Your brother and I have just spent the last hour discussing our business. I am sure he will catch you up."

Victor slouched in a nearby armchair. "Catch me up, Mummy? I hope he has good news. I hope he'll tell me you found someone to buy us out of this godforsaken business so that Wesley and I can move on with our lives and you can move on with the rest of your feeble years."

"Something like that, son," she began mockingly. "Your father would roll over in his grave if he knew what we were considering. Selling off the bank after all the work and money he put into it?"

Victor's eyebrows shot up in attention. "Money he put into it? Did I hear you right?"

She rolled her eyes at his aghast expression. "We don't have to get hung up on the specifics, Victor. You know that your father worked hard to leave a legacy for you boys, and you are just determined to throw it all away. But I suppose it's for the best. Your brother seems to believe that now is the time to get out of it."

"It is," Wesley added after he cleared his throat. "We can't liquidate enough to get ahead. I think it's a sign that things are changing. If we sell to Mags' person soon, we can at least give ourselves a little nest egg and maybe a restart."

"Exactly, Wesley. It's not about who put what money in and when; it's about being comfortable and getting out."

Victor couldn't help but comment again. Mags' eager sales speech annoyed him. "Comfortable? The last I checked, there were only two Carlson Brothers who have valid shares."

Mags' eyes narrowed as if she could slice him with her eyelids. "That may be so, but as we've discussed so many times in the past, you horrible boy, it was always my late husband's intention that I was taken care of after his death. You boys are the ones who tied up his money in his estate. I didn't get anything."

"And the other husbands you killed off? Will their estates be forever indebted to you?"

"I'm still owed my money! You cannot negate that!" Lord, she was easily riled.

Instead of relenting as he should, Victor continued, "Don't worry, Mummy. We plan to pay you a handsome sum that will keep you on Lafayette Street so you can continue to lie to your social buddies about your financial affairs.

Suddenly, a sweet smile appeared on Mags' face. "Your brother said as much, but he had the couth to put in much more delicate terms. I am not so surprised that you put things as thus. *Pish*. The Carlson Brothers. How your father handled your differences, I will never know. One is the brain, and the other is the beauty. One, astute on all matters and the other, a mannish whoremonger with the gall to treat me as if I am one of the simple women in his harem. And stop mocking me with that name."

"Mummy?"

"Yes!"

"But you told me to call you that when you were raiding my trust fund. Remember?"

Wesley stirred in his chair to calm the brewing storm, but it was too late. Victor waved his hand at him to quell his reaction and sat up to face Mags head on.

"Dear Mags, you have me all wrong, I'm afraid."

"No, I have you quite right, Victor. You are the weak link in this setting. Your philandering ways will be the family's downfall. I could bring the likes of the Vanderbilt's to the table, and they would still run away once they find out that the other half of the Carlson Brothers is a low-life philanderer. I can't say I would blame them for not wanting to align themselves with a male tart who can't keep his little friend in his pants. Your reputation precedes you. And you run in far too many of the wrong circles for my liking. Your nightly gallivanting from night club to whorehouse has dragged the Carlson name into the disgusting gutter."

"Little friend? Come now, Magsy baby. We've given you too much money over the years for you to lower yourself with cheap shots. Little friend?" Victor asked with a bemused smirk.

Victor's brother, Wesley, cleared his throat as he stood quietly by the window. "Mother, while Victor's extracurricular tastes might be offensive in some circles, they have nothing to do with our business. Whether you like it, he is one half of The Carlson Brothers Bank for a reason. His business sense should not be ignored, nor diminished in this endeavor. Our offer to you still stands. If you find someone to buy us out, we will make sure you have enough to retire. But I will not be parting from my brother as you so delicately suggested in his absence."

"Plotting on my demise, Magsy?" Victor asked in a mocking baby voice. "I'm surprised."

"I told Wesley that he is better off without you."

"Little friend?" Victor repeated from the rear of the room, where he was now arranging another glass of scotch. He repeatedly stabbed at the block of ice to shave a piece for his glass, causing an annoying tic in Wesley's eye.

"Victor!" he yelled over the building noise.

Mags would not wait for Victor to settle down. She rose to meet Wesley at the window, hoping to reason with him.

"Wesley," Mags began with a gentle voice. "I know it is hard for you to conceive this, but your brother has always held you back. I only speak the truth."

"Truth?" Wesley's voice reverberated against the oak wall paneling of the parlor. "With all due respect, you have done nothing but repeat rumors and conjecture. But I will give you some truth, Mother. Your own lifestyle has been bleeding us dry for years. You have overspent for the sake of keeping up with your neighbors. I put up with it because I want only your happiness, but you need to acknowledge that we built your lifestyle off Victor's back. You also need to acknowledge that times are changing. The Carlson Brothers' Penny Savings and Loan Bank will be worth pennies in a few years if we don't move things around now. Our offer is more than generous. So rather than discuss silly rumors, let's bring our lawyers in and talk money."

Mags pressed her lips together in a tight frown because her son had just bested her. Victor swiveled the ice in his glass loud enough to bring both sets of eyes to him.

"Fine. I will do it. I'll bring Mr. Marbury to the table. But..." She drew Victor and Wesley's attention with her dramatic voice inflection. "... with one small consideration. Mr. Marbury is a very conservative man. I've always known him to shy away from scandals and anything that would tarnish his good name."

"Get on with it, Mother. What is it?" Wesley demanded.

"Mr. Marbury will more than likely inquire into the bank's holdings, but he will also wander into our personal lives. It doesn't matter in business what one does behind closed doors, but Mr. Marbury isn't like everyone else. He's very religious, you know. He is a person who won't like the idea of making a deal with Negroes who ride around in flashy cars with white women."

"Ha!" Victor blurted.

"Mr. Marbury is one of those separatists. He does not believe in racial mixing, and he would be shocked to find out one of our own has been doing so. Now he has been generous over the years, but he will want to make sure we are the kind of Negroes he likes."

Wesley's patience was nearly gone. "He sounds like an ass. And? What does this have to do with the color of our money?"

"Fine, I'll get right to the point. Your brother needs to find a wife, and he needs to do so quickly."

"Sheeeiiit"! Victor replied, drawing blank stares from both of them.

"Done," Wesley declared.

"Done my ass. Wesley, don't be stupid enough to fall for another one of your mother's games."

"It's not a game," Mags hotly returned. "Now, I doubt you can convince a reputable girl to marry the likes of you. So there you have it. Take it or leave it. This is our ticket out. And if you want to be on this train, you will do what you need to do."

"Magsy, I am sure I could get any naïve virgin to be my wife in no time. Reverend Buckner's pocked-faced daughter passes out in church every time she sees me. I could make her play the little wife, while I carried on as usual. Now that you mention it, a wife doesn't sound all that bad. Is this a deal? If it is a deal, I think I will march right over to the good reverend's house and make his daughter's dreams come true."

"Don't you dare. Leave the innocent out of this."

After Victor expelled a loud yawn coupled with an ostentatious stretch. "Then I guess I'll call up Ms. Anderson."

"The biggest whore in Sandcaster? On a better thought, I will choose the woman for you."

This time both men laughed.

"Mother, you can't be serious," Wesley sobered while Victor fell onto the nearby chaise with laughter.

"I am quite serious. If you can't manage it, then we have no deal."

Victor rose from the chaise, still laughing. "Yep, no deal. Well, this has been a fun meeting. Unproductive, but fun. Mummy, please let us know when you will have a serious conversation about this made-up Mr. Marbury."

Victor continued to chuckle to himself as Wesley escorted Mags out of the room. When Wesley returned, Victor's chuckle had turned into an outright laugh.

"Victor," Wesley warned.

"You know, if I didn't know any better, I would think you are considering marrying me off just to appease Ms. High and Mighty."

"I don't think it is a bad idea. It wouldn't kill you to settle down."

"No, it wouldn't kill me. But I don't plan on letting you or that blue-haired devil decide when I do. And you of all people can see that this is just another distraction that she has cooked up. Even if I were to fall into this plan to fool her racist friend, she'd still find another way to weasel out of giving us anything. Have you forgotten the infamous event surrounding our father's will?"

Wesley let out a puff of annoyance and rolled his eyes heavenward. "I remember. But Victor, you have not made things better with her. You antagonize her on purpose. I bet you cause scandals and misbehave in public just to aggravate her. But you know we need to tie up loose ends with her. We have too much to lose. We have so much riding on this... our business, our legacy, our—"

"Legacy? Or our lack thereof, you mean?"

A dark shadow crossed Wesley's face as he narrowed his focus on Victor. "Our past is our past, but we have built something here, and that means something to my children and me. It should mean something to you. It should mean enough to you to be on time for our business meetings. It should mean enough for you not to act like an ass with my mother. It should mean that you will not propagate your lifestyle to the world through gossip rags. It would be nice if you were a little conservative or even discreet. We are bankers, for God's sake. It would be nice if you acted like one instead of a randy playboy. You have to admit that everything that woman said is right. This showboating around town with money, expensive cars, and women is getting ridiculous. It is almost as if you are trying to bring unwanted attention to us. I question your loyalty at times because I feel you are trying hard to sabotage us."

Finally, Victor's good humor vanished. "My loyalty? Have you forgotten, dear brother, that I bear the scar of my loyalty to this family, to this legacy?"

Wesley's stance finally eased as he let out a puff of air. "I know that you have sacrificed much—"

"I sacrificed far more than you could imagine, brother," Victor sternly interrupted. "I sacrificed all of it. And for what? So you and she can turn your nose up at what the hell I do with the rest of my miserable life?" He drank his last swig and slammed his tumbler down onto the glass table, wishing at that moment that it shattered into a million pieces. He got his wish.

≈

As BIANCA SAT NERVOUSLY in the back of a small classroom, watching her best friend, Hiram Coleman, finish his lengthy lecture on economics, she exhaled to slow her beating heart. She was nervous. Why? Because Mags' Christmas soiree was in two days and she could not figure out how on God's green earth could she show her face. She had no fiancé and no dress. The dress was an issue that her sister Cecilia had taken on since she was the more fashionable one. But the fiancé...

Of course, she had considered just marching back over to Mags' townhouse and delivering her regrets with a "no thanks" written across the front. But her mind got the better of her. Mags' stupid opinions annoyed Bianca's pride, but Bianca thought perhaps she should not let pride impede her aspirations. And that was precisely the logic that had landed her in the back of Hiram Coleman's classroom.

Hiram. Bianca smiled as she watched him enthusiastically explain the boring subject of economics. His antics were not dramatic; they were born out of how he felt. Hiram loved the subject. He talked about it ad nauseam wherever he went and to whoever he could. That was what Bianca loved about him. He could be himself with her, and in return, she was always herself around him. There was a comfortable joy in knowing that he knew her quirks. No one was lucky enough to have such a friend. And while other women ran scared, looking for a man who would love them to no end, Bianca had only to smile for she knew that she had Hiram. Hiram loved her. He said as much during their many intellectual conversations. Well, maybe he had not said it in the most romantic light, but he had said it. And love is love, isn't it? Besides, they were beyond silly romantic conventions like flowers and courtship. Their love was more of an intellectual love. One where they both fed each other's mind.

Once the flood of students exiting the tiny classroom died down, Hiram spotted her. He tilted his spectacles to be sure.

"Bee!" he exclaimed by showing his gap-toothed grin.

He'd called her Bee since they were children. It was his shortened version of her full name: Bianca Elizabeth Eubanks. Bianca smiled at the childhood endearment. She was Bee to him since the day he had taught her the logic of poker.

"To what do I owe this pleasure?" he asked. "How did your meeting go with that investor? Were you persuasive? I will say that I am truly excited about the prospect."

"Well, about that..." she began with a puff of air. There was no point in beating around the bush with Hiram. He knew her well enough to know that trick.

"Well? What is it? Did you point out the importance of the newspaper?"

"I did. I did."

"And?"

"Hiram... do you remember when we were little we always said that if we did not get married to someone by twenty that we would marry each other?"

Hiram's thick eyebrows bunched and then relaxed. "I recall our childish musings."

"Umm... well, you aren't married, and I'm not married..."

Hiram let out a loud guffaw before sobering. He wiped the tiny laugh tears from his eyes before saying, "You are so funny, Bee. I can't help laughing. I mean, could you imagine such a thing?"

Bianca blinked before she nervously laughed to save face. She soon joined him in his exuberance.

He continued to gurgle with laughter as he searched his desk for papers. "That's why I love you, Bee. You keep me laughing."

Bianca smiled again, realizing her smile had not made it to her eyes. "Us being married would be funny... wouldn't it?"

"The funniest," he added. "I mean, with you being you and me being me."

"Right... me being me." After a short pause, she followed up with, "What does that mean exactly? I am strictly asking for academic purposes."

Hiram laughed again. "Is that why you came to visit today? To give me a laugh? You are you. You are Bianca... eh... you wear pants. Most women at your age are having babies and shopping for the best dresses. But you are beyond that. You are simple in form and dress."

"Simple?"

"Sure," he answered her with sincerity. "Simple. But I like that about you. You look over trivial female silliness so you can focus on things like a man would. It is why we have the relationship we have."

Bianca tried her best to hear Hiram's words. They revealed that this whole time Hiram was her friend because he saw her as a man. What an odd arrangement of feelings she was having lately? Unable to sort them, Bianca cleared her throat of hurt feelings and ventured on for clarification. "A man?"

"Why, yes. A man is logical and un-swayed by emotion. That is you. I mean you swear, smoke cigars... even your hair is practical. Only a man would make such a decision."

"I cut my hair because my sister burned it with lye two months ago."

"And aren't you better for it? You don't take hours laying down the hairs on your head. You are above face powders and dresses. And you are sound in your logic because you don't have those feminine things clogging your judgment. As I said, Bee, you are you, and I am me."

"And you are?" she asked with sincere curiosity.

She had no question of who she was. There was never a doubt in her mind. Hiram was right in that regard; she was who she was. And perhaps he was right about her seeing little value in waiting at a hair salon every other day while they straightened the life out of her curls. She was fine with letting a hot comb go through it once or twice a week. She did enjoy smoking cigars, and she had an affinity for bourbon on a cold day.

And pants. She wore pants when she felt like it. Until recently, she had not considered that pants were an issue for some folks. Her pants were practical in every way. She spent long hours working at her father's hospital, and she had to do a lot of physical labor on print day at her newspaper. Dresses got in the way with all that, so she donned a pair of pants. Evidently, pants were hallmarks of a personality she had not considered. Mags called her a spinster, and now her best friend in the entire world was calling her a man. Both expressions suggested that the fabric she covered her legs with made her unqualified and unworthy. Odd.

"Hiram," she said, interrupting his murmurings about who he was. "Unfortunately, I don't have the luxury of seducing you with make-up and straightened hair. I wish I could be a little more subtle about what I need, but I cannot. Ms. Edison has invited me to her Christmas Soiree in two days and she is expecting to meet my fiancé there."

"Your fiancé? I didn't know you were engaged. To whom?"

"I'm not. But I could be to you."

"What?"

"Ms. Edison seems to be of the strange belief that I need to be connected to a man in order to run a successful newspaper. This has nothing to do with her willingness to loan me the money for the newspaper, but it has some strange bearing on her ability to trust a woman like me."

"That sounds like the stupidest thing I have ever heard."

"It is the stupidest thing you have ever heard," Bianca returned dryly. "But I need to get on this woman's good side and quick. If something is not done, I won't be able to buy the building to grow my business. I won't be able to pay my staff for Christmas, and I might have to declare bankruptcy."

"Well, we don't want that. You still owe me money from last month," Hiram grumbled. "So... you need me to play the part of the fiancé just to get his woman to trust you so she can loan you the money, right?"

"Exactly."

Hiram's eyebrows bunched together as he sat back against his desk in thought. Just as she was about to close the deal, Hiram's eyes flickered over her shoulder, giving Bianca the impression that something had caught his eyes. She was more convinced of this when he signaled someone behind her. Bianca turned, and a vision of loveliness appeared before her in the form of a bouncing and shimmering woman. A melodic giggle expelled from her throat as she worked her voluptuous body around the maze of desks.

"Honey bear!" Bianca heard the woman call out to no one other than Hiram as he blushingly waved her over.

"Ah. It seems that you are just in time to meet Harmony Rodgers... my fiancée." Bianca stared at his beaming smile as he looked lovingly on this golden fairy princess, with her perfectly coifed hair and her red lip paint and her red silk dress. This was who he was. And she was who Bianca was not. Oddly, instead of feeling entirely saddened by the idea of losing her best friend to a majestic goddess, she was humored by what she had proposed. How silly must she have sounded?

Bianca grabbed Harmony's hand with a firm handshake and a wide smile. It was a pleasure to meet her, but it would be even more pleasurable to leave this almost embarrassing situation.

"Ahem," she coughed to interrupt Hiram's lengthy chattering.

"I'm so glad to have met you. But I must be going. I just stopped by to give a laugh to my friend over here."

Hiram laughed nervously this time. "Oh, yes! That was a good laugh."

All three of them fell in line to a moment of awkward silence before Bianca coughed again. "Well... take care," she said almost over her shoulder before she bravely walked away, knocking a wooden desk out of its alignment. She quietly pushed it back in line while Hiram stood quietly, watching her. Not one to let embarrassment have the last say so, she turned back with a gleeful smile and waved to them both.

Well, apparently, that was that, and she was who she was. It was a silly plan, anyway. Who was she kidding? There are no shortcuts to financial freedom. For her, there was no savior investor, no rich husband, and apparently, no friendly unattached men who will save the day.

CHAPTER 3

THE PERCEIVED INEVITABLE

Bianca blew a long and blustering sigh as she made her way to the *Baltimore Beat*. She blew raspberries whenever she was nervous or frustrated. It was an unladylike habit, but she had no other way of expressing her worry. Christmas was in three weeks and she had to be the one to deliver the news to her small staff that there would be no paychecks today or next week. She had failed them. She had failed to convince Mags or anyone else who was stupid enough to invest in a silly gossip rag ran by four Negro women. The thought of their disappointed faces was enough to make Bianca turn around and run home. Before Bianca could really consider tucking tail and running, her secretary, Kizzy, appeared on the front stoop of the *Baltimore Beat*.

"Hey, boss lady!"

"Hi, Kizzy," Bianca returned.

"I am so excited about today. Ms. Ginny told me not to get all excited because we never know what's gonna happen, but I told her I have nothing but faith in our fearless leader. That's you, by the way. I know you know that because you are so smart!

I know I'm talkin' too much. Ms. Ginny says I talk too much, but I don't worry about—"

"Kizzy..."

"I know, I know too much talkin'. I won't go on and on and because I'm sure you got plenty of business to get to and papers and all that. But my husband got up early this morning before he went down to the railroad. He was worried about how we gonna have enough money to be on our own with this here baby and how we gonna get out of my mama's house. I told him the same thing I told Ms. Ginny. Ms. Bianca got it all under control. She gonna get us an investor who gonna pay all of our paychecks, and then that big ole investor is gonna fix that dang gone hole in the roof, and then we all gonna be fine. Ain't gonna be no more standing in the back of the bread lines. And you know they give the Negroes less than they give the white folks. Oh no. No, ma'am. She gonna take this here newspaper national. We fixin' to buy this here building and get even bigger and better. Then we will... "

At some point, Bianca found her way inside and to her desk. She sat there, rubbing her face to the background of Kizzy's rant.

"All right now, Kizzy. Sit yo'self down somewhere and get out of her face," Ms. Ginny said from around the corner. The gray-haired woman waved little Kizzy away from Bianca's desk before settling down on the edge to look Bianca square in the eyes. "You didn't get it, did you?" Her eyes emphasized her matter-of-fact tone by glaring over the rims of her small glasses.

For a moment, Bianca considered lying as she had lied to Mags, but she couldn't lie to Ms. Ginny. The woman had birthed seven children during her lifetime. There was no lie she couldn't see through. So, Bianca swallowed a bullet and nodded in the affirmative.

"Of course, you didn't. Mags is the cheapest ole' bag in all of Baltimore. She won't spend a penny unless it makes her look good. Old foolish fart. I bet she spends money on her young men friends. I bet that much. Alight, then. No need in crying over spilled milk. We will manage our own stead."

"I'm sorry, Ms. Ginny. I feel so bad because when I started this paper, I took all of you off of jobs that could have been paying you right now. And I convinced you to stay even when things got rough on the strength of this venture."

Ms. Ginny let out a deep grumble before she returned, "That might be true, young lady, but there is no helping it now. We will manage. We will survive. I know my sister can pull a few strings to get me back on the sewing line, and I might be able to get Kizzy a job too. Her being pregnant and as big as she is shouldn't be a problem."

Bianca forlornly considered her words until a thought entered her mind. "And what about Daisy? Where's Daisy anyway?"

Daisy had always been Bianca's closest friend and supporter. A friend since childhood, Daisy had never left Bianca's side. She was loyal enough to quit her job and help build the Baltimore Beat up from the ground. But sadly, Daisy, a talented, college-educated woman, who was a brilliant journalist, had a knack for detouring and choosing paths that were rocky and full of holes.

Ms. Ginny's posture straightened as she rounded her shoulders. Kizzy joined back next to her with a sad face as she held her belly.

"He got her again," Kizzy said gloomily.

"That bastard?" Bianca hotly returned.

With her hands neatly folded in her lap, Ms. Ginny spoke again. "No sense in being surprised. It is the same cycle as always. He tosses her out like a piece of garbage when he's used her all up; we find her, feed her, and fatten her up, and then he comes back around, wooing her so he can use her again."

"I guess it wasn't hard to woo her back when things have been so tough around here, huh?" Bianca asked.

There was no need for an answer. Ms. Ginny and Kizzy's silence spoke volumes.

Their silence also spoke to the countless sacrifices they had made in their individual lives for the sake of this little dream Bianca had. Bianca had plucked all of them from their everyday lives where they were not so much thriving, but at least they survived.

Bianca sat still to focus her thoughts. What could she do? She had to do something. She couldn't go to her father since he was on the edge of his own financial ruin. She had failed to convince Mags of anything. She had to think of something; it could not be over yet. And before her mind could visualize an answer to her problems, Kizzy spoke again. She always had a knack of interrupting Bianca's thoughts.

"Um, boss lady, there's a man here to see you. Oh, I guess I should have said gentleman. He's handsome. Is he your gentleman friend?"

Miss Ginny answered first. "Did you get the man's name, Kizzy? We can't just let any ol'body in here."

"He didn't say. But he said Ms. Bianca knew him. He asked me about the hole in the roof and asked how we keep it so warm in here. I told him we keep it warm with love. He laughed. He has a friendly laugh. Is he your gentleman friend, boss lady?"

No longer able to take another second of Kizzy's prattle, Bianca rose to meet this mysterious man. At the end of the long hallway leading to the front door stood a familiar figure, indeed.

"Hello, Bee," Hiram said with a polite smile once she reached him.

"What are you doing here, Hiram?"

"Your secretary is a little chatty. Did you know that? In the few seconds of our meeting, I learned that she and her husband live in her mother's flat in Sandcaster, along with her five sisters and brothers. She is with child, and she is looking forward to moving out whenever she receives her Christmas bonus from you, but all that depends on whether you were able to persuade your silent investor."

Bianca openly cringed at Kizzy's antics. "She loves to share. What are you doing here?"

A sober expression appeared on Hiram's face as he removed his hat from his head. He did not bother to remove his wool overcoat. Bianca noted that his professional attire had probably seen better days.

"I've given some thought to your proposal," he declared.

"My what?"

"Your proposal. The other day? Your investor's demands?"

"Ah! That one," replied with feigned discovery. Bianca knew good and well what proposal he was referencing. She would rather just forget the whole thing entirely.

"Yes, well, I will do it."

"Do what?"

Hiram leaned in to whisper in her ear this time. "I will pretend to be your future husband."

Bianca leaned back to stare at him for a moment before asking, "Why?"

"Ahem," he began. "When I thought about... err... your proposal, I figured this is the quickest way to change things for you financially. And you owe me the money I loaned you to fix your printing press. And I want to buy a ring for Harmony."

"Ah. And you believe if I get Ms. Edison's investment, you'll get your money. Have you discussed this idea with Harmony? Won't she take exception to our engagement?" Bianca emphasized by gesturing with quotation marks.

"She would. She certainly would. But she won't know because she's leaving tomorrow to visit her mother and brothers in Texas for Christmas. She will be gone through March. That gives us plenty of time to play our roles and get Ms. Edison to give you enough money to fix things around here. Now that I think of things, it is a little drafty in here. That hole in the roof isn't safe. It will snow soon."

"Hiram, you do not have to do this. It was a stupid idea, and it won't work, anyway."

"Yes, it will. My mind's made up. You owe me, and we will do it. Okay? When is that Christmas thing? Isn't it tomorrow? I have a tuxedo. Just need to get the mothball smell out. I'll set it out tonight and meet you there. Okay?" He did not wait for Bianca to respond. He pressed a hard kiss against her cheek, squeezed her hand, and hurriedly walked out of the door.

Bianca blew another raspberry at the closed door.

VICTOR LEANED over the gilded ledge of the Hinsdale House while he surveyed the sea of white tuxes and sparkling dresses downstairs. They were the elite invitees who were worthy enough to attend Mags' Christmas soiree. As much as he hated to admit it, and he had to, it was quite a swanky affair. Mags had outdone herself.

Victor's eyes grazed over the flow of expensive champagne, the opulent Christmas décor, and the menagerie of absurd entertainments and rolled his eyes. She had really put on a show. He watched her at the top of the stairs, accepting each guest as if she were the queen of England.

Victor snorted after he reminded himself that not two days before, she had barreled through his townhouse door, promising to ruin him if he didn't attend. She knew he had no intention of making an appearance. Not that he didn't enjoy a good party. He loved a good party. And he had predicted that there would be plenty of women wearing ridiculously scandalous frocks to catch his eye. And he was right, there were. But he really had no intention of supporting anything Mags created.

Her words from the other day struck him. He was not sure why. He had always known that his father's wife was a horrendous human being with a tongue capable of bringing down empires. Over the years, she had developed a nasty habit of regarding him with sincere contempt. Still, despite all the horrible things she said, her mocking him and branding him the weakest link stung.

However, no matter how much Victor loathed to breathe the same oxygen as Mags, he still had a part to play. That was what Wesley reminded him while he nonchalantly smoked his cigar in his townhome's front room.

"I don't care how much you hate the blue hairs on her head, we still need her," Wesley barked at him as he ate his morning steak and eggs. "Victor, there's a chance Mr. Marbury could be there. We need to keep up appearances. He wants to invest in a family business, and he will want to see a happy family. Maybe if you just play the nice son and get on her good side and for once in your life, she might forget about this petty marriage thing."

So, at the absolute last minute, Victor shrugged on his white tux and tails and then donned his top hat and white gloves. He wouldn't play the part of a loving son, though. Not like his groveling brother. He wouldn't. Victor Andrew Carlson might have been many things, but he was no liar. He could barely contain the contempt and disgust on his face, much less lie to others. That was why he kept his distance upstairs and away from the crowd. Deep within his vexed mood, Victor plotted an early departure.

He swiped a glass of champagne from a random waiter's tray. Champagne always helped him see clearer. And he was seeing things he hadn't seen before. The space of the missing glass on the waiter's tray revealed a yellow sparkle that grabbed Victor's attention. At closer inspection, that yellow sparkle belonged to a shapely yellow dress. To whom the dress belonged, he could not tell since the waiter had not moved on. Victor glared at the waiter and pointedly nodded his head in the opposite direction. After the waiter took Victor's blunt direction to move on, the yellow dress reappeared. But the woman's back faced him. And what a nice back it was. Her entire back was scandalously bare. Since she wasn't looking in his direction, he saw no reason he shouldn't allow his eyes to drift down to the soft roundness of her rump. Whoever this woman was, she possessed a perfect set of brown legs and an awful pair of black shoes. She ruined it all with the black shoes. He should go over to her and tell her as much. Before he could make his move, he heard a familiar voice behind him.

"Well, I was almost wrong," Mags declared with an air of satisfaction.

He refused to allow her to goad him, so he continued to stare at his new fascination in the yellow dress. Yellow dress was looking for someone. He wondered who.

"Do you know what I told Wesley this morning?" Mags continued.

"I'm sure you will tell me."

"I said that you lacked the ability to care for anything other than your own miserable self."

"You weren't wrong."

Mags whipped around to his front. Her tall headdress of peacock feathers blocked his eyesight of the yellow dress. Now his face revealed his consternation. She smiled in approval. "There you are. I knew the real Victor would show up."

"Careful, Magsy. We don't want to make a scene, do we? Where's Mr. Marbury? Did you get him to sign away his money?"

Her eyes danced wildly back and forth as she considered who might be listening. When Victor made the move to go around her, she grabbed his arm to stop him. She now had the ability to whisper into his ear.

"Well, I am glad you could make it, but you should have told me that you were coming. At my last spiteful minute, I invited Edmund and Angel Talley. They are my neighbors, you know. And you know how much Mrs. Talley loves Negro causes. I was sure she would make a hefty donation to the chosen charity of the night. Normally, I would love to watch you squirm. But we are being watched, so please do your best to act like you are a Negro who knows his place. Stay away from that woman."

Victor pressed his teeth together in his jaw so hard that he feared they would shatter. How he hated this woman. He should make a scene and embarrass her in retaliation, but that would only make Wesley angry. And when she pointed to Edmund and Angel's slow approach in his direction, he decided there was nothing left to do but to retreat and fight his opponent another day.

"I wish you a safe journey, son," he heard her loudly say behind him. It was loud enough for those around her to hear, he noted.

Victor made his way down the long stairs and headed for the coat check. He had no intention of getting tangled with Angel's husband again. As he rounded a marble pillar, a sight stopped his feet. It was Miss Yellow Dress standing at the back door, waiting. Who was Miss Yellow Dress waiting for? And who in their right mind would keep a woman with those legs waiting? Perhaps she was ugly. Maybe he should see for certain. No! This was precisely the problem with him. He had a marked destination and something or someone would distract him. Was it greed? Or just a sheer curiosity that led him astray? He was not sure, but there was a mysterious invisible string that pulled him to Miss Yellow Dress and her lovely feminine, sun-bronzed back.

"Looking for someone?" It was the first thing that came to his mind to ask. Perhaps he should have been a little less obvious. Maybe a "may I help you" would have been better. It didn't matter. It was too late as he had startled her enough to drop her purse along with its contents all over the floor. Jumpy little thing, wasn't she?

"I'm sorry, I didn't mean to startle you," he said while bending down, intending to pick up her bag.

She stopped him with her hand on his shoulder. And that was when he saw her face.

"You," they both said in unison.

CHAPTER 4

THE WELL-INTENDED MISUNDERSTANDING

"Well," he began with a big grin, "It's good to see you again, Miss..."

It was her. The mysterious woman from the other day. There was no mistaking that same scowl of displeasure to see him. One of her eyebrows rose in expectation. He still could not recall where he knew her from, but he knew her from somewhere. *Shit.* And she looked almost beautiful tonight. The dress from the front was even better than the back. The bodice dipped low and draped against her lush bosom. The eye-catching yellow dazzled him until he realized that she was growing into an outrage, watching his eyes rove her entire body.

He felt himself chuckle in embarrassment. "Okay, Miss Yellow Dress. You won't remind me of your name, but the night is young, and I have many resources available to me."

She exhaled a long breath and rolled her eyes in exasperation. "If I tell you my name, will you go away?"

"Maybe."

"If I tell you my name and how we first met, will you go away?"

"Possibly."

"If I tell you my name, how we met, and how I will gladly knee you in the bullocks, will you go away?"

"Yes," he said with a grin.

"Fine. My name is Bianca Eubanks. We met a few years back. You are friends with my brother-in-law, Joseph Carpenter."

"Good Ole Joe! Ah, yes," he blurted. The wheels in his mind turned, and a vision of Miss Bianca entered his mind, giving him the satisfaction of a refreshed memory. "You slapped me the very first time I met you, much like you did the other day."

Her chin lifted high in the air. She smiled. "I did. You were being obnoxious."

"I've been told I have a knack for being that. However, it was hardly a fair meeting. As I now recall, you slapped me, and I didn't even get to be as bad as I could be."

She smiled again. She had a delightful smile; he decided. Her teeth were incredibly white, and she had dimples that came alive on each of her cheeks. "I didn't get the chance to be as violent as I could be. Shall we try it again? You say something ridiculously callous, and I'll do something different like squeezing your balls in a vice grip."

"You have a sincere fascination with my genitals. Care to get aquatinted?" To his delightful surprise, she laughed again.

"Victor Carlson. Unlike the harem of women you tote around …" Her words became lost when she spotted someone across the room. Instead of politely excusing herself like a lady, she took her two hands and pushed, no, shoved him out of the way.

"Get away, already," he heard her say as his feet involuntarily stumbled beneath him.

Now that was rude. Still, his curiosity would not allow him to leave the scene, no matter how much she detested him. Victor found a hidden spot behind a nearby marble pillar that gave him a view of Miss Yellow—no, Miss Bianca, as she waved down a man heading her way.

"Hiram," Victor heard Bianca say. "Where have you been?

The party is almost over. I've been waiting all night. Mags has asked me three times already where my fiancé was. I know that she thinks I'm a liar. I've made up at least six stories, and none of them make any sense. If she asks, you have an astounding knack for numbers and have a growing investment portfolio. You also spent your formative years in Africa, where you lead a mission to feed starving children."

Fiancé? She was engaged? And to this scrap? This shabby soul with thick spectacles won Miss Bianca over?

Hiram cleared his throat nervously. "Bee, there has been a small hiccup in our plans."

"Hiccup? I should say so. My girdle has been riding up my you know what all night, and I will kill someone if I don't find this Mags woman, point her to you, and go home to take it off."

Victor watched this Hiram person look over his shoulder. "There is something I need to tell you. It's urgent, Bee."

"Oh, it is no time for that. Here she comes," Bianca growled with a tight smile as Mags approached. Now he should hide.

"Dear Miss Eubanks. Has the time finally arrived? Are you ready to introduce your fiancé? I've heard so much about you, Mister..." Mags could not finish her words, for she was now being shoved aside by a curvy creature on fire with sheer anger.

"*Fiancé?*" the woman screeched. "Hiram! What is the meaning of this??"

"Harmony?" Bianca called to the woman to sound pleasantly surprised. "What are you doing here? Hiram never mentioned you would be here? Hiram, why is she here?"

Hiram jabbed his finger in the tight space of his collar to collect some air. "Ahem. I might have left the invitation on the table, and Harmony might have found it. Isn't she a clever girl?" He and Bianca laughed out loud with tight expressions on their faces. "And my little buttercup refused to leave my side and go to Georgia as she promised she would. Isn't she just wonderful?"

Victor watched with great embarrassment while Bianca's features rose and fell within seconds.

It was now Mags' turn to talk. "I gather what this is all about. This isn't your fiancé, is it, Miss Eubanks?"

Poor Bianca's shoulders drooped down to the floor as she replied, "No, it isn't."

"What do you take me for, Miss Eubanks? Some senile old woman? I know everyone and everything in this town, and you will have to get up early in the morning to fool Mags Edison. You tried and failed to orchestrate all of this to gain my investment in your ridiculous business venture. And now look at you. Ruined. I will tell everyone who needs to know it what sort of liar you are."

From behind his marble pillar, Victor watched morbidly as the drama unfolded right before him. He felt bad for the girl and anyone else who had the misfortune of tangling themselves with Mags. Her bite was just as bad as her bark, and this poor Miss Eubanks was about to find out how sharp her teeth really were.

Victor made his move to back away and be on his merry way to find his coat. Too bad for Miss Yellow Dress. When he whipped around to face the coat check, his shoulder crashed into what felt like another gentlemen's shoulder.

"Pardon me," he said instinctively.

"No harm done," the stranger returned before squarely looking Victor in his eye and making the startling realization that Victor was Victor. It was Angel's husband, Edmund. The man stared at Victor with a new awareness.

Victor knew Angel stood next to him, but Victor wouldn't dare move his eyes to her in front of her husband. He was already growing incensed by the second. No words passed between them, and the only thing heard was the nearby conversation had by Mags and Bianca. That caught Edmund's attention.

Edmund's eyes settled on Bianca, remembering that Victor told him she was his wife. Victor inwardly cringed when they both overheard Mags call Bianca "a lying spinster." Upon hearing as much, Edmund's eyes darted back to Victor with a new vengeance. Victor really didn't want to have to fight Edmund. Or shoot Edmund. He didn't really want to be bothered with the whole thing. But damn it, if he wasn't trapped in a hairy predicament.

"There you are, love of my life, where have you been?" Victor bellowed in Bianca's direction. In two strides, he made it to her and lifted her stiff and shocked body in the air and planted a big, fat, juicy kiss on her full lips. He did it right there in front of a sea of partiers, Edmund, Angel, that Hiram fellow and best of all, Mags.

Mags sputtered in disbelief as Victor spun Bianca around so that her back faced his front and so he could place his arms tightly around her waist. He planted another kiss on her neck before pretending to notice that Mags was standing there.

"Oh, it's you, Mummy. Have you met my fiancée, Bianca? She's a lovely girl, isn't she? Oh, this must be your friend, Hiram, you were telling me about, darling." Victor grabbed Hiram's hand and shook the hell out of it. He gave Harmony's hand equal treatment.

"So, Mummy, what do you think of my little angel?"

Out of all the words that could have come out of Mags' mouth, he had never predicted she would say what she said at that moment. "She... perfect."

"Yes, she is," Victor said again with another kiss to Bianca's temple.

What the hell was he doing? Whatever he was doing, it was working, because Edmund had now turned away. However, Angel looked over her shoulder, sad and forlorn. There was no time to nurse hurt feelings, he decided. The show must go on.

Mags spoke next, "Victor, you never mentioned you were engaged. We had a full discus—"

"Yes, I recall our discussion the other day, but you know how I can be. Plus, we wanted it to be a surprise. But then my little sweetie told me how you wanted to meet me, so it inclined me to spill the beans. Isn't that right, darling?"

It was now Bianca's time to talk. The success of this façade now rested on her.

"That's right, my love," she said with a resolute vigor. "Mrs. Edison, please meet my fiancé."

Mags gave her a leveled look but soldiered on for the sake of the surrounding audience. "Wonderful news. I hope you will join me for a light lunch and tea tomorrow so we can discuss all the... interesting details of your engagement."

Victor's hands still wound around Bianca's middle. It was a good thing, too, because her legs had gone limp.

"I would love to," she replied, almost weakly.

After being abandoned by Mags, Harmony, and Hiram, Victor finally released Bianca. He could tell there were many things she wanted to say. He also had a few things to say, but this was not the time or place to say them.

"Gather your things. I'm taking you home, my love." He intended for his words to be final.

She accepted his extended arm and allowed him to escort her out. Good job, Miss Yellow Dress.

❧

BIANCA STAYED in character and played the role of the loving fiancée right up to the very point where Victor helped her into his brand new Studebaker and slammed the door. That was the exact moment when she covered her face in her hands and let out a muffled scream. How in the world did her little lie grow into such catastrophic proportions? Oh, that's right. She let Hiram talk her into nursing her little white lie into a small child. And once Victor barged in to help, the small child grew into a full-grown man. Two arms, two legs, and a very, very, very handsome face.

Okay, it was always her intention to lie. She had planned to tell Mags her lie about Hiram. She staged a premeditated farce that would have been an arm's length away from Mags' scrutiny, but close enough to gain her favor. But no, Hiram had to mess up her plans, and Victor... well...

She considered being mad at Victor. But she had to admit that although he had roped her into another one of his lies to protect his foolish hide, he had saved her. Mags was just about to release her ax into Bianca's neck. Neither she nor the *Baltimore Beat* would have survived her social punishment. But Lord in heaven, who knew that the fool sitting next to her driving like a deranged maniac was Mags' very own son? How was Bianca to manage an arm's-length lie now?

"Jesus!" Bianca gasped as Victor nearly ran over an old woman in the street. "Why are you driving like a madman? And what the hell is eating you?"

He was angry. She could tell. She could see the indentation of his jaw muscles move from his stone profile. His hand gripped the steering wheel so tightly that his knuckles were turning white. He continued to zig through traffic with furor until he finally pulled over and slammed on the brakes. She had to brace her hands against the dashboard to avoid flying through the window.

"What the hell?" she barked after falling back against the seat.

"What the hell is right," he growled. "Can you tell me what just happened?"

"Maybe you should ask yourself the same question."

He growled again while roughly ripping his bow tie loose from his collar. "I don't know what happened. But I now know you are a liar."

"*Me?* Isn't that the pot calling the kettle black? You started this lie when you lied to save your ass from being shot by your mistress's husband. How else did this happen here?"

"Well, that lie would have laid right where it was, had you not attended Mags' party to lie to her about your love life. And why did you lie to her? Let me guess; you needed a leg up into her social circle, so you lied about your marital status. Did you even know that fellow you propped up like he was your intended?"

She took a deep breath before she spoke through her gritted teeth. "I do know him. He's a friend of mine, but our relationship is... well... complicated—"

"Complicated? That is not what his actual fiancée had to say."

Bianca pursed her lips at his interruption and continued her explanation, "I might have given Ms. Edison the impression that Hiram and I were engaged. But I would have been able to dissolve the purported relationship with no one getting hurt at a later time."

"Except his actual fiancée," he said with a leveled look.

"Listen, we can go around and around about who lied first, but the truth is that we both lied. And whether you like it or not, you owe me."

He grumbled again. "Now we need to figure out how to get out of this mess. I have no interest in being shackled to anyone. Not even on false pretenses. You might have to resort to such drastic measures, but I don't."

"What's that supposed to mean?"

"It means... never mind. Are you going to tell Mags, or should I be the one?"

Bianca straightened the folds of her dress under his gaze. "I will be the one. I have no intention of being shackled with you, so don't worry. It was Hiram I wanted, remember?"

Although he didn't respond directly to her, he let out a snort.

"I would hate to be the one to spoil your reputation," she added.

Victor looked at her as if a light went on above her head. "Thank you," he said with sincerity.

She couldn't help but roll her eyes again. "I will go to this luncheon tomorrow and explain everything to her. I will explain that you just wanted to save me from embarrassment, so you jumped and sacrificed yourself like a real gentleman."

Victor let out a deep growl from the base of his throat. "She won't believe that last part."

"Why wouldn't she? You are family. She'd believe you were just being helpful."

"No, she won't. We're related, but only by circumstance. She will never believe that I would do such a selfless thing. You should tell her the truth. Tell her I did it to save my ass. That she will believe."

Bianca blinked at his sudden candidness. "Very well."

He stared at her for a moment and then turned back to the steering wheel to resume driving. "Home?"

He drove her home without saying a word after she gave him her address. He got out of the car to open the door for her, but she was already out by the time he made it around the hood. She could have sworn he rolled his eyes. As a final goodbye, he gave her a sendoff salute then drove away. Bianca refused to watch his car speed away. No, it was better to lift her chin in dignity and march on. Tomorrow she would tell Mags the unadulterated truth and leave the fate of the *Baltimore Beat* up to chance.

CHAPTER 5

THE UNINVITED

The next day a strange warming wind touched down in Baltimore. The snow that blanketed the ground two days before had melted. The sun's morning rays revealed what had been long forgotten once the weather changed. Bianca noted a medley of soggy fall leaves, paper, and various trinkets frozen in the December's winter, now on display for everyone's viewing. Bianca's life was similar. She had almost forgotten the soggy state of her financial affairs. For a moment, she believed that her problems had disappeared with the presence of a beautiful possibility. She would get the investment funds, pay her debts and her employees, and all would be grand. But just like the snow, Mags' investment was a fragile thing, easily melted away by the bright light of truth. And now that the sun had come out; it was time to address the forgotten.

Bianca made her way to Mags' townhome on Lafayette with a plan. She would tell the truth about Victor and then empty the last of her savings to pay her employees and file bankruptcy. She would move back into her parents' home and rebuild.

Before ringing Mags' doorbell, Bianca looked down at her

wide-legged pants, wrinkled blouse, and coat and almost laughed. Today she barely bothered to iron. What was the point? She hadn't bothered to put on any makeup, either. There was no longer need for pretense. Her life, her finances, and her appearance were what they were.

A gray-haired gentleman opened Mags' large oak door. He had kind eyes; she noticed. "Are you here to see Mrs. Edison?" he asked.

"Yes. I shouldn't be long. I can wait in the front hall if that is okay."

He furrowed his brow before responding. "My instructions are to escort you to the library for tea," he declared.

"Oh, no, no. That won't be necessary. I can just wait right here next to the door."

"Young lady, you can't very well expect me to pull the Missus out of her luncheon to make her come out into the hallway."

Bianca peevishly cursed under her breath and then gave a tight smile back to the man. "I suppose not. Lead the way."

After a maid whisked her coat away, Bianca was immersed into the opulent, and frankly, ostentatious world of Mags Edison. Every entryway and door had bright gold, ornate trimmings. Each wall had its own elaborate mural of Mags. Mags dancing, Mags smiling in the clouds, Mags looking like the queen, and Mags looking like a young girl standing in a meadow. Bianca blinked at each one, unsure of how to process such a celebration of one's self. Bianca wrinkled her nose behind Mags' butler's back as he strode to the double doors at the end of the hallway. Once he arrived, he gave Bianca a gentle smile and opened them. The bright light from the six massive windows in the room almost blinded her.

"Come forth, dear," Mags demanded. "For heaven's sake, don't stand there like a tree."

Bianca stumbled into a room with several sets of eyes watching her. She surveyed the room, recognizing some faces from the social circles she reported on and others she did not.

One woman, incidentally, was the landlady of her flat on Druid Hill Street. She had been dodging the woman for weeks and darn it if the woman was not right in front of her, no doubt wondering where this month's rent was. *Great.*

Mags sat in the center next to a vase set with a freshly cut arrangement of pink roses, bearing a tight expression. Her eyes moved up and down Bianca's attire from across the room. Bianca involuntarily fidgeted under her assessment.

"Is this her?" one older woman seated next to Mags asked.

"Yes, Pauline. This is Victor's fiancée. Or so she says."

"Why would she say if it were not true, Mags?" Ms. Pauline patted the seat next to her, gesturing for Bianca to sit. "Come girl. Mags can be a mean snake. My name is Pauline Dilworth. I'm pleased that someone has finally pinned the tail of that wild dog."

Bianca accepted the seat while they all watched her. But not before she had her say. "Nice to meet you, and thank you, ma'am. But I don't plan to stay long. I just wanted a word with Ms. Edison."

"Oh?" Mags asked.

"Yes, would you mind if we spoke privately?"

"Privately? Now? Could it not wait until after lunch? We waited for you. We're hungry, you know?"

"I didn't wait," Ms. Pauline interjected. "I've been eating the sandwiches Carmichael put out. They were a bit stingy with the tuna if you ask me."

Bianca cleared her throat. "I'm sorry about being late, but I would like a word now, please."

"How demanding," Mags commented with a frown.

"She has grit; I'll give her that," Ms. Pauline chuckled as the butler entered the room with a tray of food. "She'll give you a run for your money, Mags. Can't roll over on this one."

Mags stared at Bianca, almost contemplating Ms. Pauline's words. "What do you want to discuss privately, girl?"

Bianca swallowed her emotions. Fine, if this was how she wanted it, out in the open for all to hear. She came this way to tell the truth, and damn it that was what she would do. Bianca licked her lips nervously and then straightened to her tallest posture as she sat in her pink cushioned seat. "It's your son. He is not—"

Bianca did not finish her words. She could not. The double doors burst open as if the intruder kicked the doors down, sending a burst of cold wind into the room, nearly blowing out the fire in the nearby fireplace.

"Mummy!" Victor yelled as he stood in the middle of the doors' entrance.

Wide eyes stared at him as he confidently strolled in wearing a perfectly tailored brown-tweed suit. He threw a walking stick to the floor and his hat onto a nearby table and extended his arms as if he were greeting an old friend.

"Victor!" Mags barked. "How dare you burst in uninvited?"

"Uninvited? Come on, Mummy. Do I really need an invitation to save my sweet, darling fiancée from your roasting? What kind of man would I be if I sent her to her slaughter? I came to protect my little buttercup." When he finished speaking, he took his place behind Bianca and held her in the chair.

Bianca craned her head up at him, searching for an ounce of common sense. What the hell was he thinking? She searched his eyes as he argued with Mags over the rudeness of his presence. He did not wink at her one time. He gave no casual gesture signifying a prank or joke. And what he did next almost made Bianca fly out of the room.

He picked her up. He plucked her entire body off the chair and kissed her. Once again, he caught her off guard. Her body initially reacted by pushing his face away, but she remembered people watched them. There was nothing left to do but kiss. The heat of his body radiated against hers, and she felt something that she had never felt before. His eyes met hers with a quiet, promising fire. Feeling intensely vulnerable, Bianca pushed against his chest to force her release.

"Put her down! You awful, rude boy," Mags huffed. "You are embarrassing our guests."

The ladies in the room giggled and whispered at Victor's antics.

"I'm not embarrassed," Ms. Pauline remarked. "This is the best party you have ever had, Mags."

"Agreed," Bianca heard another woman say as Victor held her waist possessively.

"How did you meet?" one asked.

"You look so different," someone commented.

"Well, you do know opposites attract?" Ms. Pauline informed the group.

Opposites? Victor and Bianca were more than mere opposites; they were on different planets. Bianca being from a practical earth, and Victor from this awful Martian planet where judgy black women sat in whimsical libraries with silly murals of their likenesses painted on the walls. So in true Bianca fashion, she gripped three of Victor's fingers and squeezed until he yelped and released her from his hold.

"I came to have a word with you, Ms. Edison," Bianca announced.

Mags, who had been quietly nibbling on her tiny sandwich, dabbed the corners of her mouth and then quietly placed her napkin in her lap. "Did you?"

"I did. And I don't think I can wait any longer. Victor and I are not engaged. There. I said it."

Everyone around her blinked at her truth for just a moment. It was Victor who broke her truth's spell. He stood still and very tall, but his deep voice echoed through the room. He looked at her soberly and with no sign of gest. "Darling, I know we had a spat last night, but that is no reason to call things off. You were angry because I spilled the beans about our engagement before you could announce it properly to your parents. In my eagerness to be near you, and forever bound to you, I forgot to consider your wishes."

Bianca closed her eyes against the almost sincere admission of love and fidelity. Her ears ached from the horrid sounds of the ladies cooing, oohing and aahing. She opened her eyes to witness Victor's massive build crouching down on one knee before her. She watched with wide eyes as he pulled a small red box from his coat pocket and opened it. She stood there, looking at the face of opulent beauty in the form of a large emerald surrounded by smaller white diamonds. He plucked the ring from its holding place and gently held Bianca's hand.

"Will you ever find it in your heart to forgive me, my love?"

Bianca later realized that all the ladies, including Mags, had surrounded her and stood on her side, watching and waiting with bated breath for her response. Bianca glared at him with narrowed eyes before looking around her and catching the looks of the other women, her landlady included.

"You are giving her that ring?" Mags asked.

"Can't you find it in your heart to forgive him, dear?" one of her friends asked.

"Just look at that face," another said.

Perhaps it was his handsome expression adoringly begging her to say yes, or perhaps it was the unfair pressure she felt from the surrounding women, but Bianca's mind pulled into the fantasy, and before she knew it, she said, "Yes."

Without waiting another minute, Victor pressed the ring onto her finger, stood, and hugged her tightly. The room erupted in elation and clapping.

So much for the damn truth.

FOR TWO LONG HOURS, Victor danced several jigs around the truth for the sake of Mags and her fellow cronies. Thinking on his feet came naturally to him, but even he had to admit that creating a massive farce and gaining Bianca's compliance was one of the hardest things he had ever done. He never enjoyed lying. And yet since the day he had met Bianca Eubanks, all he had done was lie. Although each time he had lied for a moral reason, this time, his purpose was more self-serving than the last. When he arrived home from Mag's soiree on Saturday, his brother Wesley surprised him with his presence and greeted him with a proposition.

"You left before meeting Mr. Marbury," his brother began. "He's not so bad. We spent a long time discussing his purchase of the bank. He sounds very determined to buy it."

"Good," Victor returned dismissively.

"But..."

"I hate buts. At least grammatical ones," Victor remembered commenting.

"But," Wesley finished. "He alluded to some rumors he has heard around town. Unfortunately, you and a certain senator's wife came up."

"Did you remind him they are all just rumors?"

"They aren't rumors, Victor, and you know it!"

"Is it the wife part, or is it the white part?"

"Both!" Wesley replied impatiently. "We ought to thank our lucky stars you put on that show with that little woman from the party. It saved all of us."

"It wasn't on purpose," Victor had gruffly replied. "Too bad our little engagement didn't survive past the night. It was all a ruse to get Angel's husband off my back."

"I saw. And so did Mr. Marbury."

"And?"

"And you need to make this engagement thing a thing."

"Hell no."

Victor watched Wesley do his best to calm his rising temperature. "Perhaps you can give the impression of marrying her. Just enough to fool Mags and Mr. Marbury. He will buy us out of the bank, and then we can move on with a bigger plan."

Victor inwardly rolled his eyes. Bigger plan. Bigger plan. There was always a bigger plan with Wesley. Instead of reminding him of this, Victor gave him a triumphant smile. "The lady isn't interested. Can you believe that? She doesn't like me. Will wonders never cease?"

Wesley's eyes darted back and forth in befuddlement. "Of course she does. All women do. I even catch my wife looking at you dreamingly from time to time. Not that she would—I know she wouldn't—forget I mentioned that last part. And if you ever—"

"Never in a million years, brother."

Wesley's composure relaxed as he let out a lengthy sigh. "Brother, I know I have asked a lot of you over the years. We all have. But this is a chance for all of us to move on before things go really bad. And if you can show that little miss a good time in the process of helping your family then... it would mean a lot to me."

That Victor could never say no to his brother, was evidenced by his march up to Mags' townhome. Unfortunately, this morning, there was no time to explain his change of mind with Bianca since she was in the process of telling the dreadful truth to the very person who couldn't know the truth—Mags. So, with serious haste, Victor made his way to Mags' townhome on Lafayette Street. The same street on which Angel and Edmund lived.

Coincidentally, the two of them were leaving for church this bright Sunday morning. Angel was stunning as always as she descended the stairs. And Edmund... watched Victor carefully as he made his way to Mags' house. Edmund did not see the tiny smile on Victor's face as he thought of how many times Angel used going to church alone as a ruse to see him. Suddenly, Victor cringed at how much of a dog he had been. Still, without rocking the boat, Victor pretended not to notice the couple getting into their car. There was no time to go through his past misdeeds. It was now time to create new ones, he thought morbidly.

Though Bianca quietly pinched the shit out of him while he held her during the luncheon, he kept his facial expression as loving as he could. When he got the chance, Victor pinched her back and dared her with his eyes for her to holler out. To his surprise, she had not. She just pinched him harder. This silent argument lasted the entire duration of the lunch until they were outside and away from the ears of others. As it would happen, Edmund and Angel were returning from church just in time to see Bianca shrug out of his arms and throw her very expensive ring in his face. *Just great.*

"Darling, we shouldn't argue publicly," he declared loud enough for their ears to hear.

Bianca caught his quick glance in the couple's direction and laughed. She then made a slow and obnoxious applause. The gesture was not lost on him. He waved his hand in her direction.

"All right, all right. We have a lot to talk about, I know. But can we please do it elsewhere?"

"Elsewhere? Victor Carlson, I don't want you to come near me again. Now I will get in my car and drive away. You go tell Mags what you want to tell her, but I am done with this." She said the last part while furtively waving her finger in Edmund and Angel's direction, then to Mags' townhouse, and finally to him. She marched to her car, causing her heels to bang loudly against the cobblestone road. When she realized he was following her, she turned briskly around. "I have better things to do, you know. I have a business. I have employees; I have— Listen, stay away from me, you—"

A rash of curse words fell from her mouth as she got into her car and slammed the door in his face. Of course, her car did not start while he watched. But once she gave the gas pedal a harsh push, her trusted steed reared up and trotted along as Victor stood there watching her.

Unfortunately, Victor had no choice but to jump into his roadster and follow her home. It was wrong. He knew it. But he had no choice. The woman would not give him a chance to explain anything. She was always doing things like slapping him and pinching him. She was truly the strangest and most violent woman he'd ever met.

Victor took special care to remain out of sight all the way until the moment she opened the door to her apartment. She nearly screamed when he pushed his way in with her and shut the door.

"What the hell?" Bianca didn't wait for him to explain himself; she ran into the kitchen to grab a knife. "Son of a bitch, if you think you will come in here to rape me!"

"*Shh*! "Victor said with his hands up in the air. "No one is raping anyone. I just want to talk. I followed you because you wouldn't give me a chance to explain myself outside at Mags'. There was no other way. We need to talk. I didn't mean to scare you. I'm sorry. But just give me a chance."

Bianca's body froze in one spot. She was still in fight mode, but he could tell her brain was trying to calm down.

"Please... put the knife down," he beseeched her.

With a puff of air, Bianca placed the knife on her dining room table, crossed her arms, and waited.

"I would like to come to the table with an offer. Can we sit?" He pointed to her dining table with the knife on it and slowly advanced in her direction. He pulled out a chair, causing it to scrape against the floor. He winced. "Sorry," he offered under her glaring eyes. Without further delay, Victor sat down and waited for her to do the same. He didn't have the courage to tell her he was thirsty and that he would appreciate a drink of water.

"I would like to apologize first," he began; her eyebrow perked to attention. "I'm sorry for everything. All of it."

"And just what is it you need to apologize for? I'm curious if you even know."

Oh, she would make him work for it. *All right, then.* "I apologize for roping you into my drama. I'm sorry for accosting you several times. I'm sorry for pinching you on your arm today, although you pinched me first. I'm sorry for following you home and scaring you, and I'm sorry for my overall obnoxiousness. There. I'm sorry."

"You forgot insulting."

"I didn't insult you."

"Never mind. I can't waste my time explaining anything to you. Too slow."

Victor rubbed his head in frustration. This woman had the wit of a one-armed bartender. She was a formidable foe and not easily won over. But he needed to win her over. That was his frustration. He exhaled and gave her a gentle smile to ease the tension in the room.

"After I dropped you off on Saturday, I got to thinking about things."

"Did you now?"

"Yes, I did. I thought, what if we just tried?"

"Tried what?"

"Tried to go through with the purported engagement." He was hoping she would throw him a bone. But as he watched her lean back against her chair and cross her arms, he realized she would do no such thing.

"Why did you want Mags to believe you were engaged? You said to secure her business investment, right? I know how she loves matchmaking and wants to see everyone on this damn planet married, so I understand. So now you can do that. You can secure your investment because not only are you engaged, but you are engaged to a member of her family. If I know her, she will make sure she covers your business for appearance's sake. And all will be well."

Bianca wiped a tiny crumb from the table and then yawned.

"A few days ago, you would have flipped for this opportunity. The woman at the party on Saturday was more than desperate."

"That was before I got to know your family," she said dryly. "This lie never set right with me, anyway. I have resolved in my mind that a brick of truth is better than a wall of lies. And no one will believe it, anyway. You and me? Ha!"

"They did today. I know we're different. You being you. And me being me. Maybe if you wore dresses like you did the other day, or maybe if we get that gossip columnist on our side somehow... what's her name? Madame Noire?"

"Let me just stop you right there. My showboating for these bourgeois-ass Negroes ended today. And what about you? Why do you care about my business and my financial affairs? What's in it for you?"

He knew it would come to this. He knew that he had to answer, but what could he say? Bianca, I am trying to manipulate you into being a pawn for the Carlson Brother's big plan? No, that would not go over well at all. "Angel," he replied instead.

"That white woman? Your mistress?"

"Yes. This arrangement works for us. My being engaged throws her husband off and makes it much easier for us to be together."

Bianca tightened her lip to hold in a fury of words. She stood, walked to the door, and then opened it, gesturing for him to leave. Victor could not fight her stoic demand. He got up to leave, but not before quietly placing her ring on the table.

CHAPTER 6

MUDDLED CLARITY

The morning's sun peeked through Bianca's curtains, alerting her it was Monday. Doomsday. It was the day she had dreaded for weeks. It was the day that she had desperately tried to avoid. She had gone through lengths and suffered much to avoid this day. But there was no avoiding it.

At least she was ready for it now. Before, she was afraid of her employees' faces when she informed them that this week's edition of the *Baltimore Beat* was their last. She was afraid to tell them that despite it being Christmas, they were out of their jobs. But she was not afraid anymore. She was just sad.

Bianca bathed and dressed, rehearsing her speech to her employees. She ate a small plate of boiled eggs and toast before grabbing her coat and hat. She made a quick stop at the mirror in her foyer to give her reflection a confident nod and opened the door. Bianca's legs were ready to move to the nearby stairs, but the argument her landlady was having with her next-door neighbor stopped her in her tracks.

"That's it! No more chances!" she exclaimed over Bianca's neighbor's begging. "No way! I've had it."

Bianca thought about tucking herself back into her apartment, but she reminded herself that today was the day to confront her problems and stop running from them. With her mind made up, she shut the door, alerting the landlady of her presence. The woman stopped barking and noticed Bianca. A disarming smile appeared on her face.

"Ahh! Ms. Eubanks. Soon to be Mrs. Carlson!" Her landlady girlishly giggled. Bianca had forgotten the woman attended had Mags' luncheon the day before.

"Mrs. Sawyer, it's good to see you again. But I have bad news. I won't be able to pay last month's rent or even this month's rent. Don't worry about kicking me out and all that. I hope to have my things out by the morning. You can give my furniture to the next tenant if you like or sell it."

"Girl, what are you talking about? Your fiancé was just here yesterday. I caught him walking out. He paid for everything. He even paid you up for the next three months."

"I'm sorry, what?"

"I said your fiancé paid your rent. I guess he wanted to keep your apartment until the wedding. When is the wedding? Everybody has been bothering me since I came back from the tea. Girl, you found a good one. It's like Cinderella with her handsome prince."

Bianca began walking before she said the wrong thing. That dolt had once again overstepped a boundary and inserted himself where he did not belong. But instead of getting angry, Bianca focused her mind on her task for the day. She decided she would kill him another day. But not today.

A bright and crisp December morning greeted her outside. The streets buzzed with movement. Bianca greeted the old man on the corner and the mother pushing the carriage down the street. All was well, and all would be well, she decided. She looked around the corner to find her vehicle but noticed a strange thing. The hood of her car was up with two gentlemen dressed in overalls bent over, studying its entrails. Bianca blinked a few times to make certain she was seeing what she was seeing with her own two eyes. It was her car, all right. The dent on the left side was unmistakable.

"Excuse me, gentleman," she said.

They both looked up with dark smudges all over their faces and hands.

"Mrs. Carlson!" the older one exclaimed. "My name is Jimmy Hayden Senior, and this here is my son, Jimmy Hayden Junior, and we are Hayden and Son, the best mechanic shop on this side of the Mississippi." Mr. Hayden Senior wiped his hand on a dirty cloth and pushed his hand out to shake.

Bianca gave him a small shake to be polite and then got right to her question. "What are you doing with my automobile?"

"Oh! Your husband sent us over to look at this fine machinery of yours."

"My husband?"

"Yes, misses," he replied with a bright smile. Bianca closed her eyes to roll them. She gnashed her teeth so hard she thought her jaw would break.

Junior caught her irritated composure. "Ma'am, we are all done. She gonna purr like a little kitten now," he said as he slammed her car's hood.

Bianca got into her car while they stood and watched. She noted the bouquet of red roses with a note attached on the seat next to her.

Have dinner with me?- Victor

Bianca threw the flowers out the window onto the ground. And just as Junior told her it would, her car started up with a soft purr. That was when she decided that she would kill Victor today.

In addition to being Doomsday, it was also printing day at the *Baltimore Beat*. Print day was the day Bianca hated the most, because it required the most sweat equity. Three of her nephews always came to help work the press' arduous and tedious shifting of papers and sorting. Bianca, Ms. Ginny, and Kizzy, if she was feeling up to it, would always arrange the papers for delivery. The work would last for at least five hours without breaking. That was if there were no plate mistakes and if her press did not choke as it was wont to do. At least the tedious work would get her mind off the fact that today would be their last day to print. Bianca decided that after they stacked the last stack of the papers onto the delivery truck, she would pay each employee with what she had left and make her formal announcement.

As her car turned the corner of the building, Bianca realized that she would have to say goodbye to her alternate ego, Lady Noire. Five years ago, Bianca figured out people loved lies better than they enjoyed reading the truth. So she concocted this personality of sophisticated wisdom and named her Lady Noire, to signify she was a black woman of distinction.

Her column was usually about the small circles of elite black folks. As speakeasies sprang up all over town, her older nephews figured out that the drinking crowd enjoyed discussing the exaggerated details of her weekly gossip. In no time at all, Lady Noire was a hit and a must-read.

The demand was too much for Bianca to handle at first because she and Lady Noire were nothing alike. First, Lady Noire cared about everybody's business, and Bianca couldn't give a shit about what people did with their lives. Second, Lady Noire was a sophisticated snob, and Bianca was not. But rather than get caught up in semantics, Bianca figured out a way for Bianca and Lady Noire to coexist. She paid butlers, maids, bartenders, and bar hops for scoops on the comings and goings of the elite. They were always helpful when coin was involved. As far as Lady Noire's expert elocution, Bianca simply repeated the same babble she learned during the finishing school lessons her father made her take as a child. And as time went on, Lady Noire turned out to be a fun derivative of Bianca's mischievous personality. No one was safe. Even her sister, Cecilia, fell victim to Lady Noire's taunts. It was all in fun. And sadly, the fun was over.

So, in the quiet and stillness of the upper floor of the *Baltimore Beat*, Bianca sat down at her trusted typewriter to say goodbye.

"Alas little doves, the time has come to bid you adieu. Goodbye is never easy for anyone, but we all must say it one day in our lives." Under the cover of Lady Noire, Bianca wrote about her sincere love of Baltimore. She then charged each person to live each life to its fullest and to never quit on their dreams.

After she wiped her tears, Bianca set up the plates for the column and readied herself for her employees. They arrived within minutes, flourishing the suite with excited enthusiasm. Ms. Ginny announced that Kizzy went into labor that morning and expected the baby any hour now. Excited about the new baby, they spent their time working and guessing if the baby would be a boy or a girl and if the baby would talk as much as Kizzy. Kizzy's labor made them all forget their blues. And Bianca was happy about that. But she still had the task of ending the day with bad news.

And when the time came, Bianca set the last stack of papers onto the delivery truck, and inhaled the chilly air before declaring, "I have an announcement, Ms. Ginny."

"I'm sure you do, baby, but it will have to wait," Ms. Ginny returned. She was pointing across the street to a sight that Bianca hadn't expected at all that day.

Across the frozen street, Bianca and Ms. Ginny watched Bianca's estranged employee, Daisy, limping up the sidewalk with one shoe. Her clothes were hanging off of her, stockings torn. Despite her dishevelment, Daisy limped away as if she were the queen of Baltimore. She looked immune to the crisp weather. Experience had taught Bianca that Daisy was high on something. No person in their right mind would carry on like this in the cold if it were not for a false awareness. Daisy's behavior was a common occurrence, unfortunately. When sober,

Daisy was a brilliant staff writer. But when the wind hit her the wrong way and shadows of her past crept into her consciousness, she would step into the dark side of life.

Bianca and Ms. Ginny crossed the street to collect Daisy as they had done so many times before. They hadn't seen Daisy in weeks and figured the streets had her. The poor girl had no family to speak of except Bianca and the rest of the *Baltimore Beat* staff.

"Daisy?" Ms. Ginny called as Daisy limped along.

"Oh, no, no! Don't come by me talkin' all your Jesus stuff, Ms. Ginny. I'm high, and I means to stay that way today!" Daisy yelled as she picked up the pace.

"Daisy," Ms. Ginny sternly repeated.

"No! No, Ms. Ginny! Imma go up to Hanky's house and get me somethin' to eat. Imma eat. I promise. You ain't got to worry 'bout me. I stole five whole dollars off this trick."

"Daisy..." Ms. Ginny and Bianca stopped walking behind Daisy. Finally, Daisy stopped her running and collapsed against the cold ground.

"I hate you, Ms. Ginny. You kills my high every fucking time. Big Joon-Joon gonna marry Tea Baby, and I got me a shitload of hash."

"I have no idea who Big Joon-Joon is, and I don't care if he is going to marry Tea Baby. You will get your narrow ass off this ground. I don't want to hear about no hash."

"Oh, Ms. Ginny," Daisy sobbed as she laid herself prostrate in the soggy snow.

Bianca and Ms. Ginny struggled to get her to stand. Daisy cried, screamed, and moaned, but she didn't fight them. Remarkably, she held each of their arms as they escorted her across the street.

Bianca shoved her car keys into Ms. Ginny's other hand. "Here, take her to my father's hospital. Have him take a look at her. After he releases her, you know what to do. I'll lock things up here and catch a cab home."

As they gathered Daisy into the back of Bianca's car, she continued to babble on about Big Joon-Joon, Tea Baby, and Jesus. "Dear Lord, keep me near the cross..." she sang.

Once Bianca turned off every light and locked every door of the *Baltimore Beat*, her body released an awful cry in the middle of the dark stairway to the building's front door. She cried. She hated crying. And yet here she was doing something that was absolutely pointless. Thank God, the blustering wind outside was cold enough to freeze every tear on her face.

Bianca wiped the last of her tears with her knitted scarf and shrugged her hands in her pockets. She lifted her sagged shoulders up and braced herself for a two-mile walk to her apartment. She had told Ms. Ginny that she would catch a cab, but the truth was she didn't have cab fare.

Bianca looked out over the street and up to the dusky sky. It was pink with slashes of orange. When she looked back down, that was when she saw him. He stood on the other side of the street outside of his obnoxious, bright-red roadster, standing tall against the pink skyline. In his hand, he held a dozen, or so red roses bunched in a bouquet.

A tiny smile crept up the edges of her mouth. After covering her smile from his sight with her scarf, she lifted her chin and firmly walked in his direction. She grabbed the flowers out of his hand and threw them over her shoulder onto the ground. Ignoring his miffed expression, she placed herself in the passenger seat of his car. "Don't stand there like an idiot, Carlson," she said. "I need a drink. A stiff one, preferably."

Victor didn't waste another second. He jumped in on the driver's side and sped away.

§.

VICTOR HAD some apprehension over taking Bianca to a seedy place like Dusty Anne's. He took one look at the inside and one thought came to his mind—dusty. Tiny granules of sand hissed under his wing-tipped Spectators as he escorted Bianca into the basement bar and restaurant. Bianca didn't mind. Her informal greetings to everyone from the bouncer to the nervous busboy wiping a dirty rag on their dining table gave Victor the impression that she was a regular.

Victor would have preferred a more... sanitary environment. His goal for this dinner was to change the course of his bumbled wooing with something a little more... romantic. His assistant made a private reservation with the best Italian chef on the East Coast. A candle-lit dinner would have served as the appropriate backdrop to Victor's planned proposal. He had wooed beauty queens, actresses, and singers with the slight of his hand, so he knew confidently if he put his mind to it, he could get Bianca to trust him and go his way on this engagement thing.

But Bianca Eubanks was a special case. She, he was learning, would take some thinking and measuring. She was a puzzle, not at all swayed by his handsome features or money. What was even worse, she didn't think highly of him. And what was even stranger, he cared what she thought.

It was a desperate Hail Mary that made him hire a private detective to follow her and wait patiently for her to emerge. Once she did, he forced himself not to approach her as he could see that something had visibly upset her. He steadied his feet and waited for her to notice him. He guessed she would rebuff him on sight as she had done before. It shocked him to see her peacefully get into his car. And once she was secure in his passenger seat, there was no way he would press his luck by insisting on a romantic dinner. If she wanted to go to Dusty Anne's, that was where he would take her.

"Any menus?" he asked wryly, knowing full well there weren't any damn menus at Dusty Anne's.

She gave him leveled gaze and then smiled. "Two house specials!" she yelled to whoever was listening.

"Two house specials!" the bartender yelled to the tiny window behind the bar.

A hefty middle-aged man stuck his face out the window and shouted, "Two gizzards coming right up!"

"House specials? Sounds de-lish!" Victor said with a smile. He noticed that she was watching him as he looked about the room, and the same busboy set down two glass mugs filled with a dark ale.

"House special too? We didn't order this," Victor told the boy.

"He can't hear you. He's deaf." Bianca gave the boy a silent gesture signifying a thank you, and the boy moved on. "Just drink it, Carlson. It's the house's recipe. But sip it slowly."

Victor gave the glass a casual sip and bit down a robust need to spit the entire concoction out of his mouth. He wished he could inform Bianca and Dusty Anne that he had visited hundreds of speakeasies all over the east coast, and this moonshine was the worst he had ever tasted. Instead, he swallowed the disgusting liquid and shakily smiled.

The house special was much more appetizing. It was an assortment of fried gizzards and potatoes on a bed of white rice with a side of okra. Victor dug in under Bianca and the busboy's careful watch. It was good. So good, he got comfortable by taking off his jacket, loosening his tie, and rolling up his sleeves. Bianca gave an apathetic shrug before voraciously digging in to her plate.

He thought he had better break the ice because Bianca would happily sit there and enjoy her food with or without his company. What could he talk about? He refused to rile her by bringing up his engagement proposal, and he barely knew anything about her. Maybe he would start with a question that had perplexed him for days.

"You said I insulted you the other day."

Her eyes rose to meet his and then shyly slid back to her plate.

"But when I asked you what I said, you said never mind."

"Yeah. Never mind."

Victor figured he had best move along. "So... have you brought your fellow here before?" he asked as he tried once again to swallow Dusty Anne's moonshine. The liquid shook him to his core. However, he could now breathe out of both nostrils when a few minutes ago, he had a stuffy nose.

She chewed for a moment and then asked, "My fellow?"

"Yeah. Your fellow from the soiree."

"Ah. Hiram. Yes, Hiram has been here with me a few times."

He had a few more questions about Hiram and their relationship that burned on the tip of his tongue, but he dared not ask them. He chose a different course instead. "Have you received any strange treatment since the soiree? People who might have heard about our... engagement?"

Finally, she stopped eating and put down her fork. "I'm sure you know full well what kind of treatment I have received. I'm paying you every dime back, by the way."

"No! I wasn't referring to that. Listen, please don't mention it. I was just wondering if anyone around town has mentioned it to you." He had no clue why he was asking this. It really had nothing to do with anything, except to know if she was considering the idea.

She chuckled this time and sent a look over his shoulder. "If you must know, I have been getting a few looks from women around town who are more than likely upset about your being plucked off the market. Like this one behind you. I think it's safe to say she is planning my immediate execution."

Victor looked over his shoulder and groaned as he looked back at his plate.

"Friend of yours?" she asked with a fake sympathetic smile.

"Old friend." *Shit.* Of all the times for Belle Anderson to show up with an angry ax to grind, this was the worst.

Over the years, he told her the truth about his lifestyle and his unwillingness to settle down. She had tearfully claimed she understood. He mastered the art of ducking her sporadic declarations of love and fidelity by pacifying her with jewelry and monetary gifts. And it worked. Not one time in the last six months had Belle brought up the idea of marriage. She had not even brought up his other mistress, Angel. She was content, and so was he. That was until he got into this debacle with Ms. Bianca, who, for all intents and purposes, did not want to be in a debacle with him or Belle, or Angel. Apparently, the news of Victor's purported engagement had reached Belle, and she was not happy.

"It must be difficult for you, having so many friends," Bianca said with a mocking hum.

"I don't have that many friends," he grumbled.

"Your reputation precedes you, Mr. Carlson," she added.

"Unlike your Hiram? I don't think I have ever seen that fellow around anywhere."

A dreamy expression appeared on her face that he, for some odd reason, didn't like. "Hiram is a special soul. You wouldn't have noticed him because he is unassuming. But he is a lion in many ways."

Victor's thoughts ran rapidly with sarcasm, *Lion? Ha! He wasn't a damn lion the other day when he left you high and dry when his other woman showed up. Your Hiram was a mewling baby lamb.*

"You were crying when I saw you today. Why?" Victor asked, hoping to change the course of the discussion and crack her wall of distrust.

"None of your business," she replied, but with none of her usual venom.

"Fine. You won't tell me how I insulted you, or why you were upset today. Can you at least tell me what your favorite flower is?"

"Huh?" she asked with her fork frozen in her hand.

"I take it you don't like roses. You keep throwing them out. I just want to get to know you. Tell me which flower you won't throw away. Why are you making it so difficult?"

"Because I have no interest in being a conduit for your adultery? Because I would rather you stay your nose out of my business? Because all of your flowers are self-serving? Admit it, Carlson. You don't really care to know me and would have never met my acquaintance if I hadn't been at the right place at the right time."

He leaned partially across the table to shoot her one of his famous smoldering looks. "If all that is true, then why are you here with me now?"

"Because you happened to be at the right place at the right time. That's it, and that's all." She chuckled as she resumed eating. "Tell me, Carlson. Do you really think this little idea of yours will work? What do you think Little Ms. Angry behind you will do when she finds out?"

"She will understand." His voice was low.

Bianca sat back and studied him for a moment. "How ironic. I imagine that your looks and money have afforded you the company of thousands of women. "

"Thousands?"

"All right, fine. Hundreds. I'm sure there have been many. And the funny thing is that you still don't know them. Just like you don't know me."

"We can agree that I don't know you... yet. But I know that every woman has a price—even you. So what is it going to be, Bianca? How much are you going to cost me?" Suddenly, a strange feeling washed over him. Had he doubled down too early? Judging from Bianca's facial expression, it looked like he had. He expected her to slap him or a rant about respect, but did nothing of the sort.

She stood up and called over to a man standing by the bar. "Lennie?"

"Yeah, baby?" he replied.

"You going west?"

"Yeah, baby."

"Take me with ya?" She made her way out of the door with that Lennie fellow and never looked back in Victor's direction.

Well... shit, he thought to himself.

CHAPTER 7

THE INVESTOR

"Like I said, Mr. Finkel, my printing press is worth much more than a measly one hundred dollars. You should be able to pay off all of my creditors with the sale of the press alone." Bianca had said this to her attorney with the *hope he* would see reason as he accompanied her to her to the Baltimore Beat to price assets for bankruptcy.

"I understand what you are saying, Ms. Eubanks, but you should be happy to accept ten cents on the dollar," he returned as he scurried behind her march.

"Ten cents? You and the rest of these folks are out of their damned mind if you think they will sell me off for nothing."

They continued their debate until they arrived at the front door of the building, where they stood and watched as delivery men walked several boxes into the buildings. Bianca and Mr. Finkel followed two delivery men to her upstairs office.

"I don't know what game you are playing with your creditors, or with me, Ms. Eubanks. But it doesn't look like you need bankruptcy."

Bianca heard Mr. Finkel's announcement as she entered the room, but she really couldn't respond. She was too busy trying to understand the patched ceiling before her. She blinked several times before realizing that the massive hole in the ceiling of the *Baltimore Beat* was no more. It was closed up and sealed with a fresh coat of white paint. A dark man with white paint on his face moved in her eyesight, wearing an enormous smile.

"Like brand new, ain't it?" he asked before walking out the door with his bucket and brushes.

Bianca's mouth was still agog when she realized that other parts of her office looked brand new. The floorboards were secure, and no longer creaked. Her eyes moved over to her staff's desks and noticed that there was a brand new typewriter on each one along with a fresh set of stationery paper and a bouquet of fresh red roses. To her left, three men stood in the middle of her printing room, tinkering around her antique printing press.

Victor! she screamed his name in her head. He was bound and determined to buy her. With damned red roses, no less. She would kill him when she got her hands on him.

Her sudden anger caused her to slam her fist against Kizzy's desk, knocking a folded card to the floor. When she picked up the card and read its contents, her eyes bulged beyond their usual size. She heard Mr. Finkel say something about leaving, but she couldn't give him her full attention.

Dear Bianca:
I'm sure you already know this by now, but your investor gave everyone the day off after handing us our Christmas bonuses. I will finally get my sister off the sewing line. I give you a hard time, but you are such a good boss. I hope you get a day off too.
Love, Ginny

Bianca bunched her lips together to stop a litany of curse words from falling from her mouth. However, she could not stop her feet from stomping into her newly secured floorboards, doing her best to break through to the first floor. She expected no one to react to her outburst, not even the men working on her printing press. But when a haunting voice emerged from a dark corner of the room, she almost jumped out of her skin.

"Surely, you can find a better way to exorcise your emotions than stomping around like a horse, Miss Eubanks," said the shrill voice of Mags Edison.

Bianca knew that voice anywhere. Everything she said sounded like high-pitched judgment. "Mag- Err... Ms. Edison? I'm sorry I didn't expect you to be here."

Mags removed herself from the window and eased behind Ms. Ginny's desk. "I don't have the time for niceties, Ms. Eubanks. I am here to oversee the changes to my investment."

"You? Your investment?"

"Good gracious, you are slow for a newspaper editor. Did you not come to me asking for an investment?"

"Yes, but—" Bianca stammered.

"Oh, gracious," Mags said as she rubbed her white-gloved finger along the edge of Ms. Ginny's desk. Her mouth dipped into a frown as she inspected the tip of her finger covered in brown dust particles.

Bianca inhaled to calm her nerves and crossed her hands at her lap. "Ms. Edison, I solicited your investment. But that was weeks ago. A lot has changed since then. I have changed since then."

"You have changed... in some ways." Mags' eyes traveled down the length of Bianca's pants and then back up to her face before she said, "But in other ways..."

"Ms. Edison, while I am grateful for your contribution, I never got around to agreeing to accept it. I've been in business long enough to know that investment agreements are agreements. We did not discuss terms. What's your rate of return?"

"Rate of return?"

"How much do you expect back?"

Mags smile revealed all of her teeth in the most insincere fashion. "Gentleman?" she called to the men in the other room. "Give us a moment, would you?"

When the men exited the suite and shut the door, the lukewarm veneer of Mags' disposition evaporated, and the coldness of her eyes appeared before Bianca. "Let us discuss this rate of return, Lady Noire."

Bianca's chin raised at the sound of her alternate ego's name. Bianca didn't have time for these games. She had respected Mags for her age and achievement, but she was never one to let respect impede her from speaking her mind. "Ms. Edison, I am sure my employees are grateful for your initiative. But we didn't negotiate any of this. I have never been one to allow someone to give me something I can't pay back. That is just my upbringing. So I ask you again, what is the rate of return that you expect? Shares? Money?"

"I don't want your money, Ms. Eubanks. If that is what you are worried about. I think now that you are in the family way, you can appreciate that."

So, that is what this was about. Victor. Bianca let out a loud snort before sitting on the edge of Kizzy's desk. "Ms. Edison, you don't really think I am in the family way, do you? I will never marry your son. I hate to be frank, but—"

"Please do," Mags pertly interrupted.

"I hate him. He's an obnoxious whoremonger who doesn't care about anything but himself. Now he has set it in his head that we are engaged, but that was all from I lie that I created to deceive you. When I met with you a few weeks ago, you talked in nonsense circles about how I needed a man to validate me. You had me there for a bit. I almost swallowed that shit. Excuse my French. But I have since had some time to think about it, and my mind has changed. I don't need a man, and I don't need your unsavory son."

Damn, that felt good, Bianca thought to herself. Stupid, but good. She had no idea how the almighty Mags Edison would react, but Bianca was long ready to take the gloves off. Speaking of gloves, Mags was locked in a daze of pulling off her white gloves at an unbelievable glacial pace. It was several awkward seconds before the woman looked up at Bianca with a special gleam in her eyes.

"I agree."

"Beg your pardon?"

"Victor? I hate him too. He is beyond the pale; however, there are plenty of women who would jump through fire to just be near his beautiful face. But I have chosen you."

"Me?"

"Yes. I had wanted to connect Victor to the right woman for a long time. And then you came along with the perfect mixture of all the right things."

Bianca pursed her lips and narrowed her eyes. "Really? Me, a spinster with no money?"

"Yes, you. You are nothing like Lady Noire. Lady Noire is a shallow, vapid, and unscrupulous individual. You are a smart, young woman whom I have the greatest admiration for."

"What? That's not what you said before."

"I know what I said. Things have changed. It's time for candid conversation, don't you think? I believe you are smart enough to know when a deal is on the table. And I have a deal for you."

"Deal?"

"Yes. Yesterday I inquired into an interesting piece of real estate. The owner, as it turned out, practically begged me to buy. Said he was fed up with his tenant. Some lousy newspaper that barely paid its rent on time." Mags unfolded a piece of paper marked DEED, long enough for her to read its contents.

"You bought this building yourself? You knew that's what I wanted to do? You knew I wanted to own it to expand the *Baltimore Beat*."

"Yes. And if you do everything I tell you, you will. You will own this building and more. You will have a newspaper big enough to rival that *Journal*. By the time I'm done, you will be a very rich woman indeed."

Bianca's breathing slowed as she finally saw Mags in all her evil glory. "Just what is it that you want me to do?"

"Marry Victor."

"*What*? What is this with you people? That pretty bastard can marry any floozy he sets his eyes for, and you and he are stuck on me. I don't want that dumb ox."

"Lower your voice," Mags hissed as she stood to her full height behind Ginny's desk. "Divorce him later; I don't care. But you will do as I say for as long as I say."

"For *what*?"

"When the *Journal* fired you, I bet they thought you were just another colored woman who couldn't cut it. Don't you want the last laugh? I can give you that. With more room, you can expand the *Beat* and grow it into something that will make the *Journal* look like fire kindling. Come, love, it won't be so bad. He might be as dumb as an ox, but he is pretty. And the word on the street is that he's a good romp in the sack, so he will at least keep a smile on your face."

Bianca pressed her hands against her ears to stop the madness. "This is crazy. Lady, you have got to go. Thank you kindly for paying my creditors, and all, but the buck stops here. I'm not interested in making any deals with the devil, and I'm sure you have something evil planned for that poor dumb soul, but I don't plan to be a part of it. I'm not sure how I can pay you back all of your money, but I'll find a way."

Bianca found herself at the door, beckoning Mags to follow. But she hadn't moved a muscle. "I acquired something else recently. My private investigators located a young woman by the name of Daisy. What a colorful tongue she has when she is high on hash. We didn't pay her ranting any mind when we caught her slipping out of your apartment the other day."

Bianca felt an intense surge of goose bumps flood her arms.

The room narrowed and closed in on her. "Where is she?" she asked.

"She is safe. Don't worry. She is being cared for and well-fed. Isn't that what you wanted?"

"Let her go, Mags!"

"I don't think I can. Not yet, anyway. I could release her when I am sure that I have your cooperation. Do I have it?"

Bianca nodded slowly, but her heart was beating a mile a minute.

"Good. I don't care how repugnant you find Victor, you will accept his proposal, and you will marry him. When the time is right, you will have a brand new building, and your little friend Daisy."

"I could just go to the authorities and forget about all this shit," Bianca snarled.

"Again, Daisy is getting what she needs and where she needs it. You better not even think about going to the police, or this will get very ugly. I can do much more than hold an addict hostage. I was hoping to keep your parents out of this, but I can be persuaded."

"Fine. Tell me what you want me to do."

"First things first. You prepare your heart and mind to be Victor's happy fiancée and future bride. You will tell no one of our arrangements, especially Victor. I will see to it that you are assured of Daisy's perfect wellbeing. And when the time is right, I will give you more explicit instructions. And once you have complied with absolutely everything that I have asked, I will deliver Daisy to you along with the deed to the building."

Bianca felt a cold wind cross her as Mags moved to the door of the room to leave. When she reached the door, she turned for the final time to address Bianca. "I am hosting a small family dinner party tomorrow evening. Your presence is required. And cheer up, darling. I can think of a hundred things worse than marrying the prince of Baltimore, having a successful newspaper, and paying off all of your creditors."

Bianca eyed the closed door in front of her before murmuring, "How about kicking you in your wide ass, Margaret Edison? Is that on your list?"

CHAPTER 8

THE GUEST OF THE HOUR

Victor watched his niece and two nephews play a game of hide and seek in the parlor of Mags' townhome. His nephews were a robust set of seven-year-old twins, who had a knack for knocking down anything in their way. This was how they played their game. But Victor's four-year-old niece, Whitney, played with strategy and skill. Whitney watched her brothers bump around and stomp from one room to the next, while she skillfully slipped from one hiding spot to the next.

This game is going to go on forever, Victor thought to himself as Whitney slid behind the grand armchair he was sitting in. When she gestured for Victor to keep quiet in the most adorable way, Victor nodded, trying his best to contain his humor.

"Whitney, where are you?" her brother, Winston, bellowed as he marched into the room.

"You won't find her that way, Winston," Victor said. "I think I saw her go upstairs."

"Thanks, Uncle!" he said with a salute and before screaming for his brother to join him.

Victor heard a tiny giggle behind him before the heavy footsteps of the children's mother came in.

"I hope you are not encouraging them, Victor," she chided. "I dress them in their Sunday's best and now they are running around the house like wild animals. Mags will be here any minute and their father... well, you know how he is."

"Anna, I don't know what you are talking about," he said with a wink.

"Whitney, I can see your feet sticking out," Anna said with her own giggle.

The boys came down the stairs and saw Whitney's feet too.

"Ah-ha!" they both yelled before they all erupted in screams of surprise and laughter. Their collective moment of joy lasted until Victor's brother walked into the room.

"That's enough," Wesley said in a deadly calm voice. "Winston and Warren, straighten your suits. Whitney, go to your mother. This behavior is unacceptable. Anna, take the children to the kitchen while I talk to Victor."

They all left the room in a quiet, somber march. Victor eyed his brother's demeanor and knew that this conversation would take him out of the jovial mood the children had just conjured for him. He stood and adjusted his dinner jacket and walked to the standing bar at the end of the room. It was his first non-verbal warning to Wesley that he was not in the mood for his high-handedness today.

"Brother?" Wesley growled behind Victor's back while he gazed into the robust fire.

Victor shrugged off his thoughts and turned to his brother's expectant face. Victor knew that his brother was looking for Bianca's presence. According to Wesley's plan, they were all supposed to attend Mags' annual Christmas Eve dinner. Every single damned year, they forced Victor to attend Mags' while she berated and badgered him for every slight and sin he had committed. And now here his brother was asking, no begging that he bring another victim to this annual slaughter.

"She isn't here," Victor said with a shrug before gulping down his favorite scotch. "Can't say that I blame her. I don't want to be here either. I hate this shit."

"Victor," Wesley replied in his usual voice of warning while looking over his shoulder. "I don't like these things either, but we must stick with the plan."

"Plan?" Victor returned in a harsh whisper. "With you, it is always a plan, little brother. Has it ever occurred to you that rich or poor you and your family will be fine? You don't have to be a slave to money. Look at your children. They were actually having fun, and it didn't cost you anything. But you can't see that, Wesley, because you are too busy plotting your next venture."

"It's a good thing, too," Wesley snarled. "Were it not for my planning and plotting, we would all be in the breadlines. But I guess you don't care about that. You're too busy sticking your pole in every whore in the city."

"Every whore? Not yet. But I have my goals," Victor returned with a grin.

Wesley shut his eyes against Victor's impertinent disposition. "Victor," he began, with his calm restored. "We need to get out of this business. Our investments are failing. We extended credit to every poor Negro farmer, and we have nothing to show for it."

"Oh, poor Wesley," Victor mocked. "He's mad that he hasn't had the chance to throw all the poor Negro farmers out into the street. I guess that means we won't have any money. *Boohoo.*"

"You're a fool," Wesley said as he walked away from Victor in search of his family.

Victor shrugged and resumed his scotch. He couldn't help but agree. He was a fool for dealing with the likes of Mags for as long as he had. He was also a fool for letting Wesley manipulate him into playing Mags' games. This marriage idea was the line in the sand. He had no idea what the two of them were cooking up, but this was the end of the road. This was so much the end of the road that he had already planned to leave town soon, regardless of the bank's sale. He didn't care. He was gone. The two of them could fight over his share. He no longer cared. He no longer cared about living this lifestyle anymore. What had it really brought him? Not a damn thing.

Victor was so far into planning his escape from Mags and his brother that he barely heard her butler announce Mr. Marbury. He took a double-take to assure himself that it was him in the flesh strolling in. This was Mags' angel investor? He hardly looked like an angel anything. In fact, something in Victor told him that there was something very devilishly familiar about him. But looking at his tan and weathered face, he couldn't put his finger on it.

His bald head beamed under the foyer's light, while his stern expression radiated from his blue eyes. There was something about this one, for sure.

Perhaps it was the way he walked in, acknowledging no one. He took inventory of Mags' extravagant furnishings and trinkets. And then maybe it was the way he directed his intense focus on Victor as he arrived at his side. It was on the tip of Victor's tongue to say something crass to knock the glower off his face, but Wesley arrived just in time to save Mr. Marbury from Victor's boorish ways.

"Mr. Marbury. I cannot tell you how pleased my mother will be when she learns that you accepted our dinner invitation," Wesley said.

Mr. Marbury adjusted his composure and the direction of his gaze to Wesley. "And where is your mother? I don't got all day. I don't visit the darker sides of town often."

"I know a whore named Fat Tootsie who says different." Victor was not sure why he said what he had just said, but he sure enjoyed the looks on their faces when they heard it.

It wasn't a lie. He knew a whore named Fat Tootsie who had bragged about a rich cowboy-looking white trick named

Marbury. Word traveled around, and it was just as well that Marbury found out. And besides, since Mags wanted to police Victor's morality, they might as well know their blessed white investor had a taste for chubby black prostitutes.

Wesley must have known the rumor to be true as well since his eyes nearly bucked out of his head in fright.

Mr. Marbury, on the other hand, barely blinked. His mouth frowned, but his eyes sparkled with humor. "Eleanor does not like that name. Only her cheap handlers call her that. The special ones know better."

Wesley and Victor gaped at Mr. Marbury's confession for the longest while until he broke the spell with an alarming laugh, compelling them to join in. They laughed together until Mr. Marbury suddenly stopped as if he had evaporated all of his humor from his core. "I always believed that discretion would allow us to live the life we truly want to live. Have you ever considered that, Victor? Discretion?"

"He has," Mags sang from the entrance of the room. "Victor is all about discretion. In fact, he has made the most discrete decision to get married to a nice colored girl. Isn't that right, Victor?"

Victor's eyes narrowed on Mags' smug face. She gave him a triumphant nod and then moved away from the doorway to reveal what had been keeping her all along—Bianca.

§&

THE DINNER'S silence was deafening. Table conversation was a stark contrast to Bianca's family's holiday squabbles. The only source of noise came from the clanging of gold forks against porcelain dinner plates. Every now and again, someone would clear their throat or mutter phrases like "excuse me" or "thank you." But mostly, everyone kept their head down. It was odd.

Who was she kidding? The entire day was odd. It had begun with so much promise, Bianca recalled. She rose with plans to go on a hunting spree to find Daisy. But Mags showed up, reminding Bianca that when she said she required her presence at this damned dinner, she meant it. The woman arrived at Bianca's apartment with an excited entourage and a wardrobe of clothes to dress a queen. Mags played the part of an evil fairy godmother, while Bianca was primped and prepped for slaughter.

"Does he even know you're doing this?" Bianca remembered asking angrily while a piping hot comb fizzled next to her ear.

Mags, who was perched in Bianca's bay window, drinking a cup of hot tea made from Bianca's tiny kitchen, smiled from behind her cup.

"Doing what, dear? Fitting you with a wardrobe women would die for? Giving you a future you would not have dreamed of? Is that what you mean? If so, no. He does not know what I am doing."

The woman straightening Bianca's hair follicles began to slop an immense amount of pomade on Bianca's scalp. "So I guess that means he's ignorant to your kidnap, bribery, and blackmail activities, too," Bianca muttered as the stylist pushed her head from side to side.

They said nothing else to each other after that. Mags spoke only to her tailor during one of Bianca's dress fittings. When it was all said and done, with her corset firmly cinched and her earrings dropped from her earlobes, Bianca stood in front of a mirror to address what they had done to her. And what precisely had they done? It was only in the center of her truthful self, where she would allow that they made her look beautiful. She hated to admit it, but it was true. But one look at Mags' satisfied face reflected in the mirror told her she would die before she said as much. She reminded herself that she was the victim, how pretty she was didn't matter.

When she was later made to stand before Victor while he stared at her with his mouth agog, she felt like a lamb presented for sacrifice. After a moment of clarity settled on his face, he frowned and turned away, leaving her standing there like a dressed up ninny. Were she not in polite company, she would have socked him in his eye. Isn't this what he wanted? Wasn't this whole stupid thing his idea?

Bianca sat in the middle of the long dining table to the left of Victor and the right of an elderly man, introduced as Victor's Uncle Chito. He wasn't much for conversation as all he did was gnaw on his gums and murmur about the box he held in his lap.

Victor sat on the other side of her, as stiff as a board without saying a word. She did witness his jaw muscles jump in agitation a few times. Was he angry she was there? She did leave him at Dusty Anne's without a word the other day, but she had done worse. Oh well. At least she did her part. If Victor rejected her, it was fine with her. Maybe Mags would see the error of her misleading ways, return Daisy, and leave Bianca the hell alone.

Bianca shrugged thoughts of Victor from her mind and focused on the jungle of centerpieces blocking her view of the other side of the table. She saw movement a few times before turning her focus to the head of the table. Queen Mags sat regally while the true guest of the hour sat on the other end of the table.

The table chattered around her. They talked mostly about contracts and lawyers. Bianca thought she would get away with not having to talk when suddenly Victor turned to her and shocked her with the oddest question.

"When did I insult you?"

"What?" she whispered back.

"The other day, you said I had insulted you, but you refused to tell me when and what I did."

Bianca blinked and thought about his question for a while as she chewed on the most delicious chicken breast she had ever tasted. Was Victor Carlson capable of remorse? *Strange.*

"Dull. You said I was dull."

"I didn't say that," he almost hissed.

"Yes, you did. When you introduced me as your wife ... the very first time... to you know who."

The memory registered in his mind and on his face. And she saw it for the very first time, remorse. "I didn't mean it," he breathed. "You are actually the brightest light in this room."

His eyes held her spellbound, traces of sadness in the brown flakes in his eyes catching her off guard. But when his gaze turned into something that caused flutters in her belly, she blushed openly. And that was when the subject of the table turned to them.

"When's the wedding?" Mr. Marbury asked in a foreign Southern accent.

She and Victor exchanged quick glances, but it was Victor who answered after his brother pushed his arm. "We haven't discussed a wedding date," he said before focusing on his plate.

We haven't discussed a wedding anything, she thought to herself.

"It will be soon, I'm sure," Mags assured to counteract the awkward silence that followed Victor's words. "These two lovebirds have been on a whirlwind romance for some time now. It will be in no time."

"Humph," Mr. Marbury replied. "Good to know. I had hoped you folks were the good Christian type of Negroes. I'm looking forward to seeing a good Christian colored ceremony. Yawl understand, don't you? See where I'm from, you can't let your business dealings get tarnished with northern radical ideas, like race-mixing."

"And where you from?" asked the most unexpected person at the table. His intelligible voice echoed off the walls.

Bianca blinked her eyes to be sure the words came from the source she heard it from. Up to that point, she didn't believe Uncle Chito could put two words together other than "my box," much less say what she had just heard him say. But he said it. Clear as day.

"Where I'm from?" Mr. Marbury asked.

"That's what I asked, didn't I?" Uncle Chito asked with an unwavering gaze.

"I'm from the great state of Texas. That's where I'm from. You ever been there, Mr. uh..."

"Chito Freeman. You just keep your Texas eyes off my box, ya hear me? I'll cut 'em clean out cha head."

Over the children's giggles, Victor reached over Bianca to calm Uncle Chito down. But that didn't work. He just got even louder by proclaiming, "I don't care if he a white man. He betta not think about lookin' at my box."

"Nobody's looking at your box, Uncle Chito."

Thanks to Uncle Chito, the rest of the meal went along awkwardly. Bianca supposed this cryptic discussion had a lot to do with Mags' recent fascination—her engagement to Victor. She was sure there was more here to learn, but Bianca didn't care to inquire. All she wanted to do was go home.

The sound of a gold fork clanging against a crystal glass drew the attention of the entire table. Mags rose with her glass extended high. "I would like to make a toast. To the future Marbury Bank." Once everyone saluted their glasses, she added, "and to Victor, who has finally made himself an honest man by getting married. This family can hold its head up high in this city. To no more shame..." She lifted her glass even higher with the expectation that everyone followed. This was a toast?

Bianca felt Victor's shoulders stiffen beside her as an eerie, yet quiet, storm settled around her.

After the last course was served, Mr. Marbury took his leave, and the family remained seated around the dining room table in uncomfortable silence. When Mags returned from escorting Mr. Marbury out, Victor's hot expression greeted her.

Mags blinked in his direction innocently. "What's wrong? Don't look at me like that. I did what I had to do. Oh goodness, entertaining and saving your two asses is tiresome. I think I will lie down and rest my weary neck."

Bianca watched a shadow cross his face as he turned his sinister gaze in Mags' direction. "Margaret, if you ever interfere in my life again, the way you did tonight, you won't have a neck to rest."

"Interfere? At least I did something. You have never helped this family further its interests. Your brother has done all the work for this bank, and all you ever did was eat and screw every pair of open legs you could find. Don't you think it's high time you overcame the obstacle of your scandalous birth and lineage? I'm sure your mother would be proud to see that her little secret had finally done something useful with his miserable life."

It was the shadow of Victor's powerful hand that made her yelp. With swift precision, he knocked the massive centerpiece from in front of her to the end of the table, scaring his poor Uncle Chito into a screaming fit. Bianca and Wesley's wife did their best to console the man, but they weren't successful. It was Victor who picked up a wooden box from the floor and placed it in his hands.

"I found your box, Uncle Chito," he whispered.

The poor man grabbed at the box and finally calmed down with a sigh. Bianca watched their interaction with intense fasciation as the two of them spoke in a private language.

When they finished, Victor lifted him to stand and then turned to Bianca. In a deep voice that she was not about to challenge, he said, "Let's go." Before she could answer, he lifted her elbow to standing and pressed her in the exit's direction until a voice stopped him in his tracks.

"Don't leave on Christmas, Victor," Wesley said. "You're still a part of this family."

Victor's protective arm still held Bianca when she looked to see a wave of coolness wash over him and smooth out the lines of anger on his face. A beautiful and disarming smile appeared as he turned to his family. "Merry Christmas to all of you. My fiancée, my uncle, and I bid you good night. But before we go, we will take a few plates with us."

Bianca watched as the man strolled over to the table, grabbed the end of the pristine white linen filled with rows of dishes, utensils, and glasses, and with the most finesse a man could muster, he graciously pulled the entire length of the tablecloth until every single item crashed to the floor.

Finally, Mags' haughty demeanor morphed into one of outrage. Satisfied, Victor bowed his head and turned to Bianca. This time he placed a more gentle hand on Bianca's lower back and escorted her out of the room.

CHAPTER 9

THE OTHER SIDE OF GOSSIP

The minute Bianca stepped out of Mags' townhome, she realized that she hadn't retrieved her jacket during her hurried exit. When she shivered from the wind, she heard Victor swear under his breath. He muttered something about there being no way in hell he would go back into that house. In one fluid motion, he shrugged off his dinner jacket and applied it to her bare shoulders without asking her permission. He gathered his uncle and placed him gently into the car and then turned back to her to do the same. She wanted to tell him that she wasn't a feeble old man, and that she didn't need help, but one look at his hardened jaw told her to leave it alone.

"Home?" he asked as he revved his car's engine.

"Yes, but... aren't you going to talk about what just happened?"

He bit down on his frustration, causing his muscle in his cheek to dance. "Nothing to talk about," he replied.

She directed him to her sister's home. Everyone in her family gathered there during the holidays. They would undoubtedly look for Bianca's attendance. She did not push his silence, but

Lord, she wanted to. Although he had said his peace at Mags' dinner party, she had not. Daisy was still missing, and Mags' devilish investment was still hanging over Bianca's head. Victor's behavior may have been freeing for him, but it pushed Bianca into a deeper quandary than before.

When Victor's car slowed to a stop, her thoughts readjusted to the present. A loud crashing sound reached both of their ears. One of her sister's twelve children had crashed his boxcar into the side of the house, causing four of Bianca's nephews to gather around the broken car and argue like a bunch of old men. Bianca's sister, Cecilia, made an appearance then and yelled at the entire lot. They yelled excuses back and so forth and so on. This was a common occurrence at Cecilia's home.

Cecilia and her husband, Joseph, had adopted ten boys before having their own two little girls, and now she was pregnant with a third child. The house was in a constant state of chaos and clutter. But it was full of love. And such love was now being witnessed by Victor and Bianca as they watched Cecilia kiss the wounds of the little boy who crashed his boxcar.

The tender moment softened the angry lines on Victor's face and relaxed his tense body.

However, Bianca felt the need to explain. "Err... it is never a dull moment around here."

"I see. You are lucky to have them... your family."

"I'm sorry your mother said those things," she said.

The muscle jumped in his cheek again, and his nostrils flared. "She's no mother of mine," he replied bluntly. When Bianca's eyes danced in confusion, he added, "She's Wesley's mother. When my father was living, I suppose you could have called her my step-mother. But after he died, she just became a never-ending memory of my father's stupidity. She's been married twice since his death. Her last husband, Edison, was my father's best friend. So now she is just Wesley's mother."

"Oh," she said with a blink of realization. "Well, Wesley's mother is a bitch."

Victor laughed. She must have seen him do so a dozen times, but never like this. This time he committed the act without the air of arrogance or with pretense. Both sides of his face pulled up into a wholehearted grin, revealing his pristine white teeth. The infectiousness of his laugh drew her laughter until he broke the spell when he touched her. She nearly froze as the back of his knuckle caressed the outline of her jawbone. She felt tickles against the inside of her stomach, and she did not like it. Not from him. No thanks. When she reeled back from his touch, he nodded in understanding.

"What were you doing there anyway?" he asked.

"It's funny you ask," she bristled as she put some distance between them. "Your moth—I mean Mags had everything to do with my attendance. As you may recall, I asked her for a loan for my newspaper. Well, she did it. She spent all kinds of money. She even bought the building the newspaper is in, which is what I had wanted to do. And the crazy broad did all of this expecting that I marry you. I made a deal with the devil." It was on the tip of her tongue to tell Victor all about Daisy. She wanted to tell him desperately but couldn't risk Mags finding out.

He let out a thoughtful sound from the depth of his throat and gazed directly into her eyes as if he were reading her thoughts, as if he suspected there was more to the story.

"So," Bianca continued nervously. "I guess I should have called you to tell you I was coming, but there wasn't any time. And I figured your offer would still stand. I thought maybe we could give Mags the impression that we are together for a little while. Maybe long enough for me to pay her all the money back." Or until I find Daisy, she inwardly added. "Perhaps by then, you can sort out things with Angel."

"Who?"

"Angel. Your—"

"That white gal, boy," Uncle Chito blurted from the back seat, reminding them both of his presence.

"Oh! Yes, Angel," Victor bumbled.

"So? What do you think?" Bianca asked.

"I think..." he started before clasping her hand in his and brushing a warm kiss on the top. "Ms. Bianca Eubanks, would you give me the honor of being my fake fiancée?"

She wanted to shrug him off and or push her hand into his face, but the look in his eyes gave her pause. "Okay, see, you can't do stuff like that."

"Like what?"

"Like that, Casanova. You can't be acting like that when we are alone. Let's just be buddies. Bianca and Victor."

"Buddies? All right. And when we're not alone? How should two engaged buddies act?"

"I don't know. Like a couple."

"All right. When do we begin?"

"I guess now," she said with a shrug. "Wait—is Uncle Chito—"

"Uncle Chito won't tell a soul. Isn't that right, Uncle Chito?" Victor nearly shouted.

"Tell what? I ain't got nothing to say to nobody, especially not to that ol' dried up bitch. She betta keep her hands off my box. I know that much."

Victor gazed back at Bianca with a humorous gaze as if asking if she were satisfied.

"Fair enough," she replied.

"All right. Let's go." He was already out of the car before she realized that he meant to go into the house with her to greet her family.

"No, no, no, no." The panic in her voice increased with every step he made to her side of the car.

He opened the car door and offered his knightly hand.

"No!" she said in a harsh whisper, hoping none of her nephews noticed.

"What's wrong? I thought you wanted to start immediately. Your fiancé should escort you to family functions. And Christmas Eve is a family function." When she stared at him with wide eyes, he continued, "Or would you like me to do things the traditional way? Should I schedule a visit with your father to ask for your hand?"

Oh, dear. She had forgotten about her father. Her imagination leaped in dramatic somersaults, leaving her in a catatonic state. Her father hated Victor Carlson. He was the owner of the bank that was now foreclosing on his hospital. Oh, this would not work. Not any of it. Victor had to go away. And right now.

"Bianca?" a familiar feminine voice called. It was Cecilia. She stood at the bottom of her porch, rubbing her large belly, wearing a confused expression. As she should. Cecilia's sister was now standing outside of a shiny Studebaker Touring wearing an expensive dress with the infamous Victor Carlson clutching her hand.

"Oh, hello, Ce-Ce. Don't mind me. I was just being dropped off by this gentleman. Thank you, sir. I don't know your name, but you have been so kind. How much do I owe you for the ride?" A small smile edged on Victor's face as Cecilia approached them. "No, Ce-Ce. Don't come any farther. Don't want you to tire yourself out. Shouldn't you be sitting down somewhere in your condition?"

"I'm fine, Bianca. I just wanted to see your cab driver's car. This is quite a cab. It's been a while since I've been in a car this nice."

Victor and Bianca glanced at each other while Cecilia absently peered into the interior of Victor's car.

When she finished, she took one look at Bianca and asked, "Where are you coming from? You look so fancy."

Of course, Cecilia would notice the beautiful car and dress. Before she met her now-husband, she was engaged to the richest man in Maryland. Although she was now happy with the simple life, she was still easily dazzled by shiny things, and Victor Carlson had all the razzle-dazzle.

"You look familiar," Cecilia commented. "Do I know you?"

"I'm sure you don't know him, Ce-Ce. He's just a driver. All right, sir. Thank you. Good night."

"Why are you wearing his jacket? Where's yours?"

Jesus! The woman asked too many questions. Thank goodness Victor had a soul in that body of his. He offered her a safety net with his next words. "Ms. Edison asked me to bring your sister home after her dinner party. We didn't discover her coat was missing until just now. I can bring her coat back tomorrow if you would like."

"On Christmas?" Cecilia asked while refusing to yield to Bianca's hand, pulling her away. "That won't be necessary. I should have something in the house that will fit, Bianca. I'm sure you want to be at home with your family on Christmas day."

"Y-Y-Yes!" Bianca sputtered. "Yes! Again, thank you, sir. Good night. Merry Christmas, and all that. Shall we, Cecilia?"

"Bianca! You are being rude. I'm the mean sister, remember? What's gotten into you? The polite thing to do would be to ask to return his generosity by offering a warm cup of tea. It is Christmas Eve."

Bianca closed her eyes. In the last few weeks, she had noticed that Victor had no problem with going anywhere without an invitation. He crashed everything. He even pushed his way into her apartment. He would no doubt jump at the opportunity again. Therefore, his next words stunned her.

"Unfortunately, I would have to decline your offer, ma'am. However, I hope to see you and your family again soon. Until then, please have a joyful holiday."

Cecilia blinked in confusion. "What was your name?"

"Victor," he simply said before walking to the driver's side and driving away.

"What an odd man," Cecilia commented as she watched his car drive down the hill. "Dashingly handsome... but odd. Victor? Hmmm?"

Bianca did not offer a comment. She was already running to burrow herself somewhere in Cecilia's house.

The very next day, Bianca went on with the business of finding Daisy. Playing house with Victor Carlson was cute, but it would not rescue Daisy from the clutches of evil Mags. Bianca needed boots on the ground to sniff her out. And no one could sniff out a person better than Prince McGee. Prince was an unofficial employee of the *Baltimore Beat*. Bianca used him for the off-the-record things that would require getting hands dirty. And since Prince dwelled in the city's underbelly, Bianca knew it would be easy for him to find a kidnapped woman.

But she had to find him first. He was not the easiest to catch up with, so she had to visit his mother's house so she could send word for him. Mama must have the magic touch, because, on the third day, Prince showed up to the *Baltimore Beat* in his usual garb. A brown cap covering most of his eyes and a short industrial coat.

"How long she been gone?" he asked her in the early hours of a crisp Monday morning. She shut the door of her office to keep out Kizzy's ears. If she knew Daisy was missing, she would go nuts. And Bianca saw no point in upsetting sweet Kizzy.

"Weeks, maybe. No telling. I just found out."

"What about lover boy?" He pulled his toothpick out of his mouth to ask his question.

"Who?"

"Your lover boy? The one you hanging around town with."

Victor. He was referring to Victor. He would know about that.

"He has nothing to do with it."

"Humph," Prince murmured as he repositioned his toothpick so it leveled on his bottom lip. "Boss lady, I been knowing ya for a long time. Hate to see ya caught up with the likes of him. He's bad news.

"Fair enough. Thanks for the tidbit," she said as she handed a few bills to Prince. "If you hear anything about her, let me know."

"Will do," he replied with a pull to his cap. He was out of the door in no time, but he left his words in the room. They filled it with the stench of insecurity. Perhaps she was going about this Victor thing all wrong. Could she really trust a man like him? What if he was in on Daisy's disappearance?

"Have I got the gossip for you!" Ms. Ginny proclaimed as she dashed into Bianca's office and disturbed her thoughts. "Did you hear me?" Ms. Ginny repeated.

The hungry cry of Kizzy's baby sounded off in the distance behind her. "Oh, Lord. I don't know how you keep focus with that baby hollering every two minutes. She's just like her mama if you ask me."

"Let her be," Bianca muttered. She waved Ms. Ginny away, but the woman would not budge.

"I said, did you hear me?" Ms. Ginny asked impatiently.

"Huh? I'm working on my column, Ms. Ginny. Tomorrow is print day."

"Yes, I know. That's why I need to tell you this. You have to add it to your column." Ms. Ginny sat on Bianca's desk and childishly swung her legs.

"It must be good. You're acting like a schoolgirl. Who is your source?"

"Margaret Edison's housemaid."

Bianca's fingers froze on her typewriter. "Really?"

"Yes, really. Nannette has had nothing good to say in years. But oh my, did she have the dirt?"

"I-I-I see. And just what did little Miss Nannette have to say?"

"Margaret Edison's son, Victor Carlson, has gotten himself engaged to a young woman named Bianca Eubanks. And not only that, the two are madly in love. Isn't that something?"

Bianca expelled the air she had been holding and shrugged her shoulders. There was no keeping anything from Ms. Ginny. She was the finder of truth. No wonder she was good at reporting.

"All right."

"Is it true? Is that how you were able to win over that stingy woman? You have to marry her son? Now listen, I'm not your mother. But I'm sure she would tell you don't have to prostitute yourself to anyone. It ain't worth it. Trust me. Been there, done that."

"Prostitute myself? Ms. Ginny!"

"Hey, I don't mean to be crude, but really, Bianca?"

Bianca considered telling Ms. Ginny the entire truth. But she couldn't take the chance. Bianca couldn't risk Ginny going to the police and putting Daisy in more danger. If Ms. Ginny wanted to know the full truth, she would have to find it. It would not come from her.

"It's all a long story," Bianca said instead. "But, it's not what you think it is. We are... in love."

"In love? Just the other day, you had another beau in here. Now, what was that boy's name? Hihum?"

"Hiram."

"Yeah. Now, what happened to him? Wasn't you supposed to go with him to Mags' thang?"

"Nothing happened to him. He was already engaged and..." Bianca's words froze, and her mind fed her the best story she could think of—the truth. "Hiram's true intended showed up, and Mr. Carlson did the gentlemanly thing and saved me from embarrassment. He took me home that day, and well... I suppose it was love at first sight." Well, some of it was true.

"Love at first sight, my ass."

"Who's had love at first sight?" yelled Kizzy from the back room where she nursed her little one.

"Your boss over here," Ms. Ginny said over her shoulder, her eyes never leaving Bianca's face. "She's getting hitched too."

"*What?*" Kizzy hollered so loud she upset her nursing baby.

"You happy now?" Bianca asked Ms. Ginny with a leveled look. "Listen, the other day, when you took Daisy home, he met me for lunch. We went to Dusty Anne's, and that was that. Why are you making it a big deal?"

"Because it *is* a big deal. That man is nothing but a pretty face and a fast tongue. You're smarter than that."

"She is a lot smarter than that," said the male voice of an intruder with a pretty face that was not Prince McGee's.

Bianca and Ms. Ginny turned to see his enormous masculine form fill the doorway of the *Baltimore Beat*.

"That's why I'm working so hard to get her to defy logic," Victor said.

CHAPTER 10

PRINT DAY

At least he hadn't bothered to show up at her parents' or sister's home. She had a devil of a time blurring Cecilia's memories. Cecilia had remembered the man all right; she just couldn't place him. But it was only a matter of time before she did.

"Something isn't right, Bianca," Cecilia had said. "But then again, you are always up to something."

Thankfully, Cecilia had left the matter alone and didn't broach the subject again. Not that she couldn't discuss it, it was that she didn't know where to begin. How was she to convert this lie into something her family would believe? They were her family. They knew her. And they knew when she wasn't telling the truth. But the health and safety of her dear friend were at stake, and surely, a lie like this had a good cause. It was a good lie. And as hard as it was, it was time to stop lamenting over the betrayal behind things and pull up her breeches.

When she turned around from her desk, she saw the manifestation of this good lie standing before her in all of his dashing male glory. He stood there boldly against the backdrop of feminine disdain, immune to Ms. Ginny's scowls and Kizzy's gawking.

"Hello, my love," he said in a deep and believable tone, almost as if it were the most natural thing in the world to say.

"Hello," Bianca answered back. "What are you doing here?"

"I came to see you. And to see where you worked. So this is your business? Impressive." He directed his gaze to Kizzy and her baby and smiled. "What a beautiful child. What's her name?"

"Sharon," Kizzy replied, still gawking at the tall man.

"That's a pretty name."

"We named her that because it's my husband's aunt's name. And he loves his aunt. I mean, she practically raised him. Are you trying to marry Ms. Bianca? You know she is a good woman? It would be a shame for someone to play with her heart. Are you doing that? I hope not. I don't really like rumors, but when you are in the newspaper business, you hear things and you gotta a lot of rumors about you. You know my mama says that where there is smoke, there is fire. And I'm wondering if all your smoke is from a real fire."

Ms. Ginny spoke next from her desk's seat. "Forgive her prattling. She loves to go on and on. But I can't help but agree. You have quite the reputation, Mr. Carlson."

Victor coughed to clear his throat. "Obviously, it precedes me. I guess there is no point in riding around niceties. You are correct, ma'am. Too many rumors. But if I am not mistaken, some of those rumors started right here in this room. Tell me. Which one of you is Lady Noire?"

"We are the ones asking questions, Mr. Carlson," Ms. Ginny snapped. "Reputations and rumors are one thing, but Bianca is a good woman with a good heart. We don't want her to get tangled in any of your rumors."

"Understood, Ms...."

"Virginia," she answered.

He reached out his hand to shake hers, but she had already

moved on to a task that didn't involve him. He tightly smiled and shrugged his neglected hand in his pocket.

"What are you doing here?" Bianca asked him again.

"Ah. I came here to deliver this to you." He held out a gold envelope. When she took it, she noticed that Kizzy was still gawking. "Ahem. Kizzy, Ms. Ginny."

Thankfully, they took the hint without further challenge and left the two of them alone. Bianca opened the envelope and read the folded card, fully aware that he was watching her.

"A party?"

"Not just any party, The Dilworths' Annual New Year's Eve Party."

"But it says December thirtieth. Aren't New Year's Eve parties on New Year's Eve?"

He offered her a wickedly beautiful smile. "It's a tongue-in-cheek tradition. A way to throw off the authorities looking to catch public consumption. They love to shake up black parties and make their coin off us. So the dates are switched. We party on the thirtieth."

"Ah. A Prohibition Party. Anyway, no thanks," she said as she handed his envelope back to him.

"Why not?"

"Well…" she began in a whisper. "I don't want the word to get out just yet."

"You're serious? I've been approached by not six but seven people just today asking about my mysterious fiancée. The word is out, my dear. By the way, what should I call you? My love? Sweetie? Honey? I was thinking about a nickname for you. I thought of Bee, but I heard your male friend call you that. I want something original… for us."

Bianca shook her head ferociously as she walked back into her office. He followed her spouting more name ideas.

"I can't go anyway," she said finally. "That's print day, and we'll be too busy."

"But it's at night, my darling. How does darling sound?"

"*Mmm*, a little forced. But back to the party. I will work all day and won't have time to get ready. I'll just sit this one out if you don't mind."

"What takes all day?"

"Ack! Victor. I don't have time to explain all the workings of my business. Just like you don't have time to detail yours. I am sure it has its own intricate process."

"I think you are smart enough to figure it out. What happens on print day?"

"Well, if you must know, that is the day we have to front-load that dinosaur of a press, sort and fold papers, and get them ready for delivery. It takes sweat and organization. I already have a small staff, and I use my nephews as much as I can, but I can't afford to pay all of them. So I can only use a few. That means more work for me. There now, you see? Despite Mags' money, this is still a working publication, and we will need all hands for print day."

"All right. I will be back in two days for print day to lend my hands."

She let out a long sigh before she spoke again. "I really don't see the point in getting worked about public appearances. Mags' is on board."

"But not Angel."

"Ahh! So that is why you want to push this. Will she be there?"

"She might."

"Oh, God. Please go away, Victor. I have things to do."

"Fair enough," he said before walking over to her and grabbing her from around her waist and pulling her into an intimate embrace. His tall body enveloped her in his warmth as his hands settled on the small of her back. Why she hadn't pushed him away was beyond her. Victor would have kissed her, had she not politely maneuvered herself out of his hands. "I will see you in two days, my love," he firmly promised before walking out of the door.

Good gracious, she said to herself. She had to admit that Victor Carlson's touch was more than a woman of her standard should be allowed to bear. This fiasco needed to end soon. After Victor's exit, Bianca used the rest of the hour writing to her investigator to demand that he pick up the pace and find Daisy urgently.

Two days had passed, and December 30th had finally arrived. Just before the sun broke through the dark shade of night, Victor was where he said he would be. When Bianca discovered him, it somewhat surprised her to see his tall figure standing at the bottom of the stairs, waiting for her.

"I don't like your moving around in darkness by yourself," he said. "From now on, I'll come to get you if you have to work early." That was how he greeted her, with his mouth in a frown, and she could have sworn it deepened once he noticed her blue overalls.

"You will not," she replied as she walked past him into the building and up the stairs.

"I can't have my fiancé walking around at night and endangering herself."

"Oh, please," she dismissed with a wave of her hand as he followed close behind. "You really didn't have to come, Victor. Angel won't see you here. So there was no point. My staff and I can handle everything. We—" They both froze in the doorway when they saw Ms. Ginny face down on her desk.

"Ms. Ginny!" Bianca cried. "Are you okay?"

"*Oh,*" Ms. Ginny groaned. She sat up, meeting Victor and Bianca with a swollen face. "Please stay back. I don't know what's got on me, girl. But I feel real bad right now."

"You look bad too," Victor supplied with a frown.

"Well, no one asked you," Ms. Ginny snapped. "What's he doing here, Bianca? We got things to-to-to *achoo!*"

Bianca and Victor almost flew off the desk at the amount of snot that shot out of Ms. Ginny's nose. "I'm so sorry, dear. I know today is print day. Kizzy can't come because of the baby.

And I see the boys haven't shown. I can't leave you all by yourself."

"Ms. Ginny, you need to go home. It will be fine." Bianca eyed Victor and noticed for the first time what he was not wearing his usual dandy suit. He wore blue overalls and a pair of sturdy boots. "Victor is here. He'll help me."

"This randy dandy?" she yelled as the two of them lifted Ms. Ginny out of the room. Thank goodness her son had arrived to take her back home.

Her absence left Bianca, Victor, and two of her older nephews to do a six-person job. It was going to be a long day and possibly a long night; she surmised. But they were all up to the task. And even though he was a novice at this arduous and tedious work, Victor learned quickly, earning the respect of Bianca's nephews.

Bianca busied herself in the front while Victor and the boys worked on her stubborn print press. She peeked in at different times to spy on them when she overheard their male grunts from heavy lifting. Her press was a formidable foe against a time crunch. But Victor seemed to be ready for the challenge.

During their quiet times, Bianca looked in on them and witnessed something she could never un-see. She saw Victor unbutton his overalls and remove his shirt! Bianca's feet grew roots into the floorboards while her eyes widened in wonderment. Lord in heaven, he was a beautiful specimen. The muscles in his stomach rippled as his powerful hand ripped the bottom half of his shirt. The muscles in his arms tightened and jumped as he tightly wrapped his shirt's scrap around a metal piece as a makeshift belt for the press. When it started up again with a loud whir, Victor and the boys clapped in victory. They were all bonding over their triumph over the press until they noticed her in the doorway. *Damn.*

"We got it working, Aunty," her nephew, Tommy declared.

"I see," she replied nervously as she backed into her workspace.

"Do you need some help in here?" Victor's deep voice declared just behind her.

She never heard him walk up behind her. But there he was, an impressive foot and a half over her, sweating and shirtless.

"My apologies for being indecent," he said as he shrugged his torn shirt back on his body and re-secured his overalls.

"*Mmhm*," she murmured, doing her best to ignore his overwhelmingly male form as he loomed over her.

"I thought you said Mags paid to have the press fixed." He wiped his hands and face on an ink-smudged rag. His sweat glued his shirt to the intricate lines of his muscular shoulders and arms, causing her shakable distraction.

"I thought it was fixed, too," she snapped.

"Maybe you need a new one. I'll buy one for you."

"No, you will not! I'm up to my eyeballs in debt at this point."

"You won't have to pay me back. I want to," he whispered as he rifled through the stack of papers she was organizing.

She stopped working immediately and glared at him. "Victor, why are you here? I did not ask you to come. I have not asked you for anything, only to help me keep your step-mother appeased until I can pay her back."

A wry smile appeared on his smudged face as he gazed down on her. "And how are you going to pay her back if you don't get these papers out? Maybe you needed just a little help, Ms. Grouchy."

"Fine, fine. But once the press finishes the last batch, you can go. The boys and I will figure out the rest."

Victor didn't respond after that. He just continued to work long after the last batch was finished and long after the boys had left. He stayed by her side as she tirelessly tied each bundle for tomorrow's delivery. When it was all said and done, Bianca looked out the window and saw the sun had set and it was dark again.

"So much for your party," she said, breaking their quiet streak.

He grunted in agreement as he helped her pick up around the floor.

"Maybe I was a grouch earlier. Thank you for helping me, Victor."

Victor turned his head in her direction with another disarming smile. "What's your middle name, Bianca?"

"Why?"

"Because I need a pet name for you."

"Oh, boy. This again. Elizabeth. My middle name is Elizabeth."

"Hmmm. Liz. Lizzie. How does my Lizzie sound?"

Before she knew it, her mouth reacted and smiled at his adorable face. No matter the reason for his effort, it was sweet. Even if attending to her and pouring his affection on her was for self-serving reasons, it felt nice. Angel was a lucky woman. "My Lizzie sounds sweet."

"Good. Then it's mine. No one else can use it."

"I'm starving," she said with a yawn, hoping to change this sweet subject. "Too bad nothing is open at this time of night."

"I know where we could get the best food in town at this time of night."

"Where?"

"The Dilworth party."

"Ha! By the time we go home and get dressed to go over there, it will be midnight, and the party will be over. I'm guessing a New Year's Party on the day before still ends at midnight, right?"

"No, it doesn't. It goes even longer. But what if we didn't change?"

"And go like this? Us in our dusty clothes? Are you serious?"

"Why not? It's just a party. Who cares what anyone thinks? You don't strike me as a woman who cares."

"Because I don't."

"So... to hell with getting dressed for that uppity-ass party. Let's just go. All this work and no fun? To hell with that. Come have fun with me, Lizzie."

Bianca was not sure what swayed her thoughts. Perhaps it was that he had done a really sweet thing today by helping her. Perhaps it was the way he gazed at her as if she were the only woman in his mind and thoughts. Perhaps it was the way he stood before her, encompassing the world around her. He had filled her sight in that instant and blocked out all reason. He told Ms. Ginny earlier that day that he was trying to get Bianca to defy her own logic. And the devil if he hadn't been successful in doing so.

"Let's go."

Hours later, her second thoughts haunted her. She protested in the car on their way to the main event. Cold feet settled at the bottom of her legs and paralyzed her movement. The sights and sounds of Lafayette Street lit up with horse-drawn carriages and luxury automobiles froze her. Ladies wrapped in fur coats and gentlemen in their top hats told her that this was a bad idea. She and Victor still had black ink on their faces, not to mention their weathered clothing. But none of these points persuaded Victor. His humor had taken over all of his sound reasoning. Who was she kidding? Victor Carlson had no sound reasoning. None she could think of. For if he had it, he would wipe that quiet smile off his face.

"No good will come of this," Bianca commented under her breath as his car moved to the front of the line to allow one of the Dilworth servants to park his vehicle.

"What do you mean? They invited us, my Lizzie."

"Stop calling me that! This is a terrible idea."

He leveled a look at her nervous fluttering. "Just what makes it a bad idea? Other than our clothes. We might get some looks, but so what?"

"Well, let's see. I haven't told my parents about this... thing we are doing yet. My father will just be thrilled about the man who is foreclosing on his hospital marrying his daughter. And what about Mags?"

"What about her?"

"She will be furious. I gather she hates being embarrassed. Won't she be there?"

"I think she and Wesley mentioned it."

"So that's it? We are just going to stroll up in there without a care in the world? She'll die!"

"Good! Let's go!" He pushed his car into park and shrugged on his worker's cap. He looked over and waited for her to bundle up.

When she made no move and continued to stare at him in wonderment and sat back against his seat. She watched his Adam's apple rise and fall as he looked out into nothing.

"Bianca... have fun with me," he said as he grabbed her icy fingers.

She turned to him and was met with his dark brown eyes.

"For one night, let's forget about all the bullshit, and let's just have fun. You and me."

"Why me? You have hundreds of women who would love to throw caution to the wind and run roughshod through society. There is no point in my being here. Angel isn't going to bring her white self to this hoity-toity Negro shindig. She won't know you are here. And that's why you wanted to do this engagement thing, right?"

"Yes, but no. I have other reasons..."

"Like what?"

"You. Bianca, you are the only woman I have ever known to have gotten my Uncle Chito to mention her name."

"Uncle Chito mentioned my name?"

"Yep!" He laughed. "No fooling. He asked about you this morning. Of course, he threatened to kill you if touched his box, but he later said, that Bianca gal all right."

"You know I don't believe you?" Bianca laughed. "And it's pretty low to use a sweet old man against me."

Victor laughed again and then sobered. "I don't know. I kinda enjoyed defying the norm the other day. Telling Mags to kiss my ass was nice. I mean, I'm sick of all this shit. This need to dress up and dance around like exceptional Negroes. I don't care what they think anymore. And that's why I like this thing we got. Even though it's fake. It gives me an excuse to be your friend or as you put it, buddy. So come on, Bianca. Be my buddy tonight and let's give them all a party they will talk about in the morning. Maybe Lady Noire will be there." He emphasized that last part with a wink. "Or maybe you need some liquid courage," he added by pressing his silver flask into her hands.

After four swigs of what tasted like a very expensive whiskey, Bianca nodded for the valet to open her door. "Here goes nothing," she muttered before accepting Victor's waiting arm.

CHAPTER 11

THE NOT-SO-NEW YEAR'S EVE PARTY

The Dilworths' young butler took one look at Victor and Bianca as they stood arm in arm in a disheveled mess and nearly crossed his eyes. "Good evening, Mr. Carlson... would you care to use one of our rooms to change for the evening? I can secure you one."

"No need, Seymour," Victor replied as he brushed past the butler. Victor plucked two champagne glasses from a waiting pedestal and shared one with Bianca.

Bianca accepted the bubbling flute and drained it. With Bianca tucked neatly into his side, he greeted his friends and made his usual witty banter while overly laughing at mild jests. He attempted to appear bored by their luxuries and parade around as if overalls were the new black.

But all the while, Bianca remained quiet while the entire party gawked at her. She pressed her cap down over her eyes to hide her vulnerability. After noticing this, a strange compulsion crawled up Victor's spine that made him want to shelter her from the vile judgment of the crowd. That was why he shuffled her to the food table where he ran into his old friend George

Lewis. George Lewis was a good fellow and a long-time friend. Surely he would be a welcome ally at this party.

"Victor!" he shouted over the music with added mirth. "You sure know how to make an entrance. Did you get your hands dirty at the railroad before coming here? You're nuts!" George continued to laugh over a bed of iced shrimp while Victor accepted his jesting. "And here I was expecting you to walk in the door with the beauty of the week wearing some dead animal! When I saw you waltzing up in here looking like a factory worker, I about died! And you and your lady... Ahem. Ma'am." George soberly nodded to Bianca, at which she nodded back. "I apologize for my antics, but it's just so funny."

"What's so funny?" she asked, with her eyes peeking from under her cap.

"I-I mean. Him... you and him... I thought it was a costume. No? I thought he brought you here to be funny." George would have carried on fumbling if it were not for Victor's arresting scowl.

Bianca absently dismissed George by looking around the room. George continued to backpedal by discussing his health while Victor watched Bianca take in her surroundings.

He was sure the Dilworth mansion impressed her. It was magnificent. The entrance was three stories high and wide enough to fit her family's home. Twin curving stairs filled with partiers towered over the east and west side of the palatial foyer. At the very top, on the balcony overlooking the crowd, a well-known jazz group by the name of the Clarence Williams' Blue Five played their hearts out.

On a normal night, Victor would have relished attending this swanky affair. He would have paraded himself to be seen by arriving inconceivably late with two of the most beautiful women in town wearing an outrageously priced tuxedo and maybe his favorite chinchilla fur coat. However, just now, and looking through Bianca's lens of awareness, he had never felt as silly and superficial as everyone looked. She was right. This was a terrible idea. And looking at her tug at her worn shirt and overalls, he felt foolish. He should have never put her in a position to feel less than when she was greater than. He pulled her body tighter to his to assure her, but she surprised George and himself by shrugging out of his arms, and without a casual goodbye, she walked away.

He stood there, watching her back disappear into the crowd. Thankfully, his height afforded him a bird's-eye view to see where she was going. His eyes narrowed when he saw her target. Hiram. Was that what she called him whenever she got that dreamy look in her eyes? Victor watched the man wave Bianca to him. There was no sign of his fiancée in sight. Bianca was probably happy about that.

"You like her," George remarked, interrupting his thoughts.

"What?" Victor muttered absently because he was too busy watching Bianca share a laugh with Hiram. Apparently, her tepid mood quickly morphed into a cheery tenor at the sight of him.

"I said you like her," George pressed again, demanding Victor's attention. "You can't take your eyes off her. Interesting."

"What's so interesting about it?"

"Well... she is... different from the others. Not very frilly, I guess. And yet you are eager to go over there and deck that man in the face."

"Maybe... but not because I like her or anything. She's just different. Maybe a man tires of frill."

"Interesting," he heard George repeat under his breath.

When Victor witnessed Bianca hug Hiram, his shoes moved under his feet. He was well on his way through the crowd when a strong hand gripped his forearm. Victor turned around and stared directly into the eyes of his brother, Wesley.

"What are you doing?" Wesley asked, still firmly gripping Victor's arm.

Victor dismissively shirked his hand away. He was never one to be manhandled or controlled. That was a character trait that Wesley had made a habit of forgetting lately.

"What does it look like I'm doing? I'm enjoying the party."

"No, you are mocking this party. Or rather, Mags. And who is that man your fiancée is talking to?"

"I was on my way to find out before you stopped me. And why do you care?"

Wesley adjusted his bow tie and looked around for ears. "I care because Mags is ready for you to close this deal. She wants a wedding date so she can invite Mr. Marbury. And one sooner rather than later."

"Wedding? Hell no. This was all just for shits and giggles until you can get your little contract signed and we can get paid and move out of town."

"*Shh!* Keep it down!" Wesley harshly whispered. "Are you trying to jeopardize things? And anyway, this is for both of us. Not just me. You need to secure this deal. Just marry her and turnaround to do a quick annulment when it's all said and done. Or, if you like her, and I am picking up that you do, have at her."

"Have at her?" Victor slowly repeated.

"Take her to bed and then get rid of her," Wesley shrugged.

Victor stared at his brother for a long moment before he said, "No marriage." He was already walking away before Wesley grabbed his arm again.

"You don't have a choice, brother." Wesley's teeth gritted with every word. "We'll lose everything. There is too much at stake here. I don't understand why you can't see that."

It was on the tip of Victor's tongue to tell him that all he saw was a man on the brink of crazed desperation. But Victor decided not to say anything. In one deliberate move, he removed Wesley's hand, leaving him in a state of pique.

During Victor's hunt for Bianca, he ran into a few more friends who laughed at his attire and ribbed him about Bianca. Edging to a state of irritation, Victor shrugged them off in time for his eyes to land on Bianca. It was a good thing too. She needed salvation once again. Hiram's famous real-life fiancée had appeared at his side, wearing a smug look on her face.

"Bianca, it's not nice to see you," Hiram's fiancée said in that baby voice Victor found so annoying the first time he had heard it. "I'm still mad at what you did." She hugged Hiram's arm to her body in the most childish display of possession.

"Now, pumpkin. No need for that with Bee here. She's harmless. And just my friend. I only have eyes for you, pumpkin. Besides, I told you that the whole thing was just a show. I'm sure Bianca will tell you the same thing. Even now. Right, Bianca?"

"All action, no show," Victor announced as he possessively reached around Bianca's waist and hugged her back to his front. His large hand rested on her flat tummy as he openly nuzzled the crook of her neck. For emphasis, he added a wink to Hiram's soon-to-be and laughed inwardly when she blushed on Hiram's arm.

"Ahem," Hiram began with a cough as he held out his hand to shake Victor's. "We never got the chance to make formal introductions earlier. Hiram Coleman. It's a pleasure to meet you."

"The pleasure is all mine. Any friend of my lady's is a friend of mine." Victor had to admit that the handshake he gave Hiram was a little strong, but he could not stop himself from doing it. For some reason, he felt the need to display his rank in masculinity.

The handshake rankled Hiram, but he did his best to recover under Victor's hooded gaze. "Well, I suppose that is true. Bee is a dear friend of mine." Hiram's fiancée pulled his arm to warn him, but he paid her no heed. "Bee and I have been friends for a very long time. Childhood, isn't that right?"

Bianca gave him an endearing smile and a nod of encouragement.

"How long have you known each other?" Hiram asked Victor.

"Not long. We just met. But when you have that certain something, you don't need a long time. Isn't that right, my Lizzie?" He silently dared her to give him anything less than the same sweet yes she gave Hiram.

"Yes, my love," she said back with no hint of sweetness, causing Victor unfounded agitation. Although his reasons were invalid, he was still livid at her reserved response. But mad or not, he would never let a man like Hiram see him sweat. Instead, he recovered with a bright smile and hugged Bianca even closer to him.

"My Lizzie?" Hiram asked.

Victor gave a rich chuckle before responding, "She likes it when I call her that."

"I see," Hiram replied with heavy skepticism as he eyed Bianca as she conformed her body to Victor's hold.

"I wanna dance, Hiram," the woman next to Hiram cried. "I'm bored."

"Ah sure," Hiram replied, remembering finally that she was there. "Excuse us?"

"Of course," Victor graciously replied before attempting to walk away with Bianca in tow.

She refused to budge. "What was that all about?" she demanded. He leaned over to give her a kiss, but before he could get near, she backed away. "When we leave, we have a lot to discuss."

"Agreed," he dryly replied. "I would love to begin our discussion with my lack of appreciation for your throwing yourself at your ex-lover in front of everyone."

"What? Hiram?"

"Yes!" His ire now painfully clear to him and everyone else. "How do you think it makes me look?"

"Oh, that's rich. Now you're worried about appearances."

"My women don't wander to other men," he hissed.

She finally shrugged away from him, bumping into another random partier. She turned her cold eyes on him and smiled. "And who said I was one of your women?"

"You did," he answered, matching her coolness. They stared at each other, daring the other to take this dispute to the next level, but neither of them did. There was no time, in fact. Mags suddenly appeared with her bottom lip turned upward. A strange childhood memory flooded back to him, reminding him that her thin bottom lip was always upturned into a rounded frown—especially when he was around.

"I would like for the two of you to follow me, please." She walked away, expecting them to follow her to a pair of double doors beneath the staircases.

Victor followed behind Bianca as she walked through the doors and into what appeared to be a parlor. He shut the door behind him, fully expecting Mags to erupt the moment they were out of public eyesight. Just as he predicted, she opened her mouth wide, ready to extinguish vile insults from the pit of her gut, but when the door to the parlor opened and shut, she froze. They all turned to see the matriarch of the Dilworth family, Pauline Dilworth, walk into the room and plant herself on an empty sofa.

"Well, go ahead," Ms. Pauline declared with a shrug.

"Pauline, what are you doing in here?"

Pauline laid her cane against the side of the sofa and smiled. "I'm here for two reasons: one, it's my house, and two, I'm being nosy. So carry on."

"Pauline, I understand that this is your house, but this is a family matter. We will only be a minute."

"Oh, stop it, Mags," Pauline dismissed. "There are probably twenty people standing outside this door eavesdropping. Tongues are wagging right now. Lady Noire is probably out there just salivating for the scoop. You need someone who will get the story right."

"Don't worry about Lady Noire," Mags replied in a cool voice. "I plucked a flower of hers recently, and I can assure you she won't do anything but paint this ordeal in a positive light."

"Is that right?" Pauline asked, now standing to leave. "Well, if I am not wanted, I will just stand outside. Be sure to speak up so I can hear everything. These ears fail me even if I press them hard enough against the door."

When Pauline shut the door, it felt as if she took all the air out of the room. A suffocating tension oppressed them as they turned to Mags. She bunched her lips tightly and narrowed her eyes venomously. "So, the two of you want to mock me in public? I don't think so. This is a game the both of you know I will win."

"What game, Mummy?"

"Stop calling me that."

"All right, Margaret. What game are we playing? You wanted me to stop being a philandering womanizer and settle down with one woman. Why? You don't care about me. You don't give a shit what I do."

"That is absolutely true, little boy. But you have me wrong. Your getting married has nothing to do with my care or concern for you. It has everything to do with my care and concern for Wesley and his children. For some odd reason, he has a soft spot for you. I can't imagine why. Seeing how your mother was a low-down bitch who nearly destroyed his father's life."

"Careful... Margaret. I know your weak spot. I will gladly embarrass the shit out of you tonight if you open your mouth and utter one more word about my mother. It's funny; you didn't have shit to say about my mother once you got a hold of my mother's money."

"And I enjoyed spending every dime." She smiled victoriously. "We all did. And now that the money is gone and most of it in failing investments, we don't need you anymore. All we need from you is for you to behave, dog. But you can't seem to do that."

In a whoosh, she turned suddenly to Bianca, who was mutely standing in the back of the room, watching this exchange unfold. "Bianca, since I cannot control this fool, I want you to take the reins."

"Me?"

"Yes, you. And you know why. That little flower I plucked will wilt something terrible if you don't get it together. You will get busy planning this wedding. Spare no expense. I don't care. I am sure it is to be the event of your life. A day that a girl like you could never have dreamed of. I don't care if you invite all of your worker friends to attend. It doesn't matter. I just want it done.

"But bear this in mind," she continued, "Until the wedding, the two of you are to be the epitome of perfection... if not, then we will see how bad it can get. I am not one to be toyed with. Believe me. I am a determined woman, and I will get what I want. And do not fall victim to his handsome face. His mother was a beautiful woman too. But beauty is deceiving, and so was hers. Trust me."

After she spoke, all Victor heard was the sound of Mags' hot breathing. Enough of this shit, he thought as he assembled Bianca's terrified form. She resisted him for a moment until he picked her up from the floor and draped her over his shoulder. He gave Mags a massive grin and then headed for the door. Pauline Dilworth was right. At least twenty congregants were standing around the door, struggling to eavesdrop. He chuckled at their stunned faces when he swung the door wide open with Bianca's behind pushed up in the air for the world to kiss. He silently thanked her for wearing pants as he parted the sea of partiers and headed to the door. Seymour's eyes crossed again as Pauline Dilworth's loud cackle rose over the music and into Victor's ears.

CHAPTER 12

MIDNIGHT

The ride away from the Dilworth party felt long and oppressively quiet. Bianca consoled herself by looking out the window into the night's darkness to search for answers. How had her predicament become such an ordeal in this short amount of time? The abyss of nothingness provided no answer.

"I'm sorry."

"Huh? What?" Bianca asked.

"I said I'm sorry," Victor answered. "I'm sorry for the whole thing. Mags, your friend, me, George."

"Who's George?" Bianca asked in a dismissive tone. She really didn't care to talk at that moment.

"My friend? You met him at the hors d'oeuvre table."

"Oh, I remember. His breath stinks."

It took a moment, but Victor erupted in laughter before sobering into a sigh. "I've heard that from other women before. I just look away when he talks. He's a good man, though."

"Why don't you tell him?" Bianca asked, happy to discuss anything but the prospect of forced nuptials.

Victor shrugged. "I don't want to insult his ego, I guess." He looked away from the road in her direction when she made a small, thoughtful sound. "What was that?"

"Nothing. I was just thinking. I have never met a person like you, Victor Carlson."

His smile lines around his eyes deepened. "No? Not one hard-headed, obnoxious womanizer?"

It was her turn to laugh. "I've met plenty of those. But amongst them, you're different."

"And by that, you mean?"

"You are a kind person. I never thought I would say it. I don't think the world knows it. I am not sure if you want them to know it, but you are kind."

"And just how did you come to that conclusion?"

"At Mags' Christmas dinner, I saw you with your Uncle Chito. Even though you were angry, you were patient with him. And I've just learned that you make it a habit to brave your friend's infernal breath because you don't want to hurt his feelings." She looked over at him and realized that he had lost his good humor.

The muscle in his cheek jumped from the tightening of his jaw. "Would you think I was kind enough to meet the likes of your father?"

She flinched at that. "My father?"

He shrugged. "I figured this engagement thing might go on long enough, and I would have to meet your father."

"We won't get that far. Don't worry," she said before looking back out the window.

"I suppose not." He gave a short, thoughtful pause before clearing his throat to speak again. "What's he like? Your father? I never got a chance to meet him. He signed a loan with my father years before he passed. I've only seen your father in passing. He always seemed... intense."

"My father is only intense about his wife, his daughters, and saving lives."

"Sounds like a good man."

She didn't reply. He was a good man who did not abide by deceit. She could have told Victor as much, but any discussion about her family made her stomach churn from guilt. A dim light from the road ahead told her it was at least twenty minutes before her sister's house. That was too much time to sit in awkward silence with him and not discuss the massive elephant sitting in the back seat. "Mags... is determined to see you married. Why?"

"Shit if I know," he answered with an obtuse shrug.

At that moment, Bianca wanted to shake some sense into him. "Don't you think there has to be a reason why she suddenly wants you married?"

He eyed her thoughtfully, then shrugged. "I guess there's no point in holding this part from you. That bald white man who came to dinner on Christmas Eve wants to buy our bank. The transaction will yield enough for us to live comfortably for a long time.

"Okay? What does that have to do with me?"

"Because, you pretty little thing, Mr. Marbury does not want to be associated with Negroes who overstep their boundaries and sleep with white women."

"Why does he care who you sleep with? It should be about the money."

"It should be, but it isn't. Not when that white woman is a councilman's wife."

"So, I'm here to help give the false appearance of a Negro who follows the rules and stays within the lines afforded to him?"

"Precisely."

She watched him tightly smile and then turn to her to give her proposed conversation his wave of dismissal. He then distracted her by gently grabbing her hand, planting a soft kiss on its backside.

"A long time ago," he began. "But let's not get so wrapped up in semantics. Say, do you realize that it's still early?"

"So?"

"So? Midnight? New Year's? Come on, girl. You've been to at least one New Year's Eve party once, right?"

"Well, no. And I can't count tonight's party since it wasn't officially New Year's Eve."

A fire lit in his brown eyes, and he looked at her as if a wicked plan brewed in his mind. He made several turns and then a last one onto a road she had never seen before. The car's headlights penetrated the darkness and showed the glimmering movement of a body of water. He hurried out of the car and then busied with opening the back seat. She heard fumbling and movement; then, he finally appeared in the front seat with a blanket made of the softest shearling. He handed her two empty snifter glasses and planted a decanter filled with brown liquor onto the seat. She thought he would sit down finally, but he did not. He left her again and moved to the back of the car. She heard a series of noises that sounded like crunching and metal rubbing together. And before she knew it, the roof of his car folded on itself and disappeared.

She stared up into the newly revealed night's sky in wonderment and awe. Without the city's smog concealing its beauty, it sparkled over her. "Wow, have you ever seen something so beautifully complex? So mysterious and enchanting?"

When she realized that her questions went unanswered, she turned and caught his gaze. "Yes, actually. I have," he breathed.

A net of butterflies danced in her belly, and she hated it. Or she hated that she loved it? She was unsure, but since the day she had laid eyes on Victor's handsome face, she commanded her body not to have silly reactions to him. And since that day, she constantly reminded herself that Victor, a seducer of women, was a master of words. She couldn't let his brown eyes and magnetic smile hypnotize her. So Bianca shifted out of his intense gaze, cleared her throat, and looked around her. "So? Is this your idea of a New Year's party?"

A deep chuckle reverberated in his chest. "Yes," he said as he poured the brown liquor from his crystal decanter into her glass. He handed the glass to her and then clanked his glass to hers. "Will you be my date?"

"Seeing how there are no other women around, I guess you have no other choice."

He chuckled again, and this time, he gifted her with the brightest smile, "I would still choose you."

"Ha! You and I know that isn't true."

"It is!" He emphasized his words with the most offended expression.

"Stop it. I know that you would rather be here with another woman. You don't have to be that way with me. I'm just me. I'm not frilly or super beautiful. I'm just me. Your friend."

"I like you. I was hoping you would like me too." *What an odd arrangement of words*, she thought. He almost sounded sincere.

"I suppose you've grown on me. You are not as awful as I thought you were. Especially when you aren't doing stupid things like staring at me with smoldering intensity."

He blinked for a minute and then burst out laughing. "What are you talking about? I don't do that."

"I mean that you always pose your face and body in such an aggressively handsome way—"

"Aggressively handsome?"

"Yes! You do it. Especially when you know you are being watched. You do it to get your way with women. You even did it to that Old Lady Dilworth tonight when you escorted her out of the room. It is your masculine way of batting your eyelashes."

"What? I don't bat my damn lashes."

"You know what I mean. I mean—"

"Okay, so when I look like this..." he began as he sat upright and turned his ardent gaze on her.

"Yes! Like that!"

"Or what about this..." He gave her a more dramatic pose this time and cut his eyes in the most spellbinding way.

"Yep. That's it," she added with a tight smile before bursting out in laughter. "It's good to know you don't take yourself as seriously as I thought you did."

"Does that mean you don't hate me?"

"No, I don't hate you. It's strange. There are times you're actually tolerable."

He looked away from her this time and out to the clearing. "I'm honored you think so."

"I'm sure many women have given you higher honors."

"Yours was the hardest to gain. Therefore, it's the best. I hope one day you will give me an even bigger honor."

Bianca swallowed hard before she said, "Victor... don't ruin it. I know that after we untangle this complete mess, we both will go back to our old lives. We probably will never speak again. There's no sense in talking about a future day."

He blinked thoughtfully for a moment then said, "So you wouldn't be my friend if it were not for all this?" He gave her the look of a pained puppy.

She gurgled with laughter. "Seriously, you wouldn't have given my plain self two thoughts if it were not for all this." She continued to laugh until she realized that she was the only one laughing.

"It's too bad you think that way," he said.

"What's that supposed to mean?"

"It means that the only person in this car confused about your value is you. You seem to think a woman should go around with make-up painted on her face like a clown. Like your friend's future wife."

"You mean Harmony? She's gorgeous. What are you talking about?"

"Maybe," he said with a shrug. "I can't tell. She had so much powder on her face tonight that I thought she was a clown from the circus. I don't see the appeal with that one. If you ask me, Hiram chose foolishly."

Bianca bit her bottom lip under his half-lidded gaze while she smoothed the lines of his blanket. "He told me her appearance was more feminine. Something about me wearing pants."

"Is that what he told you? I like your pants. Come to think of it; my mother wore pants. She helped her father on his farm, just like you help your father in his hospital."

"That's not what you said the other day when you pushed yourself into my apartment! You went on and on about how I should dress better. You remember?"

"Ha! Well, you could stand a little polishing. Maybe some new pants. But otherwise, I think you are perfect the way you are. Plus, I just like to get you riled up so I can see those dimples of yours. They show up when you're angry, which is so adorable to me." He caught her off guard by reaching over to pinch her cheek, pretending to steal a dimple.

She nervously giggled through her blush and then realized that he had crossed the ocean between them and was sitting dangerously close to her.

He fished his pocket watch out of his side pocket and whistled. "It's that time," he whispered as he stared thoughtfully at her bottom lip.

Mesmerized by the aroma of sandalwood brought to her from his proximity, she did not immediately respond. "Time for what?" she asked finally.

"It's almost midnight. It's time for our kiss."

All of a sudden, the spell he cast upon her broke, and she came alive. "Kiss? As in kiss me? No, no, no." She pushed her hands against his hard chest, but he didn't budge.

"What's wrong with a little kiss? I've kissed you before."

"Yeah, but that was for make-believe and under the most extreme circumstances. Now we're in private, so there's no need to kiss me."

"No need? Don't you know its bad luck to go unkissed on New Year's Eve?"

"But it's still December. Today is the thirtieth."

"Correction! Today, meaning as of midnight tonight is the

thirty-first. Therefore, it is New Year's Eve, which means I should get my kiss. Its seven years' bad luck and loneliness if I don't."

Well, hell. Bianca's eyebrows shot up in amazement. He was clever; she would give him that. "I never took you as a superstitious man."

"Oh yeah, step on a crack, break your mama's back all of that. Now, are you gonna leave me with seven years of lonely nights, or are you going to have pity on my poor soul and lay these luscious lips on me?"

Before she could explain to herself every reason she should say no and every reason to ignore the girlish thrill of being kissed by Victor Carlson under a beautiful starry sky, he pulled her face to his and grazed his mouth over hers. And like a doe planted in the ground by the blinding headlights of an automobile, so was Bianca as she stared up at him in wonder. He gave her soft, savoring kisses that ended with a short suckle of her bottom lip. Her mouth slackened, and her head instinctively tilted forward, asking for more.

After getting all the permission he needed, Victor's mouth devoured hers hungrily with a rapid intensity that made her cling to him. Her lips parted under his hot insistence, sending a warm current between her thighs. A moan escaped her throat, and before she knew it, she was kissing him back, demanding more of his intense fire. Moments of eternity passed as the heat between them rose. His hands roved over places she would have slapped him for, and here she was almost panting from a raw need for more. It was when his enormous hand reached into her shirt and touched her bare skin that he yanked his hand away as if she seared him. He loudly groaned and backed away from her, leaving her in a confused, cold, and frazzled mess.

Damn it. She blinked out of his spell and awkwardly pull her clothes into place. What the hell had happened? How wanton she must have looked to him? He probably thought there was not a woman alive who couldn't resist his charms. *Damn it,* she repeated inwardly. Thankfully, he didn't boast in his triumph over her. Her pride couldn't take it if he dared to speak one word of victory over her broken-down wall of resistance. Instead, he pressed a single kiss on her forehead, pushed her cap back in place, and then got out of the car to push its roof back in place.

"I would appreciate it if you never did that again," she scolded as they resumed their silent drive to her sister's home.

"I can't promise that I won't try. I liked it too much. Besides, aren't we supposed to be engaged? Surely that gives me a license to kiss you."

"Public displays of affection aren't appropriate, anyway. So there is no need. Just don't do that. Okay?" She eyed his profile and narrowed her eyes as she witnessed him swallowing his smile.

How dare he laugh? If it were not for the fact that he was steering an automobile, she would have leaped on him and scratched out his eyes. Perhaps once the car stopped, she would do so. Instead of feeding into her temptation to beat him senseless, she brought up a topic of discussion that was sure to strip his vile humor.

"Your mother wants us to set a wedding date."

"She isn't my mother," he quickly spat. "And you and I both know that won't be happening."

"Of course not! I would die a million deaths before getting tied up with someone like you."

Instead of verbally replying, he blew hot air out of his nostrils and clenched his jaw. Once he parked his car outside of her sister's home, he struck her with the most astounding declaration. "I'll pay your debt to Mags tomorrow. I don't want to hear your shit about your pride, Bianca. Tack it onto your father's loan; I don't give a shit. But let that be the end of this."

Her wind seeped slowly from her body, leaving her feeling hollowed and bereft. She had dismissed him earlier with her words, but she had always handled him dismissively. Perhaps this was his cruel method of returning the favor. Bianca was about to let her pride push her out of his car and never look back, but a quiet thought entered her mind. Daisy. She was still being held hostage by Mags. Bianca needed Victor's cooperation to get Daisy back. And so, with her pride in her pocket, Bianca attempted to apologize.

"There's nothing to apologize for," he replied briskly.

She eyed him again and realized he had put up his own wall of resistance. What could she do? She wouldn't grovel. Ain't no way in hell she would do that. "We have to stay engaged."

"No, we don't. I just told you—"

"Mags kidnapped my friend and won't release her until I marry you," she blurted.

CHAPTER 13

WHISPERS IN THE DARK

"What?" Victor asked in a deceptively calm voice.

"I said Mags is holding my friend Daisy hostage and is threatening to hurt her if I don't marry you."

"*What?*" he asked again, but this time with the outrage Bianca's words deserved.

"I said—"

"I heard you! What the hell? Why would she? Wait. Wait. Tell me everything from the beginning. When did this happen? What did she say? What in the hell?"

Bianca took a deep breath before licking her lips. "It was after her luncheon. She agreed to invest in my business all right, but on her terms and with my friend as collateral. Daisy is a good girl with a tiny addiction to hash. Ms. Ginny and I had just taken her off the street and got some food in her belly and then suddenly, she was gone. We thought nothing of it because she always disappears. But then Mags told me she had her. I don't know where she is holding her or what kind of condition she is in. All I know is that I need to proceed with the engagement and marry you."

"Why?"

"Why?" Bianca repeated. "I don't know why. She's your mother. I have no clue why your family needs to involve others in their family squabble shit. But it would be nice to be left out of it."

"She. Is. Not. My. Mother."

"True and sorry. But she is a relation. I'm too afraid to think about it. I don't know what she is capable of."

"I do. I know what she is capable of." Victor recounted in his mind the countless times he remembered how far Mags Edison would go to get what she wanted.

"You and she have some real bad blood. How did that come to be?"

Victor's head tilted back in a soft chuckle. "Sun's coming up soon. We don't have enough time to talk about how Mags, and I became enemies. We go way back. I think as far as my birth."

He was right. Pink rays from the sun had crept up the edges of the hill in front of them. But Bianca had decided that she couldn't waste another minute wondering about Mags' motives. It was time to learn her enemy. "I have all the time in the world to learn about my future in-laws. Tell me."

He gave her a sidelong glance and continued, "You might have guessed, but I am the result of a long extramarital affair. My mother and Robert Carlson were lovers for years."

"Hence why Mags hates your mother," Bianca said.

"More or less. I believe they were friends at some point in time. So maybe betrayal and jealousy. It's hard to say. I know my mother was a wealthy woman. She was beautiful too. Mags, as I understand it, was poor and plain. So imagine if the girl across the way, who has everything, has now gained the one thing you had, your husband."

"But a child is an innocent party. You didn't ask to be born."

"No, I didn't. But as I look back over my childhood, I can see why so many things upset her. I had the finest education, and Wesley went to school in his bare feet. I spent my afternoons after school in piano lessons, while Wesley spent his afternoons on their small farm. We lived on an estate that sat on a hundred acres of land while they lived in a shotgun shack near the river."

Bianca smiled tightly and silently conceded that Mags' hatred was born out of inequities.

He silently agreed and then responded. "But that doesn't absolve her. She refused to allow me to have a relationship with my father. It was out of the question. So I never had a real relationship with my father until the day my mother sent me to live with him."

"And when was that?"

Even though the morning sun lit up the confines of Victor's car, a dark shadow covered Victor's face. "I was thirteen. I had an incident. I say incident because that was the word my father told me to use whenever I brought up the event. I won't talk about it. I don't think I have ever been able to. But it's still with me."

Bianca watched his mind leave his body and travel down a bumpy road to the past. And when the memories bore too much for him, he snapped his body to attention and sat up straight. "Nonetheless," he continued, "It was what brought me into Mags' home. When my mother showed up with me on the night of the incident, she promised to give them enough money to move away as long as they took Uncle Chito and me with them."

"Why couldn't she just leave with you herself?" Bianca asked.

"I don't know. To this day, I wonder why she didn't just take me. Well, anyway, she gave them some money and papers with information about my trust fund. I asked her..." Another dark cloud of sorrow descended on Victor's mind, causing his words to lodge in his throat. "I asked her if I would ever see her again, and she said... no."

"What happened to her... your mother?" Bianca carefully asked.

Victor eyed Bianca for the first time speculatively, as if he wondered if he should say as much as he had already said.

Bianca read his thoughts and responded with, "I understand if you don't want to say anything to me. It's so personal. And we hardly know each other, I guess."

"It's strange. I never felt close enough to anyone to talk about this stuff. I guess I always just bottled it up. I could never tell Wesley, and Uncle Chito is Uncle Chito. I don't know. Maybe I feel like I can trust you."

Could he trust her with his truth? The biggest gossiper on this side of the Mississippi? Bianca took one look at the vulnerable man sitting next to her, who had just revealed his troubled beginnings and felt the instinctual need to protect him.

"You can," she assured him in truthfulness.

"I believe she was killed shortly after we left Oklahoma. I wasn't allowed to go to her funeral or even visit her grave."

"I'm sorry."

He shrugged and gave her a tight smile. "She left me a hefty sum of money in my trust fund that I would have use of when I turned eighteen but..." Before he could answer Bianca, Victor's mind recoiled to the very day he signed over his entire trust fund to his father. He had just turned eighteen. Even then, he could not keep his thoughts straight because of the female sex. His young, handsome face brought him an influx of pretty girls with soft curves. And with so many lovely choices before him, how could he be in the right mind to fight for his own birthright? Perhaps his father knew this when he called Victor forth with his proposition.

On that particular day, Victor noted every single strange detail. He recalled walking into his father's study after having kissed Dolores Scott in the backyard. It was his brother, Wesley, who broke up their embrace to inform him that their father wanted him in his study.

"Come on in, boy," his father commanded from behind his mahogany desk.

Victor entered the wood-paneled room and noted Mags' presence in the room immediately.

"Sit down," his father had said. He placed a piece of paper in front of him that was mostly blank with a scribbled number written in the middle of the page. "That there is your future, boy. You will be rich beyond your dreams. If you think these little fast neighborhood girls are something, wait till you become a rich man. You can have more women than the law should allow. All you gotta do is what we tell you to do."

"You want me to sign this?" Victor remembered asking after being handed a stack of documents. "What does it say?"

His father gifted him with a wise and fatherly smile. "Son, your mama, God rest her soul, sent you to live with me after your incident back home. I knew then that all that money she put up for you would be too much for an eighteen-year-old, but she wouldn't listen."

"It sure isn't. He can barely keep his little pecker in his pants," Mags commented. "Just like his father," she added.

His father scowled in her direction and moved on. "I think her point is that nothing makes a man lose his money faster than a woman. The concern is that you may be too young to be in charge of your own finances."

"But I'm eighteen now. The trustee said I could have it. I figured that when I got my money, I could go back to Oklahoma with my mama's family and start up a business there or something."

"Startup a business? What do you know about being in business? And leave? Why would you do that?"

Victor had shrugged, not understanding his father's confusion. "I just figured that you would be happy with that. Or other people would be happy with that." Everyone in the room knew that he pointed his comment toward Mags' obvious disdain for him.

"Margaret?" His father prompted the stoic woman.

And on cue, she responded. "Oh, Victor. Don't be so silly. We love you here. I know that the two of us have had our shake-ups, but you know that I care for you like a son."

Victor witnessed the woman's mouth unthaw and mechanically morph into a tight smile. She was younger back then and more attractive. But even then, Victor knew that bitterness froze her pretty face in such a way that it always looked like someone had painted a lovely face on a rock.

"Boy," Mags said as she approached him. "You know I have been working down at the bank. I know about the market and investing. They are giving Negroes opportunities. You could invest this money and turn it into something real that will last."

"Invest?"

"Yes. Invest."

"But, the trustee told me to save my money for a rainy day."

"Are you going to listen to a white man who has been taking a piece of your money for years, or are you going to listen to us?" his father asked, fully expecting Victor to choose him.

"But it's been a while I've seen my family back home. My grandma is still there."

His father waved a dismissive hand. "Those folks are long gone, Victor. They all took off after your incident. You see that you ain't received a letter in years. Listen, boy; you need to hear Mags. She has a real opportunity to change things for us. We can set up things for you and Wesley. Picture it... Carlson and Sons Bank. It has a ring to it, don't it? Negroes will come for miles around to bank with us."

Victor remembered swallowing his disappointment before answering. After four hard years under his father's roof, he longed for nothing more than to go home. He had wished to go live in the house his mother had raised him in so he could be closer to her memory. And most of all, he wanted to get away from Mags.

"And?" Bianca asked again in the present, disturbing his dark memories.

"And? And I signed my rights away under my father's pressure."

"How much did you give them?"

"All of it. We became Carlson and Sons Bank, and then after his death, we were the Carlson Brothers Bank."

His father was right. Victor became wealthy, and he had more women than the law allowed him. But as his brother has politely pointed out to him so many damn times, their father's ambitious investments crumbled over the years, pushing the Carlson Brother's Bank to the edge of bankruptcy. Mags has known for some time that their family's future lifestyle was on the verge of collapse. So Victor presumed this was the reason Wesley proposed they find a buyer for the bank and get out of the business. In both of their minds, this was a proposition in which everyone would win.

"We'll get your friend back," Victor said with finality. "But we can't go to the police. We're better off trying to find her ourselves. And once we do, we tell Mags and Wesley the deal is off."

"What? Why? What about the bank? Don't you still want to sell it to Mr. Marbury and at least get your money back?"

"I don't care anymore. Mags and Wesley have made enough money off of me over the years. I don't care to give them anymore. Until then, dimples, you're stuck with me."

"Dimples?"

"That's my new name for you. My Libby doesn't suit you. I like Dimples. Anyway, you and I will have to go along to get along. We'll have to play Mags' game, at least the engagement part. Let's play the role she wants us to play all while we will dig around to find Daisy."

"What if Mags catches on?"

"She won't. You and I will paint the picture of a couple thrown together by circumstance but are now making the best of it. We will fall hopelessly in love in her view and the rest of the world's view."

"The rest of the world?"

Victor waited for the concept to settle in her mind before answering. "Yes, the rest of the world. Families too."

"Shit," she muttered before blowing a long raspberry.

Victor chuckled at her response. "I like that you are a little unladylike."

"You do, huh? I suppose I will need to figure out how to break the news to my father."

"After our show at the Dilworths' Mansion, I'm not sure how much breaking you will need."

"Ah! But you forget that I'm Lady Noire. And if Lady Noire didn't see it, it didn't happen."

"I get it. You don't want me to meet your father. I guess I can understand that. My reputation and all. And then I guess it doesn't help that I own the bank that's foreclosing on his hospital."

Bianca bristled for a moment before responding. "It's that, and it's also my father. No one is good enough for his daughters. With an exception to my brother-in-law, Joseph. He's practically perfect. And he's a doctor, too."

"Good old Joe," Victor commented with a smile as he thought of his old friend Joseph Carpenter.

"Yes, but you... are you. I don't know how he will react to.... well, you. And I've never brought a man home before."

"No? No one has come calling after those dimples of yours?"

"Okay, please don't refer to my dimples, around my father, or any other physical part of my anatomy. Jesus, I'm starting to sweat just thinking about it. Okay... okay. Give me a few days to figure out how to approach him."

"Well, time is ticking on your friend's kidnapping. Maybe we should get to it." He didn't let her respond this time. He reached down to grab her hand and kissed the back of it.

She numbly acknowledged his sentiment and got out of his

car in the darkness of the early morning to climb up the stairs leading to her sister's home. Victor looked up at the sky's hints of sunrise and realized that revelation was coming. He was not sure when it would come, but he knew that just as the sun would illuminate the earth and highlight its dark corners, so would the truth come forth in his life and blank out the darkness of his past. He just needed a little woman with big dimples to help him to it.

CHAPTER 14

THE TALENTED MR. CROSS

Obadiah Cross never missed a day of work in his life, and he was not about to end his streak today. He peered down the empty business street and shrugged. Let them sleep in their bed, he thought before turning his key into the wrought-iron door of the Carlson Brother's Penny Savings and Loan Bank. His work ethic would not let him waste a perfectly good day all because it was New Year's Day. His mentor, God rest his soul, the old Robert Carlson, always used to say that rest was for the dead.

Obadiah turned on the master switch to the building, disturbing the hollowed and quiet peace of the empty building. Every footstep he made echoed from one side of the main floor to the other. And as he had done many times before, Mr. Cross stopped in the front entrance to gaze into the primary banking area and marvel at its glory. The Carlson Brother Penny Savings and Loan Bank was not as large as its white investment peers, but the two-story building still had a commanding presence. Illuminated by electric brass sconces and hanging crystal chandeliers, the white Italian marble floors and walls glowed.

They built each bank teller cage with Tiffany stained glass and the highest quality mahogany wood. And yet the splendor of the entire building was from the mosaic tile vaulted ceiling above.

The Carlson Brothers' father spared little expense in its architecture and design so that, in his words, "Every Negro customer can feel a sense of pride." And looking around at what the bank had become, Mr. Cross would say that old Mr. Carlson had achieved his goal. Over the years, Obadiah watched seamstresses, miners, maids, and farmers, worn down from the turmoil of life, lift their shoulders and raise their chins from the moment they entered the building. For so many, the Carlson Brother's Bank was not just a place of opulent grandeur; it was a beacon in a dark, oppressive world and a symbol of promise for a better future. This was why Mr. Cross didn't mind tending the store while others slept in their beds. It was all for the greater good.

As soon as Mr. Cross opened his office door, he readied himself for a day of work. He flipped on his yellow visor, shrugged his armband over his shirtsleeve, and pulled the string to his desk lamp. Just as he was about to pull from the stack of red ledgers on the side of his desk, he heard a noise in the outer hallway. His body froze to attention once he realized that the noise came from footsteps banging against the marble floor. Obadiah routinely locked the doors on days when the bank was closed, so someone who had a key was making their way to his office at a determined pace. Finally, and without further delay, Mr. Cross' company made himself known. Mr. Victor Carlson stood before him in the doorway wearing a frown and a long wool coat.

Mr. Cross immediately stood at attention regarding his young boss, but the man only waved at his gesture and motioned for him to take a seat.

"Mr. Cross, isn't it?" taking his own seat across from Obadiah.

Obadiah blinked at the young man and realized that although

he dedicated most of his waking hours to his cause and had watched him grow from a boy to a man over the years, Victor Carlson had vaguely known who he was. Instead of pointing out the irony, Obadiah politely replied, "Yes, sir."

Victor tiredly rubbed his bristled chin and uncombed head in thought. In Obadiah's opinion, the man looked tired. He assumed his disheveled look was from the night before since most of the city danced until dawn on New Year's Eve. The young man pulled his driving gloves off and flopped them onto Obadiah's pristine desk, disturbing the perfect alignment of his intentionally placed pencils. Obadiah decided that it was rude to point out his boss's lack of consideration for his workspace. Instead, he discreetly shifted the gloves to the side and pushed his pencils back into place.

"Do you know who I am?"

"Yes, of course, sir. You are Mr. Victor Carlson. Is there something I can help you with, sir?"

Victor raised his pointer finger to gesture a pause while his face stretched into an oblong yawn. Obadiah steadied himself despite his gross anticipation. There must be some reason why the man was there on a closed banking day.

"My apologies. I'm a little tired," Victor said while rubbing his face. "I wasn't sure if someone would be here today. Are you always here, Mr. Cross?"

Obadiah blinked again before saying, "I try to be, sir."

"Hmm? You have been here for a long time, haven't you?"

"Of course, sir. Fifteen years, to be exact."

"You were here when my father opened these doors, weren't you?"

"I remember it like it was yesterday. It was a good day."

He did not reply in words, but the young man's eyes told Obadiah that he would have disagreed if he were at liberty to speak plainly. Obadiah sat awkwardly quiet while Victor's thoughts ran through his mind.

Finally, Victor said, "I am looking for something."

"Yes?" Obadiah began thoughtfully before his realization set it. "Are you looking for the same thing your step-mother came here looking for months ago?"

A moment passed, and a current of understanding passed between the two of them. "Perhaps," Victor replied as he searched Obadiah's eyes for more understanding.

Obadiah looked away and bristled to himself. He nervously adjusted his pencil's alignment several times. This is why he liked numbers. Numbers were what they always were. They never had hidden meanings or private agendas. And the Carlson family had never been plain as numbers. They were full of anomalies that he could never compute. And while he marveled in the glory of the Carlson family successes, he knew their successes came with a price. He knew that they made some of their deals in the dark and signed them in blood. He knew that they greased the hands of politicians and shook hands with the mafia. And they built most of it, if not all of it, on the back of the very man sitting before him. And here he was, sitting there in front of Obadiah, expecting for him to open the safe and show him what his father had done so many years ago.

"It isn't here," Obadiah finally answered.

"What isn't here?"

"The same thing your step-mother and that white man came looking for a few weeks back. Your trust documents. Your father... he..."

"Go on."

"Was a complex man," Mr. Cross finished.

"I know who my father was. You needn't paint a picture of a hero for me. What I would like to know is where my documents are."

Obadiah bristled again under Victor's expectant gaze. He took a deep breath and continued, "He stored them in the safe for years until one day when some men showed up here. No one, including myself, thought anything was unusual about this. Your father talked to many people, from politicians to..."

"Mobsters," Victor finished.

"Ahem, yes. But these men weren't mobsters. They were friendly and persistent businessmen. Your father turned them away at first, but they came right on back. Asking the same thing, I suppose. And I guess one day, whatever they had to say was enough to convince your daddy. He emptied the safe, signed some papers, and that was the last I saw of them."

"Does Mags know about this?"

"I'm not sure if she does. But she sure came hunting for whatever was in that safe with that white man. She is... not a kind woman."

"Nor has she ever been," Victor drawled dismissively. "What did she say when she came here?"

"Well... it was not so much what she said but what she did that caught my attention. She came here on an off day early in the morning, just like you. She didn't see me, but I saw her rifling through your father's safe deposit box. Then when she saw it wasn't there, she went into your office and rifled through your office. She threw papers all over the floor and on your desk."

"Interesting. So why are you telling me this now?"

"I am telling you this because there is a nasty rumor floating around that you and your brother are going to sell the bank and all of us will be out the job. You might call what I'm doing self-preservation."

Victor Carlson picked up his gloves and his hat and rose to stand. He was in the middle of adjusting his coat when a thought came to his mind. "And has my brother been snooping around as well?"

"No, sir. Not that I know of, sir."

Victor nodded his head, shrugged his hand into his pocket, and pulled out a crisp twenty-dollar bill. "I'm sure you know that this is a sinking ship. You are right; these numbers don't lie, so I can't promise you a job. But, I can pay you to be my eyes and my ears around here. Will you do that?"

Obadiah stood, shooting out his hand to shake Victor's. He

noted the folded twenty-dollar bill in the middle of their handshake. "You have my loyalty, Mr. Carlson. You have always reminded me of your father; you know that?" Obadiah offered.

"How is that?" Victor asked.

"He really was an exemplary man. He may have made mistakes in his life, but I believe in his core, he was a kind man."

Victor snorted quietly. "There is an awful rumor going around that I am a kind. Please do your best to dispel it, would you? It is not a valuable family trait." And with that, he shut Obadiah's door, leaving him confused by his words.

BIANCA'S EYES opened to bright and unfiltered sunlight pouring from a nearby window. She peeked through a narrow slit of her squinted eye and noted that someone had pushed her window's curtains wide open. But the curtains and the window were not hers. Where was she? Ah yes, she had spent the night over her sister's house after her night under the stars with Victor. She closed her eyes to get her bearings and then got a strange feeling that she was not alone. And she was right. Seated at the foot of the bed was her sister, Cecilia. Cecilia's husband, Joseph, stood to the end of her bed with his arms crossed. They both wore uniform frowns as they stared at her.

"Ce-Ce," Bianca started with a yawn. "What's wrong? Did I wake the house last night? I tried to be quiet. Good morning, Joe. What's with the somber faces? Did something happen?"

"Have you lost your mind," Cecilia asked without delay.

"Hmm?" Bianca murmured into her feather pillow as she closed her eyes against the sun.

"I asked you if you lost your mind," Cecilia asked again, obnoxiously enunciating each word. Too bad Bianca's brain waves were still fuzzy from exhaustion to understand her.

"What are you talking about? Lord, it's bright in here. Can someone close these damn curtains?"

"It's bright because it's two o'clock in the afternoon," Cecilia answered. "We've been waiting all day to talk to you. You better get up now because your father is on his way."

"Why?"

"*Why?*" Cecilia repeated after almost standing to attention, but her round tummy and her husband's assuring hand had impeded her movement. "Why because we received a visit early this morning from Mr. Percy Swain and his wife, Loretta. They were so excited to give us the details of their night at the Dilworth mansion."

Bianca's mind finally framed the world around her. Her sister and her brother-in-law finally came into complete focus. "And?" she asked, knowing full well what was on the other side of her question.

"They both had a lot to say about your entrance and scandalous exit of the party. They claim that you showed up arm-in-arm with Victor Carlson." Cecilia gave a short, expectant pause, waiting for Bianca to deny it, and when she didn't, Cecilia added, "Do you know what the most outrageous part of their story was?"

"Lay it on me."

"That you and that ridiculous whoremonger are shacked up together and that his mother is now demanding you get married. And after we dismissed the Swains, imagine our surprise when three other people called our telephone, giving similar stories. One person said that you had gotten yourself in trouble with that man."

"Since when do you believe rumors, Ce-Ce?"

"Hardly ever. But when Reverend Davis called, I considered it. He wanted to know if he should put in a word of prayer for you since you have started, and I quote, 'wallowing in the miry clay with heathen men.' And by heathen men, he means Victor Carlson!" Her voice rose an octave with each syllable of Victor's name.

"Well... "

"It's true, isn't it, Bianca? The other day, that man who came here, that was him, wasn't it? I thought I recognized him. I knew he was someone we knew."

Bianca opened her mouth, but before she could answer, Joseph cleared his throat to give his two cents. "Bianca, Victor has been my friend for years, but even I wouldn't trust him with my female dog."

Bianca cringed. "Sheesh. That's harsh. What's wrong with Victor Carlson?"

"Wh-what's wrong?" Cecilia stammered. "Let's start with the fact that his bank has tried to foreclose on our parent's home twice and the hospital once. And then let's finish with the fact that he is a womanizer and a louse. He gave Teresa Brady the disease you get from going to bed with a man like himself. No one's heard from her since he left her on the clinic's doorstep."

Bianca shut her eyelids before rolling them. "Teresa Brady got knocked up by Paul Gibson before he left town to join that no-name jazz band in Harlem. Her mama made her leave town to hide her bump. Just wait, she'll be back in the fall with a little baby. She will tell the rest of the world that the baby is an orphan she adopted."

"How would you know that?"

"I know everything, remember? I'm Lady Noire. I thought I reported as much two months ago."

"Even Lady Noire makes things up. You did it to me, remember?"

"No, I embellish the truth, which is entirely different from making things up. I never did that to you. Your scandals were all true."

"Yeah, and you told them to everyone."

"I sold papers and paid bills."

"What has gotten into you, Bianca? Maybe Reverend Davis was right. Maybe you are wallowing in the miry clay with heathen men. Oh my goodness, you aren't with child, are you?"

Bianca rolled her eyes heavenward for the second time and

then rose to sit on the edge of the bed. After two stretches made under Cecilia's glaring watch, a thought came to Bianca's mind. "Did you say our father was coming here?"

Finally, Cecilia's humor returned. She gave Bianca a satisfied grin. "Oh, yes. Daddy is on his way. And he wants answers. I would clean myself up if I were you. Is that what you wore to the Dilworth party last night? You stink to high heaven. I guess you might as well go get one of my dresses. It won't be good for him to see you looking like a worn-out trollop."

"Cecilia," Joseph gently chided as Cecilia followed Bianca around the room.

Bianca was too busy looking for her missing shoe to respond in kind. She had to get out of there. There was no way she would talk to her father. She was much too much of a coward. Perhaps she could muster enough courage to tell her outrageous lie, but not today. When Bianca nabbed her hiding shoe from under the bed, she headed for the same window that woke her from her peaceful slumber and lifted it open.

"What are you doing?" Cecilia shouted as Bianca crossed her leg through the window and then the other one.

Thankfully, they were on the first floor, so it was not far to jump down. She braced herself on the ledge for a moment, catching Cecilia's outraged face. Joseph was too busy laughing to look outraged.

"Tell Daddy I'm not shacked up or knocked up. I'm just engaged and... well... it couldn't be helped."

Bianca said nothing else before jumping down the small foot to the ground floor. She ran all the way to her trusted jalopy. In the distance, she heard Cecilia yell out the window, "What the hell is that supposed to mean?"

CHAPTER 15

A WILD LEAP

On a cold Friday night, Bianca sat at her small kitchen table happily eating a healthy bowl of black beans and white rice. In her opinion, the supper was just as good as any French chef's cuisine. And as far as she was concerned, it was the perfect ending for an exhausting week.

She spent the first half of her week dodging her family's questions about Victor and the other half of the week dodging Victor.

But at least the week had been productive. She did manage to dig up some information that could lead to Daisy's whereabouts. Bianca decided that the best way to figure out where Daisy was, was to get more information about her abductor—Mags. All she had known, up to a week ago, was what Victor fed her. And that wasn't enough. Bianca needed to know everything about her enemy and maybe, just maybe, turn things around. Perhaps Mags should have a taste of her own blackmailing medicine.

For this challenge, Bianca went to her favorite sources—the help. And after learning that Mags' maid, Ingrid, had a lot to say about Victor's fiancée, she probably had more to say in general. And boy was Bianca right. Bianca and Ms. Ginny learned a lot after greasing her palm with just three dollars. She sang like a canary about Mags' meals, her wigs, and, most importantly, her visitors. Ingrid, the maid, gave very detailed descriptions of her frequent visitors. One visitor she described sounded distinctly like that Marbury fellow. The other person was her lawyer.

"He come over all the time," Ms. Ingrid said. "Her and that Mr. Marbury be up in that library just arguing about when this gonna happen, and when that gonna happen. And then they be talking about a deed. A lot of talking about a deed."

"A deed?" Bianca asked, her interest finally piqued.

"*Mmhmm*. I heard her as clear as day. Her and that man, looking for a deed."

Bianca and Ms. Ginny paid the girl another three dollars for future information and said their goodbyes, but Bianca couldn't get her words out of her mind. Victor had told her that Mr. Marbury was supposed to be buying the bank. If that was the case, why in the world would Mr. Marbury be interested in a deed when he is supposed to be buying the bank? Bianca wondered if this little gem had something to do with her pending nuptials.

Bianca spent most of her night pondering over this discovery. After a long bath and donning her warm cotton nightgown, she decided she had mused over Mags and her visitors long enough. It was time to go to bed and leave it all behind. But just as she lifted her bed sheet to climb in, a loud ring of her telephone in the kitchen blared throughout her tiny apartment and scared the living daylights out of her. Who on earth would be calling her at this time?

She marched to the kitchen in a fury and yanked the receiver off the hook.

"Hello?"

"Dimplessssss."

"Victor?? What in the world? Do you know what time it is?"

"I do. Do you know what time it is?" His words were slurred.

"Are you drunk?"

"Nope. Just tipsy. Been thinking about you. Wondering why you been dodging me."

"I've been busy."

"Too busy for your fiancé?"

"Yes. Too busy for my fake fiancé."

"Aw. I hate when you talk like that, dimples. But you owe me some quality fiancée time. Meet me downstairs in twenty minutes."

"The hell I will. I don't owe you shit, Carlson."

She heard him chuckle on the other side. "I love your dirty mouth. Listen, I have reason to believe that some of Mags' goons hang out at the Blue Room on Dauphin Street. Let's go. Maybe we can get some useful information on your friend."

"Wouldn't they be loyal to Mags? Why would they tell us anything?"

"Too many questions. We can talk about them when I get there."

"No! You bett—"

The dial tone interrupted her. She blinked in shock as she realized that he had hung up and that he was on his way to her apartment. She briefly glanced over at a nearby mirror and grew horrified. She looked terrible. He wanted to go to a speakeasy where everyone dressed in their finery.

"Son of a—!" she yelled as she paced the room. "I should just let his ass stay downstairs. No, if I do, he might wake the entire neighborhood with his obnoxious ass. And then he might come to my door. I don't need that nosy-ass landlady talking shit about me. Okay, so the best thing to do is just get dressed and go outside. Get dressed?"

Bianca's panic mounted as she looked at the twists and coils in her hair. She was supposed to have her hair pressed the next day. Oh God, she hated Victor Carlson. And her dress. She only had one good dress to wear, and that was the yellow one she wore to Mags' soiree. He would think it was her only dress.

"So what?" she asked herself. "You shouldn't give a damn about what that imbecile thinks. But you don't want to look a mess again the second time they see you with him."

"No, you don't," Bianca answered herself as she reached her closet. She donned the yellow dress along with her expensive long silk gloves in no time. All that was left was her short-cropped hair, which on a normal day would have been just fine, but the Blue Room called for more than just fine. *A hat maybe?*

Bianca threw almost every single hat out of her hatbox until she came to a white silk turban, Cecilia gave her over the summer. Bianca brushed her hair back and slid the hairpiece over her head. When she stopped in the mirror to put on a pair of dangling earrings, she said to herself, "Not too shabby, dimples. Ack! Dimples? What am I saying?"

She continued to ask herself similar questions under her breath as she grabbed her coat and made her way out the door. "What am I doing? What am I doing?" she asked herself.

Once she made it outside and witnessed Victor turn around in his black tuxedo, she understood exactly what she was doing. She was running off a dangerous cliff that would probably end in humiliation, but the flight down would be nothing short of exhilarating. All of her primping and rushing to get ready had all been for this moment. All so he could look at her as he was looking at her right now.

"You look ravishing," he said as he took her hand to escort her into his chauffeured, shiny black car. "That might not be the best thing," he huskily added once they settled into the back seat.

She eyed him with her smirk and focused on putting on satin gloves. "Let's just get on with it, Carlson."

"Ah, not before we are appropriately dressed," he said as he reached down to gather something from under his seat.

"I'm about as dressed as I will be. And if you don't like it, you can take this entire night up your—" She couldn't finish her words because Victor had placed a velvet box on her lap.

He didn't bother to wait for her to open it or even ask what it was. He opened it and revealed a brilliant necklace filled with yellow and white diamonds.

"It's on loan from a bank client," he said to her as she gaped at the regal necklace. "But I hoped you would wear this little yellow number. And you did. If you are to be my fiancée, you have to look every bit the part."

Fine, she told herself. *Just for tonight,* her mind said. She would wear these beautiful baubles and dance with this handsome prince just to say she did it. And when the clock struck twelve and her world turned into a big pumpkin, she would not regret one bit of it.

And that was what she told herself the entire night. She enjoyed the crowd parting to gape and awe at the two of them. She heard them marvel as Victor whisked her around the dance floor until she was breathless. She basked in his unwavering affection and loved every one of his kisses. Yes, kisses. He wouldn't stop kissing her. Or was it that she wouldn't stop kissing him? There had been a lot of champagne, so it was hard to tell left from right. It was a good thing that Victor kept her on his lap. Otherwise, she would have taken a tumble onto the floor.

His friend, George, appeared out of nowhere with a huge smile on his face. "Miss Eubanks," he screamed over the blaring jazz band. "Good to see you again. My compliments. You look beautiful tonight."

"Thank you, George. Your breath smells better too." Had she just said what she had heard she just said? The look on George and Victor's face told her the answer was yes.

Thankfully, George laughed. "Thank you! Say, I'm about to go over to the craps table. Would you two care to join me? You might be lady luck tonight."

Bianca agreed and happily accepted George's waiting elbow.

The two of them walked ahead of Victor through the crowd. Although she swayed a few times, he held her steady as they walked.

Bianca accepted her seat at the craps table and laughed inwardly. No one in the building knew that she had the luckiest hand on that side of the Mississippi. She played a similar version of the game with her nephews and beat them mercilessly every single time. She took their pocket money and coveted knick-knacks with no sort of guilt. She told herself she would do the same thing tonight.

And win she did. Before she knew it, a crowd gathered around her, singing her praises. Victor stood proudly by offering his protection and his breath to blow on her dice whenever she called upon him to do so. He merrily obliged her as he smoked his cigar. However, he did once leave her side to talk to someone. After leaving George to protect her, Victor wandered to the far side of the room to speak to a man whose face was hidden from Bianca's view. She tried a few times to get a good look, but she couldn't spare the loss of focus on a winning hand. When he finally returned, he surprised her with a soft kiss at the base of her neck as his hand slid down the curve of her rump. He gave her a wink, reminding her of their ruse.

At the end of the night, after she had won a purse full of money, she sashayed out of the club, still high on thrills.

George greedily took the honor of escorting her to the car before Victor could do so. "I'm glad you came out tonight, Miss Eubanks," he said. "You are unlike any woman I've met before."

"Bianca. Just call me Bianca, George."

"I think you are the most exciting woman Victor has ever brought around."

"Is that so?" Bianca asked with a sidelong glance.

"It is so. You know he's a good man, don't you? When you get down to it, and he is a good person. He's not what everyone thinks he is."

"All right, George," Victor interrupted. He pulled Bianca out of George's clasp and hugged her body next to his. "Stop hogging my fiancée. Lady luck is with me. So, you and the rest of these losers can eat their hearts out."

Inside the warmth of the backseat, Victor burst into laughter. "What a night, dimples! Who would have thought it? You and me? We do well; you know that?"

She heard herself giggle, and for the life of her, she couldn't make herself stop. He watched her laugh like a silly schoolgirl and then said something that knocked her sober.

"I swear, there's no other woman like you. After this is all over, maybe you would consider something more with me?"

He caressed the soft traces of her mirth with his knuckle and rubbed his thumb against her bottom lip. Without asking again, he kissed her in a primal fashion. Although they had shared kisses all night long, something about this kiss seemed awfully strange. So much so that she shrugged out of his hold and slid away from him.

"Something more? Like what?"

He slid closer to her, closing in on her. With her back against the door, she had nowhere else to go. "Like lovers," he huskily replied as he leaned over to kiss her again. His hands roved up one of her legs until it found her garter. Hearing it snap woke her up.

"No, no, no, and no," she said as she calmly removed his errant hand and pushed his body back to his side of the car. "I won't be no one's mistress. Sorry, Carlson. I may be a virgin, but I'm not naïve to your antics."

"Virgin? You're a virgin?"

"Yeah, and so?"

"I'm so sorry, Bianca. I-I didn't mean—We just had such a good time tonight, and everything was so good, and I'm sorry."

"Its okay, Carlson. I'm still a good sport. I guess you'll have to keep up with Angel for now. Or the other one. What's her name again? Never mind. Tell me who was that man you talked to tonight. Do you think he will help us find Daisy?"

Victor, who still looked miffed from her confession, took a moment to realize what she was talking about. "Oh! That was one of the De Lucas. If something is going on in the streets, he would know. He gave me a few leads. Hopefully, they will pan out."

Bianca wanted to ask him more questions, but she couldn't. Her eyelids were betraying her. They kept closing even though she willed them to open. Finally, they stayed shut, and she finally succumbed to sleep.

ॐ

THOUGH HE SHOULDN'T HAVE, Victor took the liberty of removing Bianca's clothing to put on her nightgown. During their ride home, she threw up on the floor and all over his favorite yellow dress. She quickly passed out after that. So, since she was in this terrible state, he had no choice but to peel everything off her body. Luckily, she slept soundly through the entire process. She barely flinched while he applied a warm rag to her face, chest, and arms. And thankfully, she would never know how much he had enjoyed taking in every intricate detail of her soft body.

A virgin? Damn. And what a fine one she was. She might have been small, but every part of her was perfectly drawn. Especially her breasts. Perky and full. He wondered if he put his hand to measure, would he—No! What was he doing? His sweet Bianca didn't deserve to be pawed on while she slept. Victor quickly pulled her thick, cotton nightgown over her head, over her supple breasts and down her torso.

"A virgin, huh?" he whispered as he stood watching her sleep. It shouldn't matter. He liked her, didn't he? He wanted her, didn't he? Yes, he wanted her. The hard rock inside his pants told him so. But primal needs aside, he wanted to be around her. Tonight, he had felt more alive than he had ever felt in his life. And it wasn't just him. Her wit and sarcasm won over his friends. Even they could see what he saw. She was wonderful. Why someone hadn't claimed her long ago was beyond him.

It was a strange fascination, he admitted, for he had never entertained a woman like her. His friend, George, had accused him of liking her and damn it if he hadn't called it. He liked her a lot. Her profanity-laced vernacular charmed him. Her snorts tickled him. She was small, but she wasn't fragile. She opened her own doors and left the room whenever she damned well pleased. There was no expensive perfumed smell following her from room to room, yet when he got close enough, he would always catch the aroma of fresh linen off the clothesline. He had forgotten how much he loved that smell until Bianca. And when she smiled... ah... when she smiled, his dreary world brightened.

So if Bianca were so wonderful, why couldn't he just claim her for himself? He could just court her like a normal person. Meet her father and bring flowers to her mother. And then he would, he would—no, he couldn't do any of that. Because all that would lead to him actually marrying her. And that he couldn't do. He couldn't marry anyone.

Victor continued to count all the reasons he couldn't marry her while he tucked her under the covers. Later, he plucked around her apartment, looking for aspirin. His Bianca wasn't very neat, he determined. He added that to his list of reasons but then took it off because he thought her little messes were adorable. She was too busy running a business to think about cleaning.

He could afford to pay for these trifles for her. A housekeeper, and maybe a new wardrobe filled with pants tailored just for her. He would have to buy her a fur coat and some new shoes. A new car and then—*no*! He was doing it again. He imagined his life with Bianca and thinking of reasons he should marry her when he should think of reasons he couldn't marry her.

When he removed her head wrap, a mass of curls and coils revealed themselves. The dampened edges pressed against her temples and framed her serene face. She sighed in her sleep from the release of tension. He felt his mouth tug into a half-smile. Lord, his Bianca was delightful. Maybe he could convince her to be his mistress.

Victor shook that idea from his mind. An arrangement wouldn't work, either. Too bad, he thought as he removed the diamond necklace from her neck. Spoiling her would be so fun. Victor placed a glass of water and two aspirins on her bedside table and walked out of her room. He would have to solve his Bianca problem another day.

Back inside his car, Bianca still occupied his mind until Victor's driver stopped the car. Victor looked up to the front seat, wondering why. His longtime assistant and driver, Sylvester, looked back to explain.

"Hey, boss. Need to use it real bad."

"Now? We're almost home."

"I know, suh. But it ain't gonna wait. I gotta go now. If you don't mind, I can go around that building and be back in no time."

"Fine, fine," Victor responded with the wave of his hand.

Sylvester shot out of the driver's seat like his behind was on fire. Victor watched him run behind an abandoned building. Victor stared at the building, taking in its eerie details. In fact, the entire street was oddly quiet. He found it all troubling for some reason.

Victor resolved to push down his paranoia and think about something that made him happy, like Bianca. He laid his head against the seat, looking to the ceiling. Visions of her in his arms danced in his head until he heard the distinct sound of a soft and horrifying click that only came from a revolver. Victor's body froze as he became keenly aware of said revolver pointing at his head through his open window.

"Get out!" the gun owner declared.

Victor moved carefully out of the vehicle with his hands in the air. This was just another robbery. He had been robbed before. In his experience, robbers just wanted an easy take without a struggle. "Take what you want," he said. "Check my pockets. I won't make a fuss. But my driver will be back soon, so you better get what you need and get out of here."

Dawn's early light gave Victor a good view of the man's face. He could have been any man Victor would have passed by or spoken to at the bank. So it was not his features that made him distinctive; it was the look of fear that caught Victor's attention.

"Shut up and look away!"

"Look away? Just take what you want, man! What are you waiting for?"

"I said, shut the fuck up! Turn your head!"

This was no robbery, Victor determined. This was a slaying. Someone had sent this little boy to murder him. But they should have sent someone who had the guts to look a man in the eyes when he pulled the trigger. This one just trembled as he tried to muster up some courage.

"All right," Victor replied. Victor pretended to turn his head to the side, but he made a swift move and grabbed the gun from the side. The weapon discharged into Victor's car. It didn't take much brute force to gain the upper hand, but Victor managed to yank the gun out of the man's hand. The man struggled against him, determined to get the gun back, but Victor ended their dance by striking him on the top of the head with the butt of the pistol. The man's body crumpled on the wet ground floor.

"Boss!" he heard Sylvester holler behind him. "What happened? You okay, boss?"

All Victor could feel was his heart beating in his chest and his ears ringing. He eyed Sylvester for the longest while he stood over his assailant's body. "That was a very long piss," he said.

"I-I came as quick as I could. Was he trying to rob you?"

Victor shook his head. "No. He didn't want anything. Just me dead."

"Is he dead? Did you shoot him?"

"No. He's just knocked out. But we don't have time to deal with this. Let's get out of here."

"But what about him?"

"Leave him. Although I would love to find out who sent him, I don't think it's going to be worth the trouble of torturing him."

"I'm sure we both know who's behind this," Sylvester returned.

Victor eyed his assailant again. "Let's get out of here," he said.

❧

MAGS EDISON WAS capable of many things—kidnap, extortion, blackmail, and maybe theft. But even a woman like her had her limits. Someone should tell this to her lunch guest.

"You will not kill Obadiah Cross," she scolded him.

Her guest grumbled loudly and remained in his consternation. On this sunny afternoon, her guest arrived unannounced, barging in on her tranquil tea with demands that she speed up her plan.

"Why not?" Her guest shouted. "He's spying for Victor. I know it."

"Maybe so. I wouldn't be surprised if he is. His loyalties have always been with the boys and never me."

"But if he is spying, that means Victor is on to us. He might already know everything, and then what happens to our plan?"

Mags pursed her lips in thought, and her guest looked on. "He might know something, but he doesn't know everything. He doesn't have the trust documents. He never did. So he wouldn't know that title will only pass to his wife and not to him. Nonetheless, you need to be patient and stay the course. It will all work out soon. How about some tea instead of rambling on about killing people?

"Must I keep reminding you," she continued, "If we go about this too fast, the two of them will catch on. It's enough we had to resort to kidnap." She was just in the middle of pouring hot tea from the teapot when her guest's very fragile emotional state erupted into an outburst. He slammed his fist down on the small table, nearly burning her with scalding water.

"Where's my deed, Mags?" he barked. "I've put up with this charade long enough. You told me I would have it, but all I keep getting is excuses. I'm running out of time and money."

"Maybe you should stop spending the money I give you on cheap whores," she suggested.

"What and who I spend my money on is none of your goddamn business," he snarled. "But I know one thing, I ain't leaving here empty-handed. I'll be leaving with that deed, one way or the other."

Mags expelled a deep breath. "But as I told you, it is not as simple as giving you a deed. For one, the actual letter of the boy's trust precludes it, and two, we don't even know where the deed is. That is why we need to stay the course. Get them married and then proceed as planned."

"I better, Magsy. Or I can't promise you what will happen if I don't." He rose to leave, but not before taking a sip of his tea. As he sipped, he studied her posture. "I suppose you haven't changed much in all these years. Still got a pretty face. But that Kinta, Victor's mama..." He finished his meaning with a whistle. "Man, was she was a looker. Prettiest nigra in Kingfisher County. Stand up woman, too. Kept her chin high in the air. I respected her. But I know that Kinta Freeman been dead for years. In fact, all those Freemans are dead and gone. So you can imagine my surprise when I find out Kinta's son is still alive and well."

When he didn't get the response from her he wanted, he knocked her entire tea table down to the floor in one fluid movement. "No more games, Mags. I want them married. You hear me?" He didn't wait for her answer. He marched right out of the room without looking back.

CHAPTER 16

EAST PRESTON STREET

Bianca stared at the note she had received earlier while at the *Baltimore Beat*. A man in dark clothing delivered an envelope secured in a waxed seal and embossed with a big letter *M*. Bianca quickly determined that *M* stood for Mags. Or Margaret Edison, for the faint of heart. The devil herself had sent a note written on the finest of stationary to remind Bianca that their deal was still on. With perfect penmanship, she wrote:

I demand your presence at my house today. -M

Bianca shoved the note into her pocket and looked over her shoulder for Kizzy or Ms. Ginny. Once she realized they were out of sight, she thanked the man who had delivered the note and opened the door for him to leave. But he would not leave. He stood there as if he had more to say.

"I am to see you to Ms. Edison's," he said.

"But I can't just leave right now. I'm working." She eyed his expression and realized this was a non-negotiable discussion.

Less than twenty minutes later, she arrived at Mags'

townhome. Her escort for the day held a firm grip on her upper arm despite her protest. He rushed her past the butler, maids, and all of Mags' portraits of herself all the way to her library. This time, it was not as airy and bright as Bianca remembered. It was dark, but Bianca spotted Mags immediately.

Mags pointed to the empty chair and said, "Sit."

Bianca's escort pressed her into the room and attempted to push her into her appointed seat, but Bianca had decided it was enough. "Would you kindly tell this bruno I can manage on my own from here on?"

Mags set down her teacup on the marble side table and dismissed her ruffian with the wave of her hand. Once he shut the library door, Mags addressed Bianca in the same tone she had written the note. "What have you been doing?"

"What do you mean? I've been working. Did you not read my last issue?"

Mags didn't immediately respond. She threw a small box tied in a glittery ribbon in Bianca's lap and gestured for her to open it. Bianca lifted the box's lid and frowned at its contents. The box was filled to the rim with hair in its natural African form. "What's this?" Bianca asked.

"What do you think it is?"

"Someone's hair... Oh my God. Daisy's?"

"Don't play games with me, Miss Eubanks. We have a deal, and your lackadaisical method of completing your end of our bargain is trying my patience."

"Lacksi—what did you expect for me to be doing right now?"

"You were told to marry my stepson. But since we had our little chat, you have been conducting your life as usual with my money. In fact, I think you and that boy think this is all a game."

"Game?"

Mags' lips pinched tightly together, pronouncing all the tiny lines around her mouth. "Your behaviors at Christmas Eve and New Year's said as much. I heard about your dalliance in the nightclub last week. Don't think for one moment that I will allow you to mock me. I am not to be toyed with."

"But why the hurry?"

"That is none of your concern right now. You should be preparing for your wedding."

"To Victor Carlson? That's like telling me to climb a mountain in high heels. It's never been done. And surely some other contenders are trying to climb the mountain of Victor Carlson as we speak. Why didn't you blackmail them? Why me?"

"As I have explained to you before, you are what I have chosen. Now let us move this train along."

"How? I can't make him do anything."

"How could you, looking like you do? Despite my best efforts, you are still walking around like a crumpled piece of paper. You don't even wear his mother's ring that he gave you."

Bianca blinked as she digested Mags' words. The ring Victor gave her was his mother's? Why had he done such a thing? If she recalled it well enough, she had thrown it in his face when he appeared at her apartment a while back. It reappeared in its emerald glory on her kitchen table after he had left. She had stuck it in her dresser drawer and had not seen it since. She would have surely been more careful about its care if she had known its origin.

"I didn't know," Bianca humbly replied.

"You need to plan a speedy wedding," Mags continued over Bianca's thoughtful state. "On second thought, I'm not sure if we have time for a wedding. You should get yourself with a child so he will see the need for your marriage."

"Get my— Get myself? *What?*"

"It doesn't have to be his child. Use your professor friend if you like. But you need to make this happen soon. I don't believe Victor would volunteer to go down anyone's aisle. You must make him do so."

"You're crazy."

"Determined. Now, my bruno, as you called him, will see you to his house."

"Whose house? Victor's? Now?"

Mags erupted in frustration by slamming her fist down onto her desk. "Yes, now, Miss Eubanks! Do you think I have all day to wait? You haven't told him of our little arrangement, have you?"

Despite the truth, Bianca whispered, "No."

"Good. I don't want him or Wesley to know. My actual son would be heartbroken, and that would make me furious. You have thirty days to walk down the aisle with Victor. If you do not meet this demand, I will deliver a box containing Miss Daisy's body parts to you daily. I think a finger will do nicely next."

"I'm going to the police."

"Oh, the police?" Mags laughed. "Please tell Commissioner O'Donnell I said hello. We go way back. Before you go, my maid will see that you look decent before your visit. Now you may go. I can't bear to look at your wrinkled state any longer." She waved her fat hand and turned her back on Bianca.

The big lug enforcer came back into the room to pull Bianca out as gently as he had pushed her into it. This time she did not fight him. She was too weak to fight.

BIANCA STARED at Victor Carlson's stained glass door for the longest before she got the courage to knock. His townhome on East Preston Street was the last place on earth she wanted to be. She had vowed she would never speak to Victor ever again. Oh, she would tell him to kiss her ass, and then she would never speak to him after that.

Five days ago, she woke up in her bed wearing her cotton nightgown with no memory of how she had gotten there. All she had was a sore throat and a splitting headache. But when she turned to her bed table, she saw the glass of water and aspirin.

As the day rolled by, she learned more and more about what had happened to her and came to the horrifying conclusion that during their night out on the town; she had thrown up on herself and that Victor had cleaned her up. She was even more mortified after realizing that to undress her and redress her; he had to have seen her naked.

And if he had seen her naked, why hadn't he bothered to call that day? Or even the next day. On the third day, she did receive a package from him, but it was nothing she expected. It was a box with her yellow dress. The note under the dress read:

Hopefully, this dress is back to its original glory -Victor

Bianca flipped the card over to make sure he meant to be this brief. She couldn't believe that after their wild night of kissing, this was all he had to say. She could not wrap her mind around the fact that after seeing her naked, all he had to give her was an awkward note about her dress.

On the fourth day of Victor's silence, Bianca's humiliation morphed into outrage. How dare he? How dare he not send one word of explanation to her. She would slap his face the next time she saw him; she would. But she hadn't planned on seeing him for a long time. At least much longer than Mags had planned. So here she was on the fifth day of Victor's silence, standing outside his door, dressed like a trollop, and seething with anger. Oh, he would rue the day he ever got mixed up with her.

Mags' goon waited patiently for her to go inside as he sat in his automobile down the street. He had expected her to do as Mags' required, which was to throw herself on Victor. She gave the door a firm knock and held up a middle finger in the air toward Mags' enforcer. Bianca stowed her middle finger and rehearsed what she would say to him when he opened the door. Perhaps a good ole fashioned "kiss my ass" would be nice? Or a "you dirty, rotten son of a bitch," might be even better.

But when the door opened, it was not Victor who opened it.

An older brown woman stood on the other side. "May I help you?" she asked.

Bianca did her best to recover with, "Yes. Is Mr. Carlson home?"

"Not at this time. Would you like to leave a note?"

"Can you just tell him that Bianca came by?"

"Bianca?" The woman repeated but with a strange familiarity. Her eyes inspected Bianca from the top of her head to her shoes. She was probably eyeing Bianca's exaggerated dress and makeup while making the sound judgment that Bianca was just another strumpet looking for Victor. It wasn't her fault Mags' maid dolled her up like a cheap floozy.

"Yes," Bianca answered with grit.

"Well, why didn't you say so? We've been waiting to meet you," she said before grabbing Bianca's arm and yanking her inside of Victor's home.

Bianca almost tripped over the threshold in an effort to keep up with her assailant. And before she could get her bearings on the inside, the woman had already begun relieving Bianca of her coat.

"This isn't necessary, you know?" Bianca began as the woman juggled her in different directions. "I can just come back another time if he isn't here." The woman was stronger than she had imagined.

"The mister will be here in no time. He went to the bank hours ago and should be home soon for dinner. Are you hungry? No? I'm sure you can find your appetite. Just some smothered chicken, peas, yams, and cornbread. Victor's favorite. I suppose you know that already."

"I-I-I didn't."

When the woman pushed Bianca into the direction of the foyer light, she finally stopped her fuss. "Oh, let me look at you," she said as she pressed her glasses up her nose. "Pretty girl. That you are. You don't have to wear all that make-up, though."

"Thanks. I'll try to remember that," Bianca dryly replied.

"*Mmhmm.* Wait till Sylvester finds out about this. Come on in here, girl." For the second time today, Bianca was pushed into a library.

This library looked like an old English library. Three of the room's four walls had shelves of books that almost touched the ceiling. A massive fireplace took up much of the fourth wall. A strange oil painting of what appeared to be a woman in the woods hung above the long mantle.

"I'm Ival," the woman said when she reappeared with another tea tray. "Sugar?"

No more damn tea, she grumbled inwardly. "No, thank you," she said instead.

"Oh, coffee then?" Ival pressed her.

The dichotomies of Victor's home distracted Bianca, making her unable to give Ival a real answer. Was she in the right house? This looked like the room of a learned scholar, not an obnoxious fool which she had branded him so many times before. And books. So many books. He couldn't possibly have read all of them. Not Victor. "Um, are these his books?"

The woman chuckled while she poured hot water into a golden teacup. "They are. He loves to read. He likes the classics, but he'll read anything. Sly, come out here. You got to meet Miss Bianca."

"Miss who?" someone shouted from the other side of the door.

"Miss Bianca!"

"Who?"

"Mis—Just bring your deaf ass out here."

An older gentleman swung open the door. At first, his height startled Bianca. Her jaw fell open as her head tilted back to peer up to his face. Though he was tall, the man walked to her with the grace of a gazelle. He folded at the torso and bent into a ninety-degree angle to pick up Bianca's hand and kiss it. "Sylvester Milton at your service, madame," he said.

Unsure of whether to shake her kissed hand with his or curtsy, she replied, "Thank you. Bianca Eubanks."

"Bianca?" he asked in Ival's direction as he still held Bianca's hand. "Isn't that the girl that boy is marrying?"

"*Mmhm*, that's her."

"This here?" he asked.

"Yes! I toldja it is, Sly."

When he finally brought his eyes to Bianca, his face broke out in a big grin. "Well, I'll be... In that case. I am truly at your service. If there is anything you need from my wife or me, let us know."

"Wife?" Bianca asked.

"Yes," Ival answered on the other side of the room, still plucking around Bianca's coffee. "Sylvester is my hard-headed husband. We have been working with the Carlson family for years. We share most of the work around here. 'Cept Mr. Carlson hardly makes a mess. He is very neat."

That was another peculiar thing about Victor that she didn't know. She had always assumed that since he had a messy life with messy relationships, he must have had a messy home. Not so. His home was immaculately clean and virtually spotless. It was lovely too. At least the luxurious interior was not a surprise. She had seen from his small fleet of cars he had a fondness for expensive things.

Strangely, all of this made her feel an emotion which she hated: unqualified. Over the last five days, she had fantasized about a life with him like a silly ninny, as if she could fit her rumpled self into this immaculate background. No wonder Mags suggested tricking him into marriage with a child. A plain woman such as herself had no other choice.

"I-I-I think I should go now. I feel like I'm intruding."

"Oh no, don't leave. He will be here soon, I—" Ms. Ival's words were interrupted by the noise of a door opening and shutting.

"Ival?" Victor's deep voice called from the foyer. "Is someone here?"

Ival rushed out of the room to attend to Victor. Ival's soft words were inaudible, but Bianca heard Victor's loud, clear voice say, "I told you I didn't want any visitors."

"Well... shit," Bianca blurted, causing Mr. Sly to chuckle.

He continued to do so on his way out of the room, leaving Bianca feeling strangely vulnerable and trapped. This was another terrible idea. She should not have come to his home. Bianca heard more of Ival's and Victor's hushed voices discuss her presence in the house, and then he appeared.

"Bianca? What are you doing here?" Victor asked behind her.

Bianca turned from the fireplace to face him with her chin in the air. "If you must know, I came here for one reason and one reason alone. I was here to prevail upon you the need to find Daisy and end this entire fiasco. But I can see that my presence imposes on you and your staff. I didn't mean to intrude. If you are so inclined to join me in getting rid of your psychotic step-mother and ending this unholy union, send a note."

She had already moved past him and with her hand on the doorknob before he could get a word in edge wise. It was not until his hand gently grasped her elbow, did she stop charging to the door.

"Don't go," he said. "Please?" His hand made a soft glide down her arm until it found her hand and held it there. "Don't go," he repeated. He pressed his hand against the door to push it closed.

Her eyes remained on the closed door and his large brown hand. She studied the intricate lines of his veins as they led up to his long fingers and manicured nails.

"I heard you say you didn't want company. I should not have come over unannounced. I just had heard nothing from you. And your step-mother... well, has been demanding as usual. I guess kidnappers have their deadlines."

"I'm sorry," he interrupted. "Considering all that is going on,

I should have been more attentive. I apologize. I have not been doing a good job of sorting this entire thing out in my mind. But I didn't mean to neglect you, Bianca. I'm sorry. Please don't go," he begged. "I would love nothing more than your company."

"But you reach out after that night and—"

"A lot has happened since then. And—I wasn't sure how you would feel. I didn't want to make you feel worse. I suppose I messed up even more by not saying anything at all. But at least you are here, and that makes me happy. So please stay."

She heard the grim sadness in his last pleading and turned to his eyes for the first time. She saw it as clear as day. Loneliness. And as much as she didn't want to believe his words to be true, something in her heart told her he was sincere and that he really didn't want her to leave him. She took her hand off the doorknob and allowed him to lead her by the hand to his sofa. She watched the muscles in his broad shoulders move as he guided her.

"Please," he begged before inviting her to sit next to him with a pat on the cushion. "So Margaret is being Margaret. What happened?"

"She sent a very polite escort to deliver me to her home where she demanded I marry you, post-haste. I think we should go to the police."

He sighed heavily before leaning back against the sofa. "Bianca, do you think anyone will care about a junkie with no family?"

"I care."

"Sure, you do. But the rest of the world doesn't. I doubt if any harm has been done to her. She is too important at this point."

"It's interesting you think so because Mags gave me a box filled with Daisy's hair."

Victor frowned at first and then laughed. "It's probably someone else's. We Carlsons have been in banking for a long time. And when you clean mobster money, you pick up a few tricks of the trade."

"Daisy's hair is red. Just like my sister's. There aren't too many colored girls with red hair."

"All right. So she cut her hair. At least it wasn't a body part."

"She threatened to do that next! God, Carlson, you don't seem to be taking this seriously!"

"I am. Trust me, I am. But I have dealt with Mags' scheming for a long time. I'm just trying to figure out her game. So you went to her house? I take it that's why you look so... made up?"

Bianca let out a long stream of air. "I look ridiculous, don't I? I'm supposed to seduce you."

He made a humored sound in his throat and smiled with his eyes doing most of the work. "What if I told you you've already done that?"

Bianca dropped her eyes from his disarming gaze to fiddle with her skirt. She hated that his charms disoriented her so easily. She looked over at his books instead. "Are these all yours?" she asked.

"Yep."

"And you've read them all?"

"Yes. Your little Hiram isn't the only well-read man vying for your attention."

"I didn't realize that you like to read. I'm sorry. I don't mean to offend, but you don't seem the type."

"Even obnoxious fools like to read, dimples."

"I guess you always seemed like a man who spends most of his time with the ladies."

"There is only so much time you can really devote to that area. In between, I like to read. Besides, how can a—what did Ms. Ginny call me? Randy dandy? How can a randy dandy work his way around women without quoting classical sonnets?"

Bianca snorted. "Sonnets? Like what sonnets?"

"'For you, tonight I would say:

'In the old age, black was not counted fair,
Or if it were, it bore not beauty's name;
But now is black beauty's successive heir,
And beauty slandered with a bastard shame:
For since each hand hath put on Nature's power,
Fairing the foul with Art's false borrowed face,
Sweet beauty hath no name, no holy bower,
But is profaned, if not lives in disgrace.
Therefore, my mistress' eyes are raven black.
Her eyes so suited, and they mourners seem
At such who, not born fair, no beauty lack,
Slande'ring creation with a false esteem:
Yet so they mourn becoming of their woe,
That every tongue says beauty should look so.'"

"What was that?" she breathlessly asked. "Langston?"

"No. Black women have been loved for centuries, long before Langston. That was William Shakespeare."

"Really?"

"Yes," he said with a chuckle. "Yes. Ironically, Shakespeare was upset by his lady's need to wear false makeup and paints. He laments that it is unnecessary and that it takes away from her. I can agree. My black beauty does not need makeup either."

Bianca held her breath as she gazed at the beautiful man sitting across from her. How was he an arm's length away and yet still too close? He had just forwardly quoted Shakespeare for her benefit, and all she heard was the sound of the crackling fire and her mind telling her not to fall in love with this angelic-looking man.

After twenty minutes of sonnets, Victor found his way to the window to see Mags' enforcer was still outside. "How long is he supposed to be out there?"

"Who knows? I guess Mags told him to wait until I have firmly seduced you."

"Don't say things like that," Victor grimaced. "It gives a man ideas."

"Which part?"

"The firmly seduced part."

Bianca made a thoughtful sound as she pulled away from Victor's drapes to draw back to his fireplace. "Other than not asking to be born, why does she hate you so much?"

Bianca watched Victor's eyes turn heavenward as her eyes settled on his soft lips. She wanted to kiss those lips again, but now was not the time. It was time to listen to what he was saying. What was he talking about again? Oh, yes. Mags hating him.

"Let's see," he began. "I was born. I was allegedly my father's favorite. I took over my father's affairs when he was dying and stopped her from bleeding him dry. Oh, and yes, I rejected her when she tried to seduce me. I might have laughed at her too."

Bianca had not heard him right. "She made a pass at you? When did she get around to doing that?"

"My father was dying. He had days to live, and we were all at his home. When she did it, I was in my father's study in the middle of the night, dealing with my grief. She came down in a revealing nightgown. She acted shy at first, and I tried to let her down gently. In my mind, I figured she was a woman who was working out the pending loss of her husband. But then she got aggressive, and she literally threw herself on me. We struggled for a bit until I pushed her against the wall with her hands in the air. I threatened to tell her son, and she threatened to claim I raped her. So we told no one. She has been trying to take me down ever since."

"Jesus."

"She didn't shed one tear at my father's funeral," Victor continued. "In fact, her next husband escorted her there. Wasn't that nice?" Victor didn't wait for Bianca's answer. He continued his walk around the room with his hands in his pockets until he stood before her as she sat on the sofa. "Margaret Edison will go through hell and back to get what she wants. She married man after man to keep her lifestyle intact.

Now she is too old for that. Her son's banking business is fragile and she needs money. Why not go back to ravage my trust fund for whatever scraps it has left?"

"But I thought you said there was nothing left."

"I thought so. But my father was a man who kept many secrets. The details of mother's death, her estate, and her family's whereabouts had been kept from me for years. So it wouldn't surprise me if there were something left. It's just too bad I will probably never know until it's too late. My documents are missing. Much like most of my life."

"What do you mean?"

He smiled at her and grazed her cheek with the back of his hand. "There's a part of me that remembers everything about my past. My mother, her face, and her smile. A part of me remembers our house and our life. And there is a part of me that wonders if it ever existed because it's so far away from this life. I believe that is how my father intended it. That's why so many of the pieces that connect me back home are missing. All I have now is Uncle Chito, my mother's brother."

Bianca smiled when she thought of him. "He's a sweet soul, your Uncle Chito."

"His thoughts usually blur," Victor acknowledged with a smile. "But every now and again, he brings back a clear memory for me. I'm grateful to have him. He is the only piece of my mother's memory I have left."

Bianca pointed up to the oil painting over his mantle. "Is that her? Your mother?"

The lines in Victor's face softened as he gazed up at the picture. "I had it commissioned not too long ago. It's the best likeness I could remember. I tried to remember the last day I saw her... in the woods."

"How did she... pass?"

"I don't know. I was never allowed to know. I can only guess. All I got was a curt announcement of her death over the evening's supper."

"I'm so sorry, Victor, for your loss."

A wry smile covered his sadness. "Don't worry about it, dimples. I'm a big boy. I survived living in a house with Mags, and I'll survive this too. Whatever it is. And so will you. We just got to figure out what the hell she's up to."

"My ears on the ground tell me that she has been spending a lot of time with her lawyers and with that Marbury fellow. It's just hard to believe that she believes marriage will secure their sale of the bank. Just seems so far-fetched."

Victor scoffed and shook his head. "You want to know something? When they gave me that bullshit story, I never believed it. Not in the least. That man isn't going to buy us out. It's all a ploy made up by Mags. That Marbury fellow and... well... there's something about him I can't shake."

"He certainly looks formidable," Bianca breathed. "I guess no more formidable than my father. Oh, he would like to speak to you."

"Does he?"

"Yeah. There's a pesky rumor out there that we are shacking up and that maybe you got me in trouble. Like the trouble a girl gets in if she gets pregnant."

Victor crossed to her to lift her chin with his thumb and forefinger, and without preamble or even a request for permission, he placed a sweet kiss on her lips. And she just stood there and let him, like a ninny. And when he pulled his warm, coaxing touch from her face, he said, "I think as long as Lady Noire keeps reservedly quiet about us, we shouldn't have too many problems with the rumor mill. And your father..." He let out a lengthy sigh before continuing, "I won't lie to your father about us. So I guess it's best if we just keep avoiding him."

Bianca's mind clouded for a long moment before she asked, "For how long?"

Victor stretched out his long arms, giving her an up-close view of his muscular wingspan. "Until we find Daisy. I have contacts everywhere looking. We will avoid him for as long as it takes, I guess. I don't know. This is all strange territory for me too. Look, let's not talk about this anymore. How about a nice and relaxing dinner like a normal couple? Uncle Chito usually eats in his room, which leaves me to eat by my lonesome. Care to join me? Ival has already set your place, I'm sure."

As if on cue, Ival entered the room to announce that dinner was ready. A tiny part of Bianca wanted to leave, to go home to her can of sardines and crackers for dinner for the sake of pride. But as time went on in the presence of Victor Carlson, the voice of her pride was being strangled by her innate yearning to be near him.

He sat remarkably close to her as they dined over Victor's favorite foods. They drank wine and debated over the best authors. They exchanged stories of their youth and lessons they had learned. And in between all of this, Victor showered her with his unfettered attention. He bathed in every word that fell from her lips as if he were solving a puzzle in his head. It was then that Bianca decided that being Victor's fake fiancée was not so bad. Somewhere in their entanglement, he shed the veneer of his public persona and revealed a multi-dimensional person who she was starting to like.

But liking Victor Carlson was dangerous. He had a trail of heartbroken tears behind him. And she was no fool. These moments of flirtatious hints, clever discussion, and subtle caresses had to be temporary. This was nothing she could hang her hat on, and she was fine with that. Besides, there was always his initial reason for getting involved with her.

"How is Angel?" Bianca asked, causing Victor to flinch while drinking his wine. She didn't know why she would ask him this question. "Or the others?"

He regained his composure and smiled tightly. "You know, it is not good table manners to discuss a man's mistress. But if you must know, I have not seen her since the day I proposed to you in Mags' library. Or any of the others."

"Oh. I guess you have been busy."

"That and the fact that I am publicly engaged to you. I wouldn't disrespect you, Bianca."

"But you said—"

"I know what I said!" The slam of his glass emphasized the volume of his voice. He internally chided himself for his outburst and said more calmly, "I know what I said to you, Bianca. But I... I have said a lot of things I didn't mean, and what I meant, I never said." He read her confused expression and continued, "I don't always express myself well. Shit, I never really have to. People always believe what they want to believe about me. And I don't fight it. But I suppose that has been my downfall. Maybe I let people believe the worst when I shouldn't have."

"What has that gotta do with Angel?"

"Nothing! None of it has shit to do with Angel, or Annabel, or anyone else. And all of it has everything to do with you."

"W-what?" Bianca asked as she watched Victor rub his face intensely to wipe away his aggravation. Why was he aggravated? He was the one not making any sense.

"Nothing. Never mind. Just know that I have not spoken to anyone. Not while we are engaged."

It was on the tip of her tongue to ask him what happens after they find Daisy, but she feared it might bring an answer she didn't want to hear. He had already moved away from the table anyway to build his emotional wall. The grandfather clock in the dining room chimed as it struck midnight, alerting them both that hours of thrilling conversation had come to a halt.

"I didn't realize the hour was so late," he said.

"Neither did I. I wonder if my ride is still waiting outside."

"Sylvester sent him away an hour ago. I wasn't going to let him take you home, anyway."

"So, you are going to take me home?"

"Do you want to go home?" he asked huskily.

Did she want to go home? Absolutely not. Every nerve in her body wanted to stay right where she was. But she wasn't about to admit this much to him. "I-I don't know," she said instead. "Going home in the morning? People will really believe we are shaking up if I don't leave now."

"Ha! Sounds like I'm not the only one who has created a world that they are now a slave to."

"What does that mean?"

"I built this persona," he began with a wave of his arms around about the room. "This careless playboy. I did it. And now, I am forever bound to this narrative. And you built this world of gossip. You've ruined reputations, torn lovers apart, and brought down political empires all with the stroke of your pen."

She flinched because his words felt like a slap to her face. She was not sure if he intended their impact or not. No one had ever confronted her in such a way about Lady Noire's words. Anonymity had always protected her from such things. "I'm proud of the *Baltimore Beat*. That doesn't mean I'm proud of what I did to make it what it is."

"Exactly!" he exclaimed as he eagerly snapped his fingers. "Neither am I. I imagine we have both done things we are not proud of. I had my reasons, but so did you. All I'm saying is that it would be nice to write our own stories, don't you think? Maybe Lady Noire can be the gossippee instead of the gossiper."

§.

AFTER MAKING sure Bianca was locked away from his grasp in one of his guest rooms, Victor sighed a sigh of relief. He had convinced her to stay the night by telling her it was for her safety and reputation. Thereafter, he gave her a polite good night greeting and bounded up the stairs so he wouldn't have to walk her to her room.

When he arrived in his office, he concluded that his Bianca problem was back. The woman whom he had thought about every single day since their night out on the town was sleeping under his roof and in one of his beds. It didn't help that he could still recall every intricate detail of her naked body.

Normally, the wolf in him would have acted on his impulses. He would have seen her sighs and flirtations as an invitation to something more, but in this situation, he couldn't. Something in his fascination with her morphed into affection. It was hard to believe, but he couldn't see himself contaminating her vivacious soul. He wouldn't and couldn't defile her, not after she had told him she was untouched. No, she deserved better than that.

So, he forced himself not to kiss her when he walked her to her room out of fear of his old habits. Instead, he hugged her. Her little body fit into his like a glove. He wanted to keep her there for... eternity? Yes, that seemed right. What an unscrupulous amount of time. But there was no finite amount of time to keep something he didn't even know he was missing. For instance, their conversation about classic authors and playwrights was everything he missed in his life. He never shared his thoughts with anyone, and when he tried, they laughed at him. Angel laughed. Annabel dismissed him. Bianca listened.

When he saw her standing in his living room, he became instantly delighted. But the look on her face was too much to bear. She had felt betrayed by his absence. But there was no way to tell her it couldn't be helped. Someone was trying to kill him. In fact, someone had almost done so the night he left her apartment. And since that night, it had been nothing but strange occurrences. So, he did what he knew how to do. He laid low and tightened up security. He had told Ival and Sylvester no visitors, so it was a surprise to see her.

But she was in danger. Their proximity was dangerous. But he didn't want to scare her. Just like he hadn't told her what he learned about her friend, Daisy. According to an associate of his, Daisy had somehow escaped Mags' clutches and was now on the run. Victor's associate claimed that Mags set a high bounty for her return. Everyone was looking for her.

Bianca's presence in his home presented a new dilemma. He

couldn't just send her home with that thug. And although her being seen overnight in his home could damage her reputation, it was his only way to ensure her safety.

As the hour rolled on, Victor grew weary with his thoughts. He made his way to his bedroom, but not before crossing Bianca's closed door. Something in him paused his footsteps. He imagined a scenario where he knocked. She would open it and then... and then what? Invite him in? Slap him? There was no telling. But something in him made him raise his fist in the air to knock and see. But before he could do so, the door opened. Bianca stood before him wearing a soft muslin nightgown that Ival probably gave her. Her face was fresh and free of distorting makeup, giving him an unobstructed view of the lovely, soft contours of her face. He smiled at her, but she did not return his smile. Instead, she crossed her hands in front of her and pursed her lips.

He cleared his throat. "*Ahem.* I was just stopping by to see if everything was okay. Are you comfortable? Is it cold in here? I can warm up the potbelly over there."

"The room's fine, Carlson," she clipped.

"Something wrong?"

"I'm trying to figure out why you are sneaking around my door."

"I told you—"

"I heard you all right. But listen and listen carefully. I am not a toy."

"Huh?"

"From now on, we are just going to be as we were in the beginning. Just Bianca and Victor. Nothing else. No kissing, no nothing. And I don't want you to be with me like you were earlier."

He stood there like a fool, desperately trying to understand what was coming out of those pouty lips of hers. The gas lamps lit in her room brought a soft glow to the outline of her nightgown. Her gown's ruffles chastely hid her breasts, but he could still see the promise of nature's bounty. Her hips also distracted him by swaying from side to side as she berated him with her words. When she stopped talking, she glared at him, waiting for his response. What had she said?

"What are you talking about?" he asked.

"The other night, you made me feel like... like I was a woman you would consider."

Victor's forehead wrinkled in confusion, but she continued.

"I don't want you to treat me like a play doll for your amusement. You kissed me that one day, then I didn't hear from you. Then you come by the *Beat*, you whisk me off to a party, and then you kiss me at midnight, and then I didn't hear from you anymore. And then you whisk me to another party, and then I didn't hear from you. And now, you are quoting sonnets and shit, and then you kiss me on the forehead and walk me to my room. Just cut it out. You don't have to play with me like I'm a toy."

It was then that Victor understood. "I see. And how did I give you the impression that I was toying with you?"

"Because you... when you said good night, you acted as if you were going to kiss me, and then you just turned away like I was nothing. And I know this is all temporary, but I am a human being, and I have feelings, and I'm not gonna let you toy with them. And if you think—"

He wouldn't give her a chance to finish. He couldn't hear another word. All he needed to hear was that she wanted to kiss him just as much as he had yearned to kiss her. He pulled her to him as she rambled on with declarations and false promises. He blocked out all of them as he sought the sincerity of her soft lips. His hands held her face to his as he gave in to his craving and tasted her sweet honey. His heart beat rapidly in his ribs, and his mind blocked out time. And when she lifted her arms and she slid her hands around his flanks and up his back, he lost his composure. His body rippled with a need for her in a way he had never felt before.

Before he knew it, his feet moved beneath him, backing her

into the room. He still held her mouth and her body to his when he kicked the door shut behind them. The door slamming sealed their actions, making every movement intentional. He held nothing back as he lifted her into the air, gripping her round butt cheeks in his hands. He pressed her soft body against his hard manhood, enjoying the look of surprise that crossed her face when she realized the length of him.

When he set her down on her two feet, a thought crossed his mind. *What the hell am I doing?*

CHAPTER 17

CATCHING A GOSSIPER

Bianca knew what the hell she was doing. At least that is what she told herself when she opened that door. She was doing the same thing she did the night they went to the club, taking a crazy leap into deep and unchartered water. Waters that could easily drown her. She could very well get sucked in by Victor's current and die. Or she could just enjoy this for what it is, no matter how temporary.

And so, she told herself, she would have no regrets after tonight. She would stop resisting the string that kept pulling her to him. She would no longer fight against the ache that kept her up in that bed, waiting for him, wanting him.

And so when he stood in her room and pulled back, she didn't hesitate. She slapped him.

"What was that for?" he asked, holding his burning cheek in his hand.

"To remind you why you're here. Now get out of your head and kiss me, Carlson."

She watched a firelight in his eyes, and without discussion or preamble, Victor Carlson remembered why he was there. A primal determination crossed his face as he held her and kissed her possessively while lifting her nightgown from her body. He clasped her buttocks and she, almost instinctually, wrapped her legs around his waist. He had kissed her before. Several times. But not like this. And though she had less experience than he had, she quickly figured out that this kind of kissing was a dance to a beat that was sometimes rapid and others slow.

And while their lips entwined in this heavenly dance, she had not noticed that he had walked her to the bed until she felt the mattress dip. His hand softly caressed her rib cage and then down to her hips and over her thighs. And as that hand worked its way back up her thigh, she realized quickly where its destination was. Her two hands pushed his chest off hers to gain some distance. It was too late, Victor's fingers had already found its treasure, causing her to suck in a large quantity of air. Her body jolted from the shock of one of his digits pressing into the tender folds of her femininity. A part of her wanted to push away from him, and his invasion, but curiosity and the strange tingling in her body held her in place.

He slowly retracted his finger from her before murmuring, "Are you sure?"

She nodded. He left the bed for the limited purpose of removing his clothing. And in the soft glow provided by the firelight and a few wall sconces, she watched the slow reveal of his glorious body. Shades of light danced upon the intricate lines of his muscular frame. Under his watchful gaze, her eyes roved over the expanse of his wide chest, his rippled stomach, down the oblique planes of his pelvic bones, and finally landed on his manhood. His length and girth immobilized her. And when she had looked her fill, he came back to the bed to kiss her most sacred places and rupture her sanity with amorous need.

His knee nudged her thighs open and smoothly claimed the space between them with his body. At first, she felt an invasion and did not react, but then she felt herself stretching and pressured, widening that did not feel good at all. And when the onslaught of his rigidity pressed into her center, she stopped all movement. The rhapsodic fog that she had been in dissolved into clean, dry air. She sat up as much as she could beneath his heavy body to gain a direct understanding of what he was doing.

A tight expression crossed his features before he was able to soften his face. "Have you ever spoken to someone like your mother or your sister about this part of things?" He whispered, doing his best to hold the reins of his embattled loins and soothe her at the same time.

"I know what happens here, Carlson," she whispered harshly back. "I've been to college. I've seen babies born. I know the mechanics, it's just that I never thought it would be so..."

"So... what?"

"So matter of fact. So, absolute. Shit, I don't know. All I know is that I felt good doing what we were doing until you pressed your thing in me." She noticed he didn't leave his position between her legs immediately, but he did rest the weight of his body on his side, careful not to strain her thigh. His free hand gently cupped her face.

"It only feels uncomfortable because it is your first time."

"How would you know what it feels like? You're not a woman."

"True. But I—"

"Never mind," she said to stop him from going down his long list of experiences with these things.

"Don't be scared. We'll go slow."

"Do I need to slap you again? I don't want slow."

He muffled his chuckles in the curve of her neck and then continued to nuzzle her with soft kisses. "In the early stages of things, slow is better. This is special. Your first time is special. If you aren't ready, we can wait."

"I'm just a little nervous. I guess I don't know what kind of expectations you have."

"Mine?" he asked as he kissed the back of her hand. "I

expected you to be perfect, and you have already exceeded that, dimples. Like I said, we can wait."

With that, the tension in her body left her. He kissed her again, teasing her with a mixture of soft and rough nips that traveled down her neck, over her breasts, and down the length of her belly. He inflamed every place he touched and caused a welter of heat and wanting within her. So much so that when he moved above her again, she barely noticed. Her eyes were closed when she heard him.

"Bianca, look at me."

She opened her eyes and locked her gaze on his reassuring eyes. She heard nothing but the crackling fire and their syncopated breaths. He entered her slowly. And although she suffered the pressure that came from his entry, she could not remove herself from the silent conversation their eyes were having. He met her cries of discomfort with gentle kisses and soothing promises. And once he gained her wholehearted acceptance, the pain faded into something very different. The sweet sensations of fullness and emptiness washed over her for long minutes. She savored every moment of him above her. Every groan and every shutter of pleasure captivated her. She saw his sensuality morph into vulnerability as their bodies unified. Something within her caused her hips to move beneath him. He responded by quickening his thrusts. She felt a strange resonation that lifted her above herself, and as she was just about to reach an extra height, Victor's loud roar woke her dream.

A strange, dissonant silence erupted after he collapsed over her. All she heard was his breathing in her ears. After a few moments he moved beside her, shifting her in a spooning position. He held her tightly still in front of him while her heart beat within her chest.

"Victor—"

"I'm sorry, Bianca."

Of all the words she thought she would hear, an apology was not one of them. He was sorry? "Why would you say that?"

"Let's just talk about it in the morning. For now, what's done is done."

He said nothing else. All she heard was his soft snore behind her as he slept on. She, on the other hand, remained wide awake, staring at the wall, wondering what the hell he was sorry about.

In the early morning, just before the sun rose, he got up to put on his clothes. He whispered that his reasons for leaving were for propriety's sake. She wanted to understand, but she could not stop the long, awkward silence that passed while he adjusted his clothing. He searched for his discarded shoes, and when he found them both, he held them in his hands and tiptoed out her door.

THE NEXT MORNING, Victor hustled quickly past her door, refusing to disturb her as he had done the night before. He lingered at the top of the staircase, wondering about the impact of his abrupt exit from her room. Should he have stayed? Or did she understand his need to get out of there? She had to understand. Could she really understand the overwhelming amount of guilt he had in taking her chastity when he wouldn't, or rather, couldn't marry her?

"*Ahem*," Sylvester coughed at the bottom of the stairs, breaking his thoughts.

"Yes?" Victor asked.

"You got a visitor, boss," he replied. "He says he's your employee."

When Victor found his way to the bottom of the stairs, he recognized the person immediately. "Follow me," he said to Obadiah Cross before heading toward the library.

Obadiah rushed into the room and quickly found his own seating without waiting for Victor to offer it to him.

"I don't have much time. I have got to get back before someone notices my absence."

Victor's right eyebrow perked up in alert as he poured himself a glass of bourbon. "Is it my brother you're worried about?"

"Your brother? No, I'm worried about Ms. Edison's spies. They're everywhere."

"And my brother?

"I doubt your brother has any idea what is going on. I haven't seen him much."

Victor made a thoughtful sound as he drew to Obadiah. He offered him a glass, but he declined. "Coffee then?"

"No, there isn't time. I came here to show you something." Obadiah pulled a piece of paper from his vest's right pocket and his spectacles from his left one. "I thought about things after your visit the other day. It came to my mind that I remembered years back an undocumented credit on our ledgers. It was from a lease. I asked your father what bank asset was being leased, and he told me it was none of my concern. I left it alone after that, but the lease payments were on the books for years until your father died."

"I don't see what this has to do with me."

Obadiah bristled before continuing. "Because the ledgers show the name of the payors. Sovereign Oil Company. Your father must have been leasing property rich in oil to this company. Any idea where that might be, sir?"

Victor's mind zipped into a trance where only his last memories of his hometown became visible. "Oklahoma?"

"*Mmm*. And If I were a betting man, and I had to guess who owned land in Oklahoma out of the three of you, I think I would bet on you."

"Me? But wouldn't it have shown up in my trust documents?"

Obadiah's frustration surfaced before Victor in the form of a growl. "You mean the same documents that you have not seen? Or the same documents that are now missing?"

Victor refrained from nodding in agreement, but Obadiah had convinced him. Instead, he closed his eyes against the obvious answer to his woes. His churning stomach told him the land in Oklahoma was his. Either his by title or by right, but it was his. If his father had purchased it through the bank, Victor would have known about it. But this asset was rife with cover-up and secrecy, making it clear his father had never intended for him to find out about it. The bitter taste of betrayal filled his mouth with disgust. The memory of his father's last benediction to him on his deathbed now played vividly in his mind.

"Ain't nothing for you out that way, boy," his father had said. "It's all burned to the ground now. You stay here and take care of your brother. He's all you got in this world."

Victor opened his eyes to wipe away the memory and focus on the present. He gave Obadiah a thoughtful glare. "And my brother? Is he aware of this?"

"I can't say. But I will say this; the lease is still in place. Wonder who has been taking the money."

"I'm not surprised," Victor answered his hint. "She probably forged the documents to keep the payments coming."

"So why would she care if the bank was sold now? She has money. You would have never known about the land or the lease."

Victor shrugged his hands in his pockets in deep thought. "If I know my stepmother well enough, I know that she doesn't do anything unless she is forced to do it. If she had a cash cow with land from my trust, and there was no way I would find out, then someone must have found out about it. There would be no other way she would get herself involved in the bank. She never cared about that bank."

Mr. Cross grumbled at the idea. "Then, someone should tell your brother."

"My brother? Who's to say my brother isn't also on the take? If my father could betray me, I don't see why Wesley is above doing the same."

"Your brother is a good man. I have never known him to be anything other than loyal to you. There were times when many considered you unworthy of loyalty, but Wesley Carlson never listened to anyone with the subject of you. I remember one day I overheard him talking to Ms. Edison, and he said, you were all he had in this world. He said it. Clear as day."

Although Obadiah had politely hinted around at Victor's propensity to squander his money on his lavish lifestyle and women, Obadiah's point was not lost on Victor. Yes, there were many times in which he took more than he gave. In hindsight, it was Wesley who had made sure that Victor's lights were on and his bills got paid. Victor had routinely lived above his means for his own reasons, but only Wesley could have protected him from the consequences of his actions.

"As far as the bank's investment failure, Wesley has been doing everything he can to stop it," Obadiah continued in his quest to play Wesley's advocate.

Victor grumbled inwardly. "More like do everything he can to get out of it. Hence that Marbury person who lingers around claiming that he can buy the whole thing. But I've been around banking and politics for years; he is not who he says he is. I've never heard of him."

"Neither have I. Maybe he's someone we should look into."

Victor nodded in agreement. "I can't agree more. I need you to find out how I can reach the Sovereign Oil Company. Find out what you can on the ground about this Marbury character, and I will do the same. But continue to keep quiet and stay out of Wesley's and Margaret's sight. They can't know that we know anything about what we know. I will continue as usual. I advise that you do the same. I will pay handsomely if you do this for me."

"About that. I don't really need a lot, and I really don't even want anything from you. But I'm desperate. My Misses and I need to get on out of town. I figure that whatever Ms. Edison is up to, she gonna need to cover her tracks and she gonna start with me."

"I'll protect you, but I need you here to keep an eye on the bank."

"No, my wife and I can't risk it. You think your daddy died from old age? Like the rest of her husbands?"

Victor didn't answer him. He didn't need to. The truth does not need acknowledgment. It is true all on its own.

"Unfortunately, it's all a matter of time," Obadiah sighed after moments of silence. "If you could just pay for my train tickets out of town that would be fine."

"When will you leave?"

"I need a few weeks to tie things up. I will let you know when I'm ready."

"Until then," Victor said as he stood to shake the man's hand.

When Obadiah left his home, Victor gave Ival directions to rouse Bianca so he could take her home.

§&

BIANCA REMAINED in an absolute state of mortification. The memory of the night before kept playing in her head. All of it spoiled by his slow and awkward exit from her room. How awful. When she arrived at his breakfast table, the next morning dressed in an outfit given to her by Ival, he praised her, but it felt more like an offering of pity. Victor complimented her on how lovely she looked in the green blouse and floral skirt, but she refused even to look him in the eye. On the way to her apartment, he tried to hold her hand, but her pride refused to let him touch her.

How many countless times had she laughed at women who threw themselves at men's feet? Too many. And how many times had she shaken her head in disgust, thinking of women begging to be with Victor? Too many. The irony of it all was not lost on her. Besides feeling embarrassed by her wanton behavior, she felt ridiculous for even being wroth with him in the first place.

Her mind ruffled through her range of emotions as she

looked out the window and onto the street where she lived. Under the morning sun, her apartment building bustled with its usual fervor. Women hung out windows to gossip while children laughed and played on the sidewalks below. As Victor's car slowed, Bianca recognized her landlady on the sidewalk, talking with a woman from her window. She noticed Victor's grand car, along with everyone else in the neighborhood. And when Victor helped Bianca out of the passenger side, her landlady eagerly ran to her.

"Oh, Miss Bianca, how good it is to see you," she said. "And Mr. Carlson. Hello, sir. So nice of you to escort your lovely fiancée home."

"Yes, thank you, Ms. Blakely," Bianca said over her shoulder as she moved past her.

"You know you just missed the good Doctor Eubanks. He came up here, looking for you twice. Once late last night and then this morning."

Bianca and Victor froze in their steps and turned around to face Ms. Blakely. "You-you don't say," Bianca stammered.

"*Mmhmm.* He told me to call Crestwood 6254 if I see you here. He said he was gonna come back later anyway to check to see if you came by."

Bianca and Victor took one look at each other and turned back to his car. He handed Ms. Blakely a crisp twenty-dollar bill before quietly saying, "For your discretion." She pushed the bill into her floral duster and nodded as they drove away.

"So your father is on your tail," Victor said as they drove away from her building. "Where should we go?"

"I don't know. Oh, my God. What am I going to do?"

"Why don't we go back to my place?"

"That's a terrible idea! No, no. I should go to the *Baltimore Beat*. My car is there. I can always say that I slept there last night."

"Okay," he said as he turned the car around.

"No! He'll go there too. Shit! No, go to my sister's house."

An interminable silence settled between them as they drove to her sister's home. "You know you can't run forever," Victor said finally.

Bianca gazed out the window when she replied. "I know. But I just need time. My father is different. I can't just bring home—"

"A man like me?" he finished for her with a raised eyebrow.

"No, that's not what I meant... I meant to say that..." She let her words fall to the ground as they arrived outside of her sister's house. She recognized her father's car immediately. "He's here! Back up. Go."

She expected Victor to crank the car back up and shift into reverse just as he had done in front of her building, but he did not. He sat there, staring out his windshield with his jaw tight. The muscles in his jaw jumped as his eyes narrowed ahead.

"What's wrong with you? Drive. Let's get out of here." Victor pulled his key out of the ignition and picked up his hat to press it onto his head. He meticulously fixed his tie and patted the dust off the arms of his coat.

"What are you doing?"

"Look ahead of you, Bianca. What do you see?"

What she saw was a long and shiny Studebaker Touring parked right in front of Bianca's sister's home. A black man dressed in black stood outside of it as if he were waiting for someone.

Victor confirmed Bianca's suspicion when he said in a deadly calm voice, "Its Margaret Edison's car. She is waiting for us inside, along with your father. Consider yourself trapped, dimples."

CHAPTER 18

A FAMILY MATTER

The door to her sister's house was unlocked. Obviously, there was an expectation for Bianca's presence at this gathering. Bianca opened the door to a front room full of waiting people. Cecilia and her husband, Joseph sat on the left. Their parents sat in the middle, directly facing the door. Her mother sat in a pink armchair, and her father stood over her. And sitting in the far dark corner of the room, wearing the smug expression of a cat, was Mags Edison with Wesley standing on her right.

Every one of them stared at Victor and Bianca as if they were two little children who had just gotten caught in the woods. This was silly and quite unnecessary. Before she could say as much, Victor walked ahead of her in her father's direction.

He wasted no time with pleasantries. "Hello, Doctor Eubanks," he said as he extended his hand to shake. "My name is Victor Andrew Carlson. It is an honor and a pleasure to meet you. I have absolute respect and regard for your daughter. Is it possible we could have a private word, sir?"

Her usually taciturn father paid little attention to Victor's brief speech. He did not extend his own hand to shake. His eyes never left Bianca when he said, "Not before I have a private word with my daughter. Bianca?"

"Daddy," she replied as she moved through a room full of stares to Cecilia's empty kitchen. Her father shut the door and gestured for her to sit at a small table. She sat there, unable to reach his eyes for the first time in her life and could not understand why. It was not as if she had done anything wrong. She really hadn't. But her fear was what she had to do. She would have to lie to him. There was no other way. If he knew the truth, he wouldn't stand for any of it.

He lifted her chin to make eye contact. He smiled in his knowing smile. He peered through his glasses as if he were inspecting a patient of his. "What's all this, dimples?"

Her father's nickname for her calmed her. Victor had given her the same name, unaware that her father had given her the endearment first when she was a child.

"It isn't what you think it is. I can tell you that much, Daddy."

His mustache twitched under his nose as he grumbled. "What I think is that my daughter has been running around town this way and that way and never home. You have been dodging me. Why? Is there something you're scared to tell me? Who's this man?"

"I really meant nothing by it. I just wasn't ready to face you. That's all."

He chuckled and then lifted his glasses off his head. "I guess I can understand. My daddy is eighty-seven years old, and I'm still scared of the man. Don't tell him that." Over Bianca's nervous giggle, he continued, "Bianca, you are a grown woman. I won't treat you like a little girl. Those days are over. The issue I have is that you aren't acting like the woman I know you to be. You running around town with this man. You keeping secrets from your mother and me. Miss Ginny visited us the other day.

She said the man has a woman on every side of town. I know you don't want that. Are you all right?"

Oh, gracious, she thought. So Miss Ginny and her high horse had muddied the waters? Just great. She took a deep breath, but her words still stumbled along. "No, Daddy. And yes, I'm okay. It's just that..."

"Do you love him?" It was just like her father to get right to the point.

What a strange question. She blinked several times while it rested upon her heart. And when the truth came to her, she realized that she didn't have to lie to her father about Victor. "I think... I think I do," her lips uttered. It was the truth. Her heart had signed itself away to him the moment he had kissed her under the stars. She had not realized it until it was far too late. She had unveiled herself to him in more ways than one, and when he distanced himself, she felt exposed and hurt. And why else would she feel that way about someone unless she cared about his reaction? Had she felt this way after Hiram rejected her? No, she didn't. And then there was the growing concern she had about him. This care for how the world treated him. It was all perplexing and awfully scary.

If this was the feeling of love, it was strange. From it derived a host of emotions and reactions—gladness, anger, joy, frustration... and fear. Fear being the absolute worst of them all. But fear was impossible to avoid when you loved someone; she figured because there is this risk of love unreturned. What if Victor didn't love her back?

And why was that same fear relieved every time she gazed at her side and found him standing there? She hated it; this love for him. But it had grown as constant as her heartbeat. And she had tried to turn it off and ignore it, but it was an unrelenting hold on her ability to think rationally.

And so, here she was, Bianca Eubanks, Editor and Chief of the *Baltimore Beat*, aunt of ten nephews and two nieces, daughter of Hubert and Darling Eubanks, and recklessly and hopelessly in love with a man who had more women than he could handle. What an awful position to be in. But she was in it, and she no longer needed to lie about it.

"I may love him, but I'm not living with him, nor am I in trouble," she added.

"That woman out there says otherwise," her father replied.

"I'm sure she has. She is not an honest woman."

"I gather as much. But Cecilia tells us she gave you money for the newspaper. Are you in their pockets?"

"No, no, no. I am not. I have my own reasons that have nothing to do with any of that. I promise, Daddy."

"Your sister had her own reasons for trying to marry a rich man." He paused, waiting for her to respond. When she kept her eyes on the table, he added, "I just hope he is a good man and not just a pretty face."

"No, Daddy. I assure you, he isn't. He's not perfect. I know." She couldn't say any more than that. She would have loved to say that she wished this was all real because she could see her and Victor on a life journey together. But this wasn't an actual conversation about a genuine marriage proposal. None of this was even real. And she hated tainting her first conversation about a man with her father with this fraudulent scenario. But it couldn't be helped, thanks to Mags. So now, the purpose of this conversation was to continue her deceit long enough to find Daisy. That was it, and that was all.

Her father quietly studied her as he tinkered with a silver spoon left on the table by one of Cecilia's children. Bianca watched with bated breath as her father wiped crumbs of food from the table with the side of his hand.

"All right then," he said finally. "Send him in here."

Bianca left her seat without another word. Victor stood right outside the kitchen, ready to face her father. Once he shut the door, Bianca faced the room. Her focus narrowed in on Mags as she sat in the corner in a long chair with her son, Wesley, by her side.

"Ms. Edison," she said icily. "What brings you?"

Mags chuckled at Bianca's poorly contained vehemence. "I came out of concern for you, my dear. Now that I have an investment in the *Baltimore Beat*, I can't very well let you fall to pieces over a man. I came to see if your parents could help me convince him to make an honest woman out of you."

"We are already engaged," Bianca reminded her through her curled lips. Unbeknownst to her, her feet had moved beneath her, and she was already across the room in Mags' face. Her fingers itched to reach around her neck and squeeze the living daylights out of her. Luckily, Bianca's mother pulled her arms and shoulders back from what she craved to do.

"Yes, there is your slow crawl to the altar," Mags retorted with an unbothered smile. "In the meantime, I have it from an unimpeachable source that you have been spending the night with him. Even just last night. I mean, you could be with child. Gossipers don't become gossipees. It's bad for business and it does not look good for either family."

"You know damn well that I'm not pregnant, you bitch." The room erupted in an uproar after Bianca's words scorched the atmosphere.

Mags laughed as she jumped to her feet. Everyone got between the two of them, but Cecilia was the one who pushed Bianca into a private corner, with Bianca promising more physical harm to Ms. Edison.

"Bianca! Are you sure you want to do this? Marry this awful man and into this awful family? I once thought I had to settle and marry for money, but I see now that I was wrong. You don't have to do this."

Bianca was still in fighting mode when the doorbell rang. One child opened the door to a crowd of visitors. Bianca rolled her eyes heavenward at the sight of them. Bianca's Aunt Alberita and her gang of prayer warriors stepped through the door wearing white dresses and determined faces.

"Oh, we just in time!" she exclaimed as her followers trailed behind her. "The word got out and the devil is busy. But so are we. We came to pray on you, niece." They surrounded Bianca in a circle and commenced praying over her poor soul.

"Alberita!" her mother exclaimed. "This is not the time for all that. We are discussing a family matter."

"I'm here to discuss it too. I just discuss it with prayer," she returned.

"Everyone, please!" Wesley pleaded in the center of the fray. "Mother and I aren't here to pressure anyone into doing anything. We came here to point out that these two should get married soon."

"Like how soon are you talking about?" Bianca's mother asked.

"Like the end of the month," Wesley answered. "To cut down on the talk, you see."

"But we are only meeting this man today. There isn't time to plan a wedding, a dress... and family..." Bianca's mother stopped to look at her angry face. "And there isn't time to think about things."

Before Bianca lashed out at Mags again, Victor emerged from the kitchen. The room hushed as they all watched his towering form walk over to Mrs. Eubanks.

He reached for her hand in the stateliest way. "Hello, madam. My name is Victor Carlson, and I want to marry your daughter. It would be an honor if you would give your blessing one day. Your husband has done so."

Caught off guard with his handsome face at first, Bianca's mother stumbled through her answer. "I-I-I will have to think on it if you don't mind."

"Yes, ma'am. Thank you for your consideration." He gave her a bow and then turned to Wesley and Mags. "I think you two have done enough today."

"Not before I am assured of a wedding date before the end of this month," Mags answered.

"Whatever we do will be discussed in private," he snarled back.

"So you are engaged?" Cecilia asked them both.

"Yes." Victor and Bianca answered in unison.

"And you want this, Bianca?"

All eyes and ears pointed toward Bianca, waiting patiently for her reply. She gulped a few times before letting her answer escape her lips. "Yes."

Cecilia nodded with a smile. "All right, then. Then we should have something to mark the occasion, don't you think? How about an engagement party?"

"That wouldn't be bad," said Bianca's mother.

"Ain't nothing wrong with a celebration of the union of marriage," Aunt Alberita added.

"Amen," her prayer warriors sang in unison.

Her family began planning a party that had nothing to do with the actual couple. Bianca felt her blood rising and was about to tell them so until Victor turned to her. "Can you walk me out?"

They left the house with Mags and Wesley hovering paces behind. Bianca also noticed how her entire family stood in the bay window of the front room with their eyes planted firmly on Victor.

"You don't have to do this because of last night, Victor," she told him.

"Your father isn't the first man to take me to the carpet about his daughter. Believe me. I haven't done or said anything I didn't want to. I'm sorry I didn't get the chance to hold you this morning. I botched what we shared with my overthinking. Do you forgive me?"

"Yes."

"Good."

"What did you tell my father?" Bianca asked in front of his car. "What excuse did you give? He gave you his blessing? I don't believe that."

"He gave me his blessing because I didn't give him an excuse. I told him the truth."

"The truth?"

"Yeah. The truth. Now get back in there and get yourself ready to become my wife, dimples. I want you in your finest white that day and that night..." He didn't finish. Instead, he leaned over to pull her body into the hollow of his. He kissed her with a mark of possession long and hard in front of her family, Mags, Wesley, and the entire neighborhood. When he finished, he settled her back onto her feet, giving her a few soft pecks on her trembling lips. "See ya, Mrs. Carlson."

TWO DAYS LATER...

Victor gazed out the window of his office at the bank. The day was finally over. The evening sun had found a hiding place behind a hill, but its pink and orange rays spread across the sky. News of his pending nuptials had spread the same way. Everyone knew and everyone had something to say. Victor hoped that everyone would mind their business and leave him to grieve his bachelorhood in peace, but he was mistaken. Eleven times. He counted eleven times from the sun's rising to the sun's setting, did someone prod him about Bianca.

"Bout time," Ival had said when she served him his breakfast.

"So soon?" George asked on his way to work.

"Don't do it," the janitor said while sweeping around his desk.

"Mess up and I'll kick yo' ass," his friend, Joseph, had warned over the telephone.

"You could do better," his busty employee, Miss Harris, offered with a wink and a salacious smile.

"Leave her alone," Ms. Ginny urged him during her bank visit to drop off some deposits.

"You ought to get your soul saved before you marry that girl," Bianca's family reverend told him. This visit was the most interesting because, during his office sermon, in which he forewarned of the pitfalls of heathens, he requested a small donation for the sick and shut-in. The man almost salivated as Victor pulled a twenty-dollar bill from his billfold.

"I guess you won't be interested in officiating a saved woman with a heathen," Victor drawled as the reverend pushed the twenty into his coat pocket.

"Huh? Oh. Now that you mention it. I recall that scripture in the good book that says that the unbelieving husband is sanctified through his wife." The reverend opened Victor's door to leave. Over his shoulder, he said with a wink and a smile, "Brother, Carlson. You better get on to saying I do. Your soul depends on it."

After all traces of the sun disappeared, Victor set his pen down and closed all his books. He plucked his hat and coat from the coat stand and went around his desk to head for the door. A stern knock stopped him mid-step. The knocker didn't wait for Victor to answer. He walked in with an enormous smile on his face.

"Where the hell have you been?" Victor snarled at the knocker.

Wesley had the gall to look surprised. "What are you talking about? I know Anna told you I left to take care of some business."

Victor's hands grabbed both of Wesley's coat lapels to shake his entire body back and forth. He did not stop until he threw his little brother's body against the glass-paned door. "She said as much," Victor snarled again. "Now, I ask you. Where the hell have you been?"

"What's gotten into you? I was on business! We closed the Brookline Mansion account in Idlewild and I went to Michigan to settle up. What's wrong?"

"Where is she, Wesley? Where's the girl?"

"What girl?"

"Don't play games with me, you son of a bitch. Where is the girl you and your goddamn mother kidnapped?" Wesley stared back at Victor, dumbfounded with his eyes bulged out his head. "You got what you wanted," Victor continued, "I will marry Bianca. No telling what you two will do to me after the deed is done. But there is no point in holding her friend anymore. Let her go."

"I... have... no... idea... what you are talking about," Wesley said as he shook his head back and forth. "Kidnap? What?"

Victor released his hold, allowing Wesley's body to sag against the door.

"I didn't touch anybody. Why would I—"

"So you are just going to stand there and lie to my face? And pretend like you don't know what I'm talking about?"

"No, I don't. I know that Mother can be trying but she would never—"

"You have no clue what that woman is capable of!"

"*Shh*! Keep your voice down. Just calm down for a second, Victor. Tell me what this is all about. I'm sure this is all a big misunderstanding."

"Fine. If you want to play dumb, let's play that game. Your mother kidnapped Bianca's friend to force her to marry me. She has been holding her against her will for weeks now."

"Now, wait a minute!" Wesley exclaimed in a hoarse whisper. "There must be a mistake. That makes no sense. You had already agreed to marry the girl."

"And have you ever asked yourself why she wanted me married?"

"She has said why. For Mr. Marbury's sake. He needs to see you as someone who—."

"Knows how to stay in his place," Victor finished for Wesley. "It's bullshit! That bitch doesn't care if I fuck the entire east coast. She wants me married because she wants to steal the last of my inheritance from my mother."

"What does one have to do with the other? We are selling the bank and we need you to settle down for appearance's sake. That's it."

"Obadiah Cross found something interesting in our father's records. Looks like I own more than I knew about. I wonder if this has anything to do with this discovery."

"The land in Oklahoma?" Wesley asked.

"Why would you say that? I didn't mention anything about land."

"I don't know. I figured maybe. Your mother's family owned so much down there. Why not some land in Oklahoma? Do you know how much it could be worth?"

Victor eyed Wesley carefully. "I don't know. But I bet ole Magsy knows. Looks like she and your father know more about my estate than I do. But you shouldn't be surprised, seeing how they stole every dime I ever had from me."

"Victor, please don't open old wounds. I know our father wasn't perfect, but he did the best he could. And my mother has always been ambitious. But I don't know what one has to do with the other. Mother is trying to do what's right for this family. We should thank her. And as far as your fiancée's friend goes, I think you are mistaken. My mother wouldn't do anything like that."

"She admitted as much to Bianca."

"If it's true, and I don't believe it is, why would you think I had anything to do with it?"

"Why not? You've been missing in action ever since the girl went missing. The other day at Bianca's home was the first time I've seen you in weeks."

"I've been taking care of business!" Wesley erupted. "I have been looking for other business ventures! That was the plan. Remember?"

"That fucking plan was as good as that damn paper you wrote it on because it depended on her. No one is going to buy a failing Negro bank with bad investments, not even this fake Mr.

Marbury Mags created." Victor could see his words shook Wesley. The truth had shattered all the dreams he had of surviving. "Listen, brother. You and I have been through worse things than bankruptcy. We will survive. We'll think of something. We don't need her. We never needed her. I've always told you that. She has never been any kind of mother to you. It's always been you and me, remember?"

Wesley blinked for a moment and then turned to Victor. "I can't be poor. I just can't. I was never like you. You always had it. So... I have to do what I can to fight. In the meantime, let me help you find your friend?"

Victor shook his head. There was no getting through to his brother when it came to money. Their polar opposite opinions would never change. "Okay. Let's get out of here so you can figure out how to help me get her back."

"Sure. Oh, I came in here to bring you this." Wesley handed Victor an envelope with his name inscribed in the center. The soft aroma of a familiar perfume reached Victor's nose as Wesley waved the envelope back and forth in front of him. "Looks like news travels fast." When Wesley left the room to gather his things, Victor opened the envelope and the enclosed letter.

Meet me tomorrow at the usual time, at our special place. -Love, Angel.

CHAPTER 19

THE CLEARING

Bianca gazed out of her childhood bedroom window, watching automobiles pass by. After a long promenade of various trucks, Studebakers, coupes, and wagons, a bright-green roadster appeared at the tip of a nearby hilltop. It descended the winding road to her street at the precise time in which she expected him. She pushed away from the window to visit the mirror to check herself. She mused over her new satin pants and fluffed her silk blouse before she realized that it was just Victor. She didn't have to act like a schoolgirl just because he would lay his beautiful eyes on her. But as soon as her mother called her name to announce her visitor, the schoolgirl in her bounded for the door, inhaled a deep breath, collected herself, and then appeared at the top of the stairs. He waited at the bottom with a bouquet of beautiful flowers in one hand, a box of chocolates in the other, and an admiring smile. She got lost in the fantasy of it all in that moment. Her mother coughed to break up their long moment of stares.

Ever since Bianca and Victor's engagement became official,

her father insisted on traditional courting procedures. Bianca balked at the antiquated practice. She was too old for this nonsense. She had been out of her parents' house and on her own for at least three years.

"I like the idea, dimples," Victor had commented during their discussion over a candlelit dinner, courtesy of Dusty Ann, herself, to celebrate their engagement. "I'm a master courtier, you know."

"Tell me something I don't know, Carlson," she had dryly replied.

He was right. He had proved to be a master in the game of courtship. Never mind that his manners were impeccable and his punctuality precise. He was a natural conversationalist with an astonishing knack for connecting with people. Victor's interactions with Bianca's mother evidenced this. After devouring all of her mother's cooking and begging for second and third helpings, he found her sweet spot by noting that she used fresh garlic in her roux. Her mother beamed with pride before giving a firm nod of approval to Bianca.

Victor had even seamlessly won over Bianca's father. He smartly avoided topics that circled the hospital's mortgage. Instead, he followed Bianca's advice and brought up Negroes in the military. Her father tried to hide his exuberance over the chance to engage in conversation about something he loved to talk about. He tilted his glasses and hid his smile behind his coffee cup before asking with an air of pride, "Did Bianca tell you that my grandfather was the first commissioned Negro physician to serve in the Civil War?"

"No!" Victor declared with emphasized surprise. "She never mentioned a word to me." Turning to Bianca, he said, "Why on earth would you leave out the fact that you are a part of American history?"

"You didn't tell him, Bianca?" Her father turned to Victor, shaking his head in disgust. "I wanted both of my girls to go into medicine, but this one can't stomach the sight of blood." Back to Bianca, he added, "Bianca, if he's going to be family, there are some things he ought to know."

"I don't know what I was thinking," she replied with a shrug as she covertly winked at her mother.

"Sir, would you have any items or keepsakes from his time in the Army? I love that sort of stuff. Historical artifacts and things." Dr. Eubanks didn't answer; instead, he threw down his napkin, pushed back his chair, and beckoned Victor to join him in what Bianca's mother called his war room. It was the sacred place where her father stored his collection of war memorabilia. They emerged hours later as old friends, and Bianca's heart swelled. However, seconds later, her heart fizzled when a tiny thought entered her mind. He captivated everyone too easily, and his effortlessness begged the question: was his performance all an act? Was he behaving this way out of obligation because he took her chastity?

"So where are the two of you off to this evening," her mother asked later as Victor helped Bianca into her evening wrap. It was a brand-new white mink stole Victor purchased a week ago. She remembered objecting to the cost, but he insisted it was a necessity. No one would believe his fiancée would wear less than mink to warm her shoulders.

"We're going to see Blackbirds at the Royal Theater," Victor answered her mother.

"Is that one with Bo Jangles? I saw a poster for it downtown. Oh, I can't wait to hear all about it, Bianca. Make sure you come around on Sunday with details."

"Sure, Mama." Bianca nodded before noticing her mother looking at her with a strange fascination.

"Hmm, I believe this agrees with you," her mother commented.

"What?"

"You. Him. All of this. You look fine, baby. So pretty and nice with your hair done up with your fancy clothes and your pretty fur. You even got fancy pants on. It agrees with you."

"I was just fine the way I was, Mama," Bianca replied, ignoring Victor's closeness and his warm hand against the small of her back.

"Sure, sure," her mother cooed. "But ain't nothing wrong with change. Some change is agreeable. I guess you two better get on before you miss the show."

The show, like most Negro entertainment in Baltimore, took place at the famous Royal Theater on Pennsylvania Avenue. True Baltimoreans knew it as "The Avenue," the place where those who wanted to be seen were seen. There was always a crowd of onlookers and sightseers camped outside, hoping to catch a glimpse of the beautiful and famous.

As Victor pushed his car into park in front of the theater, a crowd of folks gawked at their arrival. Bianca set her focus on a small brown woman in the crowd. "Oh, look at her," Bianca heard the woman say to her nearby friend as she pointed to Bianca. "So refined. So classy. You think she's a singer?"

Bianca's ears burned from her embarrassment. How many times had she been the one to stand outside the Royal Theater as a watcher and gossiper? More times than she could count, that was how many. She was no classy dame. She was just Bianca and this was all a staged act. She realized they weren't going to the show; they were the show.

"I hope you like it," Victor breathed against her cheek as he escorted her beneath the bright awning. His warm hand settled against the small of her back as he guided her to the gilded staircase. "We got balcony seats. Nothing but the best for my sweet dimples."

Bianca blinked her eyes as a full understanding registered in her mind. Balcony seats, mink stoles, jewelry; it was all the same. This was all an opulent presentation to the world for the simple sake of appearances. It was all flair for the dramatic and none of it showed how he really felt for her. He was pretending as he had pretended to like her mother's cooking. Nobody likes liver and onions. Nobody. Just like nobody liked her this much to put on this much. Not even Hiram.

"What gives?" he asked the same question when the curtain closed after the last encore. "What's with you, dimples? You've been frowning since we left your parents' house."

"I dunno," she said with a yawn. "Bored maybe. I thought Mr. Bojangles would be taller." Bianca was uncertain, but she could have sworn she witnessed a flash of hurt cross his face.

Whatever it was, his veneer of charm quickly masked it. "Time to get you home, dimples. Where's it gonna be? Your apartment? Your parent's home? Your sister's? My bed?"

Bianca stared down below their balcony at the abandoned stage, refusing to move. "You think it's all fun and games, don't you? Daisy is probably starving to death by the hands of your step-mother and you got the nerve to play Casanova with me. I know circumstances brought us here. I'm no fool. But you don't need to toy with my parents or me. You don't have to wine and dine me. I know that when this is all over, and Daisy is back, we're done."

"All right, dimples. Take my hand. I want to show you something."

He clasped her hand in his and marched her through the crowd waiting for the next Bojangles show. She said nothing as he drove through the bumpy Pennsylvania Avenue Street. Eventually, he turned his car down a road devoid of the city lights and sounds. She looked up at a black blanket filled with stars and remembered where he was taking her.

"I really like this place," he whispered, absent from her present frustration. "When I came here with you in December, it was my first time. I don't know what it is about it. Maybe the country part. Maybe cause it reminds me of home. But I like it."

"Good for you," Bianca returned.

"I've been back here at least six times since the first night. Not intentionally. But somehow, as I am ending my evening, I find myself on this road and right back to this very spot."

"That's all nice, Carlson. I'm glad you love the countryside."

"One night, I thought to myself, maybe you keep coming back here, Victor because this is where you want to be."

"And?"

"Just like this clearing, there is something about you, Bianca Eubanks, that keeps drawing me back. And no matter how many twists and turns I take, I find myself right here. So maybe this is where I want to be. Regardless of investments, money, and supposed abductions, I am where I want to be, which is right here... with you."

Bianca froze as the weight of his words sank her body into the seat cushion. "How-how do you know for sure this is what you want?"

Pointing to his chest, he said, "I don't know. It's how I feel in here. It's how I feel when I'm with you. It's how I feel when I'm away from you and want to be with you again. I'm in love with you, Bianca Eubanks. I may not be what you want. But maybe in time, I can be. Maybe in time, you can fall in love with me too."

She wanted to laugh at that moment because he was clearly unaware that he had already stolen her heart a long time ago, and it was only her fear and vulnerability that stopped her from loving him. The coward in her refused to move. She could only stare at the depth of his gaze. He said nothing else, but as he had done on that cold night on the last day of December, he crossed the ocean between them. His warm hand reached around to the back of her neck for the purpose of upturning her face to meet his. He bent down and grazed her lips, savoring the touch as if it were his first. He kissed her again, this time desperately searching for a return of what he felt. She could have answered his silent question with her words, but she reached up and pulled him down to her, sealing the burning heat between them. Her hands searched and found the hard muscles on his chest. A pectoral bounced beneath her caress, and his own heat scorched him. His gentle kisses and soft caress evolved into a possessive hold, conquering the last of her resistance.

And nothing else mattered within the sanctity of Victor's car, not the surrounding steamed windows or the cold wind against its doors. Victor continued his gentle but demanding kiss, and Bianca's body melted into his. His massive hands kneaded her heaving breasts, causing her to burst with rampant want. And her mind barely noticed his gentle tug to her shirt or him gently pushing her back against the seat. She paid little heed to the logistics of where he arranged her body.

All that she could do was act out her true desires. She wanted Victor. Had wanted him. All of him. She wanted to breathe him in and get lost in his scent of expensive cologne and shaving cream. She loved the sensation of rubbing her face against the fine bristles of his shaved beard. She loved the strength of him and the weight of him. She wanted it all. She smiled at him. She did it freely, without holding back and without fear. And as the air between them cooled and their breath slowed to a normal pace, she whispered, "I love you too, Victor."

His eyes lit with surprise. "I won't let you down, Bianca," he promised.

"Yeah, yeah. Just don't break my heart. Now finish what you started, Carlson." She gripped his lapels and yanked him back to her to recommence kissing again, but he pulled away. He chuckled as he closed her open blouse.

"What are you doing?" she asked.

"Yeah, we aren't going to be doing the dirty until marriage. I promised your Aunt Alberita the other day when she came to visit the bank."

"Oh my God."

Victor shrugged his hand into his pocket and pulled out a shiny familiar ring. It was his mother's ring. The same ring she had stashed away in her bedside drawer. He must have found it when he took her to her apartment the night they went to the club.

"I don't blame you for not wearing this before. I asked you to marry me on false pretenses. But now... it's real. Will you marry me, Bianca Eubanks?"

"Yes, Victor. I will."

CHAPTER 20

RESCINDED OFFERS

Hiram Coleman watched his students filter out of his classroom for the last time that day. He was exhausted. He had a stack of papers to grade, a lesson plan to complete, and a late-night shift at the shipyard. Working at the shipyard was grueling and back-breaking work, but it was the only way he could make ends meet and keep his bride-to-be, Harmony, happy.

Harmony wanted a wedding with all the trimmings and Hiram barely had enough savings to make it to the end of the week. His teaching job was fulfilling, but it was not enough to keep a woman like Harmony happy. But very little made Harmony happy. It took a while for Hiram to realize her disregard for all things simple. Everything for her had to be lavish and expensive. From clothes to shoes to hats, she wanted all things lovely and refined.

His problem was that he couldn't afford any of it. At first, he tried as hard as he could so that her groanings would stop. But as he spread himself thin, he wondered if Harmony was worth the effort. At first, she was. Her loving kisses made the mountain worth climbing. But then she kissed him less and less and complained more and more. And all the while, he grew weaker.

"Doctor Coleman!" a voice sang behind him, interrupting his tired thoughts. He turned around and saw a beautiful sight for sore eyes.

"Bee! Where have you been, girl?" he called to his longtime friend. It was not until that very moment did he realize that he had severely missed her.

Bianca strolled from the back of his small classroom with a distinct air about herself. In fact, she had brought with her a special light that almost blinded him. Was it her clothes? Her hair?

When Bianca arrived before him, he removed his glasses and narrowed his eyes. "What's with you, Bee? You look different."

She blushed nervously and waved him off. "I suppose that's a good thing."

"I don't know," he began carefully. "I liked my Bee just the way she was."

A tight smile appeared on her face and then disappeared. "How is Harmony?"

Hiram rolled his eyes heavenward. "Harmony is Harmony. Or should I say Disharmonious?"

"Oh. Well, maybe she will be more harmonious when she sees the ring you are gonna buy."

"I can't afford to buy her a ring. I can barely afford to eat these days."

A bright smile erupted on Bianca's face. "Well, I came over here for two reasons. The first reason is to invite you to our engagement party tonight at my father's hospital. And two..." She handed him a fat envelope that she had hidden behind her back and said, "Open it!"

"Engagement party?" he asked while opening the envelope. A stack of green bills popped out of the folds. "What's this?"

"It's for Harmony's ring. You remember you said you needed the money I owed you? Well, here it is, silly."

"Where did you get this money? From him?"

Bianca blinked in confusion. "Him? Victor? No. I won it playing craps. I thought you should have—"

"I don't want his money," he said, pushing the money back into her hands.

"Well, as I just said, it's not his money. It was mine and now it is yours."

"What are you doing, Bee? Don't tell me you're still running around town with him. He's a dog. A stray one. He'll use you up and throw you out in the trash. You need to get a grip on yourself and get smarter about things. You should work on your next news edition, not run the streets with mutts. The Bianca I knew wouldn't lose her head over some pair of britches."

He watched her as his words washed over her. The light she brought in dimmed right before his eyes. When the hurt flashed across her face, he crumbled in guilt. "I'm sorry, Bee. I don't mean to be harsh." He attempted to hug her, but she moved away from him. "I think I just miss you. I miss my Bee."

"Well, you sure got a funny way of showing it. You don't have to be an ass."

Hiram expelled an exhausted breath as he leaned against his desk. "I know. It's this Harmony business. I don't even think I want to marry her."

"No? But you love her. She's beautiful. And you said she fits you. What's wrong?"

"She does not fit me," he said. There it was. The absolute truth. Harmony didn't fit him at all. "In fact, the more I think about it, I realize I made a mistake."

"Mistake?"

"Yes. That day you came here, asking about our childhood pact to get married. I should have said yes. You, Bianca. You fit me."

"I fit you?"

"Yes! You fit me far better than she does! And think about it. That dandy peacock you are running around with fits Harmony better than I do. You and me, we are learned individuals. We are scholars. We could work. It took me a moment to see you that way, but now I do. And ..." His words were failing him.

She didn't look convinced. She looked horrified. "Hiram... I'm getting married to Victor. I love him."

Hiram wasn't sure where it came from, but jealousy took a ferocious bite out of his thought process. If he were thinking clearly, he would not have said all the things he had said. He certainly would not have repeated what he had heard a week ago. "You know he is still seeing that white woman on Lafayette, don't you?"

She shook her head against his words. "Hiram, stop."

"No, I'm telling the truth. One of my shipyard mates' wife cleans her house. Your pretty boy was there last week. She saw him sneaking out the back door. Perhaps you should use the good sense God gave you and get away from him before he gets you killed with his antics."

Bianca didn't immediately respond. She stared back at him with her chin raised, and her spine lifted straight. He had hoped he would hear her contrite words seeking redemption for her obvious lapses in judgment. He had just illustrated, in the clearest way possible, the error of her ways. There was nothing else left to think on. But Bianca didn't say what he expected her to say. She dropped the envelope onto his desk and walked away. She did leave him with parting words.

"Keep it. I now owe you nothing."

WHEN VICTOR ENTERED his brother's home, he went in with the sole purpose of being brief and direct. His brother requested this meeting to calm the tide between them. But Victor was finished with games. Especially Mags' games.

As always, Wesley's wife, Anna, directed Victor to Wesley's study. He declined his usual scotch on the rocks, but he kissed his niece and two nephews before making his way to speak his peace.

Wesley rose from his desk and greeted him with a warm smile. "Brother, I'm glad you came."

"I don't plan to stay long. Where is she?"

"On her way. That gives us time to talk before she gets here. Listen, things are getting real bad out there. We need to do whatever we can to sell. The market is putting things in a substantial decline. If we don't act fast, we'll all be out on the street in no time."

"What's coming is inevitable, Wesley. There is no stopping it."

"But if Mr. Marbury—"

"Let's not waste time during this meeting with that bullshit, Wesley. I don't have the time. You know just as much as I do that Mags' benefactor isn't buying Carlson Brother's Bank. It's over. All of this is over."

"That's easy for you to say, little rich boy," Wesley blurted. His face showed immediate remorse as soon as the words left his mouth. "I didn't mean—I'm sorry. I have just been on nerve lately. What I meant to say was that it is easy for you just to give up when you have another asset that will sustain you."

"Perhaps I should get that drink Anna offered me. It looks like I'm going to need it," Victor said.

"I'm talking about the land you mentioned to me the other day."

"You mean the one I know nothing about? But you seem to know something. Care to elaborate?"

"What land?" Mags asked in a high-pitched voice when she entered Wesley's study. She strolled in with her haughty chin in the air and kissed Wesley on the cheek. "Victor," she addressed him dryly.

"Glad you could make it. You're just in time to explain to your beloved son how you have been stealing from me all this time. Oh and please don't leave out how you squandered every dime of my money."

"*Pish!*" she replied with the wave of her hand.

"What is he talking about, Mother?" Wesley asked.

"Yes, Mummy, what am I talking about?"

Margaret leaned against Wesley's desk with a smile. "Someone's been talking to Obadiah Cross. He always had it out for me."

"Probably because he is an excellent judge of character. But please enlighten us on what Obadiah discovered in our records. Tell us how you could forge my mother's signature for so many years and lease land that you don't own."

"What?" Wesley cried.

"You heard me, Wesley. Your dear mother hid assets right from under your nose. That's right. I didn't need Obadiah to discover all I learned when I made a call to the Sovereign Oil Company myself. They have been digging oil on a plot of land for eight years. The same land that has owned by my family since the early 1800s. And you know how they could do so?"

"How?" Wesley asked.

"A lease. They leased that land from a woman named Kinta Freeman."

"Your mother?"

Victor never took his eyes away from Mags because he wanted to see her face as he revealed the truth. "Yeah. My mother, who has been dead for fourteen years, leased land to an oil company just eight years ago. Isn't that something?"

"I'm not going to stand here and listen to this!" Mags hollered. "Wesley, how dare you let this bastard come in here and accuse me of something that he could have very well done himself?"

Victor broke out into an obnoxious laugh. "Oh, that's good, Mummy. Blame it all on me. I did it when I didn't even know it existed? But you did."

"Is this true, Mother?" Wesley asked. His pitiful soul

wandered to Mags' side and begged for her truth. "Did you do this, Mother? Have you been leasing that land for the last eight years?"

Mags' eyes flickered with the promise of retribution as she glowered in Victor's direction. "Four. It has been four years. Your father did it for the first four."

Victor raised both hands in the air and exclaimed, "Finally! She tells the truth!"

Mags' eyes shot a flurry of daggers in his direction. "Your precious father stole from you first. That's right, little boy. You weren't his favorite son, because if you were, he wouldn't have used you like a meal ticket."

"Mother—"

"It's true, Wesley. Your half-brother was the twinkle in your father's eye only because of the money he had. But when his money ran out, your father found other ways. It was your daddy who showed me the loophole in his trust. He was the one who brokered the deal with the oil company. And when he died, I just picked up where he left off. I signed your mother's signature with no remorse. And I kept every... single... dime. And you know what? She deserved it."

"But this is splendid news! Isn't it? If there's oil, then we should be saved. Right?" Wesley asked as he stood between Mags and Victor.

"Sovereign Oil Company is going out of business. They've tanked like everyone else," Victor answered.

"Oh, then can't we sell it?"

"No, we can't." Victor grew incensed with every word. "I won't be selling my mother's land."

Mags spoke next. "That I know. You won't be selling anything. You see there, Wesley? I told you he was the weak link. Here we are about to drown and he won't do anything about it."

"Where are my trust documents, Margaret?"

Mags pressed her lips together, displaying tiny lines around her upper and bottom lips. "I don't know."

"I hear you lost the girl," Victor said as he watched for her reaction to his reference to Daisy.

"They will find her. You can be sure about that. And when they find her, and they will, she will wish she never escaped me." A slow tug of Mags' lips increased to an outright sinister smile. She even splayed her whitish teeth. "But that isn't here nor there. The fact of the matter is, the bank is still failing, and your creditors are breathing down your neck. So what are you going to do about it?"

Victor closed in on her in a vicious fury. So much so, that an alarmed Wesley had to jump between them to ensure his mother's safety. Mags' refusal to flinch under Victor's snarl increased his outrage and his desire to wring her wrinkled neck. But Wesley pleaded for him to relent. And he did, but not without leaving her with parting words.

"You better hope and pray that I find Daisy before you do. In the meantime, you stay the fuck away from me, Bianca, and her family."

He was nearly out the door when she said, "I don't know if I can do that. I've already accepted her family's invitation to your engagement party tonight. It makes sense for me to be there. I am your Mummy, aren't I?"

"Go to hell, Mags," he said over his shoulder as he swung open the door to leave.

"Gladly!" he heard her say from a distance.

CHAPTER 21

THE ENGAGEMENT PARTY

On the day of her engagement party, in the middle of the *Baltimore Beat*, Bianca did the oddest thing; she hummed. She actually heard herself do it while she clanked away at her typewriter. It was a made-up tune with no direction or melody, but it was the clear sound of a happy disposition.

Ms. Ginny noticed the sound, too, and acknowledged it in the form of a glower. "Someone's in a chipper mood of late," she said as she peered over her glasses in Bianca's direction.

Bianca was too busy humming and typing to take the bait, but Kizzy was ever eager to help fuel the top of Bianca's joyful disposition. "Boss lady hums all the time now. Love will do that to you."

"Humph," Ms. Ginny scoffed. "More like lust. Ain't been no time for love."

They both fell silent, waiting for Bianca to respond. Bianca was starting to grow weary of Ms. Ginny's callous comments about her relationship, but after her run-in with Hiram, she figured she better just get used to it. But why someone such as

Hiram or Ms. Ginny could be so emotional about her decision was beyond her. Victor was her choice. He wasn't perfect, but he was hers. At least her heart told her so.

And that bit about him still seeing Angel. She put it behind her. With no actual proof, it meant nothing. So for right now, Bianca chose to be happy.

But, honestly and truly, the life of Victor Andrew Carlson's fiancée wasn't so bad. In fact, she could not think of a better scenario for a partner. She imagined that with any other man, she would have to filter or kill her ambitions for her future husband's sake. Not Victor. He proudly wore her ambition like a badge of honor. He didn't bother her with unreasonable questions about her actions or her business. In fact, during the day, she went where she pleased and conducted herself as she liked.

But during the night, he lavished her with kisses that made her shiver the next day. He had promised her Aunt Alberita, he wouldn't touch her until the wedding day, but he often came close to breaking said promise.

And romantic. He was a terrible romantic. Just the day before, he surprised her with an outdoor picnic in the backyard of his townhome. He presented her with seven different bouquets because he still hadn't guessed which flower was her favorite. She finally had mercy on him and his pocket by informing him he got one out of the seven correct. She loved tulips. He celebrated his achievement by loving her outside on his fenced-in terrace. She balked at first from the fear of getting caught by one of his neighbors, but he reminded her that the danger of getting caught made the act all the better. Luckily, a nice April shower came to her rescue. They both scrambled to put their clothing to rights before dashing back into the house. Bianca giggled at the memory of their running through the house to avoid Uncle Chito, Ival, and Sylvester.

This was another thing she had grown to love about being engaged to him, his sense of humor. It was just as twisted and outlandish as hers was. Every now and again, he would take her out on the town, where they caused a stir with his over-the-top apparel. For the sake of his humor, she dressed just as garish and then took residence on his lap the entire evening while they cheekily smoked cigars and drank until their hearts were content.

It wasn't perfect, but it was perfect for her, at least.

So, she stuck those annoying fears about him straying to another woman or him not returning her love into a drawer and never looked back. They had no place in her fairy tale. And neither did Hiram or Ms. Ginny's seeds of doubt.

Bianca was in the middle of her thought when Kizzy screamed from the other room. Ms. Ginny and Bianca ran to her from opposite directions, both in panic. Kizzy stood in the middle of the floor, staring down at an open letter.

"What's wrong?" Bianca asked. "Who is it?"

"It's from Daisy. She addressed it to you. I'm sorry I opened it, boss lady. I open all your mail when it comes here."

Bianca snatched the letter away from Kizzy with one hand and waved her off with the other. "It's fine. Its fine, Kizzy." Her heart beat wildly as she read Daisy's letter.

Dear Bianca,

I write to you, unsure if you will ever receive this letter. The last two months of my life have been the hardest months that I have ever had to endure. As you may know, I was abducted. They held me in a dark cell for weeks with paltry amounts of food. A man whose eyes are as cold as night hurt me real bad.

By the grace of God, I was able to escape. It is with a heavy heart that I tell you that I will never return to Baltimore. I am now in Alabama with my mother and my family. I am doing much better than I was before. I go to church now, and I have a job cleaning two houses. Although, I will miss you and the girls; I think it is for the best that I stay here.

Even though I'm doing better, I am really worried about you.
The man who tortured me knows you. He said he will hurt you,
too, if he doesn't get what he wants. I never found out what he
was talking about, but I have to warn you to do your best to keep
safe. I wish you would leave town too. You can always come here
to Alabama. We have plenty of room.

I pray that all will be well with you. If you need me, you can call
me at 17488 Briarwood.

Love always, Daisy

Bianca pulled the letter away from her face. Daisy was safe. Although the letter contained more that just her whereabouts, Daisy's safety was all that Bianca wanted to know. Kizzy and Ms. Ginny stood by, waiting to hear what the letter said.

"Well?" Ms. Ginny pressed. "Where is she?"

"Alabama," Bianca answered. "She's home in Alabama."

Kizzy and Ms. Ginny rejoiced. Bianca smiled to herself as she folded the letter. She donned her sweater and purse and made her way to leave.

"Why are you leaving so soon? The party isn't for hours." Ms. Ginny said.

Bianca smiled at their surprised faces as she hummed her tune. "I'm off to make time for love, Ms. Ginny," she said before plucking an apple from Ms. Ginny's desk and taking a healthy bite from it. Daisy was safe, and her lover wanted to marry her because he wanted to marry her. Daisy's letter had freed her. Despite containing warnings of danger, it liberated Bianca's ability to finally celebrate. She was getting married to the love of her life.

She heard Kizzy's giggle as she left the room. And though she tried to hide it, Ms. Ginny's smile was the last thing she saw before she shut the door to their suite. Bianca nearly skipped down the stairs and all the way to her vehicle before she realized what was clear to everyone else; she was happy.

She made it down the stairs and out the door with the tune in her head. Pink lines were scattered about the sky as the sun made its way down below the hill. Victor stood in his usual place across the street to pick her up from work, as he did on any normal day. He stood on the outside of his roadster, as he did every time he waited to pick her up.

"Have I got news for you. Daisy escaped! She's home in Alabama." Bianca pressed Daisy's letter into his hands. He read its words and then cursed under his breath. "What? This is excellent news. What's wrong?" she asked.

"What's wrong? She's imploring you to leave Baltimore. Did it occur to you she might know something we don't know?"

"I suppose. Or it could just be one of Mags' goons."

"I don't think we should go tonight," Victor said.

"You don't think we should attend the engagement party my parents planned and spent a near fortune preparing for?"

"A party I offered to pay for, but they refused me."

"Of course, they did. They are very proud people. What's wrong with you? Are you okay?" she asked as she neared his fuming side. The muscles in his jaw jumped as they did whenever he was angry.

"Fine, dear." He gave her a hard and brief kiss on the cheek before ushering her into his car and then taking off down the street. She had hardly had enough time to put on the driving goggles and gloves he had purchased her for his roadster car rides. *And dear?* Since when did he call her dear?

Bianca decided not to let forced monikers get her down. She pulled that silly tune out of her head and went back to humming it. The world, it seemed, was hell-bent on ruining her pleasant day, and she was not going to let it happen.

But a silent storm brewed in her as he drove her to her sister's home without uttering a word. She tried to coax his emotions out of him, but he claimed he was fine. By the time he opened her car door, she had had it. "If you are going to be prickly, don't worry about coming to the party tonight, Carlson," she told him.

"What?" he asked with a dumbfounded expression that made her want to resort to violent methods of communication. "It's my engagement too."

"I said, if you are going to be prickly and strange, don't bother coming tonight. I can think of a million things I'd rather do than watch you brew in silent anger."

He blinked for a moment as he looked down at her. "I'm sorry, Dimples. I have a lot on my mind. And I don't know where to begin—everything is all over the place and the only thing that remains in the same place is you. I still love you."

"Does that mean you still want to do this? Get married?"

"I still want to be with you."

"That's not what I asked."

She watched several waves of emotions cross his face before he tightly smiled. He attempted to kiss her, but she shrugged out of his grasp and walked into the house.

As she dressed, Bianca tried her hardest not to appear upset about her collision with the disaster called Victor Carlson. She promised herself she would not show an ounce of emotion while she sat at Cecilia's dressing table in her brassiere and underwear, waiting to be dressed by her sister.

When Cecilia pulled out a bright-pink frilly dress, Bianca could only offer her a tight smile. "It's lovely. Thanks, Ce-Ce."

"What? It's gorgeous. I wish I could get into it. But this baby and this tummy won't have it. I'm so jealous. And what's with you? You've been staring into space since you got here. You're getting married. You should be happy. This dress should make you happy. Your fiancé should make you happy."

Happy? She didn't feel happy. She was not sad, either. Agitated might be a better word. Especially since she was convinced Victor was hell-bent on wrecking her emotional state. She couldn't help but rehearse his words to her when he dropped her off. And then she kept kicking herself for not demanding he clarify why he even bothered to get her family involved if he was unsure. And try as hard as she might, she couldn't help but wonder if the reason he was unsure had something to do with what Hiram had told her. Was he still seeing Angel? Was that why he was confused? She couldn't know because he was so intent on being silent about every damn thing that bothered him.

But none of these answers would be found tonight, she decided. For the sake of her parents, who had sacrificed their hard-earned money to put together a lovely engagement party for her benefit, she would not disappoint them tonight. Victor had offered to pay for the event, but her father refused his help out of pride.

Victor probably had assumed that they didn't have enough money to put something classy enough to suit him. But that was the wrong assumption. With the help of flowers and a little magic, Bianca's mother and Cecilia transformed the basement of her father's hospital into the likes of any high-class supper club. Pressed white linen draped the round tables. Every single table featured crystal glasses, polished silverware, and china plates. A feast fit for a princess covered the long tables along the wall. A small quartet played melodic tunes in the room's front. Her parents had outdone themselves.

She spied her parents toward the front. They were smiling and laughing as they greeted guests. Aunts, cousins, and various family friends congratulated them. All of them were filled with joy, celebrating the occasion because she had finally chosen someone. Too bad that someone hadn't chosen her.

Bianca's mind was on its way down a negative path when a sight stopped her in her tracks. All ten of her nephews wore their Sunday best. Someone had spit-polished every one of them. They stood in a row from youngest to oldest under Cecilia's watchful eye and instruction.

"Oh, aren't you all handsome!" Bianca exclaimed.

"Have you seen us good?" the youngest asked. "Mama says we can go once you seen us good."

Bianca laughed and kissed his adorable face, "Yes, Tock. I've seen you real good." All ten of them dispersed before she could get all her words out.

Cecilia hollered as she waddled behind them, leaving Bianca behind to laugh. She looked over the rising sea of faces and couldn't help but smile. Even if none of this was real, it was fine for her.

"Looka here, looka here!"

Bianca heard a familiar voice say behind her. She turned to find her older cousin, Georgette, smiling at her with a wide grin. Her infamous husband, Fred, accompanied her. Bianca's father would often refer to Fred as the Houdini of the family because he loved to disappear.

"Cousin Georgette," Bianca returned with a soft smile.

"I can't believe it! You getting married, girl. I never, ever thought I would see the day. You being so... so ... you!"

"Thanks, cousin." Bianca tried her best to drain the tart out of her voice.

"And where he at? How you gonna have an engagement party and ain't no groom. Where he at?"

"Right here," said a husky voice from behind Cousin Georgette. Victor stepped around Georgette with the confidence of a sultan, drawing every feminine eye in the place. Even Bianca's three-year-old niece, Trudie, fell victim to the eruption of splendid manhood.

He found his place behind Bianca, where he wrapped both arms around her, giving her an almost inappropriate kiss on the neck. He gifted Cousin Georgette a wink before he said, "Sorry I'm late."

"My Lord! You can be late for me any day! Good God! Where you find this one here?"

Bianca had already moved her body away before she could answer, pulling Victor with her.

"Excuse us, please?"

Cousin Georgette was still lusting after Victor long after he and Bianca had walked away. She could be heard all the way across the room. For some reason, the sound of someone singing Victor's praises burned Bianca's ears. She had to get away. And she almost did until Victor caught her arm.

"Dimples? Can we talk outside?"

"Why? Aren't you supposed to be the entertainment? I know how much you love to put on a good show. The world is your stage, Carlson."

"I hate when you call me that," he replied as he shrugged his hands in his pockets. "I want to talk about our misunderstanding earlier today."

She threw her head back with a rich laugh. "Misunderstanding? I think I heard you right. But I will not let you ruin things tonight. This is my family, and they are too happy right now. I will give them their joy tonight, even though they will learn the truth of my deception in the morning."

She lifted her elbow out of his grasp. He tried to take command of her arm again, but one of her cousins grabbed her for a dance, which she happily accepted. She continued to evade him for much of that night. She danced with everyone she could. Everyone except him. She engrossed herself with various conversations with the elderly and refused to redirect her attention to him, even though he practically begged for it.

Part of her wanted to end this dance of avoidance with him. After having a lengthy conversation with Uncle Chito about his box, she was just about ready to end it. But then she heard something within his usual gargling that stopped her cold. "My boy shole love you. *Mmhmm.* Yes, he do. Justa look at him. I can't stand to look at him with them puppy dog eyes. Justa lookin' at you. Look at him. Ole sad eyes. He wanna dance witcha. And you don't wanna dance wit him. You going from here to dere and over dere. Justa sad. Got that boy justa lookin' sad. Ole Lawd.

Look at him! Please Lawd. Gone over there and dance wit dat boy, please?"

Bianca tried her best to contain her mirth as she eyed Victor and his sad disposition. She had no choice when it came to him. His uncle had practically pushed her in his arms.

"That was a rotten trick," she said as he rocked to the slow melodic sounds provided by the band.

"I promise I didn't put him up to it. But he isn't wrong, Bianca. I am sad. I love you. But you can't see that." Victor was going to say something else, but her facial expression stopped him. He reached his thumb to wipe her wet cheek. A damn tear had escaped her eye.

"Please," she begged. "I know this isn't real. Just for right now, let me believe. Let me have tonight."

He nodded and gave her a warm kiss against her cheek. He hugged her body tightly against hers, accepting her call for peace. Their loving embrace caught the attention of the entire party as a round of applause resounded throughout the basement.

Bianca blushed from the attention and then broke free from Victor's arms. "All right! Enough of this love music. I want to hear some jive," she yelled to the crowd.

The band's cello player strummed at the instrument, causing the crowd to react, and the floor filled with dancing and laughter. Victor had not left her side. He danced, and so did she. She even laughed with him. And in the center of a basement filled with friends and family, they were their old selves, Bianca and Victor.

That was all until Mags made her presence known. Bianca and Victor had just finished a lively Charleston around the room when they found Mags seated at one of the tables with Wesley and that strange Mr. Marbury. The very sight of them drained the very life out of Victor. She watched him morph back into the man she saw earlier today.

But Mags was not put off by his unwelcome face. "Victor, Bianca. How lovely to see you so gay and lively. I don't suppose with all this gyration that anyone will get around to announcing your wedding date."

"Nice to see you, Ms. Edison. Is this your plus one?" Bianca asked, looking at Mr. Marbury, who stuck out like a sore thumb in the sea of brown faces.

"We just finished securing the deal for the bank. Ms. Edison told me about this little shindig, and I thought I would stop by."

"Mr. Marbury wanted to witness your love for himself," Mags added.

"How charitable," Victor said dryly. "Please excuse us. We have other guests to greet." Victor and Bianca were just about to make their way to the next table when a sound from across the room was heard over the band and loud noise.

"Ahh! I know ya. I know ya!" declared Uncle Chito as he pointed at Mr. Marbury. He marched as best as he could in Mr. Marbury's direction while everyone watched with rapid fascination.

"Uncle Chito, calm down," Victor strained, hoping to calm Uncle Chito's raging storm.

"Naw, Naw! I know him. He wants my box. Yes, he do! I know ya. I know ya! You June's boy. *Mmhmm*, I know ya! Don't you touch my box! I'll kill you where you stand, you son of a bitch!"

Though Victor and Bianca tried to quiet down Uncle Chito, it was too late. He resisted any attempt to calm him. And unfortunately, things took a turn for the worst when Uncle Chito wrestled his arm away from Victor's hold and mistakenly knocked into Cousin Georgette, who then tripped, headfirst, into one of the long tables filled with desserts and pies. The entire table split in two as piles of creamy fillings covered her head. Shock and dismay froze everyone in place as they watched Georgette slide from the middle of the broken table.

"I knew I should have stayed my ass home tonight," she said after wiping brown icing from her face.

My thoughts exactly, Bianca said to herself.

CHAPTER 22

THE UNPRESENTABLE TRUTH

"Come home with me?" Victor asked once he safely delivered Uncle Chito to the front seat of his car.

An imaginary needle pressed into her spin, causing her back to straighten to attention. She inhaled deeply before she said, "I don't think it would be a good idea. I need time."

"Bianca... please don't do that thing where you pull away from me."

"What thing?"

"You know when you do it." His eyes darted anxiously. "I need to show you something... tonight. Please? Don't pull away from me."

Bianca rubbed her face in pure agitation. "You ask too much, Carlson."

"I know. Just please come home with me?"

"Fine, Carlson. I'll let my sister know."

Bianca said goodbye to her parents and offered Cousin Georgette a heartfelt apology. She was on her way out the basement door when Margaret Edison stopped her by tugging on her sleeve.

"That was quite a show, Miss Eubanks."

"Thank you, Miss Edison. I hope you found the show to your liking. Please bring the entire neighborhood next time. Or anyone else who might upset an old man."

"Speaking of next time, when will we be completing this little deal we have? Your little friend is eager to be released."

"Mags... I know about Daisy. I know she has already escaped you. So you can stop hanging her over my head."

Tiny, angry lines around Mags' lips appeared as she narrowed her eyes in Bianca's direction. "That doesn't mean we don't have a deal, little girl. Now I have given you money, a practically new printing press, and I have agreed to give you the deed to your building when this is all over. You owe me regardless of whether I have a junkie or not."

"Why do you want me to marry him?"

"That's none of your—"

"It is my concern. Why do you care so much? And what is Mr. Marbury to you? Why is he always around?"

Mags' eyes deadened as she leaned very close to Bianca to whisper. "I will destroy your little happy world if you don't find yourself in front of the justice of the peace to say your vows by morning. I'm done with your games."

Bianca had a retort ready to unleash from her lips, but before she could, a shadow crossed both of them. Victor loomed over them, wearing a menacing frown. "I thought I told you to stay away from my fiancée, old woman!" he barked.

Some of her family stuck their heads out the door in alarm.

"Victor," Bianca began with a smile to save face. "He's just kidding, everyone. You know how family is."

But Victor's demeanor toward Mags never changed, even when Bianca pulled his massive form away from the door. Angry Victor was back with a vengeance. He didn't speak a word the entire ride to his home.

When they arrived, he told her that he needed to attend to Uncle Chito, and then he would be with her later. Bianca wandered into the front room to fall onto the chaise by the fireplace. Suddenly, an odd thought crossed her mind. Victor had to attend to Uncle Chito. But that was Ival's job. Where was Ival?

"Where's Ms. Ival? Sylvester?" she asked him when he arrived at the bottom of the stairs minutes later.

He froze for a split moment and then continued his trek inside the room. "Uncle Chito is tucked in and down for the night."

"Oh. And Ms. Ival? I wanted to see if she had some witch hazel for this cut on my finger from that typewriter I have with the missing key. I hate that damn thing."

"I'll buy you another one," he mumbled.

"I don't want another one. What's with you, Carlson? Where's Ms. Ival? And Sylvester? What is going on?"

"They aren't here. I relieved them both this afternoon. They won't be returning to this household. Ever." The depth of his voice marked his words final.

"Ever?" Bianca blurted. "You fired them?"

"I did," he replied dismissively as he struggled with the knot in his tie.

"Why? For what reason? They've been with you forever. Why would you—"

"I did it to protect you." He didn't shout, but she felt like he had. When he loosened his tie, he let it fall to the floor. His eyes remained on her while he unbuttoned his white shirt. "I fired them because I caught Ival in the act of trying to poison me."

"What?"

"You heard me. I was just as shocked as you were. Sylvester was in on it too. The two of them were being paid by a certain enemy of mine to end my life."

"I don't believe that."

"And I wouldn't have believed it either. But when your trusted security guard purposefully disappears so that a gunman can shoot your face off, you see things differently. They both had been behaving oddly. And when my source told me the actual reason, it all made sense. They were being paid off."

"By whom? Who was trying to kill you? Mags? She needs you for the bank sale transaction. That makes little sense."

"Margaret isn't my only enemy. But my source gave me her word that this person would not bother us again—"

"Her? Who is your source?"

"That shouldn't matter, Bianca."

"It matters. You brought me here. You disturb my perfectly good party—"

"It was my party too!" he almost snarled.

"And I uninvited you because you told me you didn't want to marry me. And now you bring me here claiming that you have something to show me, and then you want to evade my questions about Ival and Sylvester."

"Fine. Ival and Sylvester were being paid by Angel's husband, Councilman Edmund Talley, to get rid of me. I think you can recall that Edmund has had it out for me for a long time."

Bianca narrowed her eyes to focus on his face. "Talley? Angel's husband? Angel is your source? So you saw her recently?"

"Did you hear the part where I said her husband was trying to kill me?"

"Of course, I did. But what else is new, Carlson? Your being hunted by your mistress' husband is not news. When did you see her? How long have you two been meeting?"

"None of that matters! What matters is that you are safe and that I love you."

"Do you love her too?"

"What? Have you been listening to anything I have said? No, Bianca. You stole my heart a long time ago. But I can say that a million times and you still won't believe it. You are too busy stomping all over it. And I'm not the only one visiting ex-paramours around here."

Bianca's eyes rounded in surprise. He knew about her meeting with Hiram. "You've been spying on me?"

"Spying? No. Protecting? Yes. But what I will not do is accuse you of something when I don't have all the facts."

"All right, fine. Give me the facts, Carlson. You brought me here to show me something. Let's see it. I want to know all the facts before I die of ignorance."

Without saying another word, Victor opened his shirt, revealing his rippled chest and stomach. His eyes never left hers.

"I won't be sleeping here tonight," she blurted when she noticed him backing her into a corner.

"Did ever you notice anything interesting about my body?"

"No," she replied. Except for the fact that the gods had carved his body. But she would not admit as much to him. Not at this particular moment. "Why?" she asked instead.

He turned around to position his back for her inspection. Ah. He was referring to a defect she had barely noticed in the throes of seduction. But now, under the beaming lights, every highlighted ridge and twisted welt in the middle of his back became painfully apparent. Along the planes of his muscular shoulders, scars buckled above his skin as a testament to an imperfect past.

"What's this?" she asked quietly while she felt the textured skin under her fingertips.

"It's what happens when you are beaten with a bullwhip so you will stop struggling. Do you see my neck? That happens when the fibers of a rope slice into it."

"Someone did this to you?" she asked before swallowing her words.

He nodded his head.

Her heart broke for the second time tonight. She heard of the terror that many Negroes suffered, but she had never imagined or seen it in such a real fashion. He drew near to her so she could also see the scars on his neck. She shied away, unable to bear this painful thing.

But he would not let her avoid him. "Look at it. You never noticed?"

"I-I saw the ones on your neck once. I just didn't want to ask," she whispered through her tears. "This was your incident?"

"My incident. The whole reason I am here with you today. I'll never forget that day for as long as I live. I was on my way to Uncle Chito's house. We were going to go fishing. But I remember walking along the road, feeling like the world was closing in on me. Days before, they left a burning cross in our front lawn. Two days before that, a beheaded possum."

"Why? What did they want?"

"Compliance," he said with a shrug. "I thought I was just being silly for worrying. But as soon as I let my guard down, it happened. They had me. They beat me for trying to fight them. And when I pissed my pants, they laughed at me. They laughed at me."

Bianca watched an ominous shadow cross his face and knew this thing was far too hard to describe. "Victor, you don't have to—"

"It was my mother who saved me," he interrupted. "She ran directly into the path of the fire, so to speak. All to save me. She got me out of there and took me to my father's house. She brought Uncle Chito later that night, insisting that they take him with us to watch out for me. And we left. I haven't been back since."

"Why would someone want to do this to a little boy?"

"People don't need a reason. But they had one. Else they wouldn't have let me live through the night. They wouldn't have told me they were trying to send my mother a message."

"And what was their reason? What message?"

"This is the question that has haunted my entire life. Why? What message were they trying to send my mother? And it's not that I didn't try to get answers. I questioned my mother. I questioned my father. Shit, I even questioned Mags. But no one had shit to say. They just put me in the back of the buggy, threw a blanket over my head, and told me to keep quiet. And then when we arrived somewhere safe, I tried to ask why. That was the day I met my father's ire. He punched me dead in my face and told me never to ask again. And since that time, all I have ever done was wonder."

Victor wrapped his arm around her waist and lifted her chin to meet his face with his other hand. "Bianca... I need to go. I need to go out there and get answers."

"To Oklahoma? Now?"

He nodded. "I need to know why. I need to know why they took me. I need to know what happened to my mother. I need to know why my father lied to me... why he stole from me... I need to know. Maybe it's all connected. My abduction, that land... Margaret. All of it. I also think it's time to face my past."

"How long are you talking about? This... is a lot."

"Not long, I promise. Just long enough to learn what I need to know."

"Then I should go with you. Let me help you."

"No. This, I have to do on my own. I left there as a boy and now I need to go back as a man. On my own. I need you here to watch over Uncle Chito. If Mags finds out I'm gone, I don't trust her around him. I need you here. I also don't want to give Mags the idea that something is wrong, nor do I want her to know where I've gone. I don't even want my brother to know.

Bianca shrugged out of his arms to gain some mental distance. "Wow."

"Dimples, I know this has never been the ideal courtship. But if you give me time, I'll make it all up to you. I wasn't lying to you when I told you I love you. I love you more than you could ever imagine. But I told you I want to be the man you need me to be. Let me do that. This question has held me back my entire life. Before you, I wanted nothing badly enough to care. I never wanted a wife. I never wanted anything permanent because I was afraid that it would all be taken away from me just like that day. But all that changed when you gave yourself to me. When I look at you, I see someone that I never want to let go. I want the freedom of waking up to you every morning and hearing you snore at night."

A thin bubble of control burst inside her and formed into solid tears. "All right," she said through her tears. "Go. I'll stay here. But you better come back to me."

He lifted her face with his hands, kissing her hungrily. And just like that, her frustrations and doubts evaporated. She fell into the abyss of his wonderful, soft touch, a place where the edges of the earth disappeared.

Upstairs, nestled in the safety of his arms, she basked in their naked intertwinement, aching for his weight on top of her. She yearned for his sweat and his tears as he locked himself within her, driving her past the realm of sanity. He gave her raw and intense noises of pleasure as he plundered her being. Caught in the inescapable throes of heat, she yanked his hair to pull him closer to her. And before she knew it, her moans strengthened into high-pitched screams. And when she came down from her eutrophic cloud, her body shuttered uncontrollably. Her legs quaking, the rest of her body spent. And without an ounce of energy between them, they both collapsed against the sweat-soaked sheets and fell into a deep sleep.

His warm hand roused her in the early morning hours. She woke up to find him fully dressed. "You're leaving already?" she asked as she squinted her tired eyes to focus on him.

He sat on the side of the bed and softly rubbed her belly. "Yes," he whispered. "And although I would love nothing more than to get back in those sheets with you, I need to get going. Can you get dressed and come downstairs? I have some people I want you to meet."

Bianca yawned her yes and then dressed while he waited for her. When she was ready, she followed him down the stairs, where three individuals waited in the front room. One young woman and two men.

"Bianca, these are the people who will be here to assist you in my absence," Victor said.

Bianca smiled and nodded to each one of them as they stood in a row for her inspection.

Victor began his introductions with the most foreboding man Bianca had ever seen. Not only was he bigger than Victor, but he also had a long scar that stretched from his eye to the bottom of his jaw. "This is Theodore Marshall. But you can call him Twitch. He will provide you with personal security. Don't leave this house without him."

Bianca frowned at Victor's high-handed demand.

"Please?" he added. When she nodded in agreement, Victor moved to the next man. "This is Alston Johnson. He will be here a few days a week to handle my financial affairs. There may be some changes in the bank coming soon. He will be here to handle those changes. And this is Grace Taylor. She will be here to provide housekeeping, cooking, and assistance with Uncle Chito."

Bianca smiled at the young woman who couldn't have been older than sixteen. "Nice to meet you. Nice to meet you all." Bianca turned to Victor. "Can I speak with you?"

He ushered her to the front door. She rubbed her hands nervously while she watched him pull on his trench coat and hand his luggage to his driver.

"Just how long are you going to be gone, Victor?" she asked

He stopped moving around her abruptly and faced her directly. His hands enveloped her face and kissed her lips tenderly. "I don't plan to be gone too long, but I didn't want to leave you without support. I can't tell you how much this means to me. I love you. You know that, right?"

She gave him a small hesitant nod that made him frown.

"I promise I'll make this up to you. Everything will be fine. I promise."

CHAPTER 23

AS LUCK WOULD HAVE IT

Despite all of Victor's assurances, absolutely nothing was fine. It took only a week for everything to unravel and fall at Bianca's feet. Bianca would have to strangle Victor the moment he returned.

She would certainly have to begin her list of grievances with the Twitch fellow Victor left to spy on her. He was overbearing, frustrating, and refused to give her an inch of freedom. He practically followed her from room to room. When she pointed this out to him, he simply shrugged and informed her, "Mistuh Carlson tol me neva to tah leave yuh side."

"I'm sure he meant within reason. You can't sleep outside my bedroom."

"I'm jus tryin' tah do my job, ma'am," he shrugged.

Bianca's second grievance with Victor was his accountant, Mr. Johnson. He came every Tuesday and Thursday with bad news. On Tuesday, he clucked his head about everything from Victor's failed business dealings to Victor's debt. And on Thursday, he gave her the most dreadful news she could imagine.

"Madam," he said in a nasal voice that pinched every nerve in

Bianca's body. "I will need some instruction on how to handle these mounting debts and expenses. You know that the Carlson Brothers Bank has failed officially, correct?"

"Ahem. I didn't know it was official. But I suppose you could cut a few expenses."

"We need to sell his assets to offset the damage. I noticed your husband has a few cars under his portico. Perhaps we can begin with those, Mrs. Carlson."

"Eubanks."

"Pardon?"

"Eubanks. I'm still a Eubanks."

"Oh, I just thought with your condition—"

"My what?" Bianca almost hollered.

His tan face turned beet red under her outraged glare. "I apologize. I didn't mean. The girl housekeeper mentioned you were with child. She said that was why you slept so often. Please forgive me, Miss... er..."

"Eubanks."

"Miss Eubanks. I'm so sorry. I'll see what expenses I can cut. I will also try to settle some of these debts with your—Mr. Carlson's creditors." Mr. Johnson scurried away as Bianca continued to glower at his retreating back.

How dare he? She wasn't with child. How dare that little housekeeper insinuate such a thing? She was going to have to kill this little lie right away before it got out of hand.

Bianca wasted no time in finding little Miss Grace, who was so engrossed in peeling potatoes that she didn't hear Bianca's heavy march in her direction. Bianca stood over her as she sat on a small crate in the back of the kitchen.

"Did you tell Mr. Johnson that I was with child?"

Little Miss Grace looked up, squinting to keep the sun out of her eyes. "I-I-I might have, ma'am."

"Why?" Bianca stomped her foot.

"W-well, he was asking me where you was. And he kept wanting to wake you."

"But I'm not with child. What makes you think I am? And what do you know about babies? How old are you anyway?"

Grace looked at Bianca as if she had never been asked such a thing before. "Sixteen, ma'am."

"And?" Bianca stomped her foot again.

"A-and you was sleeping all day like my-my-my sister does whenever she's having a baby, ma'am. And you threw up this morning and yesterday morning."

Oh, my God.

And just like that, a sixteen-year-old filled all the holes in Bianca's logic of the last few days. She thought her morning sicknesses were a fluke. She figured it must have been a strange illness caused by her nervousness about Victor's leaving. There had to be a reason nothing stayed down. Not even bread. And this horrible illness had to cause her long bouts of sleep at the oddest times and in the oddest places.

Then there was the matter of her late monthly. *Oh, God.*

"Ma'am?" Grace called, interrupting Bianca's racing thoughts. "I won't tell nobody else. I promise I won't. Please don't fire me. I need this job bad. I'm trying to keep my mama out of that brothel."

Bianca shook her worries from her face and softened for Grace's sake. "Hush, dear. Nobody's getting fired today. Just keep things between us from now on, okay?"

"Yes, ma'am," she returned with an enormous grin.

Bianca turned back to go into the house with new insight. If this were true, if she were with child, then everything about all of this was no laughing matter. Nothing would be fine, she determined.

THE FARTHER VICTOR drove away from Maryland, the more he learned that it was next to impossible to travel by car as a black man. Dangerous was a better word.

He would never forget the day he so ignorantly stopped at a small restaurant in Kentucky looking to acquire gas and a decent meal. He walked in looking as he did—expecting only to order his food—the owner met him with a shotgun and a not so polite request to go around back for his meal. He should have just gotten into his car and looked for the next stop, but he would risk not finding anything for miles. His car was out of gas, and he was starving. He had to pay triple the amount for his gas and his meal.

After that experience, Victor realized he needed much more than a map and determination. He needed someone who could point out to him where he could gain gas, where he could get a meal the cook didn't spit in, and where he could lay his head down at night without being harassed by the police.

Strangely enough, the answer to his problems came after a fateful escapade with the strangest Negro he had ever met. Victor met him on the night he found a juke joint on the edge of a town he passed through. The handfuls of brown faces were a sight for his sore eyes. Victor drank, ate until his belly was full, and happily slept in his parked car just outside the establishment. But he didn't get to sleep the entire night. The barrel of a revolver and this Negro's wide grin woke him.

"Where you goin', nigga?"

"Pardon me?" Victor asked.

"Oh, shit. Pardon me. *Parlez-vous Français?*" he mocked as he waved his gun around. "I said where you goin', nigga?"

"Get the hell out of my car."

"Naw, you get the hell up out of my car. This here pistol say this my car. Oh, whatcha say pistol? You want his money too? Ahem. He wants yo money too."

"You're not taking my car."

"Oh yes, I am," he said, cocking his gun for emphasis.

Victor reluctantly edged his way out of the front seat. "You know I'm going to find you, and when I do, you better already be dead."

"*Mmhmm*. There is a long line of niggas who want to off me. You betta get to the back of the line. Now your wallet. Throw it in the window."

"Wait till I find you," Victor promised as he threw his wallet inside his car's window.

"And your shoes. Them is some nice shoes. Give em."

Victor shrugged off his pair of two-toned wingtips and threw them in the window. The thief smiled brightly. "Much obliged. I shole love it when you out of town niggas visit us. Have a nice evening." He tipped his hat and drove Victor's Cadillac Town Sedan down a dark and unknown road. Suddenly the heavens opened up, and rain poured down on Victor's head.

Victor cursed as he walked back into the seedy establishment. It was closing down. The female stood at the end of the bar, counting money. She looked up when Victor walked in the door. "So he finally got you?" she asked as drops of rain filtered into the holes in the surrounding roof.

"Ma'am?"

"Red. He finally gotcha. He was eyeing you all night. I can't say I blame him. You coming in here with your nice clothes and nice shoes. He gotcha."

"Where does Red live? Because I will bury him there."

She waved her hand at him. "No, you ain't. He's my nephew and a son of a bitch. But you ain't got nothing to worry about. He'll bring your car back in a day or two."

"I don't have a day or two," Victor said through his teeth. "And he took my money."

"Well, that's as good as gone. Just come back tomorrow and try your hand at a craps game. Till then, you can sleep in the back room. There's a bed. Ain't clean, but it's dry. At least you ain't outside with the critters."

Victor humbly accepted her offerings and planned his revenge on that Red person. He would try his hand at the craps table and win his money back. He would use some tricks Bianca had taught him.

Bianca. God, he missed her. The dismal wooden-planked room suddenly disappeared as his mind rested on her. He closed his eyes, and his dreams found her standing at the door of a church in a sea of white cascading down to the floor. Victor smiled to himself and nuzzled his head against the stained pillow as he continued to dream.

The church and its congregants became clear. His brother stood at his side as we watched Bianca and her father head down the aisle toward him. Just him.

"You look beautiful," he whispered to her when she arrived at his side.

"Thank you," she whispered back, flashing her brilliant smile and her adorable dimples.

"Can I kiss you later?"

Beneath her lace veil, he saw the smirk he had grown to love so much. "When the pastor tells you to, Carlson."

The officiant coughed to gain their attention, and the show began. He hastily repeated his vows to her like a man who was desperate to have what he wanted. And he wanted her. All of her. It was strange. His need to have her was beyond a sensual need. It was a need that grew out of the satisfying effect of completion.

Suddenly, his dream whirred past their wedding and landed at a vision of her swollen with his child. He saw laughter and adoration in her eyes as she nurtured his son. And when his mind finally settled on the old versions of themselves holding hands in the sunset of their lives, he lost it. Tears. Tears, real-life tears, fell from his eyes and dripped onto his pillow.

Victor turned over, and a new dream emerged where he found Bianca again at their wedding. She stood there stoically, wiping the wetness on his face away with her thumb.

The ceremony ended in resounding applause that echoed throughout the sanctuary. They jumped over the traditional broom and then headed down the aisle. He saw a sea of smiles and some frowns as they approached the outside doors. When they arrived at the outside stairs of the church, a blizzard of white rice and applause greeted them. He must have shaken twenty hands and kissed a dozen cheeks. But one hand caught his attention. He paused at its firm grip. He looked up to see a pair of startling blue eyes glaring at him with menacing intensity.

Victor woke from his dream in a cold sweat. Luckily, it was morning. It was the day he would find Red, hurt him badly, and then go home. And not home to Oklahoma. He was going back home to Bianca. He would marry her and figure the rest of it out later.

With a made-up mind, Victor set a plan in motion to get his car, shoes, and money back. He began on the first night shooting craps. He won a gun and five dollars. The next night he won forty-five dollars and a new pair of shoes, better than the ones he had before. They were a bit tight, but at least he was getting somewhere.

On the third night, Victor spotted his Cadillac driving up the road to the juke joint. Red got out of the car with a new suit and his hands in his pockets. Victor wasted no time in confronting him with his new gun just before he walked in.

"Whoa! Big fella!" he cried with his hands in the air. "I broughtcha car back. My Aunty told me you was looking for it. Here ya go. Just joy riding. That's all."

"Where's my money?" Victor growled.

"Now that... we gonna just have to forgive. I spent it all. I ain't gonna lie. *But*, seeing how the whole town talking about your hot hand, maybe we can work something out."

"I ain't working shit out with you."

"But you could win it all tonight. You play poker? I know another spot up the road where the booze is even better. Don't tell my Aunty. Come on, man. Whatcha got to lose?"

His mind. He would lose his mind if he stayed one more night in the shabby back room of Lady Bell's Joint. And he couldn't just keep playing craps every night. He needed bigger pockets so he could win it all.

"All right," he said after he made up his mind. "But first, give me my shoes, my keys, and your gun."

An hour later, Victor and Red arrived at the Smokin' Joe's Saloon. After introductions to the owner and several drinks later, he found himself in the middle of a tournament where the stakes in each round grew higher than he expected. But with every win, he grew more and more determined to win it all.

During the last round, he studied each of his opponents. Across the table, Red's face froze behind his cards. Victor caught the man next to him, flaring his nostrils. Did he have a good hand? Another man's eyes darted from left to right, catching Victor's attention. He had him. In fact, he had all of them the moment he put down a royal flush.

Grunts and groans were heard all over the place as Victor collected his winnings. One character pointed a gun at Victor's head, demanding all the winnings. But Red stopped him cold when he pulled out his own gun and cocked it.

"This here nigga is leaving out of here alive," he said, prompting the harasser to put down his gun.

Victor and Red ran out of there, but not before Victor stopped him. "Where are you going? I'm not going back that way. I'm headed back to Maryland."

"Hey man, I just helped you back there. If it weren't for me, you'd be dead right now."

"If it weren't for you, I'd be in Oklahoma right now."

"Oklahoma, huh? That's where you were goin'? Why didn't you say so? I'm trying to go that way too." He ran around to the passenger side and attempted to get in, but Victor started the car.

"Not in my car. I'm going back to Maryland."

"But you just said Oklahoma. Why ya changing?"

"Not worth it."

"Any dream is worth it, man. What's in Oklahoma?"

Victor didn't know what stopped him from just driving off and leaving Red right there. But something in him made him stop. "Answers. Answers are in Oklahoma. But my woman is in Maryland, so I'm going to Maryland." Victor revved the engine again.

"Hey, wait, now! Looka here, I know I caused you some trouble. But I ain't a rotten guy. Maybe you and me can make a deal. The way I see it, you can't be running down these redneck roads by yourself. You look like a shiny silver dollar out here. It's gonna be more Reds. I say you and I head down there to getcha answers. I watch your back, and when it's all said and done, you give me a few dollars. But you gotta getcha answers, man. That woman... if she a good woman, gonna be there for you when you get back."

Victor eyed several hostile patrons leaking out of the Smokin' Joe's Saloon, hoping to get a second chance at Victor's winnings. He eyed Red's ruddy face and bright smile. "Get in," he said. "And I thought I took your gun from you," he added.

"Well, pretty boy. You lucky. I always keep more than one. You still trust me to ride witcha down to Oklahoma?"

"No. But I will murder you in your sleep if you try me again."

"Oowee! Don't I know it? I just wanna see how this here story you got gonna end. Hey, I neva got cha name. You know mine. Same color as my skin."

"Victor. The name's Victor."

He ripped his hat from his head and flung it on the floor of the car. "Holy shit! Victor? I shoulda known. Only a man named Victor could win that many hands. Oh, we can't lose. We gonna get our answers, and then we got to get that woman, and I'm going to get my money! Oowee!"

Victor shook his head as he drove through the dark night. This was going to be a long and interesting trip.

CHAPTER 24

THE EVER CLEVER MR. SMILEY

Bianca read Mags' threatening letter twice to be sure she read it right. Apparently, news of Victor's disappearance had gotten back to her, and she wanted answers. She had tried to find other ways to get answers from Bianca. First, she sent her favorite enforcer to Victor's house, but Bianca's new shadow, Twitch, met him. When her enforcer came back empty-handed, Mags resorted to other measures. Someone broke into the *Baltimore Beat* to smash various parts of Bianca's printing press and halt all production of her newspaper. Bianca suspected that Mags was behind it. No one else was that evil. Today's note confirmed her suspicion.

I understand that your business is down. As your chief investor, I require your presence before any more accidents occur. -M

Lord, she hated this woman. But Bianca's problems had long eclipsed Mags and her pesky antics. She had finally settled her mind around the tiny baby in her belly. Somewhere and somehow, Bianca developed a love for a tiny being that did nothing but make her throw up and sleep. She also felt an irrepressible need to protect it from the world around her.

And what kind of world would this little person live in? The father had been missing for over two weeks. And even worse, the empire he left Bianca to watch over was crumbling beneath her. Mr. Alton met her with more grim news day after day. He had nagged her so badly that she finally agreed to allow him to sell one of Victor's cars just to keep things running. Victor would kill her when he found out.

But he had better not think about grieving that damned car to her when he left her in the middle of a fire. She had gripes of her own. She would beat him as she recited all of them to him. Then she would kiss him and squeeze him tightly because she missed his obnoxious soul. She wished she knew where he was or what he was doing.

Bianca's mind circulated several scenarios of what was keeping Victor. None of them survived her sleepy disposition. Mags' threats would have to wait. Bianca found the chaise in the front room and collapsed into a deep sleep.

When Bianca woke, she found Uncle Chito humming in his chair next to hers. Since it was still daylight, he entertained himself, looking out the window. "You hungry, Uncle Chito?" she asked him with a yawn.

"Naw. That gal fixed me a plate. When you think my boy coming back?"

"He'll be back soon, Uncle Chito."

"Where he gone?"

"I told you, Uncle Chito, he's out of town on business."

"He done went home, ain't he?" he asked, still looking out the window.

Bianca considered lying to him, but there was no point in lying. "Yes."

He hummed for almost a minute before he said, "You gonna have his baby?"

Bianca lifted her eyes heavenward. Did everyone know? "Yes. Grace must have told you."

"Who Grace? I don't know no Grace."

"Never mind," she said as she stretched her bones.

"I always know'd my boy was gonna have to go back."

Bianca regarded him. She discovered, during her temporary residence in Victor's home, that Uncle Chito had brief windows of clarity. Whenever his window opened, there was always an opportunity to learn something about the man Uncle Chito used to be. "Do you miss home, Uncle Chito?" she asked him.

He chuckled when he turned to her. "Home? I miss home every day."

"It must have been hard leaving everything behind for so long."

"I'd do it all again. We had to protect the boy."

"Is that why you came with him up here? To protect him?"

"*Mmhmm*. Kinta come to me and say... ah... she say... you gotta go with the boy to keep him safe."

"Kinta? Victor's mother's name?"

"*Mmhmm*. She give me my box. Told me to keep it safe. Now looka here, Bianca, you ain't gonna take my box, is ya?"

Bianca smiled but not because he was back to talking about his infamous box. She smiled because somewhere in his mind; he found a place for Bianca's name. She must have reminded him of it at least one hundred times. Finally, it stuck.

"I heard yuh crying in your room last night. Why yuh cry?" he asked.

A rogue tear escaped her eye as she fidgeted her hands in her lap. "I don't know, Uncle Chito. Maybe I'm a little scared. So much happening. I don't think I can stop it all."

"You ain't supposed to! Naw. You ain't supposed to do none of that. Just hold fast. Dats all. You supposed to hold fast. You strong, just like Kinta was. Dats why dat boy loves you. Stand on your own two feet and hold fast, Bianca."

"Thank you, Uncle Chito," she replied. Her tears multiplied down the sides of her face and into her neck.

"I... ah... ah... I think I'm gonna check on my box."

"Yes," she sniffled. "I think it's waiting for you."

"*Mmhmm*. Check on my box," he said over his shoulder as he left the room.

Once he was gone, Bianca wiped her face, stretched her arms, and rose from the chair. "Hold fast," she repeated to herself as she walked out of the room.

VICTOR AND RED arrived in Kingfisher County, Oklahoma, two days after beginning their journey. Surprisingly, Red proved to be a worthy driving companion. His endless stories distracted Victor from his rattling nerves. Still, every mile marker identified how close he was to the place his father forbade him to remember.

It had been a long and hard trip, but it was far better than the one he made when he had left Oklahoma. When he was a child, he was made to travel under the cover of night, hidden beneath a sack of potatoes and a blanket. As a man, he returned to his home state in the bright of day and in plain sight.

But this was not the same Kingfisher County that he left years ago. Smokestacks and oil wells lined muddy roads, clogged with horse-drawn buggies and automobiles. The air itself had changed. The stench of sulfur and other chemical agents filled their nostrils the moment his car entered the city limits. The life and sounds had changed too. He recalled a quiet town. This world had a menagerie of sights and sounds similar to any street in New York City.

"Ohwee, folks making money out here," Red commented under his breath as they drove through the traffic with their eyes bright with wonder.

"Someone is."

"So, where are we going, boss?"

"I'm going to a short business meeting. You can go where you want."

"Whatcha talkin' about? We partners."

"We are not partners."

"Okay. But we are friends. I gave you half of my slice of pie from that stand down the road. I love pecan pie. And then I sat and listened to you talking about yuh woman and yuh mama. And then I told you how my mama sent me to school for all those years, and nothing I eva learned did anything for me. And then I shot that snake and stopped him from biting you while you were pissing by the road a few miles back. So what kinda friend is you?

"All right! Fine. But when we sit down, I'm doing all the talking. Nothing from you. You got it?"

"Got it, boss."

"Just call me Victor. Now that man back there said that Sovereign Oil should be just over here." Victor pointed to a warehouse across from his car. He introduced himself at the gate as Victor Carlson. After the guardsman checked his credentials within, he let them through.

Within seconds, a thin white man in suspenders ran out to greet them. "You must be Mr. Carlson?" the man said as he extended his hand. "Richard Koransky. I'm authorized to speak for the board of directors. We sure are glad to see you. We thought you were a myth. We have our lawyer inside. Is this your lawyer?"

Victor turned to Red, who had magically dusted off his weathered suit jacket and hat. Before he could stop him from doing so, Red answered. "Yes, yes, I am. Randolph Smiley, Esquire."

"This man is not my lawyer," Victor said through his teeth.

Red chuckled as he turned to Richard. "My client has some

concerns about my fee. You know how it is. Ahem. Just show us the way."

Richard led them inside. Victor had tried several times to put Red in check and to shut up, but he kept winking and nodding with that stupid grin. When the room filled with more white men in suspenders, Victor wondered if it was worth shutting up Red.

"Good afternoon, Mr. Carlson. Richard tells me you came a long way. My name is Beaufort Ross. I was the attorney who did the original agreement with your father, Robert Carlson."

"Really?"

"Yes, sir. We dealt with him for years. We didn't learn of your father's death until recently. We thought it was odd that he had been gone for years, yet we were still getting correspondence from him."

"My father's widow," Victor dryly added.

"Ah," Beaufort began before pulling off his spectacles. "Well, you probably don't know this, but we were trying to shift our business so that we can do more excavation."

"When I called, someone told me the business was going under."

The room erupted in laughter. "No, no, no. Crude oil prices might be down because of the economy, but it will go back. Other companies are getting out. But not us. We still want to do business with you and your family. But—"

"But, sir?" Red asked before Victor could.

"Well, after learning that your father had been dead, we researched how to find you. And what we learned was quite interesting."

"Do tell," Red said. Victor gave him a hard kick under the table, but Red merely coughed. "Go on, sir."

"We did quite a search at the recorder's office on your family. Some rich history there. But what was interesting was your trust."

"You have it?" Victor asked.

"We read a hand-written copy. Our transcriber took notes. Here see for yourself."

Red snatched the documents away before Victor had the chance. He got up quickly to distance himself from Victor's menacing glare and began reading. "It says... *hmm*... and *hmm*... Oh!"

"Put that down, Red!" Victor snarled.

"Looks like you gonna have to marry that woman of yours, boss! According to this, you can't lease or title shit. Never could. Your mama put in a provision that required the land to transfer to the wife of your choosing in a life estate and then to the children of your issue."

Victor blinked dumbly as Beaufort Ross nodded his head in agreement. "That's exactly right, Attorney..."

"Smiley," Red answered with a smile. "Attorney Smiley."

"And what law school did you attend?" Mr. Ross asked.

"That would be the noble institution of Howard University College of Law, class of 1915."

He nodded awkwardly and smiled. "Good. Glad Mr. Carlson has you on retainer. Now, Mr. Carlson, we would love to continue our valued relationship with you and your family. Perhaps when you marry we can continue to our lease agreement and we—"

"Lease?" Red asked. "You was leasing this million-dollar land out?" he asked Victor. Before he could answer, he turned to Beaufort and said, "It just so happens that my client is on his way back to Maryland to marry the woman of his dreams soon. Ain't that sumthin'? In the meantime, we should turn our heads to the horizon and look for something on a grander scale."

Mr. Ross frowned. "What do you mean, Mr. Smiley?"

"Ahem. My client has recently decided to move his investments in the crude oil business. Ain't that sumthin'?"

"That is something," Mr. Ross said.

"And a pitiful lease of his family's land just won't do it, oh no, no, no. If you are looking for expansion, then we're looking to be an expansion partner."

An awkward silence filled the room until Mr. Ross broke into laughter. Victor and Red carefully followed along with Mr. Koransky.

"Hot damn! Mr. Carlson, you sure got you a real one right here," Mr. Ross laughed "Yes, you do. All right, then. Let's see what we can negotiate when the time is right. But it's all got to be legal, you hear?"

"Oh, yes. Oh, yes. Legal and sound," Red said as he rubbed invisible money in his hands.

Victor numbly shook everyone's hands as he exited the building.

Red followed close behind but was too busy sharing law school jokes with Mr. Ross. "And then I said, that must be an unborn widow!"

"*Ahh haa!*" Mr. Ross hollered as he slapped his hand on his knee. "Now you look here, counselor. You come back here when you all are ready, so we can talk business."

They continued to share jests as Victor sat in his car, waiting for Red to get in. Once he did, he took off his coat, wiped his forehead, and expelled a lengthy breath. "Whew. Sure is warm in Oklahoma," he said.

"What was that?" Victor yelled, unable to contain his outrage.

"What was what?"

"You. Acting like a lawyer."

"I am a lawyer. Howard University College of Law, Class of—"

"I heard you when you said it. We rode together for hours and you never mentioned that when you aren't stealing people's cars and shoes that you like to practice law!"

"Well... we rode for hours, and you didn't mention that you are the heir of a million-dollar estate, but I ain't mad. Shit, I told you I went to school for years."

Victor leaned his forehead on his steering wheel and exhaled.

"But you should be thanking me right now," Red continued. "And we ain't got time to talk about old-ass shit. We need to be high tailing down this road and get you hitched to that gal. And we need a drink to celebrate. We rich!"

"We are not. Besides, I can't leave yet. I have one more place to go."

CHAPTER 25

A FREEMAN

With Mr. Koransky's guidance, Victor and Red found the small enclave known to the locals as Freeman's Rowe. Victor was glad that it looked nothing like the rest of the town and more like his childhood memories. It was a pocket of green, lush forest and grass with a few modest houses scattered between trees. The pocket community slowly moved with children playing freely as men cut wood and women hung their laundry on the line. Victor's red Cadillac caught everyone's attention right away. All movement ceased as Victor's automobile made its way through the main road.

A young woman had just pulled her last sheet from a clothesline when Victor pulled up next to her.

"Hello, ma'am."

"Sir. You fellas lost?" she asked.

"No, we are looking for someone. My mother and I used to live here, or somewhere around here a long time ago. Kinta Freeman?"

She squinted her eyes at him to focus on his features. "Never heard of her. But if she is a Freeman, my Grandma Tula would know. I suppose I can take you to meet her. She's up that way."

They followed her by foot in the direction of a log cabin sitting at the edge of a stream. An older woman sat on the porch with a patchwork shawl over her shoulders. Her hair was split into two long plaits on each side of her head. She rocked in a rocking chair while fanning at flies until she heard Victor, Red, and her granddaughter approach.

"My Grandma Tula is blind," the young woman whispered to Victor.

"But I ain't deaf," Grandma Tula said. "Who did you bring this way, Fala?"

"Halito, Grandma Tula, these men say they are Freemans."

Victor cleared his throat. "Just me. Hello Ma'am. My name is Victor Carlson. My mother's name was—"

"Kinta Freeman," Tula finished. "So you say."

"You knew her?"

"Maybe. If you are the son of Kinta, what are you doing here?"

Victor blinked, looking for an answer. He stared at her, wishing he could make the reason known, but he couldn't. "I'm not sure I can put it into words."

"You've been lost for a long time."

"Yes," he breathed.

"Come, take a walk with me, son of Kinta," she said as she struggled to stand. Her granddaughter assisted her until she shooed her away. She pressed one hand on her walking stick. "Come, son of Kinta," she called to him.

He pressed her hand inside the crook of his arm to lead her down her wooden stairs.

"Yuh want me to go with yuh, boss?" Red asked behind them.

"No," Tula said without stopping. "Fala, please find a refreshment for our guest. We will be back soon."

They strolled down a dirt path. The evening sun began its retreat behind the trees. A soft wind blew through the surrounding grass. Tula hummed as they walked down their path. But this tune was familiar. He had heard it a million times during his childhood.

"Do you know me, ma'am?" he asked.

"I'm not sure. I can't see you. But I knew Kinta. I suppose if you were a child when you lived here, you wouldn't have known me. I lived on my husband's land. He died recently."

"I'm sorry."

"Nothing to be sorry for. How is Chito?"

Victor smiled brightly. "Chito is good. He's lost some of his memory, but every now and again, he comes to. Can you tell me how you know him? And my mother?"

She stopped her feet, causing him to stop. "Maybe. But first, son of Kinta, I want you to look around you. I want you to breathe the air. I want you to feel wind on your face." When he did it, she asked, "Nice isn't?"

"Yes, ma'am," he answered.

"What you are experiencing is freedom. It feels nice, right? This freedom came with a price. Still does. The currency? Life. So when you look around you, when you breathe the air, see the life that paid for it. What Kinta paid for it and what price she paid for you."

When Victor fell silent within, she continued, "Did your mother ever tell you how we became Freemans?"

"I'm ashamed. I remember something about Indians."

Tula chuckled as she resumed walking. "Youngins don't long for the old way until they become old. All right, I will tell you. Members of the Choctaw Nation owned your oldest ancestor. Just after I was born, the Choctaw signed a treaty with the U.S. Government that granted citizenship to all Negro slaves they owned. We became free. As part of that treaty, they gave some freedmen land to own. Your great-grandfather, Winner Freedman, was one such man."

"*Freedman?*"

"Yes, Freedman at first. Later turned to Freeman. Winner

was a clever soul. Yes, he was. He lived way down that way. I remember him being as tall as you are. He was my great grandfather too."

"Winner?"

"*Mmhmm*. Winner. Funny name for a slave, wasn't it? Especially one owned by the Choctaw. I believe that Granddaddy Winner was bought from a white family down in Texas. I don't know why they called him Winner. But I think his name had something to do with why your mama gave you the name Victor instead of a traditional Choctaw name like the rest of us."

Victor smiled, thinking of Red. He would howl to the moon in laughter if he knew Victor's great grandfather's name was Winner.

"Well, anyway, Winner was not alone on this land. He had a neighbor. A white neighbor named Howard Frazier. My grandmother told me they were good friends. These two friends decided to dig for oil. They figured everyone else was doing it. Well, Winner and Howard dug and dug and dug. And not a damn thing came up. They spent their last penny looking for that nasty mess and nothing. So one day, Mr. Frazier decides to cut his losses. He takes his family east. He agrees to sell his parcel of land to Winner for one dollar. And Winner agrees. But I suppose you can guess what happened next."

"Winner found oil not too long after," Victor answered.

"Yes, he did. It gushed out all over the place when it did. I remember the day. He died not too long after that. But he left a fortune to his son, Papa Issi. It was all over the papers. They all talked about them Negro millionaires down in Oklahoma. It got the entire country's attention, including that of Howard Frazier. Old Frazier cried foul play for the longest, claiming that we tricked him into selling his land. Now I knew Winner was clever, but he wasn't that clever. Howard even took Papa Issi to court. Thankfully, he lost because the land that held the oil was on Winner's side of the land, not Howard's."

"Wow."

"*Mmhmm*. The Fraziers been mad ever since. They moved back here with a vengeance. They have squatted, terrorized, and... even killed to get back what they believe they were owed. Issi tried to sell them back their parcel of land, but they decided that wasn't good enough. They wanted all of it. They were bound and determined to have it all too. Issi's daughter had a beautiful little boy. She doted on him and loved him with every fiber of her being. Then one day, those Fraziers stole that little boy. If you are the son of Kinta, you know the rest."

"Yes, I do. But Ms. Tula—"

"Call me, Cousin Tula."

"Cousin Tula, I want to know why my mother couldn't just leave with me. Why couldn't she just leave all this behind?"

"Because she knew they would never stop until they found her and you, so she had to protect you as best as she could. She sent you on with your father, who lived on the other side."

Victor nodded in somber understanding. "I found out today that she had a trust for me that is strange. She gave my wife a life estate."

"Ah. I remember this. She talked about this with everyone. We all sat at the long table at Papa Issi's house, trying to figure a way around the Fraziers, and this was the only way. We needed to protect you. One day, they would come looking for you. We knew it would happen. So we all agreed to title the land to your wife and then to your children. But Kinta wanted to add the part in the grant's language to say that she prayed you chose well. She wanted you to choose well. Are you married?"

"No. But I have chosen."

"Good. Very good. I'm glad. I hope she has your mother's spirit."

Victor thought of his Bianca and smiled. "Yes, I believe she does. Strong-willed, funny, and very beautiful to me."

"Ah. Good. Now, this is the part where you commune with her."

"Beg your pardon? Her?"

"Your mother. Kinta. She's over there, buried under that tree. Take your time and pay your respects. You came to see her, didn't you?"

Victor stared ahead at the oak tree. A strong wind kicked up and blew his hat right off his head. He felt his entire life circle under that tree. Without moving, he asked, "What happened to my mother, Cousin Tula?"

Her blind eyes closed sadly. "Let us not dwell on sadness, son of Kinta. Let us cherish the beauty of today. I can tell you this. Hearing your voice, feeling your hand, I can tell you made it all worth it. It was a good sacrifice. If her spirit is here, she can now finally rest. She will see you here, alive and well. Continue to live the Freedman's life, son of Kinta. Make your way without compromise."

He nodded with new courage and made his way to his mother's grave. His knees weakened with every step until he fell. A rush of raw tears left him as his heart opened with a rush of joy and sadness. He had finally found her. He hoped and prayed she felt the same.

When he stood up, he wiped his tears, took Cousin Tula's arm. After long bouts of silence, Victor thought of something Tula said, "Cousin Tula?"

"Yes?"

"You mentioned that the Fraziers moved back from up north a long time ago. Where did they move?"

"Oh, most of them live out on Marbury Road. It's quite a few of them."

Victor froze suddenly, causing his blind cousin to fret.

"Are you all right, boy?"

"It's nothing. I just realized that I need to get back to Baltimore, quick, fast, and in a hurry."

CHAPTER 26

THE END OF THINGS

Three days later, she was surprised she didn't wake up nauseated. And she didn't feel the need to run to the toilet after eating something as simple as a slice of toast. It was going to be a good day, she determined.

"Bout time," she said to the little one in her tummy as she guzzled down her orange juice. "I'm glad you finally see my side of things. Now can we go on to work and get to the business at hand?"

"Going to work, ma'am?" Twitch asked from behind her in the kitchen.

Bianca rolled her eyes before she turned around. "Yes. But don't worry about coming along. I have a few stops to make. I need to hire someone to fix our printing press, and then pick up some supplies downtown."

"I'll wait for you outside in the car," he said over his shoulder.

So she would have to deal with Twitch's hovering another day. That wasn't so bad. Bianca was determined to look over the countless things that had gone bad since the day Victor had left and just have a good day. The sun was shining brightly, and her little baby had settled in her belly. This day was made just for her and no one was going to ruin it.

Bianca walked out the door down the stairway to the car at the bottom of the hill. She saw Twitch on the right, waiting patiently outside of one of Victor's cars. And on the left of the street, she saw someone who she knew was going to try to ruin her good day. Wesley marched up the stairway to meet her in a fury.

"Where is my brother?" he demanded as he advanced upon her. His aggression caught Twitch's attention, who wasted no time in catching up to him.

"At this moment, no," Bianca replied evenly.

Twitch inserted himself between them by creating a massive wall blocking Wesley's reach.

"It's all right, Twitch. This is Mr. Carlson's brother... the other Mr. Carlson. He's harmless, trust me. I'll meet you in the car." Twitch removed himself, but not before bestowing an intimidating glower in Wesley's direction.

"What's he? Your bodyguard?" Wesley asked.

"Something like that. What do you want, Wesley?"

"I want to know where my brother is. He's been missing for days. Our life and blood shut down last week. And he has been missing in action, leaving me to pick up all the pieces."

"What happened to your Mr. Marbury?"

"Don't mock me, Miss Eubanks. He had his own apprehensions about purchasing the bank. And seeing how he was treated at your engagement party, I can't say that I blame him."

"Wesley... I don't know you that well. But from what I have seen, I can tell that you suffer from a condition called naiveté. Some might call it stupidity, but I won't be crass. Money talks. If your Mr. Marbury wanted to buy the bank, he would have bought that damn bank regardless of how he feels about the owners. But who am I? Just the woman you tried to pawn off on your brother to further your elaborate scheme?" Bianca moved around him as he stood there with his jaw on the ground.

"Wait!" he called to her just before she reached Twitch's side. He turned to walk over to them. "I apologize. I have not been myself for some time now. You have to understand that despite our differences, my brother has never left my side. It's not like him to do this. My world is crashing down around me and I just need my brother."

Bianca's annoyance with Wesley quickly converted to sympathy. "He'll be back soon. I can tell you that much," she offered him.

"Is he in Oklahoma?"

"I—"

"I know he went there. It's something he has wanted to do his entire life. I guess I thought eventually he would forget about it. I just never thought he would leave me."

"He left me too. But as a wise man just told me, it's time to stand on your two feet and hold fast. There will be better days ahead. New opportunities, new deals, and other businesses."

He swallowed before giving her a tight smile. "So you really want to marry my brother? As he is?"

Bianca let out a snort. "He'll do, I suppose."

"I see he has chosen well. Keep him on his toes, Miss Eubanks."

"I'll do my best," Bianca returned with a knowing smile.

He turned to his car and then stopped short. "Oh, yes. I would stay away from my mother if I were you. She's not been herself, either."

It was on the tip of her tongue to tell him that she would beg to differ, but he was already gone. Of course, she was going to stay the hell away from Mags. She had planned on keeping herself as far away as she could from the old crone. Her plans today were simple. Go to the *Baltimore Beat*, hire someone to fix the printing press, and then pick up some items. None of her planned tasks had anything to do with dealing with someone who had it out for her.

Bianca pulled out her notepad and jotted down a list of items she planned to pick up from the market while she sat in the passenger seat next to Twitch. She was so engrossed in her notes she didn't hear him call her.

"Ma'am?"

"Hmm? Are we there yet?"

"Yes, ma'am. But you are gonna want to see this."

Bianca's eyes followed his pointed finger in the direction of the *Baltimore Beat*. She froze in horror as she watched her desks and equipment thrown out into the street. Strewn papers littered the ground under the feet of Kizzy and Miss Ginny. They, too, watched in horror as gargantuan men in uniforms flung typewriters, boxes, and several personal items.

Bianca jumped out of the car, screaming, "What is going on!"

"Boss lady!" Kizzy exclaimed. "They say the owner sent them. They gave us this paper." She handed Bianca a piece of paper with the largest letters that made everything clear for her: EVICTION.

"Who's the owner?" Kizzy asked.

"Margaret Edison." Bianca snarled.

"Mags?" Ms. Ginny hollered after finding her voice. "She bought the place? Course, she did. She probably owns this one's soul too."

"Shut up, Ms. Ginny!" Bianca yelled back. "I'm sick and tired of all your negative comments. Yes, I entered a deal with the devil. Yes, I took money that I can't pay back. And yes, because I can't deliver on what we bargained, she is evicting me. And another thing, I'm sick to death of your snotty comments about Victor. He's my decision. Not yours. All I need from you is a smile and subtle nudge in the right direction!" The sounds of wood breaking and metal clanging against the ground went off around them. The wind kicked up loose paper in miniature cyclones as Ms. Ginny and Bianca stared at one another.

"All right," Ms. Ginny replied with a half-smile. "Glad to know you're still in there, girl. I thought for a minute you lost your grit. But I see you still got it. Now enough of all this. Let's stop these fools from destroying our life's work."

Bianca, Kizzy, and Ms. Ginny did their best to stop the men from going in the building, but they just pushed the women out of the way and continued plundering the *Baltimore Beat*. Bianca's body crumpled in a hopeless heap just before the cracking sound of a bullet pierced the air. Every person within a fifty-yard radius froze in place and turned to the person with the smoking gun.

Twitch brought his arm down and addressed the men first. "Get the fuck out of here."

"Hey, we don't want no trouble," one pillager said, before dropping a box to the ground. "Just trying to do what they paid us to do."

The rest of them followed by forfeiting their items. They shuffled themselves into their truck as Bianca, Kizzy, Ms. Ginny, and Twitch watched.

"Our boss will just send us back. You might want to get things right with the owner," the driver said before cranking the engine.

"Yeah? Well, tell your boss she can kiss my narrow ass!" Bianca hurled from the sidewalk as they drove away.

"Bianca?" she heard a familiar voice call. She turned to find Hiram walking across the street. He had probably witnessed her exchange with the men.

She rolled her eyes openly. "What are you doing here, Hiram?" Twitch, Kizzy, and Ms. Ginny had already begun picking up items off the street.

"Good Lord, what happened? Is this about rent?"

"Oh my God. Please leave, Hiram. I have better things to do than defend myself to every damn body."

"My apologies, Bee. I can see you are busy. I-I just came to apologize for the other day. I shouldn't have said those things to you. And as your friend, I should have come to your engagement party. I—"

"Yes, yes, Hiram. Apology accepted. You missed a smashing party. Now, will you help Twitch pick up that desk over there?"

He nodded and joined in the cleanup. They all moved in silence until Bianca said, "And it isn't about rent. I don't owe that —woman a thing. What I owe her is a piece of my mind. And that is exactly what I will give her. Hiram, I need your car."

"I'll take you, ma'am," Twitch said with finality. He had proven that he would not be stepped over or left behind, no matter how many times Bianca tried.

"Twitch, thank you, but I really need you here. Those men could come back, and I can't just leave these ladies unprotected. And Hiram can come with me. See? Just this once, you can leave my side. I promise it will be fine. I'm just going to have an itty bitty chat with the owner. Just a business matter."

He narrowed his eyes at her speculatively before he hesitantly nodded. "All right."

BIANCA SHOT out of Hiram's car as if the devil were on her back to head straight for Mags' house. This was the final straw. This was the last time she would let Mags play with her life. First Daisy, and now this? Mags would see her anger today.

She was nearly at her door when Hiram pulled her arm back. "What are you doing?" he whispered. "You can't just go storming in there."

Bianca responded by shoving Hiram with all her might out of her way as she marched up to Mags' door. "Go home, Hiram!" she barked over her shoulder, as she zealously rang Mags' doorbell.

Mags opened the door herself. Bianca didn't have time to note the distressed look on her face or the fact that she was wearing her house robe. All Bianca cared about was telling her on which train she could go to hell on.

Bianca sucked in a large quantity of air to begin her planned tirade, but Mags stopped her by putting up her hand.

"Just come in," she said.

Bianca followed her for the moment into her foyer but decided not to take another step forward. "I need not go any farther. What I have to say to you, I can say right here." Mags turned around, revealing her ashen face. She clutched her robe to her body as Bianca eyed her untidy appearance.

"What the hell is wrong with you?" Bianca asked.

"I-I-I haven't been feeling well."

"Being evil will do that to you," Bianca supplied.

"I may be evil, but I'm not wrong. I had no other way to get your attention. You've ignored every single letter I sent."

"Well, you got my attention!" Bianca's voice raised several octaves. "What is it you want to know? You want to know where Victor is? I am not telling you. You want to know why I haven't married him yet? I'm not telling you. But let me tell you this. I'm done with all of this shit and I'm done with you. You will give me the deed to the *Baltimore Beat* or I will go to the authorities and tell them what you did to Daisy."

A pained look flashed across Mags' face as she listened to Bianca's tirade. Before Bianca finished, Mags walked away and into her front parlor. She stumbled to the nearest sofa and almost collapsed on it. "Do you think you can take your diatribe down a few octaves? As I said, I'm not feeling well. I know you're angry, Bianca, but the only reason I did it was to wake you up."

"I know I've asked this at least a hundred times. But why the hell do you care who he marries? The bank is shut down. From what I can tell, Mr. Marbury is a liar. He was never going to buy the bank. And as I said, they shut down the bank. It's over."

Mags let out an exasperated puff of air and mumbled to herself. "I might as well tell her," Bianca heard her say under her breath. "Sit down, girl. I would offer you a drink, but my staff has left. I can't afford to pay them anymore. So if you want something, you better go into the kitchen and get it yourself."

"I'm fine, thank you."

Mags tightened her robe to her chest and then mused over her hair. "There is so much you don't know, and I don't even know where to begin. But... because I feel my life closing in on me, I might as well tell someone. Why not let that someone be you? I suppose you could say my part in this begins where you are. I was in love with a man who was in love with someone more beautiful and far richer than me."

Bianca did not hide the rolling of her eyes. It was for Mags' benefit.

"Scoff if you like. But you don't know the pain of years of loving a man who's heart does not belong to you. Especially when that man is your husband."

"Victor already told me he's a love child."

"Is that what he calls himself?" she snorted. "You can romanticize anything, I suppose. I guess it is easy for him to tell a lovely story about his beautiful mother. And how everybody—white, black, and Indian—wanted to marry her. But she wouldn't because she was smitten with my damn husband. I'm not sure how you put flowers on my tormented soul as I suffered their affair for years. He wasn't a love child, dear girl. Not to me. I hated him."

Bianca watched one tear escape from Mags' eye as she mentally walked through her past. "I had begged God for his mother's death. I dreamed of it. I never had the courage to do it, but I did have the courage to make things difficult for her. I knew that the Freemans had enemies. So I took advantage of what I knew."

"One enemy, in particular, had a bone to pick with Victor's grandfather," Mags continued. "He wanted revenge and I told him how to get it. I introduced the idea of kidnapping Kinta's precious little boy. I know it was wrong. It and many other things, I am prepared to go to my maker about, so you can keep your judgment to yourself, Ms. Bianca."

Bianca bristled as she stood by the window. "Fine, I'll keep it to myself. Carry on." She wanted answers. And being quiet was the best way to get them.

"My plan backfired because Kinta found the boy and brought him to live with my husband and me. And Robert took the boy in. Like a damned fool. We settled here in Baltimore and my life became worse than before. She died not soon after. But that made things worse. Because my husband became obsessed with her memory. He spent the rest of his life openly comparing me to her. I was never good enough and the son I bore him wasn't good enough. He favored Kinta's bastard over my legitimate son."

Another pained expression crossed Mags' face. "My husband, Robert, also liked the fact that he had control of Victor's money. He built his entire empire on that boy's inheritance. And just when he thought the boy's money had depleted, he found out something interesting in the letter of Victor's inheritance. He found out Victor is far richer than he originally thought. And isn't that something Miss Eubanks? When you first met me, we discussed your spinsterhood at length. Who knew you would end up being engaged to the richest Negro in the United States?"

"That-that isn't important right now. What I want to know is, why me?"

"Because his mother tailored things so he never could inherit her most wealthy asset. She kept it out of his hands to keep him safe, I imagine."

"Safe from whom?"

"From me. His father. And safe from her enemies."

"So if he can't inherit, why are we even talking about this?" Bianca asked impatiently.

"Because you can. Kinta's lands, which are rich in crude oil, will transfer to Victor's wife and children."

"Ah..."

"Ah is right, you lucky girl."

"But I'm not married to Victor. He left town a long time ago. He left me and my—he left me all alone. So there is nothing here to trouble me over. He probably found another woman somewhere or something."

Mags began a coughing spell until it looked like she would fall off the chair, but somehow she regained her composure. "Miss Eubanks... you and I both know, Victor will be back for you and his child."

Bianca's eyes darted to hers in surprise.

"I know everything, Miss Eubanks. And you know the help loves to share when you throw a few coins their way."

"That damn Grace," Bianca mumbled.

"Miss Eubanks... it may be over for the bank and me, but none of this is over for Kinta's enemies. And that is why you are here."

"What?"

"I lured you here to save my own hide. I suggest you prepare yourself for what will come next."

"What are you talking about?"

"Mr. Marbury—"

"Mr. Marbury? The man who's buying the bank?"

Mags chuckled. "You and Victor were too smart for that little ploy. He was never going to buy the bank. It was all a ruse. But he is here for other reasons. He wants that land, and he will do anything to get it, I'm afraid. Even taking Victor's precious Bianca."

"*What?*"

"I-I—" Mags' words froze in her throat as her body tightened. She gripped Bianca's arm and collapsed on the floor at Bianca's feet.

After two seconds of watching Mags' taunt body, a startling conclusion came to her mind. "Oh, my God. You're having a heart attack!" Bianca should have seen the signs in the beginning. She had seen plenty of heart attacks while working in her father's hospital. Bianca scrambled to the kitchen, remembering her father's advice in search of aspirin. Bianca ran through Mags' empty house in a panic, searching for something the woman probably didn't have. She ripped open drawers, hoping to save Mags' miserable life. She was so busy in her pursuit that she didn't hear the front door opening and closing. She didn't hear the footsteps in the front parlor. It was not until she arrived back with the pills did she find the intruder standing over Mags' body with a sinister grin.

Bianca ignored him as she ran to Mags' side. She did her best to push the pills into her mouth. She pushed her hands down on her chest, trying to remember her father's advice, but her damned body refused to respond.

"Oh my God," Bianca hoarsely whispered as Mags' life dissolved before her eyes. "She's dead."

CHAPTER 27

MR. MARBURY

"So she is," she heard Mr. Marbury say behind her. From her position on the floor, her eyes locked onto his spurred brown boots. They moved up the length of his pant leg to his belt buckle and then right into his startling eyes.

"Now that she is out of our way, you and I can have a chat about your future intended," he said.

She stumbled backward, crawling on her hands to get as much distance as she could. She scrambled up enough to run, but she didn't make it far. Mr. Marbury had already plucked her from the floor and held her against his chest.

"No!" she screamed as she earnestly fought against his tight grip.

He muffled her with his callused hand. "All right now. Calm down. You and I will walk out of here peacefully. You better not make a stir, you hear me?"

She nodded, and as a reward for her acquiesce, he put her down in front of him.

"Good girl. Now, we will walk out this door, you and me. And you will not make a sound or even put up a struggle. Do you understand me?"

Bianca nodded again. He moved around her to open Mags' front door. She eyed his back and made the impulsive decision to kick her leg out as hard as she could into the dead center of his legs. Thank goodness she wore pants that day. Her assailant keeled over in front of her from the pain she caused to his groin. However, he was now blocking the front door, leaving Bianca with no other recourse than to run farther into the house.

She ran into the kitchen headed toward the back door, but once again, she got snatched away before she could reach its handle. Their silent but violent struggle ransacked the kitchen and pushed them into a room filled with bottles of wine. Somehow, Bianca gained distance from him and yanked down an entire shelf filled with bottles. With the sound of crashing and his groans of pain behind her, she searched the area for a way out and found it in the form of a set of stairs leading down to a cellar. And yet again, before she could leave, a hand from the ground reached out and bit into her ankle. She fell flat onto a floor littered with broken glass and spilled champagne. Shards broke through her skin as he dragged her against the floor.

Bianca released a pained cry as she felt her strength leave out of her. This could not be the end. It couldn't. He could not have won this easily. She pleaded for God to help her, and He answered when an unbroken bottle rolled toward her hand. With no further thought, Bianca grabbed its handle, and with all the momentum she could muster, she swung the bottle around. She heard only a loud clink and his skull hitting the ground.

After that, the sound of her heart beating rang in her ears. But there was no time to waste; he wasn't dead. His chest was still moving. When he came to, he would come looking for her. Bianca needed to get out of there fast, but not before she retrieved a particular item. With Mr. Marbury groaning on the floor, Bianca took a risk and leaped over his body to make her way into Mags' office. After she rifled through some papers, she finally found what she had been looking for—the deed to the *Baltimore Beat*.

Outside, Lafayette was still unaware that a madman was chasing her. She ran aimlessly with everything she had in her, unsure of how far she would get, until a car drove up beside her.

"Bianca?"

"Hiram? Thank God!" she screamed before yanking open his door and jumping in.

Thankfully, Mr. Marbury hadn't given her chase. He was probably still knocked out, which meant that Bianca had only so much time to get back to the house and hide.

By the time Hiram reached Victor's home, he had exhausted all arguments as to why he should go in with her.

"No, no, no, Hiram. I'm sure Twitch is here by now. Just go home. Take care of Harmony and—just go," she briskly said over her shoulder as she ran from his car and up the stairs.

When she crashed inside the foyer, she spotted Grace coming down the stairs with an empty basket. "Grace! Is Twitch here?"

Grace gave Bianca that startled look that she often gave when she wasn't sure if she had done something wrong. "Um, no, ma'am."

"No? Shit. Okay, you have the rest of the day off today. So just get your things and go."

"Am-am-am I fired?"

"What? No, you aren't fired, girl. Just—" Bianca's eye caught Mr. Johnson rounding the corner to go up the stairs to Victor's study. "Mr. Johnson! What are you doing here?"

He gave her a confused look through his spectacles. "It's Tuesday. I review the books on Tuesday."

"Oh, yes. Tuesday. Well, I have given you both the day off. So if you please just enjoy the day and go... right now."

Grace spoke next. "But I still got to fix Mr. Chito's lunch. Is I'm fired cause I told everybody about you having a baby?"

Bianca shook her head before declaring, "I will see to Uncle Chito's lunch and—"

"And I have prepared a report for you to review today, Mrs. Carlson. Something has to be done about your husband's creditors—" Mr. Johnson interrupted.

Bianca stopped his chattering by marching over to him to give him an impolite nudge and in the door's direction. She did the same for Little Miss Grace. "Yes, yes, yes, we will all be in the poorhouse in no time. And no, Grace, I am not firing you. You should work on some discretion or even some loyalty if you intend to stay in service here. But that is neither here nor there right now. All I want for both of you to do is go home, smell the fresh air, and not come back for... the rest of this week." Bianca said the last part as she pushed Mr. Johnson's briefcase into his arms. She then ripped Grace's purse and coat from the coat stand and mushed them both in her arms. And with a bright smile, she closed the door in their perplexed faces.

Bianca collapsed her back against the closed door and let out a lengthy breath. And then a thought came to her mind. "Uncle Chito!" Bianca ran up the stairs to his room. She mustn't alarm him, but she needed to get him to see that they were both in danger. Bianca found him sitting by the window looking through the curtains.

"Where's my lunch?" he asked her when she walked in.

"Um... Uncle Chito. I don't have your lunch but—"

"I want my lunch. Where's that gal? She got my lunch?"

"I gave her the day off. But I can have your lunch ready later, but first, you have to listen to me." But Uncle Chito turned his attention back to the window, humming his usual tune and ignoring her. "How am I going to say this?" she muttered under her breath as she paced his bedroom floor. "Uncle Chito, some man is on his way here to steal your box."

"What? Who? Who tryin' tuh take my box? He betta not come in here!" Uncle Chito rose and pulled out a revolver from under his bed. He held his revolver in one hand and his box in the other. "Let's go get 'em!"

Bianca's eyes bucked wide as she watched him barrel out of the room. "Yes, let's go get them. When this is all over, remind me to say something to your nephew about allowing a senile old man a weapon. But we will work all that out later. Okay, Uncle Chito, let's get the car and get out of here."

They ran down the stairs and headed straight for the foyer, unaware of the visitor seated quietly in a chair in the front room. It was not until they heard his spine-tingling voice behind them did they stop their panicked movements.

"Going somewhere?" Bianca looked past Uncle Chito and found Mr. Marbury patiently waiting for them. "Your house girl left the kitchen door unlocked. You should be mindful of that. Someone could easily break-in."

Uncle Chito wasted no time in approaching Mr. Marbury, and poor Bianca wasn't in any position to stop him from doing so. "I know yuh. I know yuh! And I todja yuh can't have my box, Frazier." He aimed and pulled the trigger. Unfortunately, he was a poor shot. He shot his gun three times and all he accomplished was Mr. Marbury's aggressive advancement in his direction.

Mr. Marbury knocked the gun from Uncle Chito's hand and clocked him with his fist. Poor Uncle Chito crumbled to the ground as Bianca screamed in fright.

"No!" she screamed as Marbury pulled out his switchblade and reached for Uncle Chito.

"Yeah, you know me, old man," he said to Uncle Chito's unconscious body. "You know me. Now let's see what's in this damn box." Mr. Marbury pressed his knife against the small copper lock, releasing the lid. He reached his hand inside to rifle through its contents. He flung papers and photographs to the floor until he found four stacks of cash. "Ah. So this is why he didn't want anyone to get his box. This'll do for a while until that bastard shows up."

He threw the empty box over his shoulder and looked to find

Bianca, who was staring at him with her heart pounding in her chest. "Now, I asked you politely back there to join me. I didn't go through all the trouble of getting rid of old Magsy for you to be rude."

"You killed her?"

"A few drops of cyanide in her tea was just enough to wipe that smug smile off her face. She was in the way, anyway. Now I was real nice the first time. But I won't be so nice this time. I wonder if you will scream the way your friend did. What was her name? Rose?" Snapping his fingers with an awful smile, he said, "Daisy. Pretty Miss Daisy. Are you going to scream like her? I hope you do. Because I will make that son of a bitch sorry he was born."

VICTOR DROVE toward Baltimore with the devil on his back, trying his best to make it home. After firmly confirming that Mr. Marbury was never a Marbury and was always a Frazier, he had an unshakable fear for Bianca's wellbeing. Although he had left her in Twitch's hands, he still needed to put his arms around her to assure himself of her safety.

Victor and Red turned down the road leading up to his home, noticing the eerie quiet.

"Something goin' on. That's your place, boss?" Red asked.

Victor couldn't answer. His feet were already out of the car. His ears heard the screams from the bottom stair. Bianca. Victor's feet crossed three steps at a time to get to the door, praying he wasn't too late.

Locked. The door was locked. Victor struggled with his keys as his ears cringed under Bianca's screams. When he couldn't find the damned key, he lifted his foot and, with all his might, kicked the door wide open.

Inside, he saw his uncle lying on the floor near the stairs. He searched, and to his horror, he found Marbury standing in the middle of the front room near the fireplace. He had a fierce grip on Bianca's shoulders. His switchblade threateningly pushed into her neck. Victor took one look at Bianca's face, swollen and wet with tears, and he knew Marbury would die on this day.

"Don't come any farther!" Marbury shouted. "So you finally show your face. I thought I would have to take this one with me. I was wrong. All I had to do was touch one hair on this little's one head and I draw you out. I wonder what reaction I'll get if I carve a nice letter into her cheek. Or what if I slice this belly of hers?" To Bianca, he said, "Oh, he doesn't know, does he? You mean he leaves you high and dry at the mercy of a madman, and you didn't have the mind to tell this nigger he is about to be a father?"

"No time," Bianca struggled to say.

Red lifted his revolver and pointed in Marbury's direction. "You want me to put a hole in his head, boss?"

Marbury replied by pushing his blade into Bianca's neck, causing her to struggle against him.

"Stand down, Red."

Red reluctantly sheathed his gun inside his arm holster. "Ain't no niggers round here," he muttered.

"All right, Marbury," Victor yelled. "Let's talk. But let her go first."

"Now that would be stupid. So you can execute me right here? No, I won't be letting her go when I know how much she means to you. No, you and I will negotiate right here, right now."

"What the hell is going on?" shouted a voice that came from Victor's brother, Wesley. He stood there with his mouth agog as his eyes tried to believe that Mr. Marbury could attack a defenseless woman.

"Wesley, get out of here," Victor said.

"Victor, I just found my mother dead in her home not an hour ago and now this? Mr. Marbury? What are you doing?" Wesley asked again.

"I'm making sure that I get what I came for, Wesley Carlson! That's what I'm doing. I tried to tell that to your dumb mama, but she wouldn't listen. And look where she is now."

"He poisoned her, Wesley!" Bianca gasped."

"Shut up, bitch! Now, Victor, are you going to give me what's mine, or am I going to slice this slut?"

"What makes you think I have something to give? The bank's closed. I'm sitting on a mountain of debt. It's all gone."

"Don't play games, boy!" he snarled. "You know what I came here for." he snarled. "The same thing my family was cheated out of years ago."

"I will not go into old wives' tales with you. Not here and not now. Our families have been enemies for far too long. Let it end between us. Let's talk. But you have to let my woman go."

"Talk," Marbury snorted. "You're a Freeman, all right. Ain't no talking. Ain't no deal. I want every parcel of that land deeded over to me today."

"I'm sure Mags told you that that is impossible since I don't own it. I can never own it. So all of this was a futile exercise of my patience."

"Mags!" Marbury scoffed. "All she did was lie to me. She made up this fucking charade about the bank and all it did was slow me down. I should have done this a long time ago. We would have gotten down to business from the start. But I suppose you and I have come down a long road, haven't we? We were destined to meet again. You remember me, don't you?"

The room filled with staggering silence.

"You've gotten old. I didn't know at first."

Marbury chuckled. "I suppose you're right. Took you long enough. I thought your senile uncle would give it away. Mags figured you were too young to remember my face. But I sort of think it's hard to forget the man who ties you to a tree. Do you remember that day, little Freeman? I do."

Victor's eyes turned cold as he watched Marbury smile.

"Can you believe that I had made it to twenty and had never

lynched a nigga? My daddy was too soft on yawl even back then. He didn't want to string you up like I did. I wanted to watch you die for the hell of it. But he said he was just going to send a message."

"What happened to my mother after I left?" Victor asked.

"Humph," Marbury shrugged. "I guess you could say I finally got my chance once you were gone."

Blinding rage lifted Victor's gun. He pointed it. Pulling the small hammer back, one bullet slipped into the destined chamber, waiting to meet its fatal appointment. And when the crack of a bullet sounded off, he saw Marbury's arms fall limp at his sides. Bianca dashed away from him as his face settled in a mask of shock. He looked straight at Victor and fell backward against the bookshelf behind him. His back slid down until he landed in a seated position. His eyes remained wide open.

Victor blinked in confusion. His gun had never fired. He looked to his left, and Red shook his head, no, as to say not him. Red raised his hand and pointed to the other side of the room. Victor followed his finger's direction until his eyes found Uncle Chito standing there, with his gun still smoking.

A tear slid down his weathered cheek as he stood there frozen in place. "He killed Kinta," he said with his hand still extended.

It was Red who sprung into quick action. He gently relieved Uncle Chito's gun from his hand. He sat him down in a nearby seat and then closed all curtains and shutters. He did his best to shut the front door.

While he and Wesley did their best to roll Marbury's body into Victor's Oriental rug, Bianca crashed into Victor's arms. He crushed her to his body, thanking God for her safe return to him. He smothered her wet face with kisses.

"Are you really having my baby?" he hoarsely whispered.

"We need to hire a new housekeeper. The one you left me with has a big mouth."

He wasn't sure what she was talking about, he was just happy he had her back. "Whatever you want, dimples," he said as he kissed her intensely.

"Hey, you two lovebirds want to take a break?" Red asked, interrupting their blissful reunion. "Any ideas for what to do with this body? I can't be caught with no dead white man."

"Who's this character?" Bianca asked pointedly in Red's direction.

He took one look at Red, recalling all that they had endured, "He's my new lawyer. And friend." To Red, he said, "I'm not sure what we can do, but go to the authorities."

"Are you crazy? We'll all be in the clink before the sun goes down," Red returned.

"Cremate. We could cremate him," Twitch said.

"Bout time you showed up," Bianca said. "How did you get in? Where've you been?"

"I came in from the back door. It was unlocked. Ma'am, when you didn't come back, I went to that rich lady's house and then when I saw she was dead, I came here. I'm sorry, ma'am. But if you let me, I will get rid of this sack of shit for you myself."

"None of that will be necessary," said a tall white man who entered the room behind Twitch. When all the guns in the room raised and pointed in his direction, he lifted his hands in surrender. "Hey, I don't want no trouble."

"Who the hell are you?" Bianca asked.

"Charles Frazier. His younger brother," he said as he pointed to Marbury's rolled-up body.

CHAPTER 28

A FRAZIER

His name was Charles. He was the youngest of eight brothers. His mother, June Frazier, had instructed him to find his older brother, Edward, months ago and bring him home. When he found Edward in Baltimore, he was shocked to learn that Edward had adopted a false name and was on a one-man mission for revenge against the Freemans. His father had adopted this same cause. His own obsession had ravaged his soul and isolated him from his family. Legend had it that Charles' grandfather had the same condition and so did his father before him.

And where did these obsessions with the Freemans lead them? Nowhere, as far as Charles and his mother were concerned. These obsessions had stolen them from their ability to live life, love their wives, and hug their children. All Charles' life, he heard everything about the Freemans. The Freemans had this. The Freemans had that. He had often wondered what life would be like if they didn't discuss the Freemans. Would his father have been more loving?

His mother would have certainly been a happier woman.

Charles' father's hostility and lack of reason had changed her from a free spirit to a woman who was constantly locked in a state of fear.

So when his mother learned that Edward had taken on the same cause his father had and his father had before him, she begged Charles to stop him. And he had tried. He really had. But Edward was blind to anything but vengeance. He had a look in his eyes that Charles had known very well. There was no stopping Edward. Just like there was no stopping his father or his father before him.

As Charles stood amid strangers, he stared at Edward's body as the blood drained from him. He recalled the days that lead up to this. He had found Edward in his hotel room under a stack of papers. All of his papers contained long paragraphs of repeated nonsense about the Freemans, their legal ties to the oil industry, and their purported mission to destroy all Fraziers. Charles recalled what Edward had said to him after being confronted about his behavior.

"It's all here, Charles! It's all here in black and white. They fixed things to take away our legacy!" Edward had snarled vehemently.

"It may be true," Charles had returned. "It might all be true. But what I am telling you and what you refuse to see is that none of this matters. Mama June and I don't care about this. We just want you back. The rest of our brothers want you home. Hell— your wife wants you home. This shit killed our daddy, and I'll be damned if I let it happen to you too."

"You don't understand, Charles. You were too young. You don't know."

"I remember. You forget I was the same age as that boy you all took. And then, what you did to his mama? I would say it's all about even."

"I did it for you! For us! For the Fraziers! I don't understand why you can't see it?" Edward screamed at Charles. But Charles couldn't hear anymore. This ranting and raving about the same thing had become the backdrop to his life, and he was tired. His brother's mind was gone. So when he saw his brother's body rolled up in a carpet, he didn't react the way one would expect him to. Not when he died that day in the hotel.

"What are you going to do," Victor asked him, breaking his thoughts. He, along with three other men, still pointed guns in his direction.

He looked down upon Edward grimly, "Take him home. My mother would want him buried in our family cemetery. I'm afraid he was obsessed with something the rest of us are not. I'm sure you've heard stories, but all of us Fraziers are not the same. We're proud, hardworking people. I know over the years we've had our differences, but honestly, most of us just want peace."

Victor finally lowered his gun. "As do we. We want our own peace and freedom. But I'm not sure what will stop the next Frazier from coming up here and terrorizing us again?"

"I can only hope for the best. I can't speak to the future. Our history is too long."

"Then let's end it," he replied.

They placed Edward into the back seat of his automobile in the cover of night. Outside, next to his car, Victor asked to be alone with him. Victor offered him cash and food, but Charles declined.

"I'll manage on my own."

Victor nodded grimly and was about to walk away, but Charles stopped when he asked, "Do you remember me? I— suppose you wouldn't remember."

"You know what's funny? I actually do. Going back home brought some memories back to me. We were very young. I remember being... friends?"

"Yes. Yes, we were friends."

As Charles turned to step into his car, Victor stopped this time when he said, "You know I can't legally do anything about the land."

"I know. I'm not asking you to."

"But maybe, down the road, we can see about a sale of the old Frazier parcel of land. It won't be today or tomorrow, but maybe a few years down the road, the Fraziers and the Freemans can do business together."

Charles softly smiled. He nodded to a final goodbye and drove away.

CHAPTER 29

MR. AND MRS. CARLSON

The morning sun heralded the return of Bianca's smile, and Victor basked in its bright glory. His dimples was back to generously offering her unsolicited opinions about everything. She was back to making sure he didn't take himself seriously by ribbing him about his quirks. And she was back to being easily riled by his ribald references to their lovemaking and then later succumbing to his indecent proposals. She called him by his last name again and he didn't even care because all was well with the world again. He had his Bianca back.

He invaded her bath, shocking her by folding his long legs into the small porcelain tub. Despite her lamentations about spilled water, he fit himself in front of her with his knees pointing up and out of the bathwater. She lovingly wrapped her legs around his flanks, allowing his head to rest gently against her shoulder. Bianca was in the middle of wiping suds from his chest with her sponge when he glanced up to the ceiling, enjoying the pleasure of her touch. He never noticed the ornate ceiling and hanging chandelier until now.

"What did you say to that man outside tonight?" she asked him.

"Not much," he shrugged.

"I just can't believe he would just drive away as if all was forgiven. His brother is dead."

"I don't think it's that simple."

"And Wesley? Did he say anything to you before he left? I'm worried about him. His mother has died. And with his finances going under, I'm just worried."

"He'll be fine. He and I both have some healing to do. But it will take some time. And as far as his finances—he'll be fine. He has me as his brother. You know, with the bank going under, things will be... different."

Bianca snorted. "I don't know what you're talking about, Carlson. I was quite comfortable before I met you. And I never wanted you for your money. I just wanted you for that pretty face and what you have between your legs." Over his hearty laugh, she said, "I don't care about living in this house. We can move into something simpler. And I suppose I should tell you now. Mr. Johnson sold two of your cars while you were gone to pay some debt."

Victor sat straight up, sloshing water over the rim of their tub. "He did what? Which ones?"

"Oh, stop it. Leaving me here during a financial crisis was a horrible idea. You're lucky your two roadsters were the only casualties."

"My roadsters—never mind. I'll just have to get them back."

"What are you talking about? Mr. Johnson has painted a hundred different pictures of your poverty."

He chuckled and then leaned back between her legs. "Well, dimples, you must have forgotten you are about to be a rich woman. My mother had the wisdom to give my riches to my wife."

"Or insanity," she replied sardonically. "But you forget, I'm not your wife."

"No? I guess we will have to fix that right away."

※

THEY MARRIED on their own terms in late August 1929. Bianca walked unabashedly down the aisle of the St. James Methodist Church with her rounded belly on full display of everyone. She had told him she didn't care what the naysayers or gossipmongers had to say; she would not be covering her stomach for anyone. He remembered that she looked radiant in her simple lace dress with two long strands of pearls that draped past her naval.

But despite Bianca's concerns, there weren't any naysayers in the church. A small congregation of well-wishers joined them. His brother, Wesley, served as his best man, with George and Red by his side. With some strategic planning and sneaking around, he managed to get Bianca's best friend, Daisy, to come up for the wedding. To Bianca's merriment, Daisy stood as a maid of honor while Bianca's sister, Cecilia, stood as her matron of honor. When Victor was asked to state his vows, he couldn't for the life of him, repeat customary vows to a woman of Bianca's caliber. There were no words that could express the depth of his love for her or the lengths he would go through to protect her. Instead he began with, "My love, I have loved you from the day you kissed me on New Year's Eve—"

"December," she interrupted.

"Pardon?" the preacher asked.

"It was December. It was midnight in December. And I didn't kiss you; you kissed me."

"Oh, you kissed me, Bianca Eubanks. You were crazy about me."

"A damn fool is what I was then, Carlson. Just like I am right now."

"*Ahem!*" the pastor said, disturbing their sparing. "Now, back to my first question. Do you take this woman to be your lawfully wedded wife? To have and to hold? For better, for worse, for richer, for poorer, in sickness and in health, until death do you part?"

"I do."

❧

SIX YEARS LATER...

Bianca's daughter had a proficient knack for finding things. Bianca and Victor had often said that if something was lost, little Kinta was sure to find it. The girl was well on her way to being every bit the journalist her mother was. So it should not have surprised Bianca when Kinta walked up to her with a neatly folded letter one day.

"Look, Mama. I found something," she before handing it to Bianca.

Bianca opened the folds of the letter and had nearly dropped to her knees. "Where did you find this?" she asked.

"It was stuck under the banister. I saw the end of it sticking out. Did I do good, Mama?"

"Yes, baby. Yes, you did."

When Victor returned home from his trip to Oklahoma, Bianca quickly shuffled both of her children to bed so she could show Kinta's recent find to him.

"What's with you, dimples?" he asked. "You're bossier than normal."

"Because I've been trying to show you something little Kinta found today."

"What long lost trinket this time?"

"Not a trinket. A letter. This letter..." she said as she handed it to him. His eyes roved over its words in utter shock.

"What is this? Is this real—Where did you—"

"I think I can piece this together. When Mr. Marbury attacked Uncle Chito and me, years ago, he took his box and ripped it open. Money, papers, and pictures spilled out all over the place. I suppose that once Uncle Chito came to, he put what he could find back in the box. All except this. He probably didn't see it because it was stuck under the banister until now."

Victor sat back against his chair as he read word after soul-stirring word. "I'll give you some time alone," he heard Bianca say. Once she was gone, he read the letter again.

To my precious son,
I write this letter to you knowing that this will be the last time I lay my eyes upon you. You will leave tonight. I am giving this letter to Chito along with some other keepsakes to remember me by. He has promised me he will keep you and this box safe.
Because of the events that have brought us to this juncture, I will have to be brief. Yet, I must let you know how much I love you. I don't know if you will truly understand the depth of this love. It stretches far beyond state lines and city limits. It will follow you to the ends of this earth. In this life, I pray that you understand that just because you do not see me; it does not mean I am not there with you. I am guiding you. I am loving you. I am holding you. I am with you always.
I know that the time that we have shared has been short. It was not enough time. However, you are enough. I know your foundation is enough to sustain you on this journey. I know what is in you will not fail you.
You will learn later in life all that I have done to protect you. Even the matter of your inheritance was done to keep you safe. Therefore, I pray that you find a love to rival mine. I pray that she is worthy of your name and that her loyalty to you is steadfast. Choose well, my son.
My love forever,
Your mother.

That night, Victor rose from his chair and went upstairs to look for his wife. He found her nestled in the confines of their bed. He pulled back the cover and reached for her, hoping to hold her until the night became the day.

"Well? What did it say?"

"Didn't you read it, dimples, when Kinta brought it to you?"

"Some. I didn't feel right reading it. It's personal to you."

"I will say this. I hope my mother knows that I did what she asked me to do."

"What's that?"

"I chose well. Goodnight, Bianca Elizabeth Eubanks-Carlson. I love you."

The End

ABOUT THE AUTHOR

I am a lawyer by day, a mother chasing two little boys by night and a writer by late night. I live in the Chicagoland area.

I finished this book just before the death of George Floyd. During my editing phase, I remembered feeling immensely moved by my character, Kinta and her sacrifice for Victor and the sacrifice of all black mothers for their children. In the wake of the world's response to Mr. Floyd's death, I made the vow to tell the stories of Black American dreamers and believers.

If you would like to keep up with me, consider signing up for my newsletter, at www.prkeys.com. I post updates for new titles and excerpts of stuff I'm working on. It is also a place where I can engage with my readers, which I absolutely love to do.

ALSO BY P.R. KEYS

Enjoy some excerpts from P.R. Keys' September Series

The Eve of Our September

Seymour Johnson was proud that he served fifteen years under the Dilworth name. They were not the finest of the Lafayette Avenue residents, but they compensated him well. He was first hired as the late Henry Barton, Senior's valet and personal assistant. When old Mr. Barton, Sr. unexpectedly passed away, Seymour was demoted to the title of second butler underneath the old and respectable, Mr. Linus Webb. He could hardly complain. He was happy to still have a job. All was not lost on the position. With some patience, he would find his way back to his old job once Henry Barton, Jr. took his rightful place in this household. Unfortunately, his faith in that prospect withered the day that Henry, Jr. announced he was moving to Chicago to set up his practice.

Today, Seymour's faith got a boost when the widow Barton announced that Henry, Jr. was returning home today. Seymour eagerly, took special care to prepare young Henry's room. Everything had to be just right for the return of the master. He gave explicit instructions to the housemaids, Charity and Lilly, regarding the bed linens. He arranged for a special bottle of brandy from the cellar reserves. Yes, the young master returning was a good sign and Seymour was not one to miss out on such an opportunity.

Seymour was quietly polishing the young master's snifter glass when the bedroom door opened and in walked the one and only Henry Barton, Jr. Mr. Webb closely followed. Both were mildly surprised to see Seymour in Henry's room. "Oh, there you are, Seymour. As you can see, Mr. Barton has arrived. Thank you for your preparation of his room. I assume you will resume your role as valet during his stay," said Mr. Webb.

"Oh. It would honor me." Seymour beamed.

Henry waived his hand to him. "Seymour, please don't trouble yourself. It's just me. I have no intention of staying very long. I just have one small matter to attend to and then it's back to Chicago for me. Please don't go through great lengths to appease me." Seymour concealed his sinking heart and politely nodded. "I would, however, be happy if you showed me to my mother and grandmother," Henry offered.

Mr. Webb cleared his throat. "Your mother has not returned from the funeral home, but your grandmother is in the kitchen entertaining her guest, Ms. Mabel Davis. Perhaps, Seymour can escort you there and see to your afternoon lunch?"

"That would be excellent. Thank you, Mr. Webb. Seymour?"

Seymour nodded and moved out of the room. Not returning for long? That was not good. Seymour inwardly grumbled and made a quick pace to the kitchen. The cackle in the kitchen warned him that there the old Ms. Pauline Dilworth was enjoying her early afternoon brandy with her friend Mabel a tad too much.

Pauline and Mabel sat across from each other at the kitchen table in what looked to be a game of poker. Pauline looked up to see Henry stride into the kitchen. "There's my boy!" she jubilantly exclaimed. "I missed you, you foolish rascal. What in the devil possessed you to leave this old woman with your mama?"

Henry broke out into an open grin. "Well, Gram, I know you to be a tough old broad. I knew you could handle her."

"Sit down, Henry," she chuckled. "Oh, before you do, fetch us more of this here brandy. I need my medicine before your mama gets back. I don't want to hear her mouth."

Just before Henry turned toward the cellar door, he picked up the empty bottle settled between the two ladies on the table. "You know this stuff is illegal?"

Pauline reached up and lightly smacked Henry on his cheek. "Shut up, boy. I didn't pay all that money for law school for you to go on and on about Prohibition. Just get me out of jail when I call you."

When Henry returned, Pauline lifted her glass waiting for Henry to pour. "Oh, yeah- that's the stuff. I need my medicine."

Mabel greedily lifted her glass. "I need my medicine too."

Henry shook his head and smiled. Seymour knew Henry secretly enjoyed his grandmother's antics. Pauline Dilworth might have been the matriarch of this prestigious family, but she had no intentions of being burdened by society. In her old age, she had taken up smoking and would not let a brandy bottle pass without a sip. She rolled her eyes whenever her daughter reminded her of her proprietary duties. Pauline would always respond that with a shrug and giggle.

Pauline not only had an outrageous personality, she had an outrageous past too. She was richer than most colored women, but she couldn't care less about any of it. Her riches were also a mystery. The Baltimore Dilworth's would tell everyone that their vast holdings were because of the success of the Dilworth Funeral Home and wise investments in trade. But Seymour saw a few bank's deposits while cleaning Ms. Barton's office, and they were not enough to hold up the family's lifestyle.

Not that Seymour cared. He was just happy to have a job. Why should he care where the money came from? If the

Dilworths wanted to stash crates and crates of illegal bottles of liquor in the cellar; why did it matter? If Ms. Barton held secret meetings with Ramsey Bedford, the owner of Baltimore's most scandalous speakeasy; it was none of Seymour's business. Still, the true source of Pauline Dilworth's wealth was a major place of speculation, even to the white Baltimore community. It was just last week that Seymour got an earful from one of Mayor Browning's housemaids who told him she heard that Ms. Dilworth's vast holdings were because of a certain white investor from down south.

Seymour shook these speculative thoughts out of his mind. It was of no consequence right now. None of this would help his current dilemmas. Once he finished with his task of preparing Henry's lunch, Seymour carefully placed his plate in front of him. Henry was too busy playing a card game with his audacious grandmother to notice.

"Aha! Read them and weep Pauline. Pay up and don't go skip on my money this time," Mabel exclaimed.

Pauline grudgingly dug in her side purse and pulled out three dollars. "Ole bitch," she mumbled.

"What did you say? You the bitch. Don't think I did not notice you hiding cards under that bottle, ole cheatin' bitch," Mabel growled.

"Mabel," Pauline began, attempting to change the subject. "Did you notice how fine my grandson is these days?"

"Oh, I noticed all right. Henry, I know you are driving those gals crazy in Chicago."

"Stand up, Henry. Let Mabel look at you," Pauline demanded.

For some strange reason, Henry stood up and politely turned around to let that old biddy, Mabel, ogle at him. Seymour was sure the old bird would pass out when Henry turned around. Mabel's *oohhs* and *ahhs* were nauseating. *Nasty,* Seymour thought. Possibly feeling too much of the awkwardness, Henry quickly sat down.

"Pauline, do you see how he is sitting... with his legs half crossed like that?" Mabel asked.

Pauline looked at Henry and then back to Mabel. "What you saying Mabel?? Are you saying my grandson is hung?" The room was filled with silence before it erupted in screeching laughter.

Henry was up on his feet in a matter of seconds with his sandwich in his hand before grumbling, "I'm out of here"

Seymour inwardly shook his head. *Crazy*, he thought. *These women were crazy*.

They served dinner around seven. Mr. Webb informed Seymour that Mrs. Barton invited her lawyer, Mr. Sherman Billings, as a guest. It was not entirely rare for a white man to be a dinner guest in the Dilworth's home. Seymour guessed, that Mr. Billings had late client meetings with his Negro clients, so he could meet his white clients in the daylight at his office. Regardless of Billings' reason for attending tonight's dinner, he looked flustered and overly nervous.

After dinner, everyone settled in the family parlor where Mr. Webb discreetly asked Seymour to assist the family for the rest of the evening while he retired early. "These old bones are tired," he explained.

Seymour gladly took on the task. He served a sweet port to everyone. Everyone accepted but Billings. With his tray emptied, Seymour settled to the back of the room in the shadow where he took a deep swig of Billing's abandoned port when no one was looking.

"Henry, I'm glad we can finally discuss this out in the open. I know you are ready to determine the reason for all of this. First, let me say I have already discussed this with your mother and your grandmother. They wanted me to be here, so you can ask me any questions you might have."

"Please sir, continue. I am eager to learn," Henry said.

"The Estate of Archibald Dilworth contacted me. Cornel Dilworth was your grandfather and a white man," Billings explained.

"I know who the man was. Everyone in this family knows who the man was." Henry said while looking pointedly at his grandmother.

"Yes," Billings said before wiping his dripping forehead with a handkerchief. "Cornel Dilworth's son and executor informed me that he recently discovered a matter that affects your family's properties. I am referring to the properties located here in Baltimore, New York, and Chicago. Your grandfather gave your grandmother a life estate over those properties instead of outright conveying them to her in his will. This means that the properties only belong to your grandmother until her death. She cannot transfer the property to anyone, but she may use them as she sees fit during her lifetime. It is possible that something concerned him about conveying title to his uhhh... uhhh mistress. His reasons were not clear in his will."

Pauline huffed, "Bastard." Everyone looked at her for a moment but later turned back to Billings for more explanation.

"There is more. After the life estate expires, the properties would have gone to Mae as a life estate until her death. But Mae was to marry a man of pedigree and education. There is no telling what that means. But Mr. Barton, Sr. did not have a college degree and that would be a reason to challenge any title conveyance."

Henry remained still, waiting for more information. "Go on," Henry quietly said. The sweat on Billings' brow travelled to his eyes. He rummaged through his pocket for his handkerchief and continued his explanation.

"The properties will revert back to Archibald's estate because of this issue. Now, old Archie did leave a loop hole. His will offers that if his daughter, Mae, were to have a female grandchild from such a union, the properties would go to that child in *fee simple*, which means the grandchild would own all of it out right." He looked at Henry and took off his spectacles. "All this must happen no later than September 1, 1925, in order to be valid. Otherwise, the land will certainly revert back to the Archibald's estate upon your grandmother's death."

Henry ran an aggravated hand over his face and through his curly hair before finally exclaiming, "Are you joking?! You're telling me that as my mother's only son, I must produce an heir no later than September whatever date in 1925 or our family is out in the street?!"

"Yes," Billings replied.

Henry turned his eyes up heavenward and let out a loud sigh. "Why, thank you, white grandfather. Not only did you steal my grandmother's virtue, but you managed to ruin all of our lives years later."

"Henry! There is no need for that," Mae growled. "What this means is that you need to get going on a wife and then get moving on a child. This can be very easily solved."

Henry narrowed his eyes. "What is all of this, Mother? Is this your way of getting me to come back home? Are you trying to manipulate your way into getting a grandchild?"

"Henry, stop it, please! The will is legitimate. I have nothing to do with your crazy grandfather."

Billings offered that perhaps old Cornel Dilworth wanted to make sure that his mulatto daughter did not marry a man of the share cropping kind. To prevent this-he heaped a penalty on her ability to inherit. To that, Mae replied that she wished she knew all of this before she married Henry's father.

"What is that supposed to mean, Mother?! Are you saying you would have never married my father? Of all the pretentious things to say—"

"You know that is not what I meant, Henry. I am only saying that this would have been some good information when I was courting. Okay, that's not what I meant either. I was trying to say... oh never mind. I cannot even speak to you, Henry!" Mae plopped on the love seat in a huff.

Everyone in the room was so focused on the matter at hand, they forgot about quiet Seymour in the room's back absorbing all they said. Seymour looked at Pauline and noticed that she had little to say about any of it-except for the occasional 'bastard' from time to time. She just sipped her brandy and looked deep into the fire blazing in the fireplace.

Seymour continued to watch Mae and Henry yell over old Pauline for another fifteen minutes until Mae stormed out of the room, Henry next, Mr. Billings followed him. The room was suddenly quiet. On Seymour in the back and Pauline, by the fire, remained in the room. Seymour watched her silhouette stare into the orange flames of the fireplace. He dared not disturb her quiet meditation. There was something far to sacred this moment. So, he sat still for the longest until she spoke.

"Seymour?" Pauline asked.

Seymour almost jumped when he heard her call his name. "Yes ma'am? Can I get you anything?"

He watched her rise with her cane and turn to the back of the room. She stared deep into the shadow where Seymour stood.

"He might have been a bastard, but he is smart. You might get your job back soon enough." With that she turned and walked right out of the room.

Well, maybe she's not that crazy, he thought.

THE SWEETEST NOVEMBER

Carroll County, Georgia, 1909

The little girl crumpled bits of red dirt between her toes while she waited for her mama to finish hanging bed sheets on their clothesline. She usually busied herself with the task of playing with the clothespins, but that was getting boring. Her mama was taking too long.

"Can we go now?" she asked for the hundredth time.

"When I'm finished, Copper," her mama mumbled.

An unruly gnat buzzed around the little girl's eye causing her to swat anxiously. She let out a puff of air again and began to ask her mother how long her task would take but her mother's attention was far in the distance. Her mother stared far beyond their white bed sheets as if she were listening for something. But all the little girl could hear was the call of the summer locust and the winds bristling around the trunks of the surrounding pine trees.

"Go up the road and see 'bout Miss Ruby. Tell her I be up dat way directly."

The little girl was glad for the reprieve and made her way up the road, just like her mama said. As she drew nearer to Ms. Ruby's house, a strange wave of goose bumps travelled up the little girl's arm. The surrounding air was quiet and so was Miss Ruby's house. There were no children running back and forth. Usually lazy dogs would lounge around Ms. Ruby's porch, but there were none about today. It was odd.

The steps to Miss Ruby's door creaked under each step made by the little girl. She knocked three times at the screen door, and still no movement in the house. The little girl decided that she had better do what her mama said and see 'bout Miss Ruby. So, with her courage in her pocket, the little girl opened the screen door and entered the solemn house.

At first, the little girl saw no trace of anything out of place. But, as she took steps deeper into the house, she saw the bottom of a man's boot. That boot was attached to a man's leg. The man's leg was attached to a lifeless body lying face down in a pool of blood.

"Get from over there," warned a voice behind the little girl. She quickly turned around to see Miss Ruby sitting in her rocking chair with a shotgun resting in her lap like a baby. "Copper, you in the direct line of a dead man. I would move if I were you.

"M-m-m-my mama said she be up here directly," the little girl stammered.

"Oh, that's nice," Miss Ruby said with a smile. "And right after I make sure this son of a bitch is dead, your mama and I can sit down for a spell."

Ms. Ruby continued to rock back and forth in her chair. The wooden chair creaked under her weight as it moved against the floor. The rhythmic clicking sound resonated throughout the small front room. The little girl considered Miss Ruby for the longest before moving her feet to back out the door. Something was wrong with Miss Ruby. Her hair was standing on end like she hadn't combed it in days. Her white skin was black as soot. She stunk too. She stunk real bad. But she didn't know. She kept on rocking and smiling like nothing was wrong.

"Imma get my mama to come see 'bout you, Miss Ruby."

"No sense in worrying her over nothing. You know what a catfish is, Copper?"

The little girl licked her dry lips and eyed the massive body lying on the floor again.

"Uh... a fish, ma'am." She heard Miss Ruby chuckle in the distance as she watched the body move. The little girl could tell that the man was breathing because his back went up and down.

"Yes, it's a fish, but what kind of fish is it?" she asked.

"Uh... a catfish."

"Dammit, Copper!" Miss Ruby hollered, terrifying the little girl. "Now pay attention and stop being smart!" Miss Ruby's face contorted in a strange arrangement of emotions then settled back into a cool expression. She smiled again at the little girl. "Now what kind of fish is it?" she asked sweetly.

"I-I-I don't know what kind of fish it is, ma'am. I can go ask my mama and find out. Maybe I can go?"

"Don't make a move." Her face contorted again. This time she showed her teeth. "A catfish is a bottom feeder. That means that while all the other fish are swimming around in the water, the catfish is at the bottom eating everybody else's shit. But we like catfish. Don't you like catfish?"

"Y-yes."

"Did you know catfish are full of shit? I guess you don't care. Everybody wants to eat a fish full of shit, but I wonder if the catfish get tired of eating shit. I wonder if the catfish wanna swim with the rest of the fish." She hugged her gun to her chest real tight and let out a deep breath.

"I ain't about to eat nobody's shit no more," Miss Ruby continued. "That pathetic son of a bitch has fed me his last plate of shit. Now I know your mammy and the rest of you blacks think you better than me. Y'all think I'm white trash. A bottom feeder. But I'm done eating shit. Now you come here, Copper, and hold this here gun for me. And if he stirs, you shoot him."

"Oh, I don't know 'bout dat."

"Yes, you do. I heard you shot a rattlesnake last month. The whole town know 'bout dat."

The little girl swallowed and took the gun in her hand while Miss Ruby continued to rock back and forth. Moments passed, and the little girl realized that the rocking stopped. Miss Ruby's head tilted forward as she nodded to sleep. Good. The little girl crept slowly to the corner of the room to prop the shotgun against the wall. She needed to get out of there and go get her mama. The floorboards creaked under her feet as she tried to steady the butt of the shotgun against the wall.

The darn thing wouldn't hold itself. It was probably best to just leave the thing on the floor. Ever so slowly, the little girl bent down to place the heavy weapon on the floor, but a fierce grip of fingernails tore into her ankle. The grip tightened and pulled her leg. The man on the floor was now awake and trying to gain leverage to stand by using her leg. She tried her best to kick his hand off. They both silently played a game of tug-of-war with her leg, but he kept slipping in his own pool of blood.

The little girl displayed the gun and silently threatened to butt him in the head with it. He silently asked for it. She shook her head no. He pulled her leg again, but this time he succeeded in knocking her off her feet. She felt her body glide under his bloody body. He reached up for the gun in her outstretched hand. With everything in her she reared up her knee into his side. He let out a groan loud enough to stir Miss Ruby. She rose on her feet and screamed.

"I told ya, Copper. Shoot him. Now look at cha. Duke, you son of a bitch, let her go!"

The little girl and the man continued to struggle until she felt another pull of the gun. Miss Ruby was furiously jerking the butt of the gun. The man finally got on his knees. The little girl looked up to see him grab the collar of Miss Ruby's dress. He reared back and socked her in her face again and again. She had not let go of the butt of the gun. The little girl was still lying on the floor. Her legs were between the man's knees. She took a deep breath and kicked up her leg firmly between his legs and he let Miss Ruby go.

She and Miss Ruby continued to share the gun as they watched the man writhe back and forth nursing his crotch. The air in the little girl's lungs burned as she struggled to breathe. She looked up at Miss Ruby who was transfixed by the movements of the man. This would be a perfect time to let go of the gun and run home. Just as she was about to let go, the man launched himself at the two of them. The next thing she knew, a harsh boom erupted between her and Miss Ruby. The noise shook her to the core and caused a piercing ringing in her ear. The shocking white noise paralyzed all movement in the room until one body finally collapsed on the floor.